BRAIDS

Braids

Carla Helené Cornick

For sensitive readers

This book contains scenes and references that some readers may find distressing, including racial violence, sexual assault, abuse, and generational trauma. These elements are presented with care and intention, rooted in historical and emotional truth, and are essential to the characters' journeys and the broader themes of healing, resilience, and reclaiming voice.

Please engage at your own pace. Your well-being matters.

What if?

What if every life you lived was connected by a soul-thread?

What if the choices you made in one lifetime shaped your world in the next?

What if your soul remembered... everything?

A note from Carla

Nothing is perfect—which means, in my view, everything is perfectly flawed. This book may have a typo or two, and I'm okay with that. The perfectionist in me—as well as the over-achieving little girl I used to be—is healing. While my intention is always to present myself and my work with excellence, I've learned that excellence is a spectrum, defined by our deepest desires. If you're doing your best, what more can be expected?

This book, like my personal journey, has been a lesson in discovery—a discovery of self, and a healing of the traumas in my own life, reflected in the lives of the women on these pages.

Though some parts are inspired by real events, this is a work of fiction—a mashup of lived experience, imagination, and creativity coming alive in 12-point font.

So, yes—I lived this. Not literally in this lifetime (not all of it, anyway), but emotionally, energetically, intuitively. Braids came together so quickly it felt like I channeled it. The characters breathed life into themselves and then informed me of what they were going to do next. And if I'm being completely honest, in more than a few places, I was just as surprised as you might be when their unexpected decisions made it into the final draft.

This book is for anyone who has ever been silenced. Anyone who has been forced to exist in a space that felt hostile. Anyone who has had to become a version of themselves their soul did not recognize.

You are seen. You are heard. You are not alone.

The women in this book—like so many who walk this earth—are with you. I invite you to claim us, as we claim you.

We stand with you, surrounding you with love and grace.May you find strength in these scrolling lines. May the resilience, love, and joy I poured into this book find you when
you need it most.

I hope these women inspire you—just as you, the reader, inspire me.

Thank you for taking this journey with me.

With love,

Carla

Contents

Braids
A NOVEL
CARLA HELENÉ CORNICK
MEMPHIS, EGYPT
C. 693 BCE
CADIZ, SPAIN
C. 1494
RICHMOND, VA
C. 1859
DEHLI, INDIA
C. 1218
AMALFI COAST, ITALY
C. 1744
PARIS, FRANCE
C. 1934
N
W
E
S
What if your soul
remembered... everything?

Praise for Braids

"Carla Cornick's debut novel Braids will take your breath away. It is a stunning and lush burst of passion that sweeps us through centuries, with wit and wisdom, guided by a soul that alights in the precarious lives of women built of beauty and resistance. Not only will you feel like you are in the room with them, but your heart will beat along with theirs, I promise."

Gabrielle Corsaro

"Braids took my brain on a wild ride! I became emotionally involved and felt the pain, the sorrow, and the love of all the women I met throughout the journey. Their soul thread intertwined in such a magical creative way! I've never read anything like this! This book is amazing, thought provoking, and definitely leaves you wanting more!"

Jessica Breve

"The descriptive imagery in this book is fantastic. Every sentence I read I can literally just see it in my head."

Devon Coblentz

"...This is a wonderful read and I can't wait for the next book in the series."

Dr. Sharon Hunter Nikolas

"The author's style of writing in Braids is deeply lyrical, witty, lush, emotionally resonant, bordering on poetic. Carla uses rich, sensory language to convey setting and emotions of each character. The narrative is full of live, vivid imagery and metaphor. The novel is structured as a braid of stories. I love how each chapter is told from a different character's perspective, spanning centuries and continents.

Her voice adapted to suit each era, culture, and protagonist, maintaining consistent attention to detail and emotional intensity. My favorite character being Christine/Harlem. I relate to her spirit, personality, and dynamics.

Carla's writing style and the use of metaphor and symbolism inBraids—the structure, inheritance of trauma and resilience, 'hands' are often descriptive of detail, touch, violence, creation and care, 'mirrors and reflections' used to explore change, self-perception—had me reading it nonstop. The result is a novel that is both epic in scope and intimate in detail—voices and experiences braided together with artistry and heart, simply a WINNER."

Raysa Figueroa

"Such an immersive story. The narrative style made it feel as though I was watching the story unfold like a movie. Connected in ways I didn't expect... thoroughly enjoyed."

Tanea Hoffman

Braids

MS. VIOLET'S HOUSE — MID OCTOBER

Chloé sat on the hard, high-backed chair with her legs swinging and her head aching. One braid had slipped beneath her, yanking her scalp so hard her eyes watered when she shifted.

She winced but didn't cry. Not out loud.

Behind her, Ms. Violet clicked her tongue.

"Sit still, child. If I've told you once, I've told you a thousand times. Sit. Still. We almost done."

Chloé squinted her eyes and tried to breathe the pain away. It was no use. So she let her mind drift.

On the TV, Batman and Robin were mid-chase across some rooftop, their bright costumes loud against the gray skyline. BAM! flashed across the screen in bright green block letters. She loved this part. Batman came on after the after-school cartoons, when her homework was finished and her stomach was still full from snack. Ms. Violet always timed it that way, so there'd be less fuss in the chair.

The living room floor was a quilt of elbows and knees and half scribbled worksheets. Six kids sprawled out on the carpet with pencils and folders, mouths full of pretzels and Kool-Aid. Chloé's spelling was already done. She always finished first.

Ms. Violet tapped her shoulder.

Chloé blinked, snapped back into her body.

A grease-coated hand stretched out, palm up, waiting. "Gimme."

Her voice was hoarse from too many cigarettes and too much Johnny Walker Red. That's what Daddy called it. Ms. Violet called it evening juice.

Chloé dropped the bead into her palm. It was clear plastic, tinted soft pink, with tiny specks of glitter caught in the middle like stars.

Ms. Violet rolled the bead between her fingers once before slipping it onto the braid. She twisted, snapped, pulled, then folded the end up in a strip of aluminum foil so it wouldn't come loose. One more done.

Chloé exhaled and rested her hands in her lap.

Her scalp throbbed, but the braid felt good—tight, neat, right.

Like something was being put back together.

She stared down at the floor and watched the beads already hanging, sway and click against each other like wind chimes. Each one caught the light in a different way. Together, they sang. Like seagulls on a sea breeze.

She remembered the sound from summers at the beach with Grandma and Grandpa.

And Smokey. Smokey always went with them wherever they went. He was like their child —riding on the floor of Grandpa's gray Pontiac, nestled between takeout bags and beach towels.

Doggie bags were invented for him.

They never left a restaurant without bringing something for Smokey to eat on the ride home. And if there weren't leftovers? Grandpa would cook for him. Seriously. He wouldn't even cook for himself or Grandma—but Smokey? Smokey got the royal treatment. Better than any of the grandkids, if Chloé was being honest.

Ms. Violet tapped her on the shoulder again.

"Bead."

Chloé handed her another—white, this time. Another one done.

She shifted in the chair. Her legs were starting to tingle, toes going numb. She shifted again.

"How much longer?"

Her patience was slipping. She was trying to sit still. Be a good girl. But the chair was too hard, her back was aching, and her scalp was pulsing in time with her heartbeat. She already knew sleep would be hard tonight. It always was, the first night after new braids. Ms. Violet slapped some grease into the part and smoothed it down with her thumb. The tension eased just a little—enough that Chloé's eyes didn't feel pulled so tight and her neck could move again

without folding in on itself.

It wasn't that she was tender-headed. But the first day?

Those braids were tight enough to make you see stars.

Chloé wished she could wear her hair loose, but her mother wouldn't even discuss it—unless it was picture day or Easter Sunday. On those two occasions only, Ms. Violet would break out the hot comb and press Chloé's hair bone straight. When pulled smooth, it reached all the way down her back, past her butt, brushing the middle of her thighs.

She loved it.

It was her best feature, she thought—besides her honey-gold eyes.

But if she was being honest, the hot comb was also one of her least favorite things in the world. It scared her. A few miscalculated passes had left scars on her neck and arms—ones that took weeks to fade. And then, the moment it was straight, her hair would catch on everything: zippers, door handles, jacket snaps. Once, she even got gum stuck in it at lunch.

If she was really honest, having her hair out was more pain than pleasure.

But the way it shimmered in the sun…

The way it fell like a silk curtain behind her…

The way it made her feel powerful—when she usually felt powerless…

That made it worth it. Almost.

"You're done," Ms. Violet said, cigarette ash drifting like snowfall.

It landed on Chloé's shoulder, lingered a second on her pant leg, then fell to the floor in a soft swoosh.

3:45.

Record time.

Chloé was glad. Her hair was finished before her dad got there to pick them up.

Last time, he'd come early. Spent fifteen minutes honking from the street, shouting through the open window that he was in a rush and to send her out—finished or not.

But Ms. Violet, being Ms. Violet, wouldn't let her get up until the last braid was done and foiled.

"He'll wait," she said, cigarette in one hand, whiskey glass in the other.

And she took her time—slow and deliberate—twisting those final two braids with the same care she always used, no matter who was yelling outside.

She was right. He waited.

But he wasn't happy about it. And he made sure they knew it.

She and her brother, Charles, had spent the seven-minute drive home clinging to the ceiling grips—those little plastic handles above the window.

Knuckles white.

Terror in their eyes.

He whipped them back and forth across the back seat like rag dolls.

Hard turns, sharp brakes. Like a game. Like a joke.

By the time they pulled into the driveway, neither of them could speak.

They were just glad to be alive.

Mom took one look at them and scowled.

Dad thought it was funny.

"Lighten up, Shelly," he laughed, tossing her the keys and heading inside.

"What's for dinner?" he called back through the screen door.

"Brunswick Stew," she said, red-faced, hands on her hips. Then she turned to the kids.

"Go inside and change out of your school clothes." And that was the end of the matter.

Chloé stood up from the chair. Her legs were stiff.

She shook them one at a time, trying to bring the life back into them.

She picked up her coloring book and crayons from the floor and tucked them into her backpack. She zipped the big pouch and hung the bag in her cubby, next to the others.

"Tell your mama she owe me eleven fifty now," Ms. Violet said. "Dem beads ain't cheap, and the way you loose 'em… no sense expectin' any of 'em get used again."

"Yes, Ms. Violet," Chloé said. "Can I have a pink ribbon this time?"

Ms. Violet pulled a satin ribbon from the plastic pouch. She smoothed it through her fingers, feeling its softness.

"Turn around."

Chloé turned her back and waited.

Ms. Violet gently gathered the top half of Chloé's braids into a ponytail. She tied the ribbon around them, securing the section at the back of her head, letting the rest trail down her spine like a waterfall of beads.

"There."

Chloé turned toward the mirror hanging over Ms. Violet's dresser.

She looked left. Then right.

Strained to see the back of her head.

Beads shimmied and danced—tinkling like little bells at the end of a velvet cape.

She pulled the braids over her shoulder, draping them down the front.

They felt heavy on her scalp, but she didn't mind.

She swayed a little.

The beads followed with a ripple.

She smiled.

"All right," Ms. Violet said, lighting another cigarette. "Don't swing them things at nobody."

One

Obedience, Oaths, Obligations

CASSIA | MEMPHIS, EGYPT | C. 693 BCE

CASSIA'S BEDROOM

The city of Memphis stirred long before the sun crowned the eastern horizon.

From the flat rooftops of whitewashed homes to the sandstone colonnades of sacred temples, the morning light crept slowly, gilding the city in warm gold. The air was already fragrant with myrrh and blue lotus, drifting upward in soft coils from rooftop censers, prayers rising alongside the smoke. Today, every scent, every sound, every gesture was laced with sacred meaning.

A noble wedding was underway.

Not just any union, but a binding of power between two ruling houses—a joining meant to solidify control, secure heirs, and appease the gods. And the city responded as if the gods themselves were in attendance.

Bronze bells pealed from high towers, their tones echoing across the stone and sand. In the courtyards of the temple of Hathor, priestesses in indigo linen lifted their voices in melodic prayer, arms swaying in rhythm with ancient hymns invoking love, fertility, and divine protection. The great processions had already begun, weaving through the arterial streets like living tapestries.

Dancers draped in white moved with ritual precision, trailing silk banners that caught the morning breeze. Musicians played lyres, double flutes, and handheld drums, their songs bright and unrelenting in tempo. Bare-chested men carried towering trays of honeyed cakes, barley beer, roasted figs, and flatbreads into the town squares, where they would be distributed feel—gifts from the governor's house to the people of Memphis.

Children with lotus petals in their fists skipped through the dust, scattering blossoms before them like a trail toward celebration. Women adorned in fresh kohl and perfumed oil draped garlands of blue water lilies over clay statues, doorposts, and even one another, blessing the day with symbols of renewal and beauty.

The streets pulsed with life, color, and expectation.

Squeals of laughter echoed through hanging tapestries of date palms and banners embroidered in gold thread. Elder women clutched hands to their hearts, whispering hopeful omens. Even the old men who usually watched with wary eyes now grinned toothless and wide, murmuring that the gods surely smiled today. Bakers set out baskets of warm coriander bread at their stalls. A butcher decorated his door with palm fronds. A potter paused at his wheel and listened—yes, even the wind seemed to hum with promise.

High above it all, beyond the bustle and bloom, the palace compound stood quiet and commanding atop the eastern ridge—walls of pale limestone absorbing the morning sun like a slow breath while low hanging clouds kissed the walls of the outer courtyard. Inside the gates, preparations unfurled with methodical grace. Servants moved in swift procession, each one knowing their part in a ritual that had played out in the same way for generations. The central courtyard, where the wedding ceremony would be held under an open sky, was being transformed into a shrine of floral splendor and imperial power.

Palm columns wrapped in woven reeds and indigo-dyed silks flanked the space, creating a corridor to the raised platform where the bride and groom would stand before the gods, the priests, and the Cours. Papyrus finds with gold-tipped edges leaned in the corner, ready to be used by handmaidens to keep the bride cool. Dried myrrh and crushed cinnamon burned in copper braziers beside stone benches, casting spirals of sweet smoke that curled like serpents into the rafters.

In the great hall, the wedding feast was being arranged: stewed duck in honey glaze, roasted goat with pomegranate and coriander, baskets of semolina flatbread brushed with sesame oil, boiled eggs in mustard seed, platters of figs, dates, and sweet melon. Jars of date wine and barley beer stood cooling in clay cisterns, while musicians tuned their lyres nearby, their soft plucks and half-melodies floating into the sunlight chambers like hopes of celebrations yet to come.

Final linens were smoothed with burnishing stones and folded under alabaster weights. A hush of reverence hung behind every motion, the kind reserved for sacred days. Yet beneath the beauty and discipline was something harder to name.

A tension, barely perceptible.

Not everyone trusted the match. Fewer still believed it was wise. But it was done. The arrangements had been made, the contracts signed in ink and blood. The House of Menemhat, Protector of the Southern Nile, would tie itself to the rising star of Djemu, High Administrator of Temple Holdings and heir of the Iesha Line. And no one—not even the gods—would undo what had been set in motion.

Inside the eastern wing of the palace, the noise of Memphis was a softened hush. Cassia's chambers, tucked behind alabaster screens and sun-warmed sandstone walls, refined dim in the early light—thick linen curtains drawn against the brightness, gauzy and pale as milk. Shadows clung to the corners, wrapping the room in stillness.

Her bed was a low, carved ebony frame inlaid with ivory and blue faience, draped in linens dyed from indigo and saffron, embroidered with lotus and falcon motifs. The mattress, stuffed with goose feathers and palm fibers, smelled faintly of rose oil and cedar. Overhead, a canopy of linen stirred in the faintest breeze through the lattice shutters.

Cassia lay motionless beneath the covers. Awake, but unmoving. Her eyes traced the fine cracks in the ceiling plaster, following them like ancient constellations, as if one might split open and show her a way out.

The air was thick—perfumed with myrrh and rose oil, heavy enough to taste. It clung to her skin like silk that wouldn't lift. She tried to take a full breathe, but the weight in her chest pressed deeper, as though the walls themselves were leaning in.

This was the hour before becoming. Not a child. Not yet a wife. Suspended.

Her thoughts came disjointed, half-formed and fast—a tumble of fragments: her mother's stern kiss the night before. The unreadable look in her father's eyes. Djemu's cold hands. The red ink of the contract. Her mother's voice whispering, "A good marriage begins with obedience."

Obedience.

Obligation.

Oaths.

And yet—something pulled at her, quieter than fear but older than memory. A thread of unrest. Of misfit. Of feeling too much for someone who had no choices left.

Outside her door, the palace stirred. The first sounds of ritual preparation began to rise—sandaled footsteps padding across mosaic floors, the murmur of attending women, the soft splash of dawn bathwater in bronze basins. The day had begun.

And it would not wait for her.

One, two, three—three precise knocks.

"Lady Cassia," came the voice of her handmaid, Luna. Gentle, but firm. She entered without waiting. Two other girls followed with armfuls of silks, jewels, and a base of scented water.

It was time.

Cassia sat up slowly as Luna peeled back the linen curtain of her bed. The woven canopy whispered against it's copper frame, dust motes rising like spirits into the morning light.

No fanfare. No hesitation. This was the duty of a governor's daughter. Her duty. Her life.

"You are not a girl," her mother's voice echoed, as if standing just behind her. "You are a legacy. Your name is not your own—it belongs to your house. To your blood."

That lesson had come with a pinched jaw and cool fingers beneath her chin. "Men may wield the title, Cassia. But never forget—it is women who preserve it."

Cassia swallowed. Her throat was dry. A memory stirred—a younger version of herself running through the halls barefoot, laughter echoing in her chest before being swiftly silenced with a look. She had been raised not just to marry well, but to stand without error. To absorb expectation so deeply it became indistinguishable from identity.

As Luna knelt and began to pour warm rosewater over her hands, Cassia's mind steadied with purpose. She knew what was required. She would not falter.

But somewhere in the hollow beneath her ribs, something fragile remained—untouched and uncertain. A question without words. A flicker of grief for the girl she would no longer be.

Luna laid out Cassia's wedding attire and adornments with quiet precision—no need for spoken instructions. They had rehearsed this day since she was a child.

On a low cedar table near the lattice windows, a broad-usekh collar of turquoise, carnelian, and deep-blue lapis lazuli—stones traded up the Nile from Nubia—gleamed beside matching drop earrings, gold arm cuffs, and a pair of delicate anklets etched with the seal of the House of Menemhat. Each piece had been chosen with care: protection, fertility, status, and legacy woven in like a fine tapestry.

Her wedding kalasiris—a fitted, ankle length linen gown—was the color of sun-warmed papyrus, with a subtle gold sheen. It had been pleated by hand and stitched along the hems with gold thread in the shape of lotus flowers opening toward the sun—the sigil of her father's house. Tiny faience beads, pale blue and pearled like dwarfs, dotted the edge of the shoulder straps in quiet opulence.

There were no sales. No laughter. Only reverent silence, as if this were a funeral as much as a wedding.

The air itself held it's breath.

It was not grief, exactly. Nor fear. But something in the hush that felt like resignation—a collective knowing, unspoken but shared by every handmaiden, attendant, and guard in the palace: this was not a love match. This was a sacrifice.

Cassia watched Luna's hands move with ritual care, pouring oil into a bronze warming bowl and plucking fragrant rose petals to steep into the blend.

No one dared to meet her eyes.

She wondered if they pitied her.

Today, Cassia would leave behind the House of Menemhat—the name that had shielded her, trained her, marked her—and become part of the House of Djemu, heir of the Iesha Line. It was a fact. A contract. A sealing of power between her father and a man she barely knew.

Her chest ached wit the weight of it.

She had met Djemu four times in total. Once, when she was nine, flanked by her father and mother like a prize falcon perched between masters. Once at a temple festival. Once in passing at a state dinner. And once in private—ten minutes in a jasmine garden, where he spoke to her not of dreams or desires, but of duty. He had looked her over like a piece of finely carved furniture.

She nodded through each meeting. Bowed when expected. Said only what was rehearsed.

She knew what he wanted.

She knew what everyone wanted.

A son.

A bloodline to outlive them all.

it wasn't spoken aloud, not even whispered in the veiled corners of the palace—but the silence around it was deafening. Djemu had been married once before. Six years. No children. No heir.

It had never been blamed on him.

Of course not.

Cassia had overheard the gossip once, unintentionally, behind a carved screen in her father's solar. The old wife was "weak of womb." "Too thin," one courtier had said. "Not devout enough," another muttered. "Perhaps cursed." But beneath all the half-truths, there had been one grain of fear: What if the problem was not the wife at all?

Still no one dared to ask.

And now that burden was passed to her.

Cassia didn't fear the idea of children—not entirely. She had held her younger cousins in her lap, sung lullabies in the nursery halls of their estate. There was even a call flicker in her chest—a tiny hope—that she might one day be a mother on her own terms. That she might carve joy from duty, love from expectation.

But not like this.

Not like a tomb being sealed shut wit her name etched in someone else's handwriting.

She had grown up with the freedom of thought, the luxury of reading scrolls by the Nile, of listening to court philosophers debate politics and gods. She had once dreamed of traveling u the river to Thebes. Of mapping the stars. Of something that felt her own.

Instead, her womb had become the paper on which history would write itself.

***

Luna's voice broke through her thoughts, low and warm. "Come, my lady. Your bath is ready."

Cassia nodded, though her body resisted the command. She rose and stepped out from the gauzy bed curtains, the soles of her feet touching the cool stone floor like a priestess stepping into ritual.

The bathing chamber was dim, lit by oil lamps nestled in wall sconces carved with lotus patterns. Steam curled in soft trendies from the recessed pool in the floor, where rose petals floated in warm, perfumed water. One of the girls—her name forgotten, a recent addition—knelt beside the basin with a carved alabaster jug and a stack of woven linen towels.

Cassia stepped down into the water.

She didn't shiver

Not today.

The warmth embraced her, and the scent of blue lotus, rose oil, and myrrh wrapped around her like a second skin. Luna rolled up her sleeves and began washing Cassia's hair with gentle, practiced hands, murmuring quiet blessings between verses of a familiar old song. The other girls began their work—exfoliating her skin with ground date seeds, massaging scented oil into her arms and legs, scrubbing her heels until every inch of her was made radiant.

Not a mark would be left untouched.

Not a shadow unpolished.

Cassia closed her eyes and let herself disappear for a moment beneath the surface.

Silence, warmth, water.

She imagined drifting far, far away—downriver, past the marshes and reeds, beyond the reach of any title or expectation.

In that imagined world, no one knew her name.

She could walk barefoot through the market towns without attendants or obligation, tasting olives from cracked bowls and choosing her own trinkets from sun-warmed stalls. She would carry her own coin purse. Choose where to sleep each night. Rise with the sun and follow it wherever it led. Maybe he'd become a scribe, copying sacred texts by candlelight. Or study under the astronomers in Iunu, mapping the heavens and reading meanings in the stars. Maybe she would paint—walls, clay jars, bodies—anything that could hold color and story.

In that world, she belonged to no house but her own.

She would never be asked to bind her body to a future she did n't not choose.

Never expected to carry a name or a child or a treaty like a burden stitched into her skin. There, her life would not be measured in dowry weight or how quickly she produced an heir.

She might have even known love—not the brittle, transactional kind disguised in silk and ceremony, but the kind that grows slowly in shared laughter, in quiet glances across rooms, in freedom.

Freedom.

The world felt dangerous.

She opened her eyes, the last of the bathwater clinging to her lashes like a shimmer of memory. The walls around her hadn't changed. The girls worked in silence. Luna still hummed softly as she braided Cassia's hair, the sound low and steady, like a tether back to reality.

But as the moments ticked on, so too did her fate draw closer—measured not in hours, but in heartbeats.

The dream was over.

Soon, she would rise and dress and walk the polished halls not as Cassia of Menemhat's House, but as the future Lady of Djemu's line.

A symbol. A vessel. A thread in the greater loom of power.

Her childish dreams would be folded away like the linens of her youth—clean, cherished, but no longer needed There would be no drifting downriver. No stars to chart. No stories to paint in bold colors.

There was only this day, and the duty waiting within it.

It was time.

Cassia stood before the bronze mirror, her dress a cascade of ivory linen pleats, edged in gold thread so fine it caught even the gentlest light. Her neck and writs were adorned with turquoise and lapis, heavy enough to remind her of the responsibility she carried—just heavy enough to anchor her in the place the world carved out for her.

The attendants had withdrawn, and Luna lingered only to finish the final touches—adjusting Cassia's belt of gilded cord, smoothing the linen at her shoulders, tucking a final pin into her hair.

Then came the sound—quiet, certain. A familiar cadence of steps, softer than a soldier's should be.

Cassia didn't turn. She knew who it was.

"You shouldn't be here," she whispered.

"I won't stay," came Saben's voice, low and steady.

He looked to Luna—not with words, but with a nod, a glance, the kind of unspoken language shared only by those long trusted. She hesitated, then included her head in understanding.

"I'll give you a moment," she said, and slipped from the room, closing the door behind her with a soft click.

In the mirror, Cassia caught his reflection.

His formal uniform was different from the one she had grown used to—the one dusted in sand and scarred with use. Today, his harness was polished leather, dark as obsidian. A ceremonial sash crossed his chest, fixed with a bronze clasp in the shape of a falcon's wig. At his side, a sword hung in a too-clean sheath. He looked taller somehow. Sharper. Not just her friend, but a figure of command, of poise, of power.

She didn't let herself look too long. She didn't trust what she might feel.

But his eyes—always calm, always steady—were storm-dark now. He approached slowly, as if not to startle a wild bird. Their friendships had always been honorable. And they were both honor-bound. But still…

From the folds of his belt, Saben withdrew a bundle wrapped in linen the color of desert dusk.

"I have something for you," he said.

He unwrapped it carefully—no ceremony, just reverence. A dagger rested in his palms. The blade was small, elegantly curved, and the hilt was inlaid with a single oval of carnelian. Sunstone, she realized. The stone of courage. Of endurance. The symbol carved into the wild was one she recognized—it belonged to his bloodline. A mark only passed down to kin.

Cassia reached for it, but paused, her fingers trembling just about the hold.

"It's not meant for violence," Saben said quietly. "Though it could be. It's meant to remind you that you're never without power. Never without a voice. A choice."

Her hand closed around it, as if she'd always known its shape. As if it had waited for her.

"Thank you," she murmured.

"No matter what name you take today," he said, "you are still Cassia. And you are never alone."

She looked up at him then. Their eyes met—and in that charged stillness, a hundred things passed between them unspoken. There was nothing she could say that wouldn't betray everything.

The moment stretched—a breath, a heartbeat, a memory already fading into history.

Then Saben bowed, low and firm. A soldier's bow.

Without another word, he turned and disappeared into the corridor's shadows.

Cassia slid the dagger into the hidden fold of her sash. The cool.

Weight of it against her hip wasn't a burden.

It was a promise.

* * *

THE PALACE COURTYARD

The sun hung low, drenching the palace courtyard in golden light. Shadows lengthened. The air had grown cooler, the head of the feast replaced by the hush of anticipation.

At the head of the banquet table, the High Priest rose once more. His staff—capped with a golden lotus—tapped the stone floor three times.

The courtyard fell silent.

All eyes turned toward the dais as a second priest stepped forward to announce:

"Let the gods bear witness—now begins the Dance of Union. The joining of house and house, of blood and breath. As Osiris to Isis, so shall husband to wife be bound."

A murmur swept the gathering. Musicians lifted their instruments—harps, sistrums, lyres—and the first strains of the sacred melody began, low and lilting, slow enough to walk upon. A rhythm older than memory.

Djemu stood first, offering his hand to Cassia with all the solemnity of an oath. She rose with grace, every movement measured and fluid. Together, they descended the steps and entered the center of the courtyard, where the floor had been cleared and circled with woven lanterns, glowing like a constellation around them.

They began the dance.

It was formal, stylized—each step patterned after celestial myth, every turn a symbol: union, protection, legacy. At first, they faced forward, apart, their arms lifted like wings. Then, on cue, they turned toward each other, palms outstretched, barley brushing. They circled once. Then again—closer each time.

Eyes followed them. Servants stilled. Nobles whispered behind their cups. Even the wind seemed to hush.

And then, within the ritual, a moment unfolded—just for them.

Cassia's gaze met Djemu's, unwavering. Neither of them smiled.

"You wear duty well," he murmured, just loud enough for her to hear, their fingers grazing in a slow, symbolic pass.

"So do you," she replied, her voice calm, unreadable.

They stepped apart again, pivoting with the beat, only to return to center—closer now, bound by rhythm and lineage.

This wasn't the place for rebellion. But in that shared glance, something passed between them—acknowledgment, perhaps. Of what he had gained. Of what she had surrendered. And what, for better or worse, now bound them both.

As the dance neared its end, Djemu stepped behind her and lifted her hands high, as tradition required. A gesture of reverence. Of unveiling. It marked the close of the rite—and the beginning of their night.

The crow exhaled as one. The musicians quieted.

Djemu leaned in—not enough to be seen, but close enough or her to feel the warmth of his breath.

"You were born to play this part," he said softly. "Let's hope you're more than the role."

Cassia didn't flinch. Her answer came smooth, deliberate.

"Likewise… my lion."

Their hands dropped.

Applause broke like a wave.

Side by side, they turned from the floor, heads high, faces unreadable, their shadows stretching long behind them.

Cassia took his offered hand. He led her from the chamber, through the arched passage that waited like a throat of a beast.

In her mind, a single word pulsed beneath the applause.

Fuck.

Two

A Donkey and a Fig Tree

CHAHIRA | ISFAHAN, AL-JIBAL | C. 1210

THE FAMILY GARDEN — MID JUNE

On the morning Chahira turned six, the garden's peacocks screamed like prophets announcing her arrival.

Her grandmother, whom she called Teta, nodded solemnly. "A good omen," she declared.

Her father, Idris, chuckled. "That means she'll always be louder than the birds."

Her mother, Samaira, sighed as she stirred saffron into the rice. "May Allah protect us," she muttered. "The child is going to be beautiful and loud—every husband's nightmare."

Chahira was born into a house where paper whispered secrets and perfume clung like a second skin. Her father, Idris, was a calligrapher whose reed pen danced across parchment in flowing, liquid poetry. The ink carried a sharp metallic tang—so sharp, Chahira swore she could hear it's soft scratches, like whispers shared between old friends.

When Idris worked, the whole house fell silent, as if the pen commanded reverence. The letters he shaped weren't just beautiful; they seemed alive, curving and souring like birds in the garden. Six year old Chahira wanted to chase every one.

She would sit beside him, breathing in the strange mix of iron, ink, and jasmine incense as she tried to decode the world etched in quiet lines.

Her father wrote letters for noblemen, verses for poets, prayers for imams. But Chahira didn't care who the words were for—she only cared what they said. Every scroll he finished, she begged to read. Every word she read sparked a dozen new questions.

"Why this phrase? Why not another? Why a bird here and not a flame?" Her curiosity bloomed faster than her curls, which bounded wildly no matter how tightly her mother braided them.

Idris's fingers were always stained black, no matter how many times he washed. Chahira loved that—it meant he carried beauty on his hands. She wanted ink stains too. But unlike her father, she was a messy writer: her left hand dragged through wet letters, smearing words and freckling her wrists with inky constellations.

Still, she persisted.

She didn't just want to write; she wanted to understand. To shape the world as her father shaped his letters.

Her mother, ever elegant, burned sandalwood and rose incense with the devotion of a priestess. The scent cloaked their home, softening the sharp smell of ink and lending every room a dreamlike air.

For Samaira, incense was both blessing and barrier—a way to mask not just the ink but the tension that drifted in when commissions ran late or when Chahira's questions grew too bold. The fragrance was her armor, as if the right scent could ward off disappointment or danger.

Chahira didn't understand the need for armor. She thought sandalwood made the walls warmer. She loved how it clung to her mother's sleeves, how the smoke curled like calligraphy into the air.

But even then, she preferred the smell of ink. Sharper, more honest. Incense tried to soothe; ink told the truth.

Chahira often got distracted by the sounds outside: the coo of doves, the rustle of silk fro ma neighbor's laundry, the ring of her father's laughter through the open window. Her other sometimes found her staring out into nothing, stylus hovering over a forgotten wax tablet. "You'll never finish anything at this rate," she'd mutter, but even she couldn't hide her smile.

Chahira wasn't lazy—she just had too many thoughts, and the world outside always seems more urgent than arithmetic. The garden didn't test her. It let her be curious, chaotic, tender. It was her first love, her first escape, and her first stage.

Sunlight dappled the stone path like scattered coins, slipping through the tangled arms of a fig tree so stubborn it only bore fruit when property serenaded.

Chahira took this as a personal challenge.

Perched on the low stone wall that bordered the garden—her throne, her stage—she swung her legs and launched into her daily comedic monologue.

"Hey, fig tree," she began, squinting up at its bare branches, "you've got more attitude than camel in summer."

The tree, as usual, said nothing.

Undeterred, she stood, arms wide—part performer.

"I get it. You're dramatic. You're mysterious. But if I wanted drama, I'd talk to Aunt Yasmina."

She paced a little, working the invisible crowd.

"Do you know how many pomegranates out there are showing off? Meanwhile, you're over here like, 'I'm thinking about fruiting... maybe... in five years.'"

No response.

She leaned in, conspiratorial.

"Look, I'm not saying you're bitter. But last time Baba bit a fig from you, he made the same face he makes when he steps in goat poo."

She paused.

"You're not a fruit tree. You're a fig-ment of my imagination."

She cackled. "Get it? Fig-ment" That's comedy!"

Still no fruit.

Chahira huffed, plopped back down, and kicked her legs in theatrical defeat.

"Fine. Stay barren. But I'm coming back tomorrow—with fresher material and a tambourine."

She would never admit it, but when the first fig appeared a week later—fat, purple, and smug—she didn't tell anyone.

She just plucked it, took one sticky bite, made a face, and muttered, "ugh. Still too sweet."

But later that day, the fig tree got an encouraging performance—complete with a fig-themed knock-knock joke and a sarcastic curtsy.

The courtyard was always warm and full of whispers—the kind that curled around ankles and drifted up from the sun-soaked stones.

And BamBam, the old tortoise who lived beneath the rose bushes, was part of it all.

He barely moved. But he knew things.

Every afternoon, Chahira told him her secrets: who cried during prayers, who burned the rice, what she'd do if she could fly.

He never blinked—just sat there, ancient and unmoved as if storing it all for some mysterious, eternal purpose.

Chahira loved the garden best at dusk, when the sun melted into gold and the call to prayer echoed over the rooftops like a lullaby for the earth.

In those moments, the leaves deepened into emerald shadow, the roses turned the color of bruised wine, and everything smelled like dust, jasmine, and eternity.

Sandalwood smoke drifted lazily from her mother's burner, curling from the windows to mix with soil and petals.

She believed the garden knew her.

She believed everything had a name—even the stones she skipped across the path, even the. Breeze that carried gossip from the neighbor's kitchen.

She once named a one-eyed cat Dervish because he spun in circles before falling asleep.

She named ants. Petals. Clouds.

Naming was magic.

Naming made things real.

Isfahan was a city of light and geometry, but their little corner—tucked behind sun-bleached walls—felt like a secret garden dreamt by a poet.

Her parents weren't wealthy, but their home bloomed as if touched by Devine mischief: roses that climbed like they had something to prove, jasmine spilling from clay pots, and geraniums her mother swore could ward off gossip.

A vine-covered trellis shaded the back steps, where stray cats lazed in the heat and birds debated theology in the branches overhead.

By seven, Chahira could recite Hafez with the flair of a caravan storyteller—one elbow on the table, voice full of melodrama, and a mischievous twinkle that made every lament sound like a punchline in disguise.

Her Teta swore she was possess by the soul of a drunk mystic.

Her father, more generously, said she had inherited his fire.

Omar Khayyám lit small lanterns in her chest—quiet and sharp and full of questions.

She adored Rumi's longing.

She snuck peeks at Attar when her mother wasn't watching.

But it was the playful, irreverent lines—the ones that made her laugh out loud and earn a stern look—that stayed with her longest.

She'd read them anyway, giggling into her sleeve, then stand on her cushion and declare:

"Even a donkey has opinions—so why not me?"

Her favorite sage changed weekly, depending on mood, weather, and snack availability.

One month, it was Al-Farabi, whose writing on music sounded like the stars whispering secrets.

Another, it was Rabia of Basra, whose verses made Chahira feel powerful just by feeling.

She once declared Rabia the "Certified Queen of Divine Heartbreak" and demanded the household observe Her Holiness Rabia Day—complete with whispered poetry readings, rose tea, and a marigold brown she placed dramatically on her own head.

Her mother tolerated the spectacle until Chahira tried to bless the teapot in rabies name.

At eight, Chahira famously declared:

"I will never marry unless the man can rhyme my name with 'immortal flame.'"

Her parents exchanged one of those long glances they had perfected—part prayer, part panic.

"This is not a metaphor," she added, arms folded firmly.

"It's quality control," she explained. "If he can't manage one decent couplet, what hope does he have in an actual conversation? I refuse to spend my life nodding politely while someone explains olives to me."

She paced the floor like a general planning a literary war.

"And besides—'Chahira, bearers of the immortal flame' is clearly how historians will refer to me."

"It would be very awkward," she continued, "if I married someone named, I don't know… Khalid from accounting."

Her father snorted tea through his noes.

He coughed, wheezed, and flailed blindly for a napkin, tears streaming down his face.

When he finally caught his breath, he pointed at her and gasped: "If any man actually rhymes 'Chahira' with 'immortal flame,' I swear—I'll write the contract myself, walk you to him blindfolded, on stilts, while sining in iambic pentameter."

Idris doubled over in laughter again.

Her mother shook her head and muttered, "Why do you encourage her, my wild poet? She needs no help from you."

She smiled softly into her teacup, eyes sparkling with amusement.

By nine, Chahira had published her first book of poems—self-published, to be precise—each page hand-painted and stitched together with pink silk thread she "borrowed indefinitely" from her mother's sewing box.

She sealed the final page with a single almond wrapped infold foil.

"To nourish the reader," she explained solemnly.

"Because art must feed the soul. And pistachios are too obvious."

The poems themselves were exactly what you'd expect from a precocious, dramatic nine-year-old: half divine insight, half absolute chaos.

Titles included:

Ode to My Left Eyebrow

Death by Homework

And the critically misunderstood,

The Moon is a Liar and I Love Her Anyway.

Samaira called the poems 'troublesome."

Idris smiled and said they were "harmless mischief."

Her Teta asked if she'd hidden a love spell between the lines and winked knowingly.

Chahira's response?

She printed a second edition. With footnotes. In red ink.

"Because," she said, "people clearly needed help understanding the layers."

It was her finest work.

It was also her last real moment of childhood.

Because just as she began rehearsing a dramatic reading of My Heart is a Water Jug with No Handle, her world shifted.

It started with guests—men in stiff robes and softer smiles, speaking in too-formal tones and scanning her like she was part of the architecture.

Then came the whispers.

Words like alliance, honor, and opportunity drifted in from behind closed doors like incense you couldn't name but couldn't ignore.

Then came the news:

They were moving to Damascus.

Chahira was thrilled.

More cities meant more books. More perfumes. More boys to outwit, confuse, and emotionally derail with one well-timed metaphor.

Her mother was… significantly less thrilled.

"You must speak softly," her mother warned.

"But everyone listens when I'm loud," Chahira protested.

"Only fools shout in court."

"I don't want to go to your," Chahira said, wrinkling her nose. Unless I get a crown. And a scepter. And diplomatic immunity."

"You'll get training. And silk. And tutors. And—" Her mother paused, searching for the lease upsetting word. "You must be… pleasing."

Chahira blinked. "I am pleasing. Baba says so all the time He even underlined in in the margins of Ode to My Left Eyebrow."

Her mother closed her eyes. "That's not what I meant."

"Then maybe be more specific," Chahira offered helpfully.

Idris, biting back laughter, knelt beside her and tucked a curl behind her ear. "My star," he said gently, "you will always shine. Just remember not to blind the others."

She tilted her head. "But isn't that… like… the literal point of stars?"

He smiled.

Her mother sighed, eyes toward the heavens. "Ya Allah, this child."

Three

Secret Garden

CELINA | AMALFI COAST, ITALY |
C. 1741

VILLA D'ALBANI GARDENS — LATE SPRING

The sea knew her name—whispered it through olive trees, sang it through salt-bitten lemon groves, stirred it like prayer in the morning silence as she painted alone in her father's garden. Celina Fiore Albani, daughter of Rosa and Luca, born of lemon trees and cliffside salt, baptized in holy water, anointed by the wind.

She was fifteen—full of life, dreams, and quiet ambition.

She painted barefoot in a soft linen chemise the color of unripe peaches, sleeves rolled to the elbows, skirt hiked above her knees. A loose brown overdress hung from one shoulder, streaked with paint and pinned where the strap had long since given up. Her pale yellow ribbon, nearly fallen from her braid, trailed dow her back. The linen whispered around her legs as she stepped from stone to soil. Her toes kissed the warmth of the sunlit path.

Before her, a wooden panel rested on a bench of stacked stones. She leaned in, brush in hand, mapping the folds of a garden nymph's silken gown in soft, deliberate strokes. The create—half girl, half winged mystery—was nestled among lavender, foxglove, and roses, holding a lantern lit with fireflies. Beetles and bees scattered at her feet, lovingly rendered.

Behind her, the sea shimmered like a living canvas, it's palette shifting from blue to silver to pearl. Her hair glowed in the sunlight, a honeyed halo around flushed cheeks and a damp neck. One brush was tucked behind her ear. Another danced in her hand, dragging pale green into curled petal's shadow.

When she painted, she didn't speak. Words failed here colors thrived. She spoke in ochre and ultramarine, vermilion and violet—stories whispered in strokes and washes, truth etched in pigment. The image already existed inside her, whole and waiting. The brush was her wand. Each stroke summoned something sacred.

Time didn't pass; it hovered. The scent of rosemary and salt hung in the air. Each color a heartbeat. Each broth a step deeper into her private world.

She did not hear them approach.

Two sets of footsteps crunched along the gravel path: one steady and measured, the other familiar. A shadow fell across her canvas, and only then did she look up.

Her father stood before her, hands behind his back, his linen coat loose across relaxed shoulders. His dark hair was streaked with grey, his beard slightly uneven. He smelled of lemon oil, tobacco, and old paper—the scent of his study, and the armchair she'd loved as a child.

"Good morning, Celinetta," he said, his voice the warm gravel of early light. "I see the fairies are up early today,"

"Good morning, Father," she replied lightly, focused more on her canvas than the stranger beside hi. "I didn't expect… company."

Her father chuckled. "Nor should you. You're a creature of this place—I wouldn't dream of disturbing your kingdom without cause."

He turned to the man beside him. "Signore Giovanni Baresi. We knew each other long ago. He's passing though on his way to Naples and wished to see the gardens again."

Celina gave a polite nod. Her eyes lingered on Giovanni's hands—rough with paint, yet careful and clean. She knew his name, had heard it in passing. An old friend of her father's. A painter of acclaim.

"It's lovely to meet you, Bellina," Signore Baresi said. "I hope the fairies don't mind the interruption."

His linen coat fluttered in the breeze. Silver streaked his dark hair. When he met her gaze, it was sharp and steady—like the pause before lightening.

Her father beamed beside him.

"Celina," he said, "Signore Baresi asked to meet you."

She rose, brushing her hands on her apron, suddenly aware of the charcoal smudge on her cheek and the streaks on her arms. She wanted to vanish into the lemon trees. Instead, she curtsied.

"Signore," she murmured.

Giovanni stepped closer and studied her panel. The wind moved like breath through the garden. Her father waited, and Celina braced herself.

He said only, "You have a hand."

No flattery. No smile. And somehow, that meant more.

Her chest ached. Was it longing? Recognition? She wasn't sure. She only knew he'd seen something. She wanted to know what.

She'd studied without a formal teacher, guided by her mother's eye. She'd copied frescoes, memorized brushstrokes in cathedrals and merchant houses. Here canvases bloomed with Amalfi's seascapes and sirens, mountain paths and garden nymphs.

She'd heard stories of girls taken as color mixers, hidden apprentices. Of women who painted in shadow, behind their husbands' names. There was a path—narrow, hidden—but there. If you were bold enough.

She dreamed of Florence, of Rome, of the Salon in Paris. Of her name, one day, in a gallery.

Was that why he was here?

She'd heard whispers about Baresi. That he hadn't taken an apprentice in years. That he lived alone, painted privately. That maybe he was searching—for a muse, or a second chance.

Could it be her?

He turned to her father. "Yes," he said. "I believe we have an agreement—if the lady agrees?"

Celina blinked.

Wait. Was this happening?

"Oh!" She said, breathless. "Yes, of course! I would be honored to study under—"

"Celina," her father said gently.

She paused.

His face was kind, but heavy wit something unspoken.

"It's not an apprenticeship," Luca said. "He's asking for your hand."

She froze.

"My hand?"

"In marriage."

Celina turned to Giovanni, eyebrows raised, lips parting in mischief.

"Oh," she said slowly. "Well… that's even more unexpected."

A pause.

She tilted her head, narrowed her eyes, and gave him a faint smirk. "But you didn't ask me. I assumed it was an apprenticeship. You should probably… ask."

Silence.

Giovanni blinked, surprised. Then, a low laugh—quiet, amused.

He stepped forward and bowed with graceful theatricality.

"You're right, Signorina. Let me try again."

He took her paint-stained hand.

"Celina Albani, will you do me the honor of becoming my wife?"

Celina smiled. Considered.

"If I say yes," she said, "you'll take me as your apprentice. I'll paint. I'll study. You'll introduce me to your patrons."

A grin tugged at his mouth.

"You are your father's daughter," he said.

Luca stifled a laugh.

"I expect to show in Naples before I'm twenty," she added firmly.

There aw a flicker in Giovanni's eyes.

Then he smiled. Broader. Impressed.

She shook his hand—firmly.

Not a love match. Not yet. But maybe something better: an honest beginning.

Maybe love would come. Maybe it wouldn't.

Maybe she would fall in love with Naples instead—with galleries, with pain on her fingers, with light spilling across a fresh canvas.

The men shook hands like businessmen sealing a deal.

"She's her mother's daughter," Luca said with pride. "You've been warned."

Celina turned back to her easel.

The garden was warm. The sea breeze soft.

And her painting waited—half-finished, full of promise.

Four

New Year's Eve

CHRISTINE | HARLEM, NY | C. 1924

135TH STREET, JUST OFF 7TH AVENUE — 10:45 PM

The black Checker cab, it's yellow trim dulled by city grime, rolled to a halt in front of an unmarked door on 135th Street, tires hissing against a ridge of ash-muddied snow piled at the curb. Christine stepped out first, the heel of her polished black leather T-strap catching slightly as she lowered herself onto the slick sidewalk. One deep club gloved hand lifted the hem of her midnight blue velvet gown just high enough to avoid the dirty slush. The fabric shimmered like ink under moonlight. Behind her, the driver—wrapped in a heavy wool coat, cap pulled low—tipped his hat wit ha grunt.

Dot followed, all sparkle and motion, laughing as the cold kissed her cheeks red. Her gold fringe dress peeked out from beneath a pale fur wrap, and she toiled once on the icy pavement, the fridge shimmying in defiance of the winter.

The icy air hit them in the face like a glass of dry gin—sharp, bracing, clean enough to stir the back of the throat. Their breath floated in silver clouds as they took it all in: the golden windows of brownstones flickering like fireflies, street lamps haloed in mist, and the clatter of heels against pavement echoing like Duke Ellington's jazz riffs dow the block—cool, unpredictable, and full of promise.

A couple walked by, hand in hand—he in a navy wool coat with a cigar tucked behind his ear, she draped in mink with scarlet lips and laughter that danced like champagne bubbles. Across the street, a jet-black Cadillac V-63 glided by, whitewall tires slicing through a patch of snow. Somewhere nearby, a phonograph crooned out a trumpet line—lazy, brassy, and bold enough to make the air hum. Heads turned—whether for the car, the music, or the man behind the wheel, no one could say.

The sidewalk shimmered faintly with frost, catching the light like scattered sequins. Each step Christine took felt like balancing on the edge of a dream—half-gliding, half-floating in her heels, as if the night itself had lifted her off the ground. Laughter rang out across the block in staccato bursts—deep baritones, high soprano giggles, the giddy hum of celebration hanging in the air like perfume. The scent of roasting chestnuts mingled with cigar smoke and the faint sweetness of gardenia from some unseen passerby.

Somewhere down the block, a man hollered "Happy New Year!" To no one and everyone, his voice ragged with joy. A chorus of shouts answered him—"And many more!" "To 1925!"— followed by the shrill shriek of a party whistle. A boy in knickers and a knit cap dashed across the street, slipping and catching himself, laughter trailing behind him like a kite. From an open window above, someone blasted a gramophone record—jazz sharp and crackling—and then, as if in response, a trumpet called out from the shadows: two notes, quick and blue, curling up into the dark and disappearing like a secret.

They reached it slowly—that door— half-hidden between a shuttered tailor shop and a hardware storefront dark as sleep. No sign, no name. Just a red bulb glowing dimly above the lintel, casting a dull halo across the wet pavement. The door itself was black, weathered, wood swollen from years of winters, the brass knocker worn smooth by too many hands. A narrow rectangle of light leaked from the seam at its base, gold and pulsing like a heartbeat.

Though nothing marked it as special, the air around it vibrated. Laughter, bold and brassy, spilled out in bursts. Glass clinked. Someone near the door let out a deep, throaty laugh, followed by the shriek of a woman delighted or scandalized—or both.

Christine could hear the music now, full and alive. Not just from inside—though yes, the throb of jazz was bleeding through the walls—but from somewhere deeper, like the club was breathing, and the music was its pulse.

People were clustered near the entrance, pretending to smoke, pretending to flirt, waiting for someone to open the door or give the word. A man in a wide double-breasted pinstripe suit leaned in toward a woman wrapped in a red satin cloak, murmuring something that made her smack his chest and laugh. "You think just 'cause it's New Year's you get to start over?" She teased, raising a delicate brow. He grinned, unbothered. "Girl, I started over the moment I laid eyes on you."

A pair of young women hurried past Christine and Dot—one in a jade green flapper dress with fox fur draped around her shoulders, the other in sequins and feathers, gold eyeshadow catching the streetlight like foil. Their heels clicked on the slick pavement, the one in green shouting, "We're late, and I swear if Langston's already started reading, I'm throwing my shoe!"

Closer now, Christine could feel the heat seeping out from the cracks in the doorframe—sweet with sweat, gin, perfume, and possibility. She could smell orange peel and pipe smoke, spilled whiskey and wax from melted candles. Someone threw the door open for a flash—a man with a tilted fedora and a grin like he knew every secret worth knowing—and warmth rushed out in a wave, thick with music and the sharp, delicious buzz of revelry.

Dot leaned closer, her voice low and wicked. "I swear to God, if I die tonight, let it be with champagne on my breath and Duke playing me out."

Behind the nondescript door—just that brass knocker and the askew red bulb—was the real celebration. This was Marjorie's Room. The real heartbeat of Harlem: Black-owned, built by a woman, and open to every shade and stripe of dreamer, rebel, writer, lover, and ghost.

It was the kind of place where the rules changed, where nobody asked where you came from—only what you brought to the table. Jazz pulsed through the bricks, low and smooth as a heartbeat. The kind of sound that could melt ice off windows and unlace Mother Superior's spine.

Dot leaned in close, her breath warm on Christine's ear. "You ready for this?"

Christine gave a slow smile, lips painted dark as damson plums. "Born ready."

She adjusted her fur-collared coat, fingers trembling from cold or anticipation—it was hard to say which—and stepped up to knock.

The door opened with a crew and a gust of warmth that wrapped around Christine like a living thing—thick with tobacco, perfume, sweat, and the sweet burn of gin. The bass throbbed up through the floorboards, and her feet picked up the rhythm before her mind could catch it. They descended the narrow stairwell, velvet-lined walls pulsing in time with the music below.

As they reached the bottom, the room unfolded like a fever dream—gold light, red velvet curtains, bodies moving like water. A horn blared, a drum snapped, and a woman onstage flung her arm wide as her voice rang out:

"Runnin' wild, lost control.."

Laughter burst at a table near the bar. A man in a white tuxedo tried to light a cigarette for a woman who kept spinning out of reach, her beads clinking with every shimmy.

"Feelin' gay, reckless too—"

Dot grabbed Christine's hand. "Tell me this isn't heaven."

Christine didn't answer. Her eyes were too busy taking everything in: the couples pressed close on the dance floor, the gold light catching sweat on collarbones, the sharp flash of a rhinestone-studded flask passed hand to hand.

"Carefree mind, all the time, never blue..."

A waitress slid by with a tray of bubbling champagne coupes, and Dot snatched two, passing one to Christine with a wink. The stem was cold in her hand, but her blood was already warm.

"Don't love nobody—not even you..."

Christine turned toward the stage. The singer winked as she hit the note, voice like molasses and fire, the crowd erupting in cheers.

"Runnin' wild, runnin' wild—"

And for a moment, the whole room seemed to pulse with those words—like they were all running wild, together.

As the final note echoed through the room, the crowd burst into applause—tables slapped, hands clapped, someone let out a war whoop from the back.

Mamie strutted onto the stage wit the confidence of a woman who had survived five husbands and buried every one of them in a better suit than they'd deserved. She raised her hand to hush the crowd, that ruby on her finger flashing like a warning flare.

"Well, if that don't wake up every sorry soul in the room, you might as well go back upstairs and ask God for a second chance!"

Laughter rolled through the club like a ripple of champagne.

"Give it up for the incomparable—unforgivable—Bunny De-Vonne!" Mamie sang out, winking as Bunny curtsied low, one leg stretched, sequins glittering like stars falling.

Bunny blew a kiss over her shoulder and disappeared behind the velvet curtain as the next act set up.

* * *

Mamie continued her tone shifting to reverent.

"Now simmer down, my sugar-plum sinners, 'cause we're changing tempo. We got words coming' at you next—real words. No lies, no polish, just truth dressed in a good suit. You might feel a little bruised after, ut baby, that's the point."

A hush fell as the lights dimmed. Onto the stage stepped a young man in a charcoal vest and wire-rim glassed, with eyes like he'd seen too much and a voice like he'd barely recovered from it.

> *"The night does not apologize.*
> *It spills.*
> *And we go walking, wine-drunk with hope,*
> *forgetting our names in the mouths of strangers…"*

Christine leaned forward slightly, something in the cadence catching her ribs. But before the next stanza could unfurl, a glass clinked too loudly near her elbow.

She turned just in time to meet a crooked grin and a raised eyebrow.

"Didn't mean to interrupt your enlightenment," said the man beside her. He had dimples like soft traps and a hat tilted just enough to be charming, not try-hard. "But I had to ask—are you actually listening to the poem or pretending to understand it so you look mysterious?"

Christine blinked. Then laughed. "Maybe I'm doing both. Maybe I am mysterious."

A voice called from nearby, half-laughing, "Come on, don't scare the nice girls with your cheap thrills and philosophy."

Christine glanced past him—his friend, tall and grinning, lifted his drink in apology before returning to the smiling woman by his side.

The man beside her rolled his eyes. "Ignore him. He thinks sarcasm is a love language."

Dot leaned over from the other side of the table, eyes wide with mock horror. "Oh no. Did you seriously just try poetry-shaming a woman in a velvet gown? Sir. That's a crime."

The man grinned at her, unbothered. "Then arrest me. I'm clearly a menace."

"You're clearly something," Christine said, sipping her champagne, trying not to smile too hard.

He extended his hand with a flourish. "Malcolm. Just Malcolm. No middle name, no known aliases, though my sister calls me Trouble."

He was warm brown, skin like fresh coffee with a splash of cream. Hair close-cut, waves brushing the edges of his temple like quiet waves lapping the shore. His voice was deep—smoky and slow, like the first pour of good whisky after midnight.

Dot raised her glass. "Nice to meet you, Trouble. I'm Dot, and this here's Christine."

Christine gave a faint smile. "Also known as: still deciding if you're worth talking to."

Malcolm feigned a wound to the chest. "Ah, madam! You wound me. I haven't even had the chance to buy you a drink or ruin your life yet."

Christine tilted her head, her tone dry and amused. "Well, aren't you ambition. No drink, no dance, strait to ruin?"

Dot leaned in with a grin. "Jumping straight to ruin? At least buy a girl a drink she won't finish."

Malcolm chuckled. "I can work with that."

He slid into the empty chair beside them like he belonged there, long legs folding easily, hat still rakishly perched. "You two from the city?"

"We're from near the city," Dot answered before Christine could. "Close enough to get in trouble, far enough for our mothers not to hear about it."

Christine smirked. "We're house-sitting for a friend."

Malcolm raised a brow. "And you thought the best way to honor their home was to sneak into a speakeasy dressed like heartbreak and champagne?"

Dot cackled. "You should see what we left behind. You're lucky we didn't come in feathered boas and tiaras."

Christine cut a glance at her. "You were the one who almost wore the tiara."

"I still might," Dot said, tugging her coat tighter. "Midnight hasn't hit yet."

Malcolm looked back at Christine, his grin softening just slightly. "And what about you? You a tiara type?"

Christine lifted her chin, eye glinting. "Depends on who's watching."

Malcolm blinked, the grin twitching wider, "Damn."

Dot fanned herself with her champagne coupe, "Oh, we're flirting now. Should I leave, or take notes?"

Malcolm leaned in just enough to spark a thrill without being rude. "You don't strike me as someone who ever sits on the sidelines, Dot."

Dot beamed. "You're not wrong. But I am someone who orders another round. Champagne, Trouble?"

He tipped his imaginary hat. "Don't mind if I do."

Malcolm signaled the waitress with casual flick of two fingers. She gave him a nod and disappeared into the swirl of bodies and velvet.

On stage, the poet lifted the last lines of his piece with quiet gravity.

"We carry our stories
like cracked glasses—
full of light,
full of ache,
waiting to spill."

A hush lingered. Then came the snapping—sharp and rhythmic, fingers echoing across the room like raindrops on a rooftop. Scattered claps followed, not polite but earned. The poet bowed once and slipped away, vanishing into the red shadows.

Mamie strutted back onstage in her turban and her glory, one hand on her hip, the other waving down the noise.

"Alright now, don't go getting too sentimental on me. That was poetry, not a funeral. Dry your eyes, tip your glasses, and hold onto your damn hats, sugar plums—'cause this next act's about to raise the dead."

A low ripple of laughter moved through the crowd.

She leaned into the mic, eyes glinting. "We got a brand new cat in the house tonight. Just rolled in from Kansas City with a trumpet case full of fire and the kind of fingers make the Devil nervous. Make some noise for young Mister Louis Armstrong!"

The crowd burst into cheers as a skinny man in a slick suit and shiny shoes made his way to the stage, cradling his horn like it was made of bone china. He flashed a wide grin, cocked his eyebrow, and let loose a note that curved like honey around a bullet.

Christine let out a soft breath. "Oh. This is gonna be good."

The waitress returned with three fresh glasses of champagne, and Malcolm raised his to the women.

"To poetry, trumpet boys, and bold introductions," he said, then shot Dot a glance. "Especially the last one."

Dot clinked her glass to his, eyes gleaming.

"Stick around, Trouble," she said with a teasing smile. "We're just gettin' started."

Christine laughed softly into her drink, the warmth of it curling behind her ribs like a secret. The music swelled, a burst of brass punctuating her thoughts, and for a moment, she felt suspended—light, lovely, entirely present.

She turned toward Dot and Malcolm, a witty retort forming on her lips—

And that's when the air shifted.

Not the temperature, the tone. Like the entire room took a breath.

A woman entered through the side door.

She didn't walk so much as arrive, her presence rippling across the crowd before her heels even touched the floor.

Marjorie Viola Belle, tall and stately in deep violet silk, a fox fur slung off one shoulder, black hair sculpted into perfect finger waves that caught the gold light like lacquer. Her earrings danced with every step—long drops of mother-of-pearl—and her eyes? Her eyes were sharp. The kind that had seen everything and forgot nothing.

She moved through the club with easy elegance, stopping at tables, touching shoulders, laughing low, checking the corners like a queen surveying her court.

Then she spotted them.

"Well, well," she said, voice smooth and low, tinged with amusement. "Fresh faces."

Dot stood quickly, straightening her skirt. "We're honored, ma'am. This your house?"

Marjorie's smile widened. "That's what they tell me."

Malcolm tipped his head respectfully. "Beautiful place. Electric."

"Good to hear," she said, then turned her gaze to Christine. "And what about you, baby? You havin' a good time in my lil 'stablishment?"

Christine smiled, warmth blooming in her chest.

"It's like my grandmother's kitchen—only with better cocktails and a few thousand more sequins."

Marjorie let out a warm, full laugh. "Now ain't that the sweetest thing anybody's said to me in a long while."

She slid into the seat between Christine and Malcolm, her fur slipping off her shoulders with a casual flick. "So go on then—what y'all think of the show. So far?"

Christine leaned in slightly. "Honestly? It's like walking through someone's dream. The music, the words, the way everyone seems to belong here... It's not just entertainment. It's church. With better shoes."

Marjorie chuckled, clearly pleased. "Mmm, you got good eyes, baby. That's exactly it—this ain't just about passin' time. We buildin' somethin' here that remind folks they matter."

She took a slow sip from her glass, then grinned, sly and easy. "Course... don't hurt non havin' a trumpet that could set the dam walls on fire."

Christine smiled, then tilted her head. "Is that the secret, then? Make them feel like they matter, and they'll keep coming back?"

Marjorie nodded, shifting her glass, voice low and thoughtful.

"Close," she said. "But here's the real play: you build culture wit the artists, the poets—the dreamers. That's where the soul come from. Then you bump the prices just enough to bring in the folks with deep pockets."

She paused, watching Christine close.

"They eat it up—rubbin' elbows with creators, feeling' like they part of somethin' wild and alive. But you push it too far? Artists vanish. And when the art goes, baby, the magic's gone. Ain't nobody tryin' to drink in a room that's lost its soul."

Dot blinked. "So... don't price out the magic?"

Marjorie grinned. "Now you're cookin'.'"

Christine didn't blink. "That's good advice."

That earned her a gleam of approval from Marjorie, who tapped the side of her glass against Christine's.

"Well said, Port Jervis."

Christine blinked. "How'd you know—?"

Marjorie shrugged, a mischievous glint in her eye. "Didn't. Just a lucky guess."

Christine laughed. "You're good. My family's from there. It's a small town upstate, tucked between a river and a railroad. We used to call it 'the place the trains forget'."

Marjorie nodded, like she knew the place anyway. "Quiet towns make loud women. What brought you to the city?"

"School" Christine said. "Hunter College."

Marjorie's eyes lit. "Ahh, a smart girl."

"I'm trying," Christine said humbly. "Majoring in literature. And life."

Marjorie chuckled again, gentler this time. "Honey, the way this city moves? Life'll major in you."

Christine tipped her glass in salute. "Then I'm taking good notes."

That seemed to warm Marjorie in some private way, and for a moment, the two women just sat—surrounded by jazz and laughter and light—connected by the quiet truth of women who understood the balance between survival and sparkle.

Dot leaned toward Malcolm with a low whistle. "I think I just lost my best girl to royalty."

Malcolm chucked, eyes on her. "That's all right—'cause I'm sitting beside the crown jewel, ain't I?"

Dot blinked, caught off guard—but the grin that spread across her face lit it up like fireworks.

He watched Christine and Marjorie for a beat, something curious flickering behind his eyes. Then he turned back to Dot, voice low, casual.

"Thought y'all were house-sitting."
Dot didn't miss a beat. "We are."

She took a slow sip of champagne. "Also studying literature. Also trying not to starve."

Malcolm grinned, clearly impressed. "Smart, gorgeous, and resourceful. Be still my heart."

Dot smiled behind her glass, voice sweet as sugar and twice as sharp. "Don't go catching feelings, trouble." She winked.

Behind them, the music kicked up—brass blaring bold, a stand-up bass snapping in rhythm, the piano tumbling like dice across velvet. The dance floor was a blue of motion: flapper dresses swishing, heels clacking, suspenders bouncing on men who moved like they had jazz in their bones. A woman spun into her partner's arms and dipped so low her feathered headpiece brushed the parquet.

Malcolm watched it all with a grin, then turned to Dot. "You dance?"

Dot tilted her head, eyebrow raised. "You asking?"

"I might be."

She glanced toward Christine automatically—old habit—and found her friend already smirking, sipping her champagne with a shrug that said: You need my permission now?

Dot laughed. "Alright then. Lead the way, Trouble."

Malcolm stood and offered his hand like a gentleman conjured from the chorus of a jazz record—charming, bright, and already in step wit the rhythm. Dot slipped hers into his and let herself be pulled into the pulse and whirl of it all, vanishing into the riot of sequins, laughter, and music like she'd been born there.

Christine watched them go, her smile soft and easy.

Beside her, Marjorie Belle leaned in just slightly. "That one's got fire."

Christine nodded. "And lots of it too."

They sat together am moment longer, soaking in the pulse of it all—the dancers whirling, the band riffing on something bold and bright, the room glowing with heat, laughter and golden light.

Her eyes flicked again to the woman cross the room—the one laughing with abandon, her presence a quiet blaze amid the riot of sequins and brass.

She shifted in her seat, uncrossing one long leg, and the hem of her dress slid back just enough. To reveal a pair of red leather heels with a shine that caught the light like sin.

Christine blinked once. Felt something warm stir just beneath her ribs.

Then Mamie appeared back on stage, her voice cutting through the din like a trumpet call.

"Alright, sugarplums! You know what time it is—grab your sweetheart, grab a stranger, grab your glass—because we're countin' it down!"

A wave of cheers rolled through the room.

Marjorie Belle rose gracefully from her seat, fluffing her fur over one shoulder. She gave Christine's arm a gentle squeeze.

"You don't have to know where you're going just yet, baby. Just don't stop moving forward."

Christine blinked, surprised at how much those words settled in her chest.

"Happy New Year," Marjorie said with a wink, then turned and slipped into the crowd, her violet silhouette swallowed by the shimmer and sway of dancers.

Christine lifted her glass in a soft, silent toast, a grateful smile tugging at her lips as she watched Marjorie vanish behind the velvet blur of bodies.

The stem of the flute was still cold in her fingers, but her cheeks were flushed with warmth and laughter and champagne bubbles. Around her, the celebration swelled—horns blasting, tambourines rattling, someone drumming a rhythm on the table wit silver spoons.

She took it all in—the swirl of sequins, the swing of suspenders, men and women dancing like the floor had turned to fire. Laughter soared like jazz over the rhythm, and Christine let herself get lost in it, just for a moment.

Across the room, Dot caught her eye—twirling once in her gold fringe dress, then raising her own glass with a wink. A toast without words. Roommates, best friends, chosen sisters—tonight was theirs.

Mamie lifted her arms from the stage.

"Ten! Nine!"

The crowd shouted with her, voices rising with each number, bodies pressing closer, hearts thumping in sync.

"Eight! Seven!"

Someone handed Christine a noisemaker and she took it without thinking, laughter bubbling up in there throat.

"Six! Five!"

A couple nearby clinked glasses and kissed hard and fast, lipstick smudging.

"Four! Three!"

Confetti cannons were being passed out. Someone stepped on a balloon with a festive pop.

"Two! One!"

"Happy New Year!"

Cheers exploded across the room as balloons dropped from the ceiling and a storm of confetti rained down. Horns blared. Couples kissed. Glasses clinked. The whole place shimmered like champagne in mid-burst.

Christine laughed, blinking against the glitter in the air—when suddenly, the woman from across the room spun toward her.

Impossibly long legs. Sinful red shoes. Cheeks flushed, lips slightly parted, curls slipping loose from a jeweled comb. Her eyes were lit with something wild and golden.

"Happy New Year, gorgeous!"

Before Christine could answer, the woman leaned in and kissed her—quick and bold, laughter-sweet and gin-warm.

Christine startled, then smiled—something sparking behind her eyes.

"Well," she whispered, breathless. "Why not?"

She kissed her back—softer, slower, not unsure but almost reverent. For a heartbeat, time stretched. Music dulled. The room held it's breath. Then they parted—eyes still locked, an electric hush crackling between them.

The woman winked, turned, and disappeared into the blur of shimmer and smoke.

Christine stood blinking, lips tingling, one hand still lifted like she might catch the moment before it slipped.

A new year. A new breath. A new spark.

She closed her eyes and raised her glass high.

"To 1925."

Five

Strawberry Pop-Tarts

CHLOÉ | EAST ORANGE, NJ | C.
1983

THE HALL HOUSE — MID APRIL

"Chloé! Get up!"

The voice was small but shrill—her brother's—and came with a series of sharp pokes to her shoulder.

She groaned.

"You're gonna be late," Charles warned. "Mom's already called you three times."

Chloé didn't answer. She pressed her face deeper into her pillow, willing the sunlight to gold back into the night. The morning light leaking through the window was too loud, too bold, too cheerful. She yanked the blanket over her head and curled tighter into herself, searching for the place where dreams still clung like cobwebs.

"I'm tellin'!"

Before she could bargain with her body for five more minutes, the covers ripped away in a sudden, cruel gust—her brother tugging them with both hands and all his might. Cold air pounced on her bare arms and legs, a chill slap that made her gasp and flinch.

"Hey!" She snapped, eyes finally opening. "What is wrong with you?"

"You!" He huffed, hands on hips like a tiny sergeant. "Get UP!"

Chloé sat up slowly, blinking as her braids flopped over her eyes. The walls of her room seemed a little grayer this morning. The posters on her walls—torn-out pages of dancers and gymnasts and cartoon animals—Mary Lou Retton and Michael Jackson—they looked tired this morning. Even Pepper, curled at the foot of the bed with his snout buried in his paws, didn't stir.

"I don't feel good," Chloé mumbled. It wasn't a lie, exactly. But it wasn't a truth either.

Her brother squinted at her, suspicious. "You said that yesterday."

"I did not."

"Did too."

"Did not,"

He stuck out his tongue and stomped off, muttering under his breath.

"I'm tellin'."

Chloé heard him in the hallway a second later, voice stretching down the stairs.

"Moooom!"

Chloé rubbed her face and signed, the weight in her chest pressing heavier than the covers had. She used to wake up with a song in her head and sunlight in her bones. She used to sing "Tomorrow" at the top of her lungs while brushing her teeth, imagining she was Annie, belting it to the rafters of some Broadway stage. She used to leap across the room like the rug was a trampoline and the ceiling didn't matter.

Now, her feet felt heavy before they even hit the floor.

Outside her door, her mother's voice rose again. "Chloé, last call!"

She knew that tone. That was the 'if I have to come up there, I'm going to make it worth my while' tone. The 'I got enough to do this morning without fighting with your narrow, yellow behind' tone.

Still, Chloé lingered, her gaze drifting to the small bookshelf across the room. Tiger, her orange-striped kitten, sat perched like a loaf of bread on the second shelf, tail twitching. He blinked at her slowly, as if to say: You okay, kid?

She shrugged at him. Even her fur-babies knew something was off.

She didn't know how to name it, but school didn't feel like a place for her anymore.

Not since the move.

Not since the teasing.

Not since her favorite leotard had been found behind the gym—soiled, torn—and someone hissed "Light-Bright Barbie girl" like it was a curse.

Not since the world decided she was too loud, too emotional, and that her shine needed dimming to be tolerable.

Didn't matter how fast she could cartwheel.

Didn't matter how perfectly she could land a round-off back hand-spring.

No one was cheering.

"Chloé!" Her mom bellowed. Closer now. Feet on the stairs.

Chloé sighed again and slipped out of bed.

"I'm up," she called, louder this time. "I'm up."

She padded down the hall and into the bathroom, Pepper trotting in close behind before she could close the door.

She barely noticed him until she tripped over his tail. He yelped, half startle, half drama.

"Sorry, baby," she said, crouching down to kiss the top of his scruffy little head. "Should've named you Shadow, you're always un-derfoot."

Pepper was… well, objectively speaking, kind of a mess. A black with a sprinkling of white mutt with wiry hair that stuck out in tufts like he'd lost a fight with a brush. His ears never agreed on a direction, and one eye always seemed just a little more suspicious than the other. But to Chloé, he was perfect. So ugly he was cute—Oscar the Grouch meets Sandy from Annie, with just the right mix of attitude and heart.

Her dad had brought him home in a cardboard box one rainy Thursday, and from the second their eyes met, that was it. Pepper had chosen her. Chloé always said he was her guardian angel in dog form, disguised in fur and mischief.

They did everything together. Played in the yard, raced up and down the block until their legs age out, invented elaborate games that no one else understood. Chloé had even trained him to chase squirrels—though if he ever actually caught one, she was sure neither of them would know what to do next. They were nearly his size, after all.

Even Tiger, their orange-striped kitten, was nearly as big as Pepper. But size never fazed him. Pepper was fearless. Loyal. Fierce.

And every morning, without fail, he walked her to the front door. Every afternoon, at exactly 2:58 PM, he was back in place—ears perked, tail wagging—waiting for her return.

She smiled at the thought, turned the faucet on, twisted the dial toward hot, and pulled the shower pin.

Steam filled the room, curling against the mirror. Chloé pulled off her pajamas and stepped into the stream.

Warm water rushed over her shoulders, her back, her legs. It felt like a hug from the inside out, like the night being peeled away one drop at a time. She tilted her head back, keeping her hair out of the droplets and tried to let it carry away the heaviness, the whispers, the shadows that clung from her sleep.

Another nightmare.

Worse this time.

The kind that stayed with her even after waking, like ink smeared behind her eyes. She didn't remember every detail—just the feeling:

fear pressing against her chest like a weight, sweat slicking her skin, her sheets twisted and damp beneath her.

She didn't cry out anymore. Not for the last few weeks. But her pillow still caught the tears she learned not to talk about.

And now, the mirror—blurry as it was with condensation—still showed the faint puffiness around her eyes.

Proof that Chloé, the girl who used to wake up singing, the girl who summersaulted down the hallway and made friends with robins and butterflies, hadn't slept well in weeks.

She pressed her palms flat against the tile and whispered into the mist, "Please let today be better."

Pepper gave a soft whine from behind her, as if echoing her hope.

"Chloé Elizabeth! Hurry up!" Her mother called p the stairs, the clatter of heels on the tile following her voice. She was already late. Again.

Chloé pulled open her drawer and stared at the same three pairs of pants she always rotated through—two with grass stains, one with a frayed hem. She grabbed the cleanest pair and a T-shirt with a fading rainbow on it, then tugged them on, still damp from the shower. Her socks didn't match. She didn't care.

She gathered her braids, pulling them into a low ponytail that tugged at her scalp. As she turned to leave the room, her eyes landed—like they always did—on the frame hanging in the hallway.

It used to make her proud. That photo. The day it came out, the Essex County Observer had printed it in full color, right on the font page. A rare thing. You could see every detail—well, as much as a newspaper and a 35mm film reprint could manage. But her mother had the original photo framed along with the article, and that version showed everything. Too much, maybe.

The sharp creases in her father's decorated Army dress uniform. The flash of red silk lining her mother's navy cloak, worn over the crisp white Nurse's Aide uniform she'd earned while going to college full-time—between raising kids and running the hospitals entire PR and marketing department.

The article didn't mention that part.

Didn't mention that she got certified not because she wanted to, but because it gave her the authority to speak for the nurses—many of of whom were ready to strike. The hospital had started turning away patients deep in the grip of crack addiction. People the nurses knew. People they loved. Neighbors. Friends. Cousins. Sons.

The hospital liked the optics: a credentialed Black woman. A "bridge." A mother. A wife. A church usher. An extended family member of one of the most prominent Black churches in the county. A face they could put in front of a microphone when the cameras showed up.

And Chloé had been proud. Back then.

But now, the frame watched her every time she passed it. Her brother's dark, round afro and darker eyes seemed to follower her down the hallway, haunting her even when he was just a room away. She'd caught herself staring at it once, just after waking up from a dream she couldn't remember—just a heaviness in her chest and the echo of some lost sound.

Her pink-and-white lacy dress fluttered in the photo, perfectly still in the shot. Her hair had been blown out and pressed straight, slinging under the flash. Her lacy socks, her shiny black paten leather shoes. Their Sunday best, standing in front of the fireplace in their little colonial house—the one her parents were so proud to own. A Black-owned home in a struggling neighborhood.

That part had made the paper.

She hadn't noticed back then how stiff everyone looked.

Now she couldn't unsee it.

Smiles that felt like lies. Her father's arm draped a little too tightly around her mother's waist. Charlie, her little brother, squinting hard in the camera flash. And her own face—Chloé, mid-grin. Eyes too old for the girl they belonged to.

She looked away.

Downstairs, Pepper barked once. Impatient.

"Coming," she whispered, her voice rough with morning.

They'd said they were proud of how she "carried herself." How polite and articulate she was. So well-spoken, the lady from the paper had said, like it was a compliment.

They hadn't printed the part where Pepper flinched when Dad sneezed too loud.

Or how Chloé would draw the bath, then wait at the foot of the stairs, steadying her mother's arm as she climbed—knees swollen, breath shallow, after twelve long hours on the hospital floor and a week of night classes in fluorescent-lit classrooms.

The paper said they were picture-perfect.

But perfect didn't mean peaceful.

Or safe.

She slipped on her sneakers—tied the fraying laces—and grabbed her backpack.

At the bottom of the stairs, her mother swept past in a cloud of perfume, keys jangling in one hand, folder in the other. She looked tired. Always tired. But beautiful, too. Lipstick bright. Hair wrapped in a scarf that matched her blazer. Her mask.

"Finally,"her mom said without looking up. She was flipping through notes, muttering under her breath. "Today's the press follow-up. I'll be home late."

"Did they fix the vending machine yet?" Chloé asked, trying to sound casual.

"What?"

"At your job. You said it was broken."

Her mother paused, blinked. "Oh. No, I don't think so. Why do you care about the vending machine?"

"I don't," Chloé mumbled. "Just... wondered."

Her mom sighed and looked at her then—really looked. "You okay?"

Chloé nodded. Too fast. "Yeah. I'm fine."

"Okay, come straight home after school. Your brother lost his key again and won't be able to get in until you get here."

She shoved a strawberry Pop-Tart into Chloé's hand. "And there's no telling when your father will be home, so go get Charles from the neighbor's and make sure he does his homework before either of you turn the tv on."

"Ugh," Chloé wrinkled her nose. "I don't like these. I like the brown sugar ones better. These take like chemicals and death."

"Chloé, please stop being so dramatic. It was Charle's week to pick. If you don't want all the brown sugar ones gone in a day, don't eat them all in one sitting."

Chloé opened her mouth to argue, but one look from her mother and she thought better of it. "Okay," she said quietly, stuffing the corner of the cold Pop-Tart into her mouth. "Yuck. It's cold."

"Whose fault is that?" Her mother rolled her eyes. "You're the one who slept in. Next time, come down on time and they'll still be warm."

Chloé swallowed the dry, artificially sweet lump of strawberry and frosted crust. She didn't say anything about Tiffany. Or the girls who called her "Hollywood" because of the newspaper. Or how Mrs. Sheers pretended not to hear them.

Her mom leaned down and kissed her forehead, the scent of coffee breath clinging close. Her lipstick left a ghost of color behind.

Then the door opened. Bright light flooded in. Chloé blinked.

"Bye Pepper," she said, stepping outside.

The air smelled like cut grass and car exhaust. She could already hear the bell ringing up the street. She looked for Tiffany out of habit.

She wasn't there.

Not that it mattered anymore.

"Bye, Mom," Chloé called over her shoulder as she walked down the front walkway to the sidewalk, not looking back.

She'd better hurry if she was going to make it before the late bell.

Six

Heir

DJEMU'S STUDY

In a land where names were carved to outlast stone and bloodlines were the scaffolding of legacy, a man without a child was a man already halfway to the grave.

Four years had passed since Cassia's wedding—four years since her name was joined to Djemu's by ink, by law, by the gods. Four years since the dance of union had sealed their fate before nobles and servants alike. And still, the House of Djemu had produced no heir.

It was a quiet crisis, the sort that cracked slowly through foundations. No priests had spoken openly. No scrolls had yet called her barren. But the silence was tightening. Eyes lingered longer. Whispers clung to her footsteps. Each passing festival brought fresh offerings to the fertility gods—more elaborate, more desperate.

In Egypt, a man's name was only as eternal as the child who spoke it after his death. Without a son, Djemu's estates would pass back to the temple, his titles redistributed to younger, hungrier rivals.

His ka—the vital soul meant to live on through prayer and remembrance—would wander the afterlife alone, untethered, eventually forgotten.

And that was the death beneath death. The one men feared most. Djemu had not spoken of it—not directly. But the distance between them had grown like the drought between Nile floods. His glances were colder. His voice, clipped. He had once looked at her as if she were a divine acquisition, a crown set upon his house. Now, he looked at her as one might look at a locked door that refused to open. Cassia knew. She saw it in the way Luna tightened her lips while dressing her. In the way household servants fumbled for words they once spoke freely. In the way her mother wrote less and less, and when she did, used language carefully chosen.

Her womb had become a conversation the world was trying not to have out loud.

And Djemu—Djemu was no longer waiting for fate to change its mind.

The city of Memphis stirred beneath the weight of unanswered prayers. Gossip moved like river fog through the streets and colonnades. Market stalls spoke Cassia's name beneath layers of honey and linen. In palace halls, priests and viziers exchanged glances when Djemu passed—too respectful to confront him, too shrewd not to worry.

No child meant no future. No heir meant no peace.

Inside the estate's private walls, it meant something far more dangerous.

"It will be done during the Festival of the Flood," Djemu said, his back to her, arms crossed, eyes on the black window beyond. "Three nights of wine, combat, and celebration. The city will be too drunk to question anything."

Cassia stood still. She had not sat when summoned. She would not sit now.

"You're going to hold a competition," she repeated, as if hearing it again might make it sound less absurd. "You're going to parade our soldiers like bulls in a ring—tell them they're fighting for gold and glory, and then… offer them a woman like cattle?"

"Not a woman," he said sharply. "A slave. A faceless girl. One night. No one will know."

"A slave girl who is me," she spat. Silence.

He turned then, and his face bore none of the warmth it had once held. It was carved from ambition now, chiseled hard by shame.

"You should be thanking me," he said quietly. "This preserves everything. Our name. Your station. Your life."

"My life?" Cassia stepped forward, fury brimming. "You would have me lie with a stranger like a whore in a veil—and call that my salvation?"

Djemu didn't flinch. "Lower your voice."

"No." Her voice shook, not from weakness, but from the weight of what he was asking. "You lower yours. You're asking me to submit to this—to smile and play my part in some grotesque pantomime—so you can wash your hands of it afterward like you had no part in it at all."

He exhaled, a tight sound, like patience wearing thin. "It's not grotesque. It's a solution."

"To what?" she asked. "To your shame? To the whispers behind your back that the great Djemu, son of war, can't plant seed in the earth he claims to rule?"

That landed. A muscle jumped in his jaw.

He turned away, took a slow step toward the window. "They'll whisper either way. This way, they whisper about you."

The silence stretched between them, taut as a drawn bowstring. Cassia's voice dropped, sharp as a blade. "And that's more comfortable for you?"

"It's survivable," he said without turning. "For both of us."

She laughed once, low and bitter. "You mean it protects your power."

He turned then. "It protects everything. The house, the name, the line. Your position. The work my father bled to build, the alliances I've had to keep alive. You think you can keep that with artful speeches and clever eyes? This is how power is preserved, Cassia—not with ideals, but with heirs."

"And what about love?" she asked, more quietly now. "What about dignity?"

Djemu blinked, slowly. "Love was never part of this. We had duty. And you have done yours, mostly. But now… now you must do more." She stared at him. "By letting you sell me to a stranger in disguise?

You want me to carry a child I won't even recognize, and call it ours?" He didn't answer.

Something inside her cracked, quiet but final.

"You're not doing this for us," she said. "You're doing this for you.

You'd rather gut my honor than admit you've failed." His nostrils flared, but he kept his voice even. "You forget yourself."

"No," she said. "I remember myself. You're the one who's forgotten."

A pause. A shift.

His gaze hardened. And when he spoke, it was lower now, colder. "You swore your body to me," he said. "Before gods and men. You wear the rings. You carry the seal. I don't need your consent, Cassia. I need your obedience."

The words struck like a slap.

Obedience.

Obligation.

Oaths.

She swayed, but did not retreat.

The heat of tears stung behind her eyes. She would not let them fall.

"Then take it," she whispered. "Take what's yours. But don't ever again ask for my loyalty. You already spent that."

Djemu's jaw tightened, but he said nothing at first. Just stood there, still as stone, watching her like something wild he could neither tame nor turn away from. Then—

"I never asked for loyalty," he said at last. "I asked for an heir." The words landed like a blow.

Cassia flinched—but only slightly. Her face held.

"You think they won't find out?" she said, quieter now, but laced with venom. "The servants talk. The soldiers boast. And if a child comes of this, the blood in his face will not be yours."

"It won't matter," Djemu said, stepping closer, his voice ironclad. "I will claim him the moment he draws breath. And you will say nothing—because you need this too."

Cassia closed her eyes. It was true. As much as it curdled her, as much as it broke her spirit and violated every fiber of her dignity... she needed this.

The rumors were already circling, but not about her. About him. His pride had festered, twisted into blame. He would rather destroy her than admit the fault lay with him.

Still—still—there was a sliver of strategy in this madness. A child would protect her, keep her position secure, shield her from being cast aside like a bad harvest.

Even if it cost her body. Even if it cost her soul.

"I will not do this," she said at last, voice hollow, trembling. He stepped forward, one hand at her jaw, too firm, bruising. "You will," he said softly. "Because the alternative is worse."

She met his eyes. She saw the fear there, buried beneath layers of arrogance. Not fear of the gods. Fear of power slipping from his grasp.

Desperate men are dangerous.

And in that moment, hope fell to a whisper. There was no other choice.

If she failed—or didn't return before dawn—he would have his answer.

Cassia didn't nod. She didn't cry. She simply turned and left the room.

There were preparations to be made.

* * *

THE BARRACKS MESS HALL — ONE WEEK LATER

Sunlight struck bronze helms and bare shoulders as three soldiers circled a small fire pit, each with a cup of watered wine, the lingering taste of tension on their tongues and the low hum of anticipation winding through their nerves. The heat clung to them, thick with unease, expectation—of coin, of flesh, spectacle... of glory.

"They're calling it a reward for service," said Hamut, the youngest of the three, barely more than a boy by veteran standards, though his arms were already roped with sinew and sun-darkened from drills. "But it smells like distraction to me."

Distraction from what?" Saben asked, leaning against a support post, arms crossed, a slice of shadow cutting across his face. His wine sat untouched by his boot.

He cut an imposing figure even in rest—tall, sun-bronzed, with the hard lines of a man who knew violence intimately but didn't wear it loudly. His dark locks were tied back loosely, a few curls clinging to the sweat at his temple. The lion clasp on his chest caught the last of the firelight, glinting bronze against worn leather.

Hooded black eyes watched from beneath heavy brows, unreadable as ever. Soldiers said he could stand that way for hours, unmoving, like stone—and then strike faster than a snake when provoked. His kopesh rested across his back, a curved promise of what he was capable of.

He didn't speak much unless it mattered. But when he did, men listened. Not just out of duty—but because they believed him.

And though he could command with the weight of a king's voice, tonight, he just flicked a coin between his fingers and waited. Still. Calm. Ready.

Hamut leaned in, voice low. "The unrest in the west. Those river settlements keep testing the border. And the priests haven't blessed the Nile in weeks."

Jorek let out a dry grunt, one eye narrowing as he tore off a hunk of flatbread. A scar dragged from jaw to ear—an old Nubian blade had nearly silenced him for good. "And next you'll tell me the grain rot is a curse from the gods," he muttered. "You believe every fireside whisper, boy."

"No," Hamut said coolly, shrugging one shoulder as he sipped from his cup. "I just don't believe what they want us to. You think it's a coincidence they drag us out here for a 'celebration' a few nights after you-know-who and the wife were overheard tearing into each other about not having an heir?"

That earned a few glances.

The flick of Saben's coin stopped mid-air. Just for a beat.

He caught it clean, set it on the table, and leaned forward slightly—just enough to refocus attention without drawing it.

A slow breath. Calm on the outside. But his jaw had tightened.

He didn't speak. Didn't need to. The shift in his posture was enough for anyone paying close attention—though most weren't.

"Even the columns shook," one of the younger guards said low. "Like a quarrel in the market square. Thought he'd tear the room apart."

"Speak for yourself," Jorek said, waving a dismissive hand as he leaned back against the stone wall, scar catching the firelight. "They give me a purse of gold, a field of my own, and a night with one of those highborn silk-skins? They can call it a blessing from Horus for all I care."

"They said concubine, not wife," Hamut smirked, raising a brow. "You think one night with a concubine's enough to distract an army?" Jorek chewed his words like gristle.

"Add land, gold, and a title to it, and you'd be surprised how many start dreaming instead of thinking."

"They're calling her one of the high harem," Hamut added with a wink. "Not the usual temple whore."

Jorek snorted. "Long as she's warm, I don't care whose bed she came from."

"She won't be offering you figs in the morning."

Jorek barked a laugh. "I don't plan on being there for breakfast." That drew a round of chuckles from the others.

But not from Saben.

His coin flicked faster, the metal catching candlelight in sharp flashes. The warmth of the room no longer touched him—he felt apart from it, a breath held too long.

Hamut's words rang louder in his mind than the laughter. That shift in tone—cool, but laced with something deeper. A warning, maybe. Or a trap.

His jaw flexed once. He didn't look up.

"What about you, Captain?" Jorek asked, half-mocking, half-curious. "You going to join the game? A man like you—loyal, decorated—seems the gods would shine favor on you."

Saben's voice was quiet when it came.

"I don't gamble with things I can't stomach winning." "Ah," Hamut said, grinning, "too proud for prizes?" "No," Saben murmured. "Just careful about the price."

Jorek raised his cup in mock salute. "Suit yourself. But if I win, I'm taking her thrice. Once for the gold, once for the glory—"

He grinned, eyes gleaming under firelight. "—and once more for the story."

That drew a round of hoots and slaps to the table. "Ha! I'll drink to that."

"Save some of her for the rest of us." "Careful, Jorek—she might break you."

The men roared, cups clinking, bravado thick in the air like smoke. Their laughter rang sharp against the stone walls, easy and ignorant. None of them saw the edges fraying beneath the night's velvet. None of them noticed Saben's silence.

He didn't lift his cup. Didn't smirk.

Didn't speak.

He watched the fire instead.

The flames flickered in his eyes, throwing shadows across the hard line of his jaw. He hadn't yet decided whether this was spectacle or insult—but something about it tasted wrong. Too elaborate. Too eager. Like silk drawn over rot.

For four years, Saben had watched this household from the front row. He hadn't protested when Djemu reassigned him—promoted him, technically—to oversee the palace gates and coordinate security for court arrivals. A more prestigious post, they'd said. A reward. But it meant leaving Cassia's side.

He hadn't wanted it. He hadn't said so.

Cassia had told him to go. Her voice had been soft, her smile convincing. She said it would be better this way. Told him she was safe. He'd nodded. Obeyed. But even from a new distance, he'd seen the shift.

The slow souring of court toward Djemu and Cassia. Whispers growing teeth. Nobles who once bowed low now offered shallow nods. The absence of an heir was an open wound wrapped in silk, and it festered beneath every ceremonial smile.

And her family. Gods. He watched them too. How their support pulled back—not dramatically, but inch by inch. No more midnight visits from her cousin with gossip from the provinces. No more emissaries bringing news from her father's estates. They left her in the cold, but gently. Politely.

Cowards.

Cassia bore it all with the grace of a queen. Chin high. Voice steady. Smiling at the same men who whispered behind her back. But

Saben knew better. He had stood by too long not to see the cracks spidering beneath her skin.

He was tired of it.

Tired of watching her shrink, day by day, behind veils of duty and decorum. Tired of pretending she wasn't unraveling. Tired of doing nothing.

And yet—what could he do? She was not his. Not in any way that mattered.

So he watched. And guarded. And kept silent. It was all he had left to offer. His service. His sword. His obedience.

Now this competition—this parade of gold, land, and flesh—it was grotesque. Too perfect in its timing. And something in Djemu's eyes lately… It wasn't lust. It was strategy.

Saben stared into the fire, jaw clenched.

Maybe this was the answer. Maybe if he joined—if he won—he could take the prize and disappear. Retire to the river provinces. Breathe air that didn't reek of lies and longing.

Cassia would survive. She always did. She was too smart, too sharp, too proud to fold.

And he… he was tired of dying by inches. Watching her change and saying nothing. Seeing her from a distance carved into his bones.

Maybe this was the sign. Maybe it was time.

He couldn't offer her land. Or title. Or even a name that would matter outside the barracks.

The idea of Cassia riding off into the sunset with him—sand-stained boots and all—was laughable.

Maybe he'd go mad before she ever looked at him like a man instead of a shadow in the halls.

A sharp, two-note horn blast echoed across the courtyard, cutting through his thoughts like a knife. The southern yard. Assembly call.

Saben stood slowly, shaking the dust from his palms. Nothing good ever came from that horn.

Still, he made his way toward the barracks yard, where the others were already gathering. Armor half-fastened, blades strapped, some still chewing breakfast—soldiers moved with that practiced blend of laziness and precision only years of discipline could produce.

He found his usual place near the edge of the pack. The sun was high, hot enough to melt the sand to glass. If the gods were merciful, this was a weather warning and they could all go back to pretending to be useful in the shade.

No such luck.

Sergeant Kareth stood at the front, arms crossed like an annoyed idol, his voice already cutting through the yard.

"For those of you stupid enough to think with your swords," he barked, "you'll want to hear this."

Scattered laughter. A few chest bumps. Saben folded his arms. "This contest isn't a game. It's not a drunken wager or a street

brawl. It's sanctioned by the high court. Sponsored by the House of Ibsha. And yes"—he paused for dramatic effect—"there is a woman at the end of it. Which means half of you will lose your minds before you even swing a blade."

Groans. A smirk from Beren. Saben stared forward.

"One week from today," Kareth continued, "you'll present your-selves here. Clean. Armed. Fed. You'll fight in three rounds. Last man standing takes the prize: gold. Land. And a night with a royal concu-bine."

More hoots. Someone clapped.

"And if you die before round three," Kareth added, "I'll have your bones swept off my yard by the hourglass. Questions?"

A hand shot up. "How much land?"

"Enough to keep your mother out of your house. Shut up." More laughter.

Saben didn't smile.

He just stood there, watching the others grin and jostle and joke—and felt something cold settle deeper in his chest.

He didn't know why yet. But this wasn't just about winning. Something was off.

And whatever it was… it smelled like trouble.

Seven

A Fortune for a Fortune

CARLOTTA | CADIZ, SPAIN | C. 1494

THE MARKETPLACE — EARLY FRIDAY MORNING

The morning sun had barely crested the rooftops of the city, but already the harbor sang with the sounds of trade and temptation. Ships rocked in their moorings, gulls screamed overhead, and the scent of brine, fish, and frying oil tangled in the air like lovers in a tight bed. Carlotta preferred this hour—when the world was still stretching, when the bustle hadn't quite become chaos.

She sat cross-legged on a faded woven rug near the market steps, her full skirts a tumble of saffron and wine-colored cotton, worn thin at the hem but still vibrant, catching the light like fire through silk. A crocheted shawl—indigo-dyed and threaded with tiny mirrored discs that winked in the sun—draped loosely around her shoulders in a way that made it seem as though she didn't care who looked at her, even as she controlled exactly what they saw.

Bracelets—brass, glass, bone, and a single carved bangle painted with a red eye—layered thick on both wrists, chiming softly whenever she moved. Her eyes, kohl-rimmed and glinting like flint, were fixed on the young man seated in front of her—soft hands, velvet cloak, too much gold on his fingers for someone so young and foolish. "Your lifeline is strong," she murmured, tracing the line along his open palm. "But see how it splits here?" She pointed with one ringed finger. "A choice. One will lead to glory. The other..." She let the sentence trail off, then gave a small, dramatic shrug. "Let's hope you choose well."

The boy swallowed, wide-eyed—hazel, with flecks of green that darkened when he was nervous. Not fear, exactly, but the restless shimmer of someone both anxious and eager to be told something important. She could already see his imagination spinning tales where he was the hero, the lover, the king.

Behind him, the crowd pressed closer. Market-goers paused to gawk, drawn by the allure of mystery and the soft promise of forbidden knowledge. A perfect audience.

And perfect cover.

Just off to the side, Sofia moved like a breeze through the onlookers—innocent, curious, unnoticed. A finger brushed a pouch here, a ribbon tugged loose there. Coins vanished. Trinkets slipped silently into hidden folds. Her wide brown eyes blinked up at a merchant as she bumped into him and offered a sheepish smile. The man huffed, patted her head, and turned back to the spectacle.

Carlotta kept her gaze on her mark, but she was always aware of Sofia. The rhythm between them was years in the making—wordless, flawless. A dance.

"Your fate," she said, dropping her voice to a smoky hush, "is still unwritten, but luck, she is fickle. A coin offered may buy you favor... or at least keep misfortune at bay."

He fumbled at his belt, pulling free a silver coin and pressing it into her palm like a child handing over a secret. Carlotta gave him a smile like sunlight off a blade.

And then—

A voice, low and sharp, sliced through the moment.

"That one's light-fingered."

Carlotta's heart kicked. Her eyes snapped up, catching the source: a man leaned lazily against a sun-bleached barrel at the edge of the square. He wasn't dressed like a merchant, nor a soldier—too casual, too dirty, too sure. A scarf was knotted around his neck like an afterthought, his boots worn to the sole, a smirk tugging at the corner of his mouth like he already knew how this would end.

His eyes weren't on her. They were on Sofia.

Sofia stood a few paces behind the crowd, half-shadowed beneath a swaying awning. Her dark curls had slipped free of her scarf, and she was mid-turn—just sliding something small and glittering into her satchel when she froze. Her eyes flicked up, wide and sharp, locking with the stranger's for a single beat. She was caught.

Her eyes darted to Carlotta.

Carlotta didn't flinch. Her pulse thundered in her ears, but her face broke into an easy, languid smile. She laughed—a rich, amused sound that turned heads and bought her seconds.

"Aye, and who isn't in this city?" she said, voice light as wind off the sea. She rose with the grace of a cat uncoiling, flipping the boy's hand closed like she was brushing off crumbs. "Your fortune's told, sweet dove. Hold fast to your purse now. Cádiz will eat the foolish alive."

The crowd chuckled, a ripple of amusement shifting the gathered bodies like wind through grain. No one looked too closely. No one questioned.

But Carlotta's eyes didn't leave Sofia.

Her cousin stilled mid-step, the stolen brooch still heavy in her pocket, her body half-turned as several heads turned too—more curious now than alarmed. It was a heartbeat from unraveling.

The merchant's son blinked dumbly, caught between flattery and confusion, as if wondering whether he'd just been charmed, robbed, or both.

And the stranger—

He didn't move. He only smirked, slow and deliberate, like a man who'd just tossed a stone into a pond and was waiting to see where the ripples reached.

Carlotta's mind raced.

This was no accident. No righteous citizen crying foul. This was a test.

Another player.

Someone testing the waters. Fine.

Let's see if he can keep up.

She clapped her hands, the sound sharp as a whip crack. "Come, Sofia! The stars have changed!"

She moved fast. Too fast to think. Her skirts swept up dust as she vaulted off the step and into the crowd, ducking beneath the merchant boy's startled arm. His velvet cloak twisted like a broken sail as he spun in confusion.

"Sofia!" she hissed, barreling past a fruit cart.

Her cousin saw her, blinked, and bolted—nimble as a cat, the two of them weaving toward each other through the shifting chaos like magnets snapping into place.

"Hey!" the boy shouted behind them. "My ring—she took my—!" Too late.

Carlotta caught Sofia's hand in hers and spun them both into a knot of spice sellers. "Run," she whispered, grinning, "and try not to drop the cheese this time."

Laughter sparked from somewhere behind them—half delight, half outrage.

A woman shrieked as her basket of oranges hit the cobblestones and exploded like cannonballs.

A dog barked. Barked again. Then lunged. Carlotta yelped and hoisted her skirts. "NOPE!"

Sofia shriek-laughed, dragging her cousin sideways into a side lane. The dog skidded into a pile of onions, sending peels flying.

The merchant boy's voice hollered over the din, "Guards!

GUARDS! They robbed me!"

"¡Dios mío!", Sofia gasped between giggles. "You really took the ring?"

"He's lucky I didn't take his shoes."

Behind them, a bell rang from the watchtower. Too close.

They careened into a thread vendor's stall, sending bolts of silk into the air like fireworks. Ribbons slapped across their faces. Feathers flew. A fat hen squawked and made a break for it.

Carlotta tripped over a spool of indigo thread, arms flailing, and crashed into a crate of buttons that exploded like hailstones. She landed on her back in the soft folds of imported muslin, blinking at the sky.

"Artful," Sofia muttered, grabbing her by the elbow. "Shut up and grab the good stuff."

They stuffed scattered trinkets and beads into their skirts, half-crawling, half-laughing, half-running as the first guard turned into the alley.

"STOP! Thieves!"

Carlotta grabbed the edge of a balcony and vaulted herself up, yanking Sofia behind her. The wood groaned, then cracked—

"Don't you DARE—" It broke.

They tumbled. Through the thatch. Into someone's laundry.

The scream they met inside wasn't polite.

"Sorry!" Carlotta sang as they leapt through the front door, knocking over a pot of lentils and a startled man missing half an eyebrow.

Down the steps. Past the goats. Over a wall. And then—

Stillness.

Silence.

Just their breath and the sun and the dust of the alley. Gone.

* * *

Behind them, the merchant boy was still yelling about the injustice of it all. One guard examined an onion like it might hold a clue. Another chased the wrong pair of girls in green skirts.

And the whistle blower?

He pushed off with a lazy stretch, eyes narrowing, amusement dancing on his face like heat over stone.

He wasn't surprised they got away. He was counting on it.

He tucked his hands in his belt, and followed. Smiling.

Mission accomplished.

*　*　*

They crouched behind the crumbling stone wall, hearts pounding in tandem, backs pressed against the cool rock like it might swallow them whole if they asked nicely. A few breaths passed. Then a few more.

Carlotta peeked through a gap between sun-warmed terracotta pots and curling green leaves. The plaza beyond was a painting in motion—barterers, soldiers, shouting vendors, a chicken trotting indignantly down the steps with half a ribbon tied to its leg. But no guards. No shouting merchant boys. No smugglers with smug grins.

She dropped down beside her cousin again, exhaling the breath she hadn't realized she'd been holding.

Sofia burst into laughter—bright, uncontainable, wild with adrenaline. "You're slipperier than an eel."

Carlotta clapped her hand over her cousin's mouth with a mock-scowl, eyes dancing. "Quiet, idiota! Want to get us killed?"

Sofia peeled her hand away and whispered theatrically, "If I'm gonna die, let it be after the oranges, the feathers, and the collapsing balcony, yeah?"

Carlotta couldn't hold it in any longer. She tipped her head back and laughed until her sides ached, the wall trembling behind her from their shared mirth. They mimed the chase—Carlotta pantomiming her fall into the buttons, Sofia reenacting the dog's bark, her own shriek, and the moment Carlotta tumbled out of the window with all the grace of a startled goat.

They wheezed with laughter, collapsing into each other like they used to when they were young girls. For a moment, it was just that: two girls, alive, wild, and free.

Eventually, Carlotta stood and brushed off her skirts. "Come on. Let's count the cheese before we get caught again."

They ducked into the grove that bordered the eastern road—olive trees and dusty fig shrubs offering welcome shade. The sun streaked through the branches like golden fingers, dappling the path with warmth and light.

Sofia pulled the pouch from inside her blouse and let the stolen trinkets catch the sun—earrings, a gold brooch with a red glass gem, a few rings, and three silver coins. "Could've been worse," she said, turning a sapphire-like bead between her fingers.

Carlotta dug into her pocket and revealed the ring she'd palmed from the merchant boy's finger during the reading. A thick gold band set with a garnet the size of a grape. She slipped it onto her middle finger with a satisfied grin. "Perfect fit."

Sofia gasped. "I still can't believe you swiped that during all that chaos!"

"Of course I did. All that velvet and no brains—he'll cry to his father and never learn a thing."

* * *

THE CAMPSITE — LATE FRIDAY MORNING

The trees thinned as they approached the edge of the woods. The scent of firewood and roasting onions wafted through the air. Before too long, the sounds of their caravan floated to them—children laughing, a fiddle playing a lazy tune, the creak of cart wheels settling in soft soil.

Ahead, their camp sprawled like a patchwork quilt—tents, wagons, blankets laid out under trees, the dark smoke of cooking fires winding up into the blue. Midday had come early thanks to the chaos, and Carlotta knew the others would want to know how the morning's take had gone.

They hadn't made as much as she'd hoped. It would feed them, yes. Maybe buy a pair of boots or replace the comb she had broken detangling her braids last week. But it wouldn't change their lives.

Carlotta walked in silence, arms loose at her sides, eyes tracking the shifting light between the trees. For months, they'd been scraping and scheming toward one goal—passage to the New World. Every dockside drunk and barnacled sailor had an opinion about it. Ever since that Genoese madman convinced the Crown to send him west, Cádiz had been buzzing like a kicked beehive.

From deeper down the rooted path, closer to camp, a burst of laughter rang out—male voices, loud and swaggering. Carlotta caught the familiar refrain drifting through the trees: 'Glory and gold, boys! Enough for a man to live like a king!'

She rolled her eyes so hard her head followed. "If one more sailor tells me about his 'glory and gold,' I swear I'll shove him into the sea." Just ahead, Sofia stopped short, spun on her heel, and dropped her voice into a dramatic growl. "We'll find new lands," she proclaimed in a thick Andalusian accent, "full of riches, virgins, and pigs that roast themselves!"

Carlotta blinked, then burst into laughter. "Pigs that roast themselves? That's oddly specific."

Sofia shrugged, all innocence. "Some fellow behind the fish stall swore it on his grandmother's bones."

Carlotta was still giggling when Sofia added brightly, "And maybe scurvy," hopping over a gnarled root like a goat in boots two sizes too big, her braid swinging behind her like a banner of mischief.

"Dios mío," Carlotta groaned, grinning wide. "You're impossible."

"And you're delusional," Sofia called back, skipping backward now, smirking. "But somehow, we make it work."

"Hell's teeth!" Carlotta snorted. "That we do!"

She had heard the stories for years—rumors of lands where streets sparkled with gems, where the sun never set, where a clever girl could be anything she wanted.

It was one of the things she loved most about Cádiz. The stories.

The smugglers brought them home like trophies, passing bottles and bread around the fire while they spun tales of pythons in the trees, temples carved from mountains, cities with golden roofs. As a child, Carlotta would sit so still, hardly breathing, eyes wide. She had believed every word. Maybe she still did.

And once—just once—she'd nearly gone with them.

Three years ago, the opportunity had been real. A ship was sailing for Santo Domingo, and the captain had taken a shine to Carlotta's card tricks, her sharp tongue, and her even sharper instincts. He'd offered her a place on board—a hammock, a pistol, and a cut of whatever they brought back.

She'd said yes.

Then, two nights before departure, news came from Sevilla: her aunt and uncle, Sofia's parents, were dead. Fire.

One day, she was planning her escape. The next, she was on a train carting a skinny, grief-struck girl with wild hair and bigger eyes than sense back to Cádiz.

There'd been no choice.

Sofia hadn't cried—not once—but she'd clung to Carlotta's hand the whole ride home like it was the last solid thing left in the world.

And just like that, the hammock and the pistol belonged to someone else.

She didn't regret it.

But she hadn't forgotten, either.

She glanced at Sofia now, darting over a root with the restless energy of a spark seeking flame, her curls catching the sunlight like a dark halo of defiance.

That dream still lingered.

And one day, if they ever got the chance—they'd chase it together. They stepped into the clearing, and the camp unfolded around them like a waking animal—hazy with woodsmoke, golden in the

sun, alive with laughter and the clatter of midday.

Bright scraps of drying laundry danced between trees like signal flags. Tents in faded reds and patchwork canvas sat in irregular rows, their sides stitched with repairs and decorated with charms, feathers, and old bone beads. Someone was sharpening a knife on a flat rock; another was napping in a hammock slung between two olive trees, straw hat tilted low over his face.

A wiry boy darted past with a carved wooden sword and a war cry in two languages, chasing a goose. The goose was unimpressed.

Sofia waved at the boy. "You still owe me two buttons, Miguelito!" They passed a pair of women weaving fresh netting for La Cerrada's next run. One of them—Reyna, a tall woman with a silver streak in her braid and arms like coiled rope—nodded at Carlotta as they passed.

"Back early," Reyna said, eyes sharp. "Lose your charm or find trouble?"

"Both," Carlotta replied with a grin. "But we brought gifts."

Reyna grunted approvingly. "Fernando's on scales today. And tell him not to haggle—last time he tried to take half my coin weight."

They found Fernando exactly where Reyna said he was: perched on a low stool beside a wooden table covered in scraps of leather, a battered scale, and various pouches and lockboxes. His shirt was unbuttoned halfway, his belly round as a wine cask, and his long mustache drooped like a disappointed crow.

"Ah, my favorite little cousins," he said, not looking up from a cracked ledger. "Come to confess or impress?"

Carlotta emptied their haul onto the table. Trinkets and coins gleamed in the sunlight. Sofia added the brooch and a pair of pearl-studded pins she'd managed to pull from someone's hair without them noticing.

"Impress," Carlotta said, with a little flourish of her hand. "Naturally."

Fernando snorted, but the corners of his eyes crinkled with amusement. He was grizzled and weather-tanned, old enough to be her uncle—if Carlotta had any family left besides Sofia—but sharp as broken glass and twice as dangerous if you crossed him. Still, he'd always had a soft spot for her. Not that he'd admit it.

"You were born to drive me mad," he muttered, holding up the brooch between calloused fingers. "You, I'd never trust near my mother's grave. You'd charm the bones right out of it."

"Only if they sparkled," Carlotta grinned. "I have standards, Fernando."

"You have nerve," he said, giving Sofia a glance that was half warning, half admiration. "And this one's no better. Someone's going to cry for a week over this bit of glass."

"Then she did her a favor," Carlotta shot back, eyes flashing with mischief. "Emotion builds character."

Sofia snorted, trying to stifle a laugh behind her hand.

Fernando chuckled despite himself, shaking his head as he turned to weigh the items. He muttered as he worked, scrawling numbers with a bit of charcoal on a scrap of parchment, pausing now and then to argue with the air or squint at Carlotta like she'd offended him personally. But when he handed over the pouch of coins, it was heavier than most—less than the haul deserved, more than most would've risked giving them. A quiet thank-you, in Fernando's way.

"Lunch is with Mara today," he said, jerking his head toward the rising smoke and clatter from the cook-fire. "Stew again. Better hurry if you want meat."

Carlotta raised a brow. "Who else would it be with?"

Fernando grinned. "Could've been Luis—boiled fish and broken dreams. Or Linna—Madre de Dios, everything she cooks smells like wet rope."

"Then Mara it is," Carlotta said, pocketing the coins and tossing him a wink. "Nothing but the best."

Fernando grunted, "Bah," but the grin tugging at his weathered face gave him away. He watched them go with that amused, exasperated fondness reserved for trouble you couldn't help but like.

Carlotta and Sofia slipped back into the rhythm of the camp, weaving past wagons stacked with crates and barrels, sidestepping tethered goats and sleeping dogs. The scent of roasted fish, simmering herbs, and sweet smoke hung thick in the warm air, curling around them like a familiar song.

Near the heart of the camp, beneath a patchwork canopy of faded linens, old sails, and bits of bright cloth fluttering like prayer flags, stood Mara's domain: the cook station. It was more throne room than kitchen—if thrones were battered stools and iron pots the size of wine barrels.

Mara herself was a mountain of a woman, wrapped in layers of striped skirts and aprons that bore the scars of a hundred meals. Her dark hair was twisted up with wooden spoons and sprigs of rosemary, and her arms—thick as tree limbs—moved with purpose. One hand stirred a bubbling stew with a ladle long enough to be mistaken for a weapon, while the other swatted away a cluster of small, dust-smeared children trying to sneak tastes.

"Not yet!" she bellowed, her voice rolling like thunder across the clearing. "You're not starving, Mateo—I watched you eat three pears this morning, you little fraud!"

A few of the children scattered, giggling. One held his belly in exaggerated agony, which earned him a flick of dishwater from Mara's basin and a muttered curse in a language older than the camp itself.

Despite the gruffness, Mara was the heart of the caravan. She knew who'd arrived in the night, who was gone in the morning, who'd eaten, who'd bled, who was pregnant, and who was lying about it. People came to her for food, yes—but also for news, for advice, for comfort. She kept the caravan fed and grounded, and when Mara wasn't happy, no one was.

The stew smelled of chickpeas, smoked paprika, and salt pork—thin, but hearty. Carlotta grabbed a chipped bowl, and Sofia snagged a hunk of bread from a cooling rack when Mara wasn't looking.

They sat in the dirt under a fig tree to eat, watching the life of the camp unfold around them. A man tuned a lute and started to play softly. Two women practiced a knife-throwing game, taking bets from the crowd. A grandmother dozed beside her embroidery. The rhythm of the place was slow but alive—always humming, always turning.

Mornings were spent weaving through city streets, pockets full of stories and fingers full of secrets. Afternoons in the camp—trading goods, listening for whispers of new runs or black market buyers, occasionally washing their clothes in the river if someone started complaining about the smell. Evenings around the fire, telling tales or playing dice until the embers died.

Carlotta rarely let her guard down. But here, in this moment, in the shade of the fig tree with a bowl of soup in her lap and the taste of adrenaline still buzzing in her mouth—she allowed herself to dream.

"Do you think we'll ever leave?" Sofia asked, pulling her knees to her chest, voice quiet.

Carlotta blinked. "What?"

"Cádiz. This life. Do you think we'll really go?" She looked out toward the trees, the open sky beyond. "Find that place with mangoes and parrots and gold in the sand."

Carlotta didn't answer right away. She watched a dragonfly skim past, caught in a shaft of sun. She leaned back against the fig tree, arms draped across her knees, watching the sky shift behind the leaves.

"We'll go," she said at last, voice low but steady. "Just... not yet."

Sofia didn't press. She just nodded, resting her head against Carlotta's shoulder, the weight of it familiar and grounding.

Around them, the camp carried on—music, knives, laughter. Life spun forward, as it always did.

But somewhere—just beyond the smoke and sunlight—a different world waited.

And Carlotta was determined to find it.

Eight

Naples

CELINA | NAPLES, ITALY | C. 1741

THE DOCKS — EARLY SEPTEMBER

They cut across the Bay of Naples just past the golden hour, the late sun slanting behind them, kissing the wake of the ship with ribbons of fire. The water had been kind—calm and steady with only the gentlest rise and fall. Celina, perched near the bow, had not once felt ill. Instead, she felt suspended—adrift in something softer than reality. A dream. A painting in motion. A scene from one of her canvases. Her skirts fluttered around her ankles in the sea breeze, white muslin layered over soft saffron, her wedding ribbons still pinned in her braids. The light brown plaits shimmered with threads of gold, strands glinting like a halo where the sun touched them. Serafina had retied the ribbons mid-journey, fingers swift and soothing, as if weaving new life into each careful knot.

Ahead, Naples rose like a breath held too long.

Gray stone and pink stucco, gold domes, bell towers, narrow spines of alleys descending into ports. A city born of contradiction—art and ash, saints and scandal. Even from here, it felt louder than Amalfi. Hungrier. She smelled the difference in the air: brinier, smokier, threaded with spice and fish and the faint copper of coins exchanged at crowded stalls. The city gleamed beneath a faint haze—like oil brushed thin over canvas to soften the edges.

This will be my new home, she thought. The place I become myself.

She didn't know what that would look like yet. A wife. A painter. A student. A Naples woman.

She pressed her hand over her stomach, as if trying to still the fluttering there. Anticipation. Or nerves. Or something more ancient.

She glanced back toward Giovanni, who stood at the stern with a hand on the rail, speaking quietly with the captain. His coat flared gently with the wind, and the angle of the sun caught the silver in his hair—at his temples, in his beard, like moonlight stitched into darkness.

He was handsome, in a way that felt seasoned rather than sweet. No softness to him. He had the posture of a man who had been watched all his life. There was still something impressive in the cut of his shoulders, the length of his frame, though a slight paunch softened his middle and he sometimes favored one leg. Forty-five, perhaps? Maybe fifty? He hadn't said.

To Celina, it didn't matter. He knew things. Important things. He had seen Rome. Painted cathedrals. Shaken hands with princes.

And now—he had chosen her.

I'll be a good wife, she told herself. I'll listen. I'll learn. I'll make him proud... and Papa, too.

She imagined walking Naples as a local, not a visitor. Climbing the hills to Capodimonte, where whispers said the king was building a palace to house the Farnese collection. She dreamed of seeing Caravaggio's brushwork up close. Studying frescoes by day and painting by candlelight. Having her own corner of the studio—their studio. Maybe even taking on commissions someday, if he allowed it. If she earned it.

She felt prepared for the household—she'd been trained for that. How to manage a kitchen. How to entertain. How to speak little and listen well.

The marriage bed, though—that was different. Her mother had said little. Serafina, even less. There were only hints and silences, the way women in the village passed knowledge like folded notes in church pews.

Do your duty. Let him lead. Don't ask too many questions. You'll be fine if you're quiet.

Celina didn't know what she expected. She only knew she was expected to yield. That a wife gave her body. That she was his now. Entirely.

I'll make it beautiful, she thought. Like a painting. Like a dream I can live inside. I'll make him love me.

They reached the docks just as the sun bowed into the sea, casting Naples in its afterglow. The water here was darker than Amalfi's crystalline turquoise—a deeper, more mysterious blue, edged with the smoke of the city. The sand was coarser, the shoreline more crowded, the boats smaller and packed tighter together. Voices shouted. Gulls screamed. Bells rang.

It was louder than she'd imagined. More alive.

Horses brayed in the distance, and somewhere nearby, a fishmonger shouted over the clanging of a bell. Children darted between legs, chasing each other with sticks, skirts and tunics flying. Vendors haggled in a medley of dialects she didn't recognize—Neapolitan, Sicilian, some sharp-edged northern tongue. A dog barked furiously at a beggar. A priest passed by with a donkey cart stacked high with melons.

And the smell.

Not the clean, salty perfume of Amalfi but a pungent stew—seaweed, smoke, old stone, sweat, wine, garlic, oil. Overripe fruit. Wet rope. Living things rotting and renewing all at once.

Celina drew in a shallow breath, willing herself not to show how it hit her.

Her legs wobbled slightly as she stepped off the vessel. Though she had grown up near the sea, she wasn't a sailor's daughter—just a merchant's. She hadn't spent enough time on the water to develop proper sea legs. The stone dock felt too hard beneath her soles, too unyielding. It scraped against her countryside shoes like judgment.

Giovanni returned to her side, gloved hand outstretched, steadying her as she touched down.

"Welcome home, mia sposa," he said, voice warm but distant, smile thin and polished like a coin rubbed smooth from too many trades.

His glove was soft kidskin, elegant, creased at the knuckles. Hers were lace-trimmed cotton—a wedding gift from her mother, pale ivory and delicate. They were too fine for her, too fragile. She hadn't removed them during the crossing, unsure if it would be improper now that she was a wife. But the gloves itched. She couldn't feel anything through them. Not the cool of the wind, or the smoothness of the ship's rail, or the press of Giovanni's hand.

Underneath, her fingers were raw with quiet longing—cleaned meticulously that morning, but still rimmed faintly with lavender blue at the cuticles and rose red beneath a single stubborn nail. She had scrubbed until her fingertips throbbed, until she wasn't sure if it was her skin or her heart that had peeled.

She missed the feel of bristles and linen stretched taut on a frame. She missed the textured drag of pigment across gesso, the stickiness of oils, the way her fingers could know something before her eyes did. These gloves—symbol of her new place, her new name—had no memory in them.

They muffled her. Muted her senses.

When their hands met, she felt the brush of him against her fingertips.

Warm. Controlled. Unreadable.

She looked up at him, searching his eyes for something familiar, something reassuring.

Instead, his gaze was already elsewhere—on the men unloading their luggage. On the street beyond. On the climb ahead.

She followed his line of sight.

The street rose steeply from the dock, narrow and crowded. Balconies leaned toward each other overhead, strung with laundry and iron lanterns. Cats paced rooftops. A woman tossed a bucket of water onto the street, narrowly missing a barefoot boy.

A shout. A laugh. A curse.

And all of it—all of it—felt foreign.

The stones were darker here. Uneven and damp with fish water. The buildings leaned, casting long shadows in the late light. Naples wasn't made to charm. It pulsed. It pressed in. It demanded.

She clutched her satchel tighter, glancing back once toward the sea. Serafina stood a few paces behind, her arms looped around the smaller trunks, eyes watchful. She'd felt the shift too. Something unseen had passed between them like a cold wind in summer.

Celina stepped forward, following Giovanni up the winding street.

She didn't look back again.

✳ ✳ ✳

PALAZZO BARESI

The carriage moved slowly through the narrow, winding streets. Celina sat stiffly beside Giovanni, her gloved hands folded in her lap, fingers aching to lift the curtain and peer out—though she didn't dare. Naples was louder than she expected. More crowded. The streets were tight, hemmed in by tall, sun-baked buildings with shuttered windows and terracotta rooftops, stacked one upon the next like sleeping children in a crowded bed. The smell of baking bread, salt air, and human life—too many lives—rushed in through any crack in

the glass, chasing away the clean citrus winds of Amalfi.

The streets beneath the carriage wheels were not like the sun-warmed pavers of Amalfi—those smooth, golden stones that echoed the sea's light and cradled her barefoot wanderings. Here, the road was carved from old fire—black basalt cobblestones, wide and uneven, worn by centuries of hooves and heels. They shone dully with sea mist, like cooled embers, and clattered beneath the wheels with a hollow rhythm that felt too loud, too alive. The volcanic rock was darker, rougher, older, steeped in the weight of a thousand forgotten steps. This city didn't open to the horizon—it pressed inward, like a secret whispered through clenched teeth. In Amalfi, the sea had always called her just beyond the lemon groves. But here, Naples leaned in, its stone bones crowding close, watching, whispering stories she did not yet understand.

Laundry flapped from the balconies overhead—bright linens and underthings strung like carnival banners in the wind. Children zigzagged through narrow alleyways, barefoot and shrieking with laughter. A woman passed with a chicken tucked under one arm and a string of garlic slung over the other. Two men bickered at a wine cart, their gestures as fast and sharp as their words.

Everything was closer here. Tighter. Grayer. Even the sky felt lower—like the clouds had sagged beneath their own weight, pressing down against the rooftops. Once-vivid murals—faded rose, washed out gold, sun-bleached coral—peeled from crumbling plaster like memories too proud to let go. The buildings leaned inward at odd angles, and clotheslines stretched between shuttered windows like loose stitches trying to hold the city together. The air was thick with smoke, salt, and the faint tang of rust—like old coins left too long in the mouth.

It was Naples. But to Celina, it felt like a strangled version of home—a pale, breathless echo of Amalfi's sea-swept light.

She swallowed. This was not her garden.

As the carriage turned down a narrower lane, flanked by tall, shadowed facades, her heart tapped faster in her chest. Then—there it was.

The house.

Not grand, but distinct.

Tucked among a row of neighboring buildings that pressed close like gossiping sisters, it was three stories high, with arched windows trimmed in soot-darkened stone. The façade was once a soft ochre, though time and weather had worn it into a kind of mottled parchment. Wrought iron balconies clung to the upper windows, their curls delicate but rust-stained. A small marble plaque near the door bore the Baresi family crest—barely legible now, like something meant to be forgotten.

It was not luxurious, not by Neapolitan noble standards, but there was something proud about it. And private. It didn't call attention to itself—it endured.

Celina stared up at the house, its silhouette rising from the cobblestones like something half-remembered from a dream—not quite a mansion, not quite a cottage. It was smaller than she imagined, more weathered than expected, but it carried itself with a kind of tired dignity, like a widow wearing her best silk dress to market. Her gaze drifted to the darkened balconies, the iron railings twisted like vines. There were no lights in the windows. No music. No voices. Just the soft scrape of the carriage wheel coming to rest and the rhythmic slosh of the tide beyond the alley mouth.

She hesitated.

This was where she would live now.

Her fingers curled tighter in her lap. The lace of her gloves felt stiff, useless. As if they belonged to another girl entirely—one who still lived by the sea, barefoot in the garden, the scent of lemon blossoms in her hair.

A shift beside her broke the stillness.

Giovanni leaned forward slightly, gazing out the carriage window. And something in him... changed. His face, always calm and composed, took on a new tension. A flicker of ownership. Not pride exactly, but something colder. Possession. Calculation. Familiarity. The kind of gaze a man reserves for a ledger or a locked drawer. She'd seen warmth in his expression before—gentle smiles, thoughtful nods as he studied her work in her father's garden, even the occasional question about the plants she favored, as if trying to understand her world. He had courted her with a certain restraint, yes, but there had been a softness in it—enough to spark the quietest hope that something more than business might take root between them. But that warmth had vanished now, replaced with a distant steeliness.

He did not look at her as he adjusted his gloves, nor did he offer her his hand this time.

Celina's breath caught as she realized: this was his world. The one he had invited her into. Or rather… delivered her into.

She studied him quickly now, as if trying to learn something she should have known before. His hair, once charmingly silver at the temples, looked colder here in the city light. His hands, strong and elegant, seemed built for painting—or for closing doors. She had thought him worldly. Mysterious. Safe.

Now, she wasn't sure what to think.

Hope still lingered—a small, flickering flame, delicate against the chill that seemed to settle into the air around them—but she could feel it waver, unsteady in the draft of her uncertainty.

Would he love her here? Would he teach her to paint?

Would this house—this dark, quiet place—be a home or a cage? She had once imagined that affection might grow between them,

that Naples might soften his edges and grant their union a chance at warmth. But that imagining felt far away now.

She reached for the door before he could, determined not to seem afraid. But her fingers trembled as they closed around the handle, and her new wedding ring caught the moonlight as it moved.

A gilded promise.

A shining rock.

'Til death parts us.

Celina pushed the carriage door open. A gust of wind swept in, laced with smoke and brine, unfamiliar spices and distant rot. The city air was thicker than the salted breeze of Amalfi—earthier, more human. More lived-in.

She stepped down, her slippers touching the uneven street stones with a faint scuff. The clatter of horses and murmurs from dim alleyways pressed in around her. But her eyes lifted to the house before her.

It was taller than she expected. Narrow but imposing, its façade washed in a faded terracotta blush that once might have been vibrant. Cracks ran through the plaster like veins. Iron balconies curled above the windows, black with age and rain, potted geraniums wilting in the dark.

She stood in the street, head tilted back, staring up at the building that was now her home. It didn't glow the way her father's villa did at sunset. It loomed. Watching. Waiting.

Her husband stepped beside her.

"This way," Giovanni said, almost absently, his voice low and tired. His gloved hand touched the small of her back—a gesture that might've been comforting if it hadn't also felt like direction.

The heavy front doors were made of dark wood, reinforced with iron bands, the kind that could withstand weather and memory. There was no family crest carved above the lintel, no symbol of welcome. Just a brass knocker shaped like a lion's head, teeth clenched around a worn iron ring.

Before Giovanni could lift it, the door creaked open from within.

A man—gray-haired, sunken eyes, thin as a stork—bowed at the waist. A house servant. Behind him, a flicker of candlelight trembled in a long corridor of shadow.

"Benvenuta, Signora Baresi," the servant murmured. Signora Baresi.

It struck her, then. This was not a visit. Not a lesson or a dream.

This was her life now. Her home. Her name.

She hesitated, only a moment, before stepping forward. Into the mouth of the house.

Into the hush of candlelight and stone.

The door closed with a soft, definitive click.

The sound echoed in the narrow corridor like the closing of a casket lid—at least to her. Giovanni barely noticed.

He was tired. Bone-deep. Not from the wedding itself—he'd gone through those motions before—but from the effort of holding himself together, of performing charm and grace and sincerity in front of Luca Albani, whose judgment mattered far more than Celina's wide, admiring eyes.

Luca, his old friend. His investor. His key to salvation.

Giovanni cast a brief glance toward Celina, who stood motionless in the vestibule, eyes wide, soaking in the dim interior like someone stepping into the nave of a church.

The entrance hall was narrow but long, its stone floor worn smooth by time. A patterned runner in shades of rust and deep blue stretched down the corridor like a guiding path. The walls were a pale, yellowing cream, once vibrant, now dulled by years of candle soot and damp coastal air. Paintings—his own, mostly—lined the walls. Still lifes of fruit and fine porcelain. A portrait of a bishop whose name he couldn't remember. One of himself in younger years, too dramatic to be flattering, too expensive to discard.

The light was minimal—only a few sconces burning low, the shadows from their flames flickering like restless spirits.

He watched Celina take it all in, her posture stiff but not afraid. Just… young. So very young. And still too full of wonder. That would pass. He wasn't unkind—just realistic. Wonder softened over time. Hardened into form. That was life.

She would learn.

And she would serve her purpose.

She had been presented to him as clever and willing, with enough fire to inspire him and enough humility to follow his direction. A blank canvas, he thought, with just enough color already blooming beneath the surface to make her interesting.

Malleable.

He needed that.

The commissions were still slow. The last one—a Madonna for a chapel just outside the city—had dragged beyond deadline, and the patron was growing restless. He'd scraped by, barely, covering debts and appearances. But the art wasn't coming the way it once had. Not like when he was younger, hungrier, certain of his place in the world. He had hoped marrying would bring some stability. Fresh energy.

A wife who painted well and asked few questions was a rare treasure. And Celina, with her fair hair and salt-stained fingers, was better than he'd expected.

He could work with this.

She was eager to learn. Hungry, even.

He turned to her at last, gesturing casually up the narrow marble staircase ahead.

"You'll find the bedchambers on the second floor. Yours is beside mine." He glanced at the servant waiting in the shadows. "Your things should already be placed. If you need anything, tell Serafina."

He watched her nod, absorbing the instructions. He didn't smile.

Didn't offer his arm this time.

"We'll eat a little something before bed," he added, already moving down the corridor. "You'll want your strength. I'll show you the rest of the house tomorrow."

He did not look back.

Serafina stepped from the shadows just as Giovanni passed her by, her head bowed slightly in deference. She said nothing to him, only waited until the echo of his footsteps disappeared down the corridor before turning her gaze toward Celina.

"Come, padrona mia," she said softly, her voice wrapped in the warmth of familiarity and shared girlhood. "Let's get you settled."

Celina hesitated, then followed, grateful for Serafina's presence—the only piece of home that had made the crossing with her.

The marble steps curved upward in a tight spiral, worn slightly concave from generations of use. The stairwell was narrow, and Serafina lit a small oil lamp as they ascended, its flickering glow throwing long shadows along the walls. Tapestries hung between gilt-framed portraits—mostly Giovanni's work, somber religious scenes and portraits with heavy brows and darker palettes than she would've chosen. The textiles were dark too: thick damask in garnet and forest green, the kind that swallowed sound and dust and time.

The carpet runner beneath her feet was a deep, dull red, like dried wine. It muffled their steps. Along the second-floor hallway, Celina counted five doors—each one painted a dark, glossy green and trimmed in aged brass. She wondered what lay behind them. Studies? Storerooms? Secrets?

She didn't ask. She only followed Serafina, who walked a pace ahead, lifting the lamp as she opened the last door on the left.

"This is yours," she said quietly, stepping aside so Celina could enter first.

The room was larger than she expected. Rectangular, with high ceilings and a pair of narrow windows framed by thick curtains the color of moss. The light from the hall spilled in as she stepped across the threshold, brushing her fingers along the carved edge of a sideboard near the door.

Her eyes swept across the room:

A tall canopied bed stood against the far wall, draped in cream and burgundy, its posts carved with fluted spirals. A low chaise sat beneath one window, upholstered in a faded floral fabric. A writing desk faced the opposite wall, already topped with a small oil lamp and a stack of parchment. A washstand stood nearby, beside an iron tub already filled with steaming water—someone had been preparing long before their arrival. Lavender and rosemary drifted from the water, faint but comforting.

On a small table beside the bed, a silver tray waited with a plate of figs and cheese, half a small loaf of bread, and a delicate glass of amber-colored wine.

Her trunks had been brought in—one open, her traveling cloak draped across its edge. Beside it, folded neatly on a chair, was her wedding night attire: a soft cotton shift trimmed in lace, pale ivory with tiny rose-colored ribbons at the collar and cuffs. The fabric shimmered faintly in the candlelight.

Celina stood motionless for a moment, taking it all in. It was a beautiful room. Tasteful. Expensive.

Her fingers found the carved edge of the writing desk again, grounding herself. The floor beneath her feet was cold. The walls were unfamiliar. The bed, though inviting, looked far too big for a girl who had slept beneath the same patchwork quilt since childhood.

She swallowed hard.

"Would you like help with the bath?" Serafina asked gently, already moving toward the basin to test the water's warmth.

Celina nodded, though her voice caught in her throat. "Thank you, Sera."

Serafina smiled softly. "Everything will feel better after a good soak."

Celina nodded, but her gaze drifted—first to the folded shift laid carefully across the bed, then to the untouched glass of wine, and finally... to the door that led to her husband's chambers.

Her heart fluttered, rapid and uncertain. Her husband's chambers.

The words echoed through her like a bell struck from within.

Serafina lit the final candle near the tub, the golden glow catching on the copper's warm sheen and painting flickers of firelight across the floor. Then, with a soft hum, she moved to the chaise and returned with a pale linen shift—soft, nearly translucent in the candlelight. She laid it gently across the foot of the bed beside a folded towel and a small dish of scented oil.

Celina stood in the center of the room, arms wrapped around herself, suddenly very aware of the silence. Serafina returned to her side and reached for the buttons at the back of her dress.

"May I, Signorina?"

Celina hesitated, then nodded.

The gown slipped away like a second skin, and with it went the last physical remnant of her life in Amalfi. She stood in her chemise and stockings, flushed and uncertain, allowing Serafina to guide her gently toward the bath.

The water steamed faintly, fragrant with herbs. Serafina helped her step over the copper edge and settle in, careful with the folds of linen still clinging to her modesty. Celina settled in, gasping softly as the warmth enveloped her.

She drew her knees to her chest, wrapping her arms loosely around them as she sank a little deeper into the copper tub. The water lapped gently at her shoulders, warm and fragrant—lavender and something woodier, sharper. Rosemary, perhaps. Familiar, yet foreign.

Like everything else in this new life.

She had managed only a few polite bites of bread and cheese, but now her stomach churned with more than nerves. The moths inside her ribcage beat against the bone, frantic and furious. Was it the rich wine? The rocking of the sea still lingering in her limbs? Or the unspoken weight of what the night would require of her?

She closed her eyes.

The heat of the bath dulled the edge of her thoughts but did nothing to silence them.

She didn't know. She only knew this was expected.

She would be pleasing. She would be obedient. And it would all be fine.

Serafina knelt behind her, sleeves rolled, slowly braiding the long mass of curls that still smelled faintly of sea and sun. She worked gently, silently, as though she too understood that words could bruise.

When she finally spoke, her voice was low. "You are brave," she said.

Celina closed her eyes. "I don't feel brave."

Serafina dipped a cloth and ran it over her shoulders, sweeping away salt and childhood. "You don't need to feel it. Just be it."

A pause stretched out between them. "Serafina… will it hurt?"

Serafina was quiet for a long time. Then, "A little. At first. But not forever."

Celina turned her face slightly toward her. "What if I don't know what to do?"

Serafina's fingers paused in her hair. She wrung out a lock and tucked it behind Celina's ear.

"You are not there to perform," she said carefully. "Tonight is not about you knowing—it is about you learning."

Celina's brows pulled together. "He's my husband. He won't hurt me, will he?"

"I don't think he means to," Serafina answered. "Look, you'll lay down a girl and get up a woman. It's an age old dance."

The air between them changed. Something solemn, rooted in centuries of silence settled there.

Serafina helped her rise, wrapped her gently in a drying linen, and guided her to the side of the bed nearest the fire's glow. A delicate nightgown of pale silk awaited her, folded beside a matching robe, slippers, and a slender golden ribbon to tie her hair back loosely. Celina's hands trembled as she dressed.

Serafina fastened the buttons for her, one by one. "If he's kind, it will pass quickly."

Kind? Celina thought, what was the alternative?

"If not, think of the sea. Think of Amalfi. Home."

Celina looked down at her hands—soaked clean now and feminine. Her nails trimmed, no longer smudged with charcoal. They didn't look like her hands.

"Will I still be me tomorrow?" she asked softly.

Serafina kissed the top of her head. "You'll be whoever you choose to be."

Then, with a gentle nod, Serafina opened the door to the adjoining room.

Celina stepped inside.

Nine

Consummated

CELINA | NAPLES, ITALY | C. 1741

GIOVANNI'S CHAMBERS

She stood in the open doorway between her chambers and his.

A single candle burned low on a silver holder beside the door, throwing thin golden light across the threshold. The wooden frame was carved with vines and birds, worn smooth at the edges by years of passing hands. Celina's fingertips lingered there now, resting lightly against the wood as though it might anchor her.

Giovanni's chambers were larger than she'd expected—wide, shadowed, and quiet. The floors were dark wood polished to a dull sheen, warm beneath bare feet. A long rug ran from the doorway toward the fireplace, deep red and patterned with foreign symbols she didn't recognize. It muffled her breath, her heartbeat, the sound of her thoughts.

The walls were not painted like her room but paneled in aged walnut—rich and heavy, smelling faintly of resin, smoke, and old paper. The scent of wax, dried herbs, and something leathery clung to everything. It was not unpleasant, just... unfamiliar. Like a study, not a bed-room.

Books lined the far wall in tall, crowded shelves. A stack of papers and open folios sat on a low table beside a wingback chair. The fire-place there glowed with faint orange embers, casting long shadows across the ceiling. Tapestries hung near the windows, thick and dark, keeping the city out. The light from the hallway made the chamber feel even dimmer by contrast, as if her world had narrowed to just this room and the breath caught in her chest.

The bed stood at the center of it all—too large for one man, with tall carved posts and a canopy of midnight velvet that pooled around the frame. The sheets were ivory linen, the coverlet a deep wine red, edged in heavy gold embroidery. It looked more like a throne than a bed.

A ceremonial altar. A battlefield. A cage.

Celina's mouth had gone dry.

Giovanni stood at a sideboard across the room, still fully clothed, pouring wine into a pair of goblets. He had removed only his coat and cravat; his shirt was open at the throat, sleeves rolled up. She watched the muscles in his forearm shift as he worked the bottle, calm and practiced, like this moment was no different than any evening he'd spent alone. He had not looked at her yet.

She wondered if he was giving her a moment. Or if he simply didn't care.

The candle flickered behind her. She took a step forward.

Her shift brushed against her knees, too light to offer any real modesty. The lace sleeves slipped a little off her shoulders. Serafina had smoothed oil into her arms and back, brushed lavender behind her ears, and whispered quiet words meant to soothe. But they had not followed her into this room. Here, she was alone.

Her ring caught the firelight again. Her breath hitched.

He turned, finally, one glass in his hand. The expression on his face was unreadable—neutral, polite. His eyes moved over her without pause.

"You came," he said simply.

Celina opened her mouth, but no words arrived. Instead, she nodded once.

Giovanni crossed the room and handed her a glass of wine. His fingers grazed hers. His hands were warm. Steady. Almost comforting.

She focused on the warmth of it as it slid past her teeth, coating her throat like velvet and fire. If she could feel the wine more than everything else—maybe it would slow the wild flutter of her nerves, quiet the noise in her head. Maybe it would wash away the awkwardness of standing here in this nightdress, trembling in front of a man she barely knew.

She took another sip. Willing it to help. Willing it to work. Behind him, the bed waited.

An immovable monolith wrapped in linen and velvet, carved like something holy and dangerous. It stood at the center of the room like an altar dressed for sacrifice. Celina's gaze flicked to it, then back to the rim of her glass.

Her fingers tightened slightly around the stem. Her ring tapped the side with a delicate, accidental ting.

What now?

Would he come to her slowly? Speak gently? Or was there a sequence to this, a script she hadn't been given?

She lowered the glass. Her mouth was dry again.

She wished Serafina were here, just for one more word. One more anchor.

Giovanni was moving slowly, purposefully. Shrugging off his waistcoat, folding it with care before setting it across the chair back. His movements were calm. Not rushed. As if this moment belonged only to him, and she was a detail in the corner of the canvas he was preparing to paint.

He was calm. Completely at ease. Not like her.

Filled with stolen glances and silent questions.

She watched him under the tilted rim from her glass.

He didn't seem unkind. Or cold. But he wasn't really warm either. Just a man with plans.

A man who had waited patiently all day to arrive at this point.

A man who, perhaps, had the patience of a saint and now stood before the long-awaited reward he believed he'd earned.

Her.

He was ready. Was she?

He reached for the buttons on his waistcoat. "You may sit, if you like."

She obeyed, crossing the room in slow, measured steps, her slippers silent on the rug. She perched at the edge of the velvet upholstered chaise by the hearth—low and wide, carved mahogany, the wood cool against the backs of her knees. Her gown pooled around her like spilled milk.

But Celina couldn't feel the cushions beneath her.

Her fingers clutched the glass tighter than before, her knuckles pale beneath the lace cuffs. The wine trembled faintly with the shake of her hands. She focused on breathing slowly, evenly, but the pulse in her ears rushed like the sea, loud and unrelenting.

The room was too quiet. Too still.

The kind of silence that follows finality.

He said nothing more. He simply undid each button, one after another. Calm. Practiced. The faint rasp of fabric and clink of metal louder than it should've been in the candlelit room.

She watched him.

Not quite knowing where else to look.

What now?

Was she supposed to say something? Rise? Undress? What was expected of her?

She'd been taught to be gracious. To be obedient. To be still. But not this.

He crossed the room toward her, and her stomach dropped like a stone into deep water.

Still, she did not move.

He stopped in front of her and gently reached for the glass in her hands. She let him take it, her fingers falling away, limp now, like they no longer belonged to her. He set the glass on a small marble-topped table beside his own—still nearly full.

Two barely touched glasses. Two untouched people.

She lowered her eyes to her lap. Her ring caught the candlelight again—a flicker, a glint. Like something delicate and dangerous all at once.

She was his now.

Giovanni stepped closer, and with each footfall, her skin prickled. His shadow moved before he did, stretching long across the floor, then sliding up the fabric of her skirts, over her trembling hands, until it wrapped around her shoulders like something unseen and inescapable.

"Don't be afraid," he said quietly. His voice was low, level. Calm. He stopped directly in front of her.

The soft white of his linen shirt gaped open at the chest, the fastenings left loose—intentionally, she thought. Beneath the linen, a brush of dark curls rested against bronze skin. The candlelight gilded the deep contours of his collarbones and cast long shadows down the curves of his abdomen.

He looked… different here.

Less like the man who had stood beside her at the altar that morning, more like something molded and hidden behind curtains.

Like marble left in the sun too long. She swallowed.

Her fingers, still curled in her lap, twitched against the folds of her dress. Her heart beat an erratic rhythm beneath her breastbone, wild as a trapped finch.

And yet—she could not help but take note. The way his hips narrowed.

The sharp line of his jaw.

The contrast of light and dark, skin and shirt, man and shadow.

She traced them silently in her mind, sketching without brush or charcoal.

He was attractive, in a dark way. The way cliffs were beautiful.

The way lightning split the sky. And still, she was terrified.

But—somewhere beneath the terror—was a flicker of something else.

Curiosity. Anticipation.

A desperate desire to be good. To do this right. To prove she was capable of becoming what she was meant to be.

Hope.

She was about to have her first real lesson— Not in painting.

Not in color theory or composition. In obedience.

In what it meant to be a wife. What it meant to be a woman. What it meant to be his.

The most important lesson of all.

And perhaps… to claim him as her own. If she dared.

If she was allowed.

Celina wasn't sure what the challenge truly was—only that she was being asked to meet it without any instruction, without a map, without even knowing which direction to face. Still, some part of her wanted to rise to it—not just to endure, but to discover if something softer might grow from this arrangement. She would do her best. She would not fail.

When he extended his hand, she placed hers into it. He said nothing. Neither did she.

He led her slowly across the room, the silence thick with something neither of them named. The stone floor was cool beneath her slippers. Her pulse surged in her throat, in her chest, behind her eyes.

He stopped at the foot of the bed and turned to face her. Then, with an unexpected gentleness, he brushed his lips across her fore-head.

Her breath caught. Was that… tenderness?

He turned her around in his arms so that her back met his chest, the heat of him seeping through the thin layers between them. His hands moved to her hair, slow and sure, gathering the heavy length of it and draping her thick tresses over her left shoulder, where it fell like a veil beside her face.

She blinked, brushing a few loose strands out from her eyes straining to see clearly in the darkened room.

Then he guided her forward, carefully, until her body lay unceremoniously across the bed. The velvet coverlet was thick and warm beneath her hands, against her cheek. She felt the mattress accept her weight as she settled there, uncertain and waiting.

The silence pressed in.

She felt him standing behind her—his warmth, movement. The shift of fabric. The hush of breath. Something gave way, perhaps a belt or a button. Her heart pounded so loudly, she was sure he could hear it.

Then his hand—light but certain—traced a path up the back of her leg, lifting her skirts where they roamed. The air touched her bare calves first, then her thighs, then the small of her back. A chill shot up her spine and she flinched.

"It's better not to delay what's expected." His hand settled on the curve of her hip, firm and possessive.

He paused for a moment.

"Are you ready?" he asked, voice low, somewhere near her ear. Celina's thoughts scattered. Ready?

For *what*?

What would it feel like? Would it hurt?

Would he be kind? Would she bleed? Would he notice?

She had no answers, only instincts.

She summoned what little courage she had and forced her voice into the darkened room, the sound of it so small it barely carried.

No, she thought. "Yes," she whispered.

She knew she *had* to say yes. She left her choices in her father's garden.

She braced herself as Giovanni shifted behind her. The press of his body loomed—warm, inevitable. One of his hands settled on her hip, the other slid across her belly in a quiet claim, then moved lower, guiding her legs apart the way he wanted, positioning her limbs in a way that pleased him—granting him his desired access to take his pleasure in her warm, tight innocence.

She focused on the feel of the bedcover beneath her fingers—plush against the fine linen of her shift, against the tender skin beneath. On the uneven rhythm of her breath. On the soft crackle of candlelight behind them.

Then his hand touched her—where no one had touched her before.

That part of her had always been sacred. Unexplored. Unnamed. *Hers.*

She stiffened instinctively, breath catching in her throat, her abdomen tightening as if her body already knew what her mind could not yet name.

She didn't know what she feared, only that it was coming— rushing toward her with the gravity of something inevitable. The air changed. Time folded in.

She gripped the bedding tighter, fingers clutching the embroidered edge like a lifeline.

He leaned in behind her. The heat of his presence swelled around her, unfamiliar and all consuming. She rose slightly on her toes, instinctively seeking some kind of balance, some small adjustment to make the uncomfortable position more bearable. The height of the bed forced her forward, the weight behind her pressing her down with a demand she didn't know was possible.

It was too much—too close, too heavy, too soon. Her chest tightened, her breath shallowed.

The pressure of the day—the ceremony, the journey, the newness of everything—collapsed inward all at once, crowding her lungs with a feeling she couldn't name. Not exactly fear. Not exactly sorrow. But something sharp and tight, lodged just beneath her ribs.

This was what it meant to be a wife. What she'd been told, but never truly understood.

He shifted again—closer now. Hotter. Firmer. The pressure mounted—

The world seemed to hold its breath. Her body, her mind—everything went still for a moment.

And then—

Pain.

Blinding.

Splitting.

A white-hot thread unraveling through her.

It split through her like a blade drawn from within.

Her cry caught in her throat and was swallowed by the pillows she pressed her face into. Her fingers clawed at the coverlet, breath shallow and frantic.

Whatever this was, it was not what she had expected.

Is this what it means to be his wife?

The words repeated in her mind like a slow, measured bell toll, distant and low.

Each movement behind her pressed the lesson deeper—not just into her body, but into the corners of her mind that had never been touched. She had been told—softly, carefully—that love might come in time. That marriage began with duty and often grew into affection. That obedience was a virtue, and quiet resilience the mark of a good woman. A good wife.

Was this affection?

Her brow furrowed against the bedding, still warm from her breath. She tried not to flinch, tried not to cry, tried not to think—but thoughts had a way of slipping in, even when she didn't want them to.

He is your husband. You are his wife.

He has every right.

The pressure, the weight, the heat—it all worked together—to root her into this new truth: her body was no longer hers. It belonged to the man who now owned her nights and would soon shape her days.

A part of her curled inward, retreating just enough to bear it.

This is good.

He's teaching you. This is how you learn.

The thought frightened her, and yet, it made sense. Wasn't this what the world expected? Wives obeyed. Husbands led. This was the way life was supposed to be.

She was determined to be a *good student.*

She blinked. The sharp stinging pain slowly beginning to fade, swallowed by the rhythm of breath and movement and surrender.

She would not cry.

With every rotation of his pelvis, Giovanni drove deeper into her flesh, asserting his dominance over her body, branding her soul, immersing Celina in complete sensory overload. As he moved, his thrusts grew faster, frenzied, more hurried, brutally demanding more of her delicate skin than it had ever given before.

She turned her face further into the coverlet, masking her anguish. Lavender and old linen. It smelled like someone else's memories. Maybe now, they would become her own.

His breath quickened. She could hear it above her now... behind her—close, uneven, edged with something like urgency. She couldn't see him, only feel him: the way his body surged against hers, faster now, less precise. An unraveling rhythm.

The weight of him pressed down harder. One movement—harsh, sure. A second—sharper still. A third, almost desperate.

Then a sound—a groan, raw and guttural—and the full force of him collapsed against her back. All at once, she was crushed beneath the finality of it. His body, heavy with release, blanketed hers, forcing the last breath from her lungs.

She didn't move.

Couldn't.

Everything inside her had gone still.

The mattress creaked beneath them. The candle behind them fluttered on its dish. Somewhere outside the window, a carriage clattered past on distant stones, like the world was continuing on, unaware of what had just taken place inside these silent walls.

Celina stared ahead, eyes cracked open but unseeing. Her thoughts, scattered like petals in a storm, refused to settle. Only one thing echoed clearly in the silence between them:

So this is what it means to be a wife.

Mermaids

CELINA | NAPLES, ITALY | C. 1741

Carry me far from all I've known,
Beyond the blood, beyond the bone.
Let sorrow sink and silence rise—
I'd trade this life for bluer skies.
In darkened seas I yield my will,
May I forget.
May time stand still.

Ten

The Silk Road

CHAHIRA | DAMASCUS, BILAD
AL-SHAM | C. 1213

ODE TO MY HOOVES
(and the girl who talks too much)

"They packed me with figs, philosophical dreams,
She asked the wind if olive the trees scream.
Six weeks of dust and poetic despair —
I carried a princess who forgot I was there.
History's great, but my saddle still squeaks.
Next time, she walks. I demand six weeks."

Farheen (dictated to Chahira)

THE ROAD TO DAMASCUS — EARLY APRIL

The journey from Isfahan to Damascus took nearly six weeks.
They traveled by caravan, nestled among merchants and diplomats,
along dusty roads lined with almond trees and olive groves.

Chahira rode in a curtained palanquin for parts of the way, but spent most of her time on a small mare named Farheen, which meant joyful—not that the mare knew it.

Chahira insisted she named her that because "we are both full of opinions and faster than we look." She also claimed she could "see history better on horseback," though she mostly rode in zigzags.

The roads were a winding story of their own—quiet some days, alive with color and company on others. They passed veiled women with baskets on their heads, children chasing goats through narrow passes, and once, a traveling magician with a monkey that tried to steal Chahira's ink pot.

They slept in desert inns that smelled of cumin and dust. Her father sang songs by the fire. Her mother burned clove incense at every stop, muttering, "For protection," every time someone looked at Chahira too long.

As they neared Damascus, the roads grew busier—no longer quiet paths bordered by swaying grasses, but bustling arteries pulsing with life. Their caravan became a single thread in a sprawling tapestry of movement: spice traders from the south with jangling camels draped in faded silks; soldiers on horseback, armor dusty and expressions unreadable; a pair of monks debating philosophy so loudly their mule looked genuinely offended.

Animals moved in every direction. Parrots squawked from cages tied to carts, their eyes wild and insulted by confinement. Goats trotted beside children, nipping at anything that resembled a scroll. A peacock—yes, a peacock—strutted freely between wheels as if it owned the road, its feathers scandalously unbothered by the dust. There were tired oxen with lashes that drooped like poets in despair, proud white horses that tossed their manes like they were on stage, and an elephant who looked deeply offended to be traveling with such ordinary company, as though someone had promised it a royal procession and then handed it a traffic jam.

Most of the animals were tethered—ropes around ankles or necks, lashed to carts or loosely led by handlers—but not all. A pair of monkeys escaped their perch on a spice wagon and caused a scandal involving a stolen turban and a fleeing merchant who, in Chahira's words, "ran like someone had accused him of bad poetry."

The carts themselves were as varied as their drivers: simple wooden wagons stacked with baskets and bundles; painted carriages with embroidered curtains and tired wheels; rickety push-carts overflowing with herbs, clay pots, copper jugs, and at least one cart that seemed to carry nothing but shoes. So many shoes.

And above it all, like an invisible tide, rose the scent of civilization—cardamom, sweat, ash, honey, iron, roasted meat, and dust. Always the dust. Dust that didn't settle so much as linger, like it had opinions.

"Damascus," Chahira said, breathing it in like perfume. Then she grinned.

"Smells like opportunity and roasted lamb—I'm in."

It rose from the horizon like a palace made of mirage and myth. Towering stone walls, bleached rose by the morning sun, wrapped the city like ancient arms—strong, solemn, and full of secrets. The gates yawned wide, equally welcoming and warning, and from this distance, Chahira could already see the mosaic shimmer of a minaret winking in the light.

"Looks like a genie got bored, drank too much rosewater, and accidentally created... art! Ten out of ten. No notes."

Her father didn't laugh this time.

"No," he said, quiet and steady. "This is your future."

Chahira blinked, surprised by the weight in his tone. She sat up a little straighter, lips pursed.

"...Well," she muttered after a beat, "I hope it comes with snacks."

* * *

As they entered through Bab Sharqi—the Eastern Gate—Chahira sat taller on her mare, pretending she was part of a royal parade no one had officially declared.

The gate towered above them, carved from pale stone that caught the sunlight like a secret. Two massive towers flanked the archway, their walls worn smooth by centuries of wind, war, and whispers. Narrow arrow slits stared down at travelers like quiet judges, and the great wooden doors, though swung open, bore iron studs the size of baby fists.

A band of faded blue and gold tile work crowned the entrance—once gleaming like a jeweled diadem. Ivy clung stubbornly to one upper corner, and beneath the keystone, someone had painted a tiny crescent moon. It was almost invisible, like a secret joke only the gate was in on.

It didn't look like an entrance, Chahira thought. It looked like a mouth.

A big, stone mouth that swallowed you whole and decided who you got to be on the other side.

Then the fullness of the city's scent wrapped around her like a story.

Spices. Dust. Fire. Stewed lamb. Sweets dripping with rosewater. And sweat. So much sweat.

Chahira blinked, sat back, and fanned herself with both hands. "Correction, Damascus smells like power… and pickles."

Her mother gasped—at the smell or the sentiment, it wasn't clear. Her father coughed, covered his face with a sleeve, and muttered something about cloves.

Not quite a laugh. But not not a laugh. Chahira grinned. The gate had let her in.

But she was determined to write her own script.

The city was a festival, a riot, a wedding, and a prayer—all at once. Copper bells clanged. Merchants sang. Arguments overlapped with belly-laughter. Pigeons flapped in sudden, dramatic bursts.

And donkeys. Everywhere she looked. And a random zebra. She squinted at it.

"Someone clearly misunderstood the dress code."

Inside the gates, the streets bloomed with all the colors she'd ever seen—and a few she'd have to invent names for. Green glass bangles. Indigo silks. Saffron robes. Brass trays taller than she was.

A boy with honey on his chin and the swagger of someone who'd never been told no winked at her as their caravan passed.

Chahira rolled her eyes. "If you can't see the honey on your own face," she muttered, "you're definitely not ready to see the poetry in mine."

This time her father did laugh—low and behind his hand—but quickly turned it into a cough, as if he were choking on pistachios. Her mother pinched the bridge of her nose like she'd smelled goat cheese left in the sun too long.

Chahira, naturally, felt deeply, completely pleased with herself.

A procession passed—a local dignitary, important by the way everyone moved aside. He was draped in gold-threaded robes with a turban so massive it had its own sense of gravity.

"Farheen," she leaned in to whisper in her horse's ear, "He looks like a very fancy onion."

Her father snorted—then clapped a hand over his mouth. Her mother made a strangled sound in her throat and muttered a prayer she didn't finish.

But Chahira beamed.

Because the city had swallowed her whole.

And she had absolutely decided who she would be on the other side. Herself.

* * *

She was nine when Damascus took her in.

By fourteen, she'd memorized its alleys and moods, the scent of her mother's tea, the weight of her father's sighs, and the exact look Teta gave right before saying something wildly inappropriate.

She'd been polished like a gemstone—cut, turned, tutored, threaded, perfumed, and, most recently, taught how to walk while balancing a bowl of roses on her head.

Letters had arrived months ago, sealed in wax, wrapped in silk, and full of flowery words that translated roughly to:

She's beautiful. She's clever. We'll take her.

So now her future had a name: India.

A distant court. A mysterious sultan. And possibly, if the whispers were true, an elephant with its own umbrella.

She wasn't exactly sure what awaited her. But she'd been trained to sing, dance, debate, and survive a room full of rivals while looking like she was born to do exactly that.

Chahira did not feel nervous. She felt… prepared.

Also, slightly over-scented. But she was ready.

And whatever happened next, she promised herself this: She would arrive with stories.

And she would leave with better ones.

Eleven

Victory Lap

CASSIA | MEMPHIS, EGYPT | C. 689
BCE

THE BANQUET HALL — THE NIGHT OF THE CELEBRATION

The hall was loud with heat and laughter. Smoke curled from bronze braziers, laced with saffron and spit-roasted lamb. Music clattered somewhere in the background, half in rhythm with the clink of goblets and the jostle of elbows against linen-covered tables.

Saben sat at the edge of it all, ribs aching, knuckles split, the taste of iron still ghosting the back of his throat.

The champion's seat. He had earned it.

And he hated every second of it.

"You look like shit," Hamut said, grinning, half-drunk already. "But your sword—gods, your sword! You should've seen the way you flipped that poor bastard into the dirt. What was his name again?"

"Which one?" Saben muttered.

Jorek laughed. "Exactly."

Around them, the table burst with noise—stories from the arena re-told louder and bloodier than they happened. Panehsy, a young soldier from the east, mimed how Saben "nearly snapped his opponent's jaw" with a pommel strike. It had been a glancing blow at best, but the others howled like it was legend.

Saben reached for his cup, only to find it already empty. Again.

Flash: the searing crack of his shoulder against stone, the ground giving out under him, his vision doubled as he forced himself to rise—no time to breathe—just a blur of silver and pain and Djemu's eyes on him from the dais, unreadable.

"You're quiet, old man," Jorek nudged him. "You nearly killed three men and won yourself a fuckin' future. Say something."

Saben managed a smile. It didn't touch his eyes.

"I'm just listening," he said. "Trying to remember which version of the truth I'm supposed to tell tomorrow."

Flash: the moment the blade slipped from his hand—slick with his own blood—kicked into the dirt by his opponent's boot. His heel caught the rim of the pit wall. Winded. Cornered. And then—instinct. A dropped shoulder. A scream. The feeling of his fist connecting with something soft and vital.

"Cheers to the gods of war!" someone roared, lifting their cup. "And the lucky beauty tangled in his sheets by morning!"

The table echoed the toast. Saben stayed still.

Flash: his name called from the pitmaster's mouth. The deafening ringing in his ears. The crowd a blur of voices. Cassia, somewhere above him, veiled in shadow, unmoving.

He hadn't seen her since.

Jorek leaned over again, half-laughing. "So tell me, Saben—what will you do with your winnings? Build a villa? Stock it with wine and women? Or just lie on your back and let the gods serve you figs?"

Saben didn't answer.

Panehsy snorted. "He's gonna do what every man in this room wishes he could—He's gonna walk in there, lift that veil, and make some perfumed palace whore thank every god from here to Thebes."

Laughter cracked again. Saben didn't move.

Flash: the final kill. The last man. Not clean, not noble. Just fast. Brutal. Necessary.

He had thought victory would feel like triumph. Instead, it felt like drowning.

Because no matter how hard he'd fought—no matter how much blood he'd spilled to earn this seat at the table—it had always been a trap. A performance. A game played behind curtains and veils.

And now he was done playing.

He didn't care about silk-skinned slave girls or whispered promises behind palace doors. Let the others chase glory between perfumed thighs.

He just wanted the coin and the land. Enough to buy peace. A quiet corner of the world where no one wore masks, and loyalty didn't cost your soul.

A simple house. A warm meal. Maybe a wife. Children, if the gods were kind.

Ordinary. Honest. Real.

And if the gods were watching, they could keep their kingdoms.

He'd take freedom.

* * *

The room roared like a stadium of jackals.

Drums pounded from raised balconies, dancers spun in metallic silks, and the scent of roasted lamb and fig wine soaked into the air. The torches threw everything in gold and shadow—except the man of the hour.

Saben stood at the center of the feast, his tunic damp with sweat and wine, his shoulder freshly bandaged and dusted with resin. He didn't smile, didn't speak. But the others cheered enough for him.

He'd won.

He knelt—because that's what was required—before Djemu, who stood atop the dais with his arms wide like a conquering god.

"Tonight," Djemu said, his voice ringing through the marble hall, "we honor a soldier who fought with courage, strength, and unflinching loyalty. You have brought pride to your legion—and to me."

Applause thundered. Saben stared at the polished stone beneath his knees.

Djemu raised a goblet. "To Saben, may his blade rest, his purse overflow… and his undoing arrive in silk limbs and red lips."

Laughter, toasts, and a few well-timed whistles filled the air. Someone shoved a fresh cup into Saben's hand and slapped his back. He drank—enough to satisfy, not enough to lose focus.

He scanned the room, instinctively—looking for her. Cassia wasn't there.

His brow pinched faintly.

Djemu seemed to notice as well. After a quick scan, he leaned toward a veiled servant from Cassia's staff. She whispered something in his ear.

"Retired for the evening," Djemu announced smoothly, with a smile for the crowd. "Even queens must rest."

He turned back to Saben, beckoning him closer with a casual flick of the wrist.

"Walk with me, champion."

As Saben stood, the men erupted in a raucous chorus of hoots and applause.

"Go easy on her, Captain!"

"Don't break the silk, or you'll be paying for it!"

Tankards slammed the tables. Someone howled a lewd song about figs and thighs. Another tossed him a garland of myrrh-scented leaves that landed at his feet like an omen.

Saben didn't smile. Didn't bow.

Just nodded once and moved.

He stepped over spilled wine and scraps of roasted meat, through a haze of smoke and perfume. Past gold-lipped goblets and gluttony disguised as celebration.

Only when the firelight faded behind them did the laughter begin to rot in his ears.

The corridor ahead was quieter. Cooler. Lined with carved palm columns and latticed windows where the moon spilled silver across the stones. Djemu's pace was slow, measured — a king granting favor, or leading a lamb to slaughter.

Saben didn't trust the silence. He didn't trust the shadows. But he followed anyway.

"Quite the show," Djemu said lightly, almost like a friend. "The court loves a good fight. You made it worth their while."

"I aim to please," Saben replied, slurring just a little. He let his eyes droop and stumbled just enough to sell the part.

Djemu chuckled. "And please, you shall."

They stopped at an archway hung with heavy drapes of blue and silver, the fabric whispering in the breeze like breath before a scream. A single guard stood watch, posture rigid, hand resting on the hilt of his khopesh. His face was unreadable — but his eyes flicked to Saben's with the briefest flicker of recognition.

They knew each other. Not well, but well enough.

No greeting passed between them. No nod. Just a taut silence stretched thin as a drawn bow.

"The chamber beyond is yours for the night," Djemu said, his voice smooth, indulgent. "Everything has been arranged."

He stepped closer, close enough for Saben to smell the crushed clove on his breath and see the cruel twist of amusement in his eyes.

"The girl is waiting. She knows what's… expected."

Saben nodded heavily, rubbing his temples. "She, uh… pretty?" Djemu smiled. "Enough to keep the gods up all night."

Saben gave a dopey, drunken laugh. "Then I'd better not keep her waiting."

"Indeed," Djemu said, clapping him on the back. "Make the realm proud."

As Djemu turned and strode back toward the feast, Saben stood before the curtain.

The drunk slipped from his face like a discarded mask.

He stared at the soft folds of silk, heart thudding with dread.

Saben stood before the silk-draped archway like a man staring into his own grave.

Muted laughter echoed down the corridor behind him. The scent of wine clung to his breath. The room before him was dim, perfumed, still.

He hadn't moved.

The guard beside the door shifted his weight and cleared his throat. "You going in, or just planning to sleep on your feet?"

Saben blinked slowly, leaning a shoulder against the column. "Thinking it over."

The guard smirked. "Well, if you're too drunk to finish the night, I'll step in for you." He didn't bother to hide the grin that came with it. "She won't say no. Not with orders like these."

Saben's stomach twisted.

He studied the guard—broad shoulders, young face, wolf's hunger behind the eyes. Just one of a dozen men who would see a veiled slave girl as a nameless reward. No consequence. No memory.

He could walk away. Claim the wine had bested him. Collapse in a hall somewhere and sleep off the shame. The girl would be spared him, but maybe not the next man.

And if she told Djemu nothing had happened, it could unravel the entire arrangement. His winnings. His leave.

Saben exhaled through his nose and stood up straight.

"I've got it," he said to the guard, who stepped aside with a low chuckle.

"Your prize, Champion."

Saben opened the door, stepping into a quiet chamber lit by a single oil lamp.

The scent of myrrh and honey lingered in the air. Gold-tinted fabrics draped the walls. A low bed lay at the far end, surrounded by sheer veils that fluttered gently in the breeze.

A figure sat waiting at its edge, robed and still, her face obscured behind a delicate veil.

She didn't speak. Neither did he.

He stood there a moment, heartbeat too loud in his ears, mind running every path out of this with clean hands and a clear conscience.

None existed.

So he did what soldiers do—he played the part.

He stumbled forward, heavy-footed, swaying. Let his words slur just enough.

"Hope you don't mind," he muttered, collapsing onto a nearby couch. "Too much wine. Not enough… anything else."

She didn't move. Not toward him. Not away.

He kicked off his boots, laid back, and draped an arm over his eyes. "I'll just rest a bit," he said, loud enough for her to hear. "Then we'll see."

Still no response.

He could feel her watching.

He closed his eyes and prayed to any god still listening that she'd let him sleep. That she'd wait out the night in silence. That when the sun rose, this whole performance could be folded up and buried with the rest of his regrets.

Silence lingered a few minutes. Then, she spoke. "Saben."

His name slid from her mouth like a blade drawn in the dark—soft, careful, unmistakable.

He froze.

The room tilted. Not from wine. Not from weariness. From recognition.

He sat up slowly, like waking from a nightmare he wasn't sure he wanted to leave.

She was still veiled. Still motionless. But the voice was hers. Cassia.

Twelve

You?

THE ROYAL CONCUBINES' CHAMBERS

He stared, breath caught between denial and dread. "No."

"I'm sorry." Her voice broke like a porcelain plate dropped on stone—delicate and final. "I didn't know it would be you."

He stood, then sat back down just as fast, knees too uncertain to hold the weight of what was unraveling.

"This is—" He scrubbed a hand over his face, searching for sense. "This is some kind of trick."

"I wish it were."

He laughed, once—sharp, bitter. "You? In here? What is this, some test? Some royal joke?" His voice lowered, hoarse. "Did Djemu plan...?" His words trialed off.

She didn't answer.

And that was answer enough.

He looked away, jaw clenched so tightly it ached. "Gods."

Cassia stood, slowly, veil still in place. She walked toward him, bare feet silent on stone. "You don't have to do this. Just… stay until morning. Let them believe what they came to believe. And then leave."

He met her eyes for the first time.

Pain lived there. And shame. And something else—desperation dressed in dignity.

His voice was quiet now. "How could he ask this of you?"

"He didn't ask." Her mouth curved into a smile that wasn't one. "He gave me a duty. Just like you."

"And what? You just—obeyed?"

Her silence pressed like a hand around his throat. "You're not a prisoner, Cassia," he said. "You're—"

"I'm his wife." Her voice was calm, too calm. "And I am barren. And the court is restless. And my family is watching me disappear, one season at a time. If I do not give him an heir, I lose everything."

"You loose everything anyway."

Her hands curled at her sides. "Then at least let me choose how."

The lamp crackled softly between them, casting shadows that slithered like ghosts across the walls.

Saben stared at her and for the first time in years, he saw her—not as a noblewoman, not as a symbol of power or privilege—but as a woman standing on the edge of a life she no longer recognized, doing whatever she could not to fall.

A woman who still dared to call it a choice. His voice was barely more than breath. "Cassia…"

She took a step closer. "Don't look at me like that." Something in him cracked.

Saben said nothing—his throat thick with a thousand words he'd never be allowed to speak.

She stood before him still veiled, still wrapped in silks like some gift prepared for a stranger's hands.

He hated it.

Hated what had been asked of her.

Hated himself for walking into this room. Hated that it was her behind the veil.

And hated—most of all—that some twisted part of him wasn't even surprised.

Secretly *hoped* even.

He'd always known Djemu would destroy her.

"I thought I could do it," she said quietly. "Thought if it was someone I didn't know, it would be easier. Thought I could disappear behind the veil and let the shame belong to someone else."

"He gave me two choices," she whispered. "Sleep with the champion... or pay the price of his wrath."

Saben stared at her, throat tightening. The room tilted. "It was never going to be easier," he said.

"I know." A bitter smile touched her lips. "I didn't expect it to be you."

He laughed once, hollow. "That makes two of us."

Silence stretched again, but this time it felt less like an absence and more like a space being held.

She turned slightly toward him. "If you want to leave, I won't stop you." Her voice was hoarse, throaty.

She swallowed.

He looked at the door. The heavy bronze handle gleamed under torchlight.

"I thought about it," he admitted. "Thought about pretending I was too drunk to remember where my own feet were."

Cassia gave a soft, humorless laugh. "You should have."

"But the guard outside," he said. "He offered to take my place." Her body tensed.

"I know what that means," Saben said. "I've seen enough to know what happens when no one's watching. And I couldn't let that happen. Even to a stranger."

She went still. Then whispered, "You thought I was a stranger."

"I didn't know it would be you."

Cassia reached up and lifted the veil away from her face, letting it fall softly to her lap. The candlelight caressed her features—still royal, still sharp and proud—but worn. Thinner. Paler than he remembered.

She looked older. Sadder. Worried.

He met her eyes and saw everything—rage, sorrow, guilt, tears... and something unspoken that threatened to gut him.

"I didn't want to do this," she said. Her voice barely held together. "But there was no way to say no. So I prayed whoever it was, would be kind."

Saben closed his eyes. Kind.

He could do that.

He could be kind. Even if it killed him.

He turned to her, hands open, not reaching, just... present.

"I'll stay the night," he said. "You don't have to pretend with me. No performance. No lies. No shame. Just a peaceful night's sleep." He could offer that.

"And if they ask?"

"They'll ask." He swallowed. "And I'll say what I need to say."

Cassia's eyes shimmered with unshed tears, the kohl smudging slightly beneath her lower lashes.

"I can lie," he added. "But I won't hurt you." Even in this state, she was the most beautiful thing he'd ever seen.

"I could never hurt you."

She reached for his hand then, slowly, carefully, like touching him would be a sin she couldn't take back. Her fingers brushed his.

He placed his hand over hers.

Just that.

Not possessive. Not claiming. Simply there—solid, warm, still.

Cassia didn't move. But her fingers curled slightly beneath his palm, not to grasp, but to ground herself. The weight of his presence… it was enough. A silent promise in a world with nothing but conditions.

For the first time in a long while, she didn't feel alone. No more words came. Not right away.

Saben sat with her like that for what felt like hours, her head resting against his shoulder, his arm around hers. Eventually her tears slowed, then stopped.

She didn't speak. Just breathed—slow, shallow breaths like it hurt to take up space.

He felt every exhale in his bones.

She was so still, so delicate in that moment, it undid him. The same woman who ruled courtrooms with little more than the arch of a brow now looked like she might crumble under her own silence.

And he hated that he could do nothing. Not really.

He thought about the guard outside. About Djemu's face when he gave him that crooked smile and called it a "favor." About the performance expected of him. Of her. Of everyone.

And he thought about what would happen if nothing changed. Cassia would pay the price.

Women always paid the price.

When she finally drifted to sleep in his arms, he stayed still for her sake. Let his eyes close. Let the warmth of her soak into his skin. Let himself believe, for just a moment, that the world wasn't watching.

* * *

He woke slowly, as if surfacing from a dream he wasn't ready to leave. Eyes still closed, breath shallow, unsure if it was the wine from the night before or her warmth beside him that made the air feel too thick to breathe.

It was her.

She was already awake when he stirred. Propped on one elbow, hair tousled and curling loose around her cheeks, obscuring the caramel of her bare shoulder. She watched him. The dark of the night clung to her skin, a softness in the hollows beneath her eyes, still slightly puffy from tears shed hours before.

No veil.

No ceremony. No pretense. Just her. Cassia.

She should've looked ruined.

But in the gray hush of pre-dawn, with the linen wrapped across the curve of her hip and her bare knee peeking through the folds, she looked more goddess than woman—fierce and flawed siren, heartbreak made flesh. The kind of beauty no painter could replicate because it wasn't meant to be captured.

Only witnessed.

Her fingers moved absentmindedly across his shoulder, tracing slow circles into his skin. Not with intent. Not even with awareness.

A quiet, unthinking tenderness. Familiar. Intimate.

This was a side of her he had never seen—never been allowed to see.

This woman beside him was real.

It wasn't a dream.

And he…

He didn't know where to look first.

The soft chaos of her hair, wild from sleep.

The warm glow of her skin in the pre-dawn hush.

The bare line of her throat, the slope of her shoulder, the shadows beneath her lashes.

"You stayed," she whispered. Not surprised. Just quiet.

"I said I would."

Cassia sat up slowly, the sheet sliding down her back, pooling around her waist.

The movement revealed the thin, near-transparent slip of gauze still clinging to her body—one strap fallen askew on her arm, the fabric doing nothing to hide the dark, pebbled circles at the center of her breasts.

She didn't pull it up. Didn't flinch.

Didn't cover herself. Just breathed.

He stared, helpless. Frozen. Drowning.

"What?" she asked softly, catching him.

Her voice curved with quiet amusement. The corner of her mouth lifted—just barely. Not quite a smile. More like the echo of one.

A spark.

A dare.

He shook his head, voice rough with sleep. "You're just... not what I expected."

Cassia arched a brow, a small spark of humor in it. "What did you expect?"

"I don't know." He looked away. "Guilt. Regret. Armor."

She lay back, eyes on the ceiling. "You're not wrong. I have all those things."

He was quiet for a moment.

The kind of silence that buzzed with everything unsaid. Then, carefully:

"What happens now?" A beat passed.

Then another.

Cassia exhaled through her nose, still staring upward like she was asking the ceiling for permission—or forgiveness.

"Now?" she echoed, her voice barely a whisper. It clung to the space between them like smoke.

He turned toward her, every muscle alert but unmoving. "Yes."

She didn't look at him. Not yet.

"Now I stop pretending I don't want this." Her eyes flicked to him.

"Not because Djemu demands it," she said, her voice low and steady.

"But because it's you."

She waited. Just long enough for doubt to sink its teeth in. Her voice faltered. "Unless... you don't—"

"Don't."

His voice was low. Firm. But his chest ached with the weight of it.

She blinked, startled — and maybe a little scared. She hadn't meant to sound so desperate.

His hand found hers, strong, certain — but inside, he was reeling.

This wasn't battle. It wasn't strategy. This was her, trusting him in the dark.

And for one suspended breath, he didn't move. Couldn't. Afraid touching her would collapse whatever fragile truth was blooming between them.

Then — slowly, carefully— he reached for a loose curl brushing her cheek, his fingers meeting skin instead of hair. A simple touch. A thousand implications.

Her breath caught.

The curl slipped behind her ear, and still he hovered, like he was waiting for gravity to give him permission.

"Cassia," he murmured, not even sure what he meant to say.

She turned toward his touch. Her breath skimmed his knuckles.

Her lips parted, soft and close.

She closed her eyes. One beat.

Two.

Three.

He cupped her face — not possessive, not coaxing. Just there.

Searching. Holding her like she might vanish if he let her go.

Her eyes opened slowly. They met his, steady now. Unapologetic.

He exhaled, jaw tight. "You know what this means."

She didn't answer.

His thumb grazed her cheek. "If we do this…" The words caught between want and warning.

He was searching — for her truth, for permission, maybe for his own.

"I can't be another secret you carry," he said, voice low. "Or a regret you bury."

She shuddered — just slightly. Her lashes dropped. A breath held. Swallowed. Her fingers curled into the sheet, gripping something she couldn't say aloud.

His hand never left her face. Thumb lightly trailed her bottom lip. Still tethered.

"And if a child comes of this..."

His voice fell away, not from doubt but gravity.

If a child comes of this...

The words echoed—not as threat or warning—but as truth. A possibility so real it felt like a shape in the room with them.

Her lips parted. She exhaled. Pulse thrummed in her throat.

She should've panicked. Should've felt the ground tilt beneath her. Instead, something inside her tilted. Shifted. Ignited.

Like a knowing. Like she'd been here before. Like she'd already said yes.

To the ache. To the risk. To him.

If a child came of this...

It would solve everything.

The thought echoed between them—unspoken, undeniable. Cassia.

As the mother of his child. The air left his lungs in a rush.

He hadn't meant to think it. Hadn't dared.

But now that it was there—real and full and possible—he couldn't look away.

Her eyes. Her breath. The bare line of her collarbone disappearing behind the gauze.

His child. Their child. Something cracked inside him.

A dam, a cord, something he'd knotted down and buried deep just to survive. Gone.

He reached for her—no pause, no breath—fingers tangling in her hair as he pulled her to him.

His mouth found hers, and the world narrowed to heat and contact.

Not comfort.

Not restraint.

This was hunger.

This was surrender. To her.

To him.

To fate.

Forbidden fruit.

Her hands slid to his chest, clutching the front of his tunic like she feared he might disappear. "I don't know how to ask for what I want." He gathered her sheet wrapped body and pulled her onto his lap.

Her thighs wrapping around his hips closing the space between them. He kissed her.

It started gentle—reverent, restrained, like a secret passed between souls for comfort.

But when she kissed him back, something snapped. It deepened, teeth and heat and years of longing compressed into a single, trembling second.

They pulled apart, breathless, eyes locked. Time stood still.

Like in the eye of a storm, the world a hurricane of emotion, swirling around them in the deafening silence.

And then…

It took them both by surprise—the rush of passion, emotion. No more thought. No more words.

Just the raw, desperate need—the hunger of two people who never had a choice surrendering to a contract their souls had signed in some distant lifetime long ago.

Her fingers curled into the linen at his chest like she was holding on to the last solid thing in a world built on shifting sand.

Saben felt the storm rising in him, wild and relentless, demanding release.

Not yet.

Cassia's face held every emotion she'd tried to bury: The tears shed and unshed.

The pride she clung to like armor.

The fire she'd hidden deep just to survive. And beneath it all—want.

Not strategy. Not survival. Desire.

It unraveled him.

"Cassia," he said, voice rougher than he meant. "If we do this... if we cross that line..."

She didn't blink. "Shhh."

Her mouth claimed his, hungry, certain. He kissed her back—hard. "Say it."

"I want this." A tremor, but no hesitation. Then, shaking her head: "No... not this."

He froze.

"Saben. I want you." That was it.

Heat tore through him, white-hot and all-consuming. He silenced her with a kiss—not gentle now, but urgent. Aching. Like they were already burning, and only each other could temper the flame.

She moaned against his mouth, soft surrender laced with need, offering everything—and he took it, begged for more.

In one fluid motion, he shifted, pressing her beneath him, hip to hip, her body yielding like water.

A tangle of silk and breath and heat.

His mouth moved down—tracing her collarbone... lower... beneath the swell of her breast...

He circled her nipple with his tongue, teasing until it responded to his worship.

A breath of air against it—warm, maddening— She arched into him, a soft cry escaping her lips.

Her body opened beneath his touch, slick with anticipation. He slid two fingers through the velvet heat, savoring the way she clenched, tested, trembled.

Two knuckles deep.

Cassia gasped—then moaned, the sound spilling into the quiet like a confession.

He drew her nipple into his mouth again, suckling, teasing the hardened peak with his tongue, then his teeth—just enough.

The air thickened. Time fractured.

And everything that had been forbidden was now unfolding—inevitable, holy, burning.

Cassia cried out—a sound half-swallowed by the hush of predawn, half-offered to the man devouring her inch by inch. Her fingers

threaded through his locs—not to guide, but to feel. To anchor. To make sure this was real. That she was awake. That he was here.

His name spilled from her lips like a prayer, like poetry. Saben wasn't thinking anymore.

He was learning her.

The way her back arched when his mouth lingered.

The way her breath caught when his lips slipped beneath the gauze and found bare skin.

The way her hips lifted, helpless, when his tongue brushed her pearl—ripe, waiting, hers.

He worshipped her slowly. Deliberately. Each kiss a vow.

Each breath, part of a rhythm older than time.

She inhaled sharply, trying to tame the storm inside her— But it was no use.

Lightning ignited in her veins, searing upward from her core like heat pulled from the earth. Something ancient and primal stirred to the surface—something she hadn't known lived inside her.

The scent of her arousal sent Saben over the edge of restraint. Tasting her wasn't indulgence—it was ruin.

And he welcomed it.

Her soft cries echoed in his mind, mingling with the low thrum of his own desire.

Their bodies answered each other like instruments tuned to the same impossible key.

She was soft and wild and glorious. Not perfect—real.

Flesh that flushed beneath his mouth.

Lips that parted with sounds that undid him.

A body that met him, moment for moment, breath for breath. But still—before the final threshold—he paused.

Hovering.

Searching.

"Are you sure?" he whispered.

Her eyes found his. Calm. Clear. Unshaken. "I've never been more sure of anything." He pressed into her—slowly, deeply—

and the world fell away.

In that space—between breath and skin, pulse and bone—they gave each other what no one else ever had: truth.

Not the rehearsed kind.

Not the version trimmed for court. But the kind spoken in tremors.

In moans.

In soul and sweat and surrender. There was no shame.

No masks.

No roles.

Just Cassia.

Just Saben.

And for one perfect, impossible moment— Nothing else mattered.

Thirteen

You Lost, Sailor?

CARLOTTA | CADIZ, SPAIN | C. 1494

DOWN BY THE RIVERSIDE — EARLY FRIDAY AFTERNOON

The river bent like a silver ribbon through the trees, its banks heavy with reed grass and shaded by low, leaning branches that trailed their fingers in the current. Carlotta knelt at the water's edge, sleeves rolled past her elbows, hands red and raw from scrubbing linens. A faded chemise clung to the flat rock beside her, half-washed and heavy with suds.

She wasn't thinking about laundry, not really. She was replaying the morning—over and over again like a bad joke. The market, the mess, the stranger with the sharp eyes and sharper smile.

The way he'd *watched her with interest* that wasn't just curiosity.

That had been a move.

Ratting out Sofia.

That had been a test.

Carlotta knew a test when she saw one. And she'd passed.

Now, her hands moved by habit, rhythmically wringing out a tunic as sunlight flickered off the river's surface and the humid air pressed close, thick as syrup. Her skirts—damp from where she'd waded in to rinse the soap from the garments—clung to her hips, molded to her thighs in a way that was both incidental and utterly maddening to the man watching from the trees.

She stood ankle-deep in the shallows, water lapping at her calves, the hem of her chemise trailing like pale seaweed behind her. Curls had escaped the braid at the base of her neck, sticking to her jaw, her throat. She was the picture of careless beauty—earthy, sunlit, entirely unaware of her effect. Or perhaps fully aware, and simply not bothered.

A frog croaked nearby. Cicadas buzzed like a warning. She glanced over her shoulder—again.

He hadn't made a sound, not a single snapped twig. But she could feel him.

The sensation had been crawling up her spine for the better part of ten minutes. Like breath on the back of her neck. Like the electricity in the air before a lightning strike. She didn't need to see him to know—he was watching. Stalking. Calculating.

A hunter studying his mark.

She didn't spook. Just lifted the garment in her hands and snapped it straight—hard—letting the sound crack through the clearing like a whip.

"If you're going to stalk me," she said, voice sharp as broken glass, "you might as well help scrub."

Silence.

Then, a chuckle—low and amused—from somewhere just beyond the brush.

She didn't turn. Just waited, eyes narrowed, fists tightening around damp cloth.

Vasco stepped into view with the ease of a man who feared nothing—not beasts, not bullets, certainly not women. And yet...

She was different.

He'd been watching her for weeks. At first, it had been curiosity—simple, surface-level. She moved through the market like smoke, graceful, elusive, impossible to hold. He'd seen her hustle merchants and charm fishwives. Seen her steal without lifting a finger, only a smile. He had a talent for reading people, and she was the kind of clever you didn't teach—you were born with it or you weren't.

But then came the morning's incident. The scheme. The escape. She'd outmaneuvered him, left him standing like a fool while she vanished in broad daylight.

And it had only made her more magnetic.

It wasn't just her beauty, though Santo Dios, she had that in spades. He'd laid eyes—and hands—on more women than he could count: dancers with smoke in their hips, widows with too much coin and too little company, merchant wives with silks in their hair and a hunger they mistook for love. From Lisbon to Cairo, they'd sighed after him, lips bitten, eyes tilted to the sea as his sails slipped away.

But her?

She was a siren—and her allure was irresistible. The kind whose voice echoed in your bones long after the music stopped.

He'd watched her for ten minutes—maybe longer—anchored by something he couldn't name. She moved with purpose, wringing out a tunic in the shallows, the afternoon sun dripping off her skin. Her skirts swirled in the river like sea foam, clinging just enough to make his breath hitch—and other parts stir to life, insistent and inconvenient. The way the wet fabric hugged her hips, the dark line of her bodice outlining the swell of her breasts, the lazy roll of her shoulder as she flicked water from her wrist—Dios mío. He shifted his weight, adjusting the ache in his breeches with a practiced flick of his thumb.

She was temptation made flesh.

And temptation, Vasco knew, was always the most efficient kind of bait.

He'd told himself she was just a mark. A piece of the plan. Useful.

But now… he wasn't sure if he wanted to recruit her or fall at her feet.

What would she look like bathing? The image hit him like a musket ball. Lifting her arms, water running down bronze skin. Would she be private? Secretive? Or would she be brazen? Stare him down and dare him to keep looking?

He shook himself.

Focus, Vasco. You're not a lovestruck cabin boy.

But Santo cielo, the fire in her voice—sharp, teasing, dangerous. Like flint striking steel. He liked the way she spoke to him. Like she had a dagger tucked behind every word. She didn't flinch. Didn't fawn. Didn't give a damn who he was or what tales chased his name from Sevilla to the Barbary Coast.

He liked that.

More than he should.

"You lost, sailor?" she asked, not bothering to stand.

"Depends," he said. "If I found what I was looking for, does that count as lost?"

His voice was smoother now, less theatrical than it had been in the market, but no less dangerous. He was measuring her. Testing the waters again.

Carlotta dipped the fabric back into the river and began scrubbing anew. "If you're here to apologize for this morning, I prefer coins."

"I was going to offer a bottle of wine and my eternal admiration," he said, stepping closer. "But coins do make good company."

He shook a small leather pouch, the dull clink of silver inside punctuating the offer.

She looked up then, slow and deliberate, eyes sharp as the blade at her hip. "Is that your angle? Wine and flattery?"

"No," he said, smiling faintly. "My angle is opportunity. But I figured wine might soften the pitch."

He held up the bottle, letting the sun catch the dark glass. A good vintage, by the look of it. Not local.

That made her pause.

Her hands stilled in the water. A ripple slipped past her fingers.

Then, without breaking eye contact, she stood. Water dripped from the linen as she flung it across her shoulder, unbothered. She was taller than he expected. Sharper in the light.

The sort of woman who could dress wounds or slit a throat without flinching—and might enjoy doing both.

"I'm not looking to be pitched to," she said flatly. "Especially by the kind of man who ruins a perfectly good scam for sport."

His grin widened. "Wasn't for sport. I wanted to see how quick you were."

Her eyes narrowed. She stepped toward him—not enough to threaten, but enough to make the air between them tense like a drawn wire. "And?"

He didn't flinch.

"Too quick for me to catch alone," he said, almost like a confession. The words hung there.

The cicadas chirred. A dragonfly skimmed the water, and a breeze stirred the reeds behind them. The scent of damp linen, river clay, and heat pressed in around them.

They stared at each other.

A breath passed. Maybe two. Then he reached.

Not fast, not rough—just a hand lifting toward her face like it was something sacred. His fingers, scarred and sun-darkened, paused inches from the loose curl clinging to her cheek.

She didn't move. Didn't flinch.

But her jaw tightened. Her eyes flashed.

And for a second, he thought she might slap his hand away, draw that dagger and pin his palm to the nearest tree. But she didn't. She stood her ground—daring him to touch her, daring him to find out what would happen if he did.

His fingers brushed the curl. Lightly. Reverently.

It was a whisper of contact, no more than a breath, but something shifted. A jolt—barely there, but unmistakable—passed between them like static before a storm.

Her breath hitched. Just a little. Just enough. She caught his wrist.

Not to push him away. Not yet.

But to hold him there. Still. Contained.

Her fingers wrapped around his with a grip like iron beneath silk. She studied him, eyes unreadable, and he couldn't help but wonder if she was measuring the strength in his hand… or the restraint.

"Careful," she said at last, voice velvet and smoke. "You don't want to play games you're not ready to lose."

His grin returned, slower this time. Crooked. Heat and challenge all tangled together.

"Darling," he murmured, "I never play fair." She held his gaze.

Unblinking. Unapologetic.

Then, slowly—so slowly—her lips curved. Not into a smile. Into something darker. A warning dressed in velvet.

"You brought a pebble to a knife fight, sailor." He didn't have time to process what that meant. Not before he felt it.

A whisper of pressure, low and sharp and very precise—just beneath his belt.

His eyes flicked down.

She'd palmed a second dagger.

He hadn't seen it. Hadn't sensed it. Hadn't even dreamed she was armed with more than the one on her hip—and he was never caught off guard.

His breath left him in a short, stunned exhale.

The dagger's tip rested against the most vulnerable part of him with surgical intimacy. A hair closer and she'd draw blood. A twitch and he might never recover.

Her other hand still held his wrist. Trapped. Disarmed. Played.

She leaned in—barely—but it was enough for her breath to ghost against his ear.

"You have two minutes," she murmured, the words like silk dipped in arsenic. "Then I castrate you."

And just like that, she stepped back. No flinch. No flourish.

She tossed the damp linen over a branch and reached for the next one, humming under her breath like they hadn't just danced at the edge of violence and seduction.

He stood there, stunned, adrenaline pumping.

A slow laugh crawled up his throat—quiet, breathless. Santo Dios.

He'd been outplayed. And holy hell, he liked it.

He stood there, momentarily stunned, the ghost of the dagger's kiss still tingling at his groin. She was back to scrubbing linen like nothing had happened—like she hadn't just threatened to castrate him in broad daylight while humming some Andalusian lullaby.

Vasco exhaled slow. Then, he laughed. Low. Warm. Genuine.

Not the arrogant bark he wore in taverns or the half-drunk roar of a bet gone sideways. This one came from his gut. From the place that recognized when a storm was too beautiful not to sail into.

He rolled his shoulders back, schooled his breath, and let the mask slide back into place—only now it gleamed a little different. Less predator, more supplicant. Still dangerous, but willing to play a longer game.

"You know," he said, stepping to the edge of the water, "I should probably be furious."

She didn't look up. "You don't strike me as the easily wounded type."

"I'm not," he said, crouching to skim his fingers across the river's surface. "But you did just threaten the most valuable part of me."

Now she glanced over. Not a smile, exactly—but her mouth twitched.

Progress.

"I've met all kinds of women, Carlotta," he went on. "The ones who bat lashes to get what they want. The ones who cry until someone else swings the blade. And the ones who run because they don't know their own power."

He met her eyes again, steady and sure.

"You're none of those. You know what you are. And that terrifies people."

Another beat. Another ripple of wind through the reeds.

"But me?" he said, voice dipping low. "It makes me want to build something around it."

She arched a brow. "Is that supposed to impress me?"

"No," he said, standing again. "It's supposed to interest you." He took a step closer, slow and deliberate.

"I have a plan. One that pays in coin, power, and freedom. You won't be taking orders. You'll be giving them. And I want you on board—because I've seen what you can do."

His voice dropped, rough with truth.

"And I'd rather have you as my partner than my rival." A beat passed.

She studied him—really studied him. Not just the easy confidence or the tilt of his grin, but the way he stood like he already owned the next move. Like he thought charm and coin were enough to buy her time, her talent, her fire.

Carlotta had known men like that.

She smiled then—a slow, wicked thing. Tilted her head, gave him one long, assessing look like a queen weighing the value of a pawn, and said:

"Time's up, sailor."

She stepped back, dipped her linen into the river, and began scrubbing as if he'd never interrupted her day.

"Go bother someone else. I have work to do."

Vasco opened his mouth to reply—but something in the set of her shoulders, calm and unbothered, told him he'd lost this round.

So he turned, coin purse and wine still heavy in hand, and walked back up the narrow footpath that twisted between riverbank and trees.

He didn't look back.

But he'd be back.

Fourteen

India for the Win

CHAHIRA | DELHI, INDIA | C. 1218

"You ask an elephant to hold an umbrella for shade as if he's not already giving off shade the size of a country."
Chahira, Queen of Shade & Occasional Mischief

THE DELHI SULTANATE

It wasn't just the heavy scent of jasmine and cardamom in the air, or the way the mirrored domes of the palace caught the sunlight and flung it back into the sky like a challenge—it was the sheer orchestration of it all. Every step, every scent, every glance had been curated for effect. The palace was vast—more like a series of connected dreams than rooms—each one glowing with color: saffron, lapis, emerald, gold. Light bounced off the walls like it had nowhere else to be.

The garden was symmetrical, with channels of water that caught and reflected the moonlight like veins of silver. Lanterns hung from orange trees and carved marble arches, lit with scented oil and flickering low, casting a golden web of light. Low tables and silk cushions were spread across the grass and beneath rose arbors, allowing guests to recline and mingle. Musicians played under a canopied alcove — the soft twang of the sitar, the heartbeat of tabla, and the old weaving through the jasmine-scented air.

The smell was a rich tapestry: jasmine, rosewater, grilled lamb with pomegranate glaze, incense smoke and freshly baked cardamom-saffron bread. Silks rustled, gold bangles clinked, and laughter bubbled from veiled courtiers and the Sultan's sons. It was both elegant and teasingly relaxed — a carefully curated illusion of comfort and ease.

That night, the feast was held in the Sultan's inner garden, a walled paradise known as a bath, tucked behind the palace. It was a formal, private space reserved for intimate court celebrations — luxurious but with a sense of breath and breeze, unlike the stuffier palace halls.

Chahira had been bathed in rosewater, wrapped in layers of silk so fine it whispered when she moved, and led barefoot through a garden that smelled like crushed mint and orange blossoms. The new arrivals — Chahira and the other young women who had traveled with her — were seated together under the watchful eye of a palace matron, being gently observed from every angle. Chahira sat between Yasmina, a sweet, nervous girl from Persia with wide eyes and a soft laugh, and Zohra, a more seasoned beauty from Bukhara who already understood the game and had begun strategizing.

They whispered observations and jokes as young women do, biting fruit and watching the princes with wide eyes and folded fans.

The Sultan was seated on a raised dais beneath a silk canopy, his viziers and senior wives nearby, the gravity of power cloaked in floral silk and soft smiles. His sons roamed freely — charming, greeting, stirring whispers wherever they passed. But above the girlish giggles and drifting silks, the architecture of power loomed — elegant, immense, and impossible to ignore.

The court was larger than any space Chahira had ever seen beneath a single roof. The domed ceiling arched overhead like a sky of marble, its height dizzying. Latticed windows cast slatted sunlight across cool stone, and the air was thick with the perfume of incense, sweat, and anticipation. The mirrored domes of the palace shimmered like a desert mirage, but it was the eyes that shimmered more

— hundreds of them, watching her, weighing her, wrapping her in the velvet hush of judgment and expectation.

A servant passed by with a tray of jeweled goblets, and Chahira took one without thinking. Just a sip, she'd told herself. Just enough to calm the riot in her chest. But the wine was sweeter than she expected — honeyed and floral — and far too easy to drink.

Servants stood like statues. Musicians played something both hypnotic and mischievous, their melodies winding through the tension like silk threads through a loom. Along the length of the elevated dais lounged the princes — five of them, as confirmed by the Vizier's sonorous introductions. They were dressed like gods who'd grown bored and decided to try being handsome instead.

The eldest, Prince Jalal, was unmistakably the heir. He radiated the kind of regal confidence that could not be taught — it was born, not bred. His gaze drifted over the room with disinterest, touching on each of the young women awaiting presentation. Even his falcon, tethered beside him, looked unimpressed — a sleek creature with a golden hood, clearly annoyed to be caged in such a glittering room when it should be slicing the sky above.

I feel you, pretty bird, Chahira thought, before shifting her gaze to the man seated just beside him.

Prince Samir, the second son, was courtly perfection incarnate. Handsome in the deliberate, practiced way that comes from knowing precisely how handsome one is. Not a single fold in his turban was out of place, nor a single hair misaligned. He smiled with polished ease, a diplomat's charm in every gesture, his manicured fingers toying with a dagger that sparkled more than it threatened.

Stuffed peacock, Chahira decided.

"Vain enough to kiss his own reflection and mean it." She mused under her breath.

Next were the youngest — Prince Karim and Prince Zayd — who clearly had no patience for the ceremonial posturing. Their eyes flitted toward the sword-dancers, then toward each other, as if daring one another to slip away for a sparring match. Cute, yes — chaotic, certainly. Chahira hoped they stayed distracted and far from her. She didn't need their energy complicating anything.

And then, there was the other one, the middle one—Prince Rashid.

She'd caught sight of him earlier, seated quietly to one side during the meal, half-shadowed by a carved marble pillar. He hadn't mingled. Not really. He watched. From beneath heavy lashes and an unreadable expression, he scanned the room like someone counting cards, not guests.

He seemed closest to her age, by her estimation, though there was a gravity to him that made him feel older — or maybe just deeper. When she first entered the court, she was certain she'd felt his gaze on her, the prickle of attention so sharp she'd almost flinched. But it had passed — no more than a flicker, lost in the tidal wave of stares that washed over every girl presented tonight.

Still, something about him *lingered*.

He didn't perform like the others. He didn't preen or glint or sparkle. He was… still. Like a pool of dark water, too deep to guess the bottom. She couldn't read him — and that was the part she didn't like. Chahira could read almost anyone. It was a gift, a survival tactic —

a skill sharpened in hushed corners and fleeting glances, in the unspoken language of women who learned early how to listen with their eyes. But this prince? He was a wall. A shadow. A silent echo that pulled at her thoughts even as she swore she didn't care.

She took another sip of wine, just to give her hands something to do. It was either that or fidget. And she wouldn't fidget. Not here. Not now.

If she weren't so dazzled by the colors and sounds of India — the silk-bright saris, the temple bells in the morning mist, the scent of cardamom in the air — she'd be ready to sail straight back to Damascus. Or better yet, to Isfahan, her beloved birthplace, where she once spent entire afternoons watching Baba's pen dance across parchment like it carried the weight of the world in each inked curve.

How she missed those days — when life was simple, the sun was kind, and her world ended at the courtyard walls.

She blinked the memory away and brought herself back to the present — to the perfumed chaos of the palace, the glittering celebrations, and the aching tiredness stitched into her bones after weeks of travel and preparation.

That's enough of that, she told herself, tossing her braid over her shoulder like it might shake loose the weight of homesickness. Let the dark-eyed prince stay unreadable. Let him keep his secrets tucked behind that calm, impenetrable face.

This was her world now.

And tonight, she had a role to play — a part in a golden theatre where eyes watched and whispers followed. So be it.

Let them watch.

The chamber swelled with perfume and silk and a trace of lemon on the breeze drifting in from the garden. Musicians played softly from an alcove, their melody curling like smoke through the air. The polished floor shimmered like water, mirroring the ceiling painted with golden vines. Somewhere, a fountain murmured, indifferent to the nervous flutter twisting in Chahira's stomach.

Golden lanterns cast dappled light along the marble columns, their wicks fed with rose oil and resin. Courtiers lined the edges of the hall like lacquered ornaments—silent, jeweled, watching. The Sultan reclined on a low dais draped in crimson and indigo, flanked by his sons and favored viziers. His expression was unreadable beneath the weight of his turban, his fingers idly stroking the hilt of a dagger inlaid with lapis.

Then—a throat cleared.

The Vizier stepped forward, scroll tucked beneath his arm, his robe brushing the floor with theatrical precision.

He clapped once.

Silence fell like a silk curtain. It was time to present the gifts. First came the treasures.

Servants appeared bearing lacquered boxes and covered trays. One opened with a flourish to reveal a sword from the western frontier, etched in silver and wrapped in a brocade sheath.

Ah yes, Chahira thought, because *nothing says diplomacy like an object designed to cut someone open.*

It was probably ceremonial, but still. Men and their blades—always compensating for something.

Ambergris and saffron followed, heaped in shallow bowls from the coasts.

So, whale spit and flower dust, she mused. One to burn, one to eat. *Preferably not in the same dish.*

Though if someone made a sweet rice pudding with saffron, she wouldn't object to a taste. The ambergris, however, could stay in its bowl—smelling like poetry and dead fish.

Next came bolts of Persian silk in colors so rich they looked wet—like poured rubies and storm clouds. Even Chahira had to admit they were stunning. The kind of cloth that whispered as it moved. The kind meant to drape queens, not courtesans.

Then, a carved ivory chess set from the mountains beyond Kabul.

Tiny rooks shaped like towers. Bishops with delicate beards.

She could never remember how the horse piece moved. Still— it was a beautiful thing. Dangerous, too. All that strategy masked in quiet silence. Like women, she thought. Quiet until they checkmate you.

Finally, an ebony birdcage holding two trembling nightingales. Why were they shaking?

Was it the music? The perfume? Or did even birds know when they were being offered up like jewels?

A murmur of approval rippled through the court. Then—the scroll was unrolled.

"The court welcomes Her Highness Nasreen of Shiraz," the Vizier called, drawing out each syllable with ceremonial gravity. "An offering of delicate beauty. Of grace. Of song."

A girl with honey-brown eyes and far too much confidence stepped forward, veils swirling around her like a pink dust storm. The material floated around her like spun sugar—excessive and unnecessary, just like the girl beneath it.

"Gifted to Crown Prince Jalal, First of His Sons, Keeper of the Golden Crescent, Lord of the Five Winds, and Protector of the Celestial Order," the Vizier intoned, with a flourish that nearly made Chahira snort aloud.

Nasreen bowed deeply, arms raised with theatrical flair, then opened her mouth to sing.

The sound was just as she remembered — an unholy marriage of shrill and flat, like a peacock being strangled beneath a temple bell. Chahira winced.

Oh no. Not again.

She remembered that voice all too well. Every morning at dawn, like clockwork, Nasreen would serenade the upper deck of the ship as if the ocean itself required her offering — a songbird convinced she was a nightingale, never mind the bleeding ears she left behind.

Chahira rolled her eyes so hard it was a miracle they didn't stick. *If this is the voice of grace, then I am the moon's left shoe.*

She leaned slightly toward the girl beside her. "Maybe she and Prince Jalal's falcon will hit it off. They sound exactly the same."

A stifled snort. Then another giggle. The soft sound of laughter rippled quietly through the line of girls like wind through silk. Even one of the guards at the far pillar twitched at the corner of his mouth. Prince Jalal, regal as ever, betrayed nothing. His falcon, however, gave a single, irritated shuffle on its perch and looked away.

"Guess not", Chahira mused. "Even the falcon knows when to feign deafness."

More muffled laughter.

When Nasreen finally hit — or rather, sideswiped — her final note, the court offered a polite smattering of applause. A mercy more than a compliment.

Chahira clapped too. Quietly. Gratefully.

Thank the stars. And the falcon. And perhaps the ghost of every musician she ever offended.

The Vizier stepped forward again, scroll in hand, voice as smooth and practiced as ever—like butter over a blade.

"Lady Amani of Samarkand," he declared, gesturing with a flourish to a girl with impossibly perfect posture and a ribbon of pearls braided into her hair. "A gift of hope and harmony between our noble lands. Promised to Prince Samir, Second Son of the Sultan, Defender of the Western Gate, Envoy of the Silk Road, and Bearer of the Jade Seal of Accord."

Honestly, Chahira thought, how do they even fit all that on a coin?

Lady Amani moved forward with the eerie grace of something rehearsed—like a doll pulled by silk strings. Her bow was flawless. Her anticipation, palpable. She opened her mouth as if she might sing.

She did not.

Instead, her voice, high and soft, floated into the chamber like over-steeped tea—delicate, warm… and entirely flavorless.

She began her poem:

> *"O Prince, bright as the noonday sun,*
> *Your gaze does burn, yet I do not run.*
> *For in your eyes I see the spring,*
> *And in your voice, the sparrow sing."*

Chahira blinked. Did she just rhyme *"spring"* with *"sing"*?

> *"Each breath I take is drawn for thee,*
> *My heart is bound, my soul set free.*
> *Let me be moon to your endless night,*
> *A candle trembling in your princely light."*

Chahira couldn't help herself. Under her breath, just loud enough for the air to catch it, she muttered—

"If I were *that* candle, I'd blow myself out."

A deep, unexpected sound answered her—a rich, rumbling laugh, low and unguarded.

She froze.

The laugh came from just behind her. She turned slightly, horrified… and there he was.

The dark one.

Unreadable eyes with midnight secrets. Standing far too close for comfort.

Prince Rashid.

She hadn't even noticed him approach—which only made it worse. His expression was amused, lips curled, eyes sharp with intelligence and something she couldn't quite place.

Their eyes locked. Heat rose to her cheeks like fire on parchment, but she refused to look away. You've already embarrassed yourself. At least don't flee like a frightened rabbit.

She lifted her chin. Met his gaze. Respectfully. Cautiously. Brazenly.

Rashid's smile lingered, and for a flicker of a moment—just a moment—she swore she saw something shift in his expression.

Approval?

Delight?

Danger?

She wasn't sure. But the air between them crackled.

Chahira turned back toward the dais just in time for Lady Amani to curtsy and flutter back into line, blissfully unaware of the comedic undercurrent she had unknowingly inspired. The court applauded. Chahira clapped too. Still red-cheeked. Still pretending she hadn't just insulted a princess in front of a prince. Still very, very aware of the man standing behind her.

Two down.

Maybe she'd be sent to a library. Maybe her "assignment" was to copy scrolls. Or tutor the royal parrot. Or—

"And next I am honored to present," the Vizier boomed,

"Chahira of Qamar al-Nisa — daughter of the Crescent Ladies, scholar of Isfahan, and ward of the House of Learning in Damascus."

She stepped forward. Her robe shimmered. Her heart thundered. "A rare mind," the Vizier added, casting a meaningful glance toward the Sultan.

"And a sharp wit, or so the letters claimed. A gift to His Grace's third son, Prince Rashid."

The air shifted.

Chahira blinked.

Wait—what?

Behind her, Prince Rashid arched a single brow. A smirk tugged at the corner of his mouth, like a man handed a pet tiger for his birthday and unsure whether to feed it... or set it loose.

Fantastic, she thought. They've wrapped me up like a sweet and served me to the only man here who looks like he collects knives and names storms for fun.

Still, she bowed low. Swallowed her panic. And muttered to herself, steadying her voice with each breath.

Before she could straighten, the Sultan leaned forward beneath his golden canopy. His voice was smooth, resonant—laced with curiosity and dangerous amusement.

"They say your mind is as sharp as your tongue, girl of Damascus. Let us see. What wisdom would you offer my son on the eve of your meeting?"

A hush rippled through the chamber. Not judgment—anticipation.

Even the musicians faltered, the notes hanging like stunned birds in the air.

Chahira's pulse kicked. She hadn't expected a test. Not yet. And certainly not like this.

She glanced sidelong at Rashid. He raised a brow, delight dancing in his eyes, clearly enjoying every moment.

She inhaled.

And offered softly—almost shyly—but with a smile that shimmered like a blade wrapped in velvet:

"They say silence is the language of the wise... I was trying to appear brilliant."

A beat.

Then—behind her—Rashid's voice: velvet and stone. "What's the matter? Cat got your tongue?"

A ripple of laughter swept the court—hesitant, scandalized, thrilled.

Shoulders stiffened. Eyes flicked between the prince and the girl like watching flint strike steel. Chahira straightened. Heat rose in her cheeks, not from embarrassment—but from the fuse it had lit.

She turned, just enough to meet his eyes. "Not at all, Your Highness. I was merely deciding whether to use my tongue... or my claws." The chamber inhaled—one collective breath, sharp and suspended.

Silence.

Thick enough to slice with a dull butter knife. A single cough. A beat.

Then—

Rashid laughed.

Not politely.

Not reserved.

But full-bodied and unrestrained—a sound that cracked the tension like monsoon rain hitting hot stone.

The Sultan chuckled, eyes gleaming.

"At last," he said. "Perhaps the most difficult of my sons has met his match. This should be very… interesting."

Chahira exhaled. Whew. That was close. The prince had a sense of humor. So did the Sultan. And the court hadn't erupted into scandalized gasps or called for her immediate beheading. That was promising.

She smiled. Bowed, smooth and slow. And then—without thinking—heard herself say: "Well. I've insulted a princess, sparred with a prince, and dared the Sultan… All in under ten minutes and you haven't cut off my head yet. I've decided that India may not be so bad after all."

Silence.

Then— the Sultan burst out laughing.

"Well said!" he roared, clapping his hands. "At least you're efficient, girl."

More laughter followed—rolling, raucous, delighted.

Rashid, still grinning, inclined his head with exaggerated grace. "Indeed."

"Let it be known," the Sultan declared, "Prince Rashid's gift comes with wit sharper than any sword.

And perhaps… a touch of madness." All eyes returned to Chahira.

She tried not to melt into the marble.

Rashid's voice drifted over her shoulder, low and amused: "I've always preferred a little improper fire to boredom."

She smiled. Slow. Gracious. Dangerous.

Then bowed again—just a breath too long to be humble. "Then I shall do my best to keep it… interesting."

Chlóe Hall - 5th Grade Report Card

REPORT CARD

FRANKLIN ELEMENTARY SCHOOL
ACADEMIC YEAR 1984-1985

Student : Chloe Hall - #358204

Grade : 5th grade

Teacher . Mrs. E. Coazie

Subject	FINAL GRADE
READING & WRITING	A+
MATH	B-
SCIENCE	C+
SOCIAL STUDIES	A
MUSIC	A+
PHYSICAL EDUCATION	A+

ATTENDANCE

DAYS ABSENT: 3

DAYS TARDY: 7

Comment :

Chloe is a gifted and inquisitive student with a vibrant imagination and a sharp intellect. She often contributes thoughtful insights during discussion and excels particularly in Creative Writing and Social Studies. However, she has a tendency to drift into daydreams, often gazing out the window during independent work time. If she channeled her full focus into her studies, she would easily qualify for High Honor Roll. With maturity and continued encouragement, Chloe has the potential to be a better student.

--Mrs. Eleanor Coazie

Fifteen

Big Girls Don't Cry

COLETTE | RICHMOND, VA | C. 1843

"Big Girl Don't Cry."
**Bessie Smith (aka my mama, on teaching me to
stay alive 'for I even knew what it meant to be
livin')**

Thursday, 12th of October

5:52 PM

The door shut with a quiet click behind him. She didn't move.

The silence pressed in like heat. The smell of pipe smoke and
something else—bitter, coppery, thick—curled in the air. She lay on

the rug, cheek and tummy pressed against the polished wood floor, her arms slack at her sides, her dress bunched around her waist.

Her legs wouldn't close.

A slow sting burned between her thighs. Sharp. Raw. The ache pulsed in time with her heartbeat, cruel and rhythmic.

Her body ached in places she didn't know could hurt. Her ribs. Her throat. The inside of her arms where she'd tried to push him away.

She didn't have the words for what had just happened—only the dull understanding that something had been taken.

Not just her dignity.

Or the ease with which she once breathed in her own skin. It was deeper than that.

Like part of her soul had been scraped out, scooped from her center and tossed aside.

Fragments slowly began to return—not memories exactly... Impressions.

His smell.

His weight.

The grunt in her ear....

She could still feel her cheek burn from where her face smacked the floor.

Cloth ripping.

Fingers clawing to get away. The deafening silence after...

Somehow she knew — what had been done wouldn't be undone. Colette was no longer a child.

She blinked up at the ceiling, tracing the edges of the coffered beams. Dust hovered in the waning sunbeams like ghosts. Her chest rose and fell in shallow, shivering breaths.

Big girls don't cry.

She heard her mama's voice say it. Or maybe it was her own now.

Big girls don't cry.

A tear slipped down the side of her face, tracing the curve of her cheekbone until it disappeared into the hair clinging to her skin. She swallowed hard. It was just one. It didn't count. One didn't mean she had broken.

A painting on the wall drew her attention. The woman on the chaise watched her—unblinking, unmoved. Her gaze was tilted just off center, not quite meeting Colette's, as if she were looking through her. Or beyond her.

What was behind her eyes?

Colette studied her. Her ivory skin and perfect lips glowed pale under the lamplit. Eyes, large and round like a drops of honey—what was the painted woman thinking? The brushstrokes gave her presence, but not life. She was quiet. Had she always been quiet?

Had she seen this before? Had she been a silent witness to all the things that had happened in this room?

How many girls had the painted woman watched disappear into the same stillness?

Colette slowly pulled her dress down, hands trembling. The fabric clung to her skin—damp, twisted. Her underthings were missing. Her hair, once in a neat braid, had come loose. She reached for the ribbons. She had to look decent. She didn't know why. She just knew it mattered.

There was a soft knock. The door creaked open. "Colette?" It was Mattie.

The older woman's face appeared in the crack, cautious, then grim. She stepped inside and shut the door behind her, moving swiftly with a basin and cloth.

"We gon' get you cleaned up, baby," Mattie said, her voice thick but steady. She knelt beside her, hands practiced and gentle. "Don't talk. Don't think. Just breathe."

Mattie dipped the cloth in warm water. She pressed it to Colette's face, wiping away the sweat, the blood, the invisible stain of what had been done.

"Lift your arms for me."

Colette obeyed. Her limbs moved like someone else's.

Mattie didn't ask questions. She didn't need to. She'd seen this before. Too many times.

"You a house girl now," Mattie said softly, more to the room than to her. "He got plans fo' you."

Colette wanted to ask what kind of plans, but her mouth wouldn't work.

Big girls don't cry.

Mattie helped her into a clean dress—simple cotton, pale blue. She braided Colette's hair, then tied a yellow ribbon around it, creating a bun at the nape of her neck, and once again leaving a few tendrils loose around her face. "He likes it like this," she murmured, brushing one of the wisps gently.

Colette blinked again. Her body clean now, but still heavy. Hollow.

She sat on the edge of the sofa and looked at her hands. They were shaking.

Mattie placed a hand on her shoulder. "You strong, girl. You gon' make it."

Colette didn't answer. She just nodded once, slowly. And in her head, the words returned.

A whisper. A spell. A rope.

Big girls don't cry.

* * *

4:35 PM

The early afternoon sun filtered hazily through the heavy gray clouds as the carriage rumbled down the dirt road, wheels kicking up plumes of dust that clung to the legs and skirts of the passengers inside. It was just past harvest season in 1843, outside Roanoke, Virginia, and the wind had that sharp, dry bite that scraped the inside of one's throat when breathed in too deeply.

Colette sat on a wooden bench bolted to the side of the open cart, her back straight, her hands clenched tightly in her lap. She had not spoken since leaving the slave market the day before. She was too afraid. Too aware. Too awake.

She was fourteen. Light-skinned. Almost delicate-looking, with almond-shaped eyes and full lips that trembled despite her resolve to be brave. Her mother had warned her that looks like hers—"high-yellow," with soft, curly hair and a fragile frame—were more curse than blessing in this world. Colette now understood.

The Keller Plantation loomed ahead, its main house a looming white monstrosity with towering pillars and a wide porch that seemed to sneer down at them. Tobacco fields stretched endlessly behind it. Colette's throat tightened. She'd never seen so much land, never smelled the bitter tang of tobacco so fiercely.

She stepped off the cart with three other newly purchased slaves. A large man with a silver chain for a watch and sun-leathered skin called out names, separating them one by one. His voice was flat, practiced. She was last.

"Colette," the man said, not unkindly. "Come now. Don't dawdle. Miss Patty doesn't like lateness."

Big girls don't cry.

Her mama's voice drifted through her thoughts.

She swallowed them down like warm salt, then followed him silently.

Inside the main house, she was greeted by an older house slave with a kind but resigned face. She had deep lines around her eyes and mouth and moved with the grace of someone who had spent a lifetime tending to others.

"This here's Mattie," the man said. "She'll show you what's what."

Mattie looked Colette over with a slow, maternal gaze and then nodded. "Come on, now. Let's get you settled."

She moved quietly but firmly through the polished hallways, pointing to various rooms.

"This here the kitchen. You might help cook now and then, but mostly, you gon' be carryin' and cleanin'."

They passed a narrow back stairwell.

"That there go up to Miss Patty's room. You gon' be her maid, so you best learn her ways. She spoiled, that one—think the whole house turn 'round her. Keep your eyes down, mind your tongue, and don't sass."

Colette nodded, silent and wide-eyed. Mattie kept on.

"That there the work room—where we iron, mend, do the sewing. You'll be in there plenty, 'specially when Miss Patty don't need you. Rest of the time, you help us keep this house straight."

They stopped in front of a room with tall windows and a washtub. "This here the washroom. You clean yourself regular, hear? And don't fret—we look out for our own."

Somewhere in the house, a clock chimed the hour.

* * *

5:00 PM

Mattie called out, and a young woman with a rich, chestnut complexion and piercing black eyes entered. Lila.

"This here Lila. She been in the house a good while now. She gon' help you get cleaned up. Master Keller'll be wantin' to meet you soon, so you need to look right."

Lila didn't smile. She looked Colette up and down with barely concealed resentment. Her posture was stiff, her jaw tight.

"Go on," Mattie said gently, retreating. "Lila'll get you sorted."

Lila didn't speak at first, just eyed the girl up and down with a curl in her lip and a quiet, simmering silence. After a moment, she sighed, "Go on and take off that dress. Gotta get you cleaned up proper."

Colette hesitated, hands fidgeting at her sides.

"Ain't nothing I ain't seen before," Lila added, softer now. "Best go on, now. Water's already gettin' cold."

Swallowing hard, Colette nodded and eased the dress from her shoulders, folding it careful and laying it aside. Her arms wrapped around herself as she stood trembling in the chill.

Lila dipped a cloth into the rose-scented basin and motioned toward the stool beside the tub. "Sit down."

Colette obeyed, her knees wobbly. Lila set to washing her with brisk, practiced strokes.

"You from Jones' place?" she asked, eyes on the task. "Yes, ma'am," Colette whispered.

"Mmm. Figured as much. He been talkin' 'bout you." Colette didn't answer. She didn't know how.

Lila wrung out the cloth and worked it down her arms. "You know what they brought you here fo'?"

"I'm s'posed to be Miss Patty's maid," Colette said, her voice just a whisper.

Lila let out a short snort, sharp and dry. "That what they told you?" Colette's throat tightened. "What... what else would it be?"

Lila finally looked her in the eye. There wasn't meanness in it—just sorrow. Maybe even pity. "You'll know soon 'nough."

She finished the bath in silence, then dried her with a worn linen cloth. From a nearby chest, she pulled out a pale blue dress—clean, if a little threadbare—and helped her into it. Then she guided Colette to a stool by the mirror and began brushing out her hair.

Her fingers were sure, gentle. She drew Colette's curls into a loose braid, coiled it into a bun at the crown, and smoothed the stray hairs at her temples. A few soft wisps she let fall, brushing the tops of her shoulders.

"He like it that way," Lila murmured. "Soft. Curled just so. You'll suit him fine."

There was no warmth in her tone. Only knowing. And weariness.

She tied the sash in a perfect bow, stepped back, and gave a single nod.

"You ready."

Somewhere down the hall, a clock began to chime.

* * *

5:30 PM

Mattie came back and laid a steady hand on Colette's back. "Come on now. Master Keller waitin' on you."

The Mountain Remembers

CI'WIS | TAIWAN | C. 824

The wind is soft here.
Not like before.
It doesn't carry heat, or grief, or flame.
It carries nothing at all, really—
just mist.
And petals.

Dark pink — wild. Like the ones from elsewhere.
Uncultivated.
They spiral through the air
like whispers,
catching in my hair...
on my skin.

They do not ask who I was.
They fall anyway.

Beneath the moss, a whisper sleeps,
where roots entwine what silence keeps.
A thousand steps, a thousand names—
the wind still hums them just the same.

I think I've been here before.

There is water.
Falling—
a ribbon of laughter braided through black stone.
Still—
a basin fed by snowmelt and silence.
It holds the sky,
and something else—
something I forgot I needed to remember.

I kneel at its edge.
A ripple moves across my reflection —
long hair, wild, heavy.
Green eyes I do not wear in this life.

I laid my sorrow in the stone,
and found that I was not alone.
The river cupped my shattered song,
and taught me how to hum along.

A mark stirs beneath the surface — a line,
a curve,
a memory inked in flesh.
I lift my arm.
The tattoo is there.
The story is mine.
Though I've forgotten the beginning,
my skin remembers the song.

Somewhere beyond the trees, an antler rattles —
Warning?
Welcome?
I do not flinch.

A white hawk calls once.
A black-feathered cousin answers.
They carry something between them —
A thread.
A name.
A flame.

A mother carved me from the clay,
with sky in breath and dusk in sway.
She wrapped me in the cedar's skin,
and bade me start the world again.

I sit in the hush,
feet kissed by moss,
petals gathering like old promises in my lap.

There's a trail beyond the trees — winding, steep, red with clay.
I know it.
My breath remembers how to take it.
But not yet.

First, I rest. I listen.
I let the water speak.

It sings of a girl
who ran like a shadow through the forest,
who hunted with silence,
who bore the storm in her throat and carved her becoming
into skin and stone.
She is not gone.

My face hovers between them — unfinished.
Unforgotten. Unwritten.

No mirrors here, no gilded throne,
just fireflies dancing over bone.
They know the shape that grief can take,
and how the dawn will never break—
unless you touch it, soft and wide,
like hunger hushed or tears that hide.

A single blossom lands on the water.
It does not sink.
It waits.

And I rise —
petal-heavy,
mountain-made,
still becoming.

I am not lost—I was regrown.
My body is a mountain stone.
And when they call, I'll rise anew,
with forest blood and rain in view.

Beneath the moss, a whisper sleeps,
where roots entwine what silence keeps.
A thousand steps, a thousand names—
the wind still hums them just the same.

And I rise—

Sixteen

Paris

MONTMARTRE DISTRICT — EARLY FEBRUARY

The train hissed as it pulled away, leaving the platform shivering behind it. Steam curled around Christine's ankles like a living thing, rising in ghostly ribbons as the wheels shrieked into motion. The Métro station was half-underground, tiled in white enamel that caught the weak electric light and echoed every cough, footstep, and muttered pardon. The air smelled of cold metal, damp stone, and coal smoke from a nearby stove. She pushed through a set of heavy wooden doors—scarred by decades of graffiti and grime—before the city opened up around her.

Christine stepped out of the Métro station and into the sharp slap of Parisian winter.

Wind tunneled up Rue des Abbesses, catching the end of her marigold wool scarf—faded from wear but still bright against her navy coat. It was the only truly warm thing she owned, a hand-me-down from her mother—thick-knit, a little scratchy, but made with love for survival. Function over fashion. The kind of scarf that had weathered New York blizzards and Harlem tenement drafts.

She tugged it tighter as the wind turned it into a sail, pulling it sideways and reddening her cheeks instantly.

The sky overhead was gunmetal gray, low and heavy with unshed snow, and the air carried that bite of cold metal and distant smoke—the kind of sky that threatened things without saying them aloud.

Paris didn't feel like New York.

It was older. Quieter. Smaller. But somehow grander.

Buildings curved where New York's stood rigid. Stone façades instead of brick. No brownstones. No stoops. Just pale limestone walls, tall windows veiled with lace curtains, and wrought iron balconies—delicate and disciplined, corseted against time.

The streets were cleaner here, but the alleys were just as dark.

Traffic moved in staccato bursts—narrow delivery trucks rattling over cobblestones, a clanging streetcar farther off, the soft clip of hooves from a vendor's cart. Somewhere down the block, a bicycle bell rang twice, fast and impatient. A black Renault's horn barked, followed by shouted curses in French that made Christine smile under her scarf.

It was nearly 11 a.m. and the cafés were on round two of their breakfast patrons.

Brass chairs scraped against stone as staff set up their terraces—yes, even in February. Thin wool blankets were folded neatly on chair backs, tiny ceramic ashtrays already in place. Men in newsboy caps and wool coats sipped espresso and read Le Petit Parisian, their gloved fingers turning pages slow.

A woman in red heels passed with a leash in one hand and a cigarette in the other. Her little white dog wore a sweater with green buttons. Her curls danced in the breeze—delicate, untamed. Christine let her eyes linger, just a moment longer than necessary.

Her new two-tone spectators clicked along the cobblestones as she climbed the hill, their white-and-oxblood leather still stiff with promise. She passed shuttered bars and the scent of yesterday's bread, breathing in roasting chestnuts from a street cart, cigarette smoke, and wet stone—a mix of charm and hunger.

She passed a florist sweeping petals off the sidewalk with slow, methodical strokes. Then a storefront with records in the window—Josephine Baker's voice slipped through the cracked door, low and sultry, wrapping around her like a silk scarf.

Paris didn't move fast. It moved deep.

Like jazz. Like secrets. Like dreams.

At the corner, a street violinist played something aching and beautiful. The notes tangled in the wind, clinging to the edges of buildings and the soles of her feet.

Everything was different from home—but the bones of revolution hummed beneath the surface here too. Posters for protests hung crooked on alley walls. Black faces in European suits passed by, speaking French touched by Wolof and Creole. A boy with dark skin and a saxophone case nodded at her as he passed.

She nodded back.

Christine paused on the corner, clutching her camera bag to her side. She looked up at the rows of cafés, the crooked buildings that leaned into one another like conspirators, the city that underestimated her—but might one day remember her name.

Today, she was Christine Miller, backup photographer. But in Paris… she could be anything.

Her gloves were already damp, fingertips stinging. She tugged her coat tighter and checked the address one more time:

"31 Rue de l'Espoir — 3rd Floor."

She stopped in front of the building. This was it—a crooked townhouse with peeling blue paint and a wrought iron gate. She looked up. Three floors. One shot.

Christine smiled to herself and whispered, "Let's go make some noise."

She checked her bag, her gloves, her camera. Then she climbed.

* * *

OFFICE OF LA LUMIÉRE NOIRE

The stairs were steep and narrow, the kind that leaned with time. The wood creaked beneath her boots, but Christine barely noticed—adrenaline had taken over, burning like a second heartbeat in her chest. Her breath fogged in the stairwell, mingling with the scent of old varnish, paper, and roasted chicory drifting from a café window somewhere far below.

Three flights up.

At the landing, the stairwell opened into a short hallway—dimly lit, with walls that hadn't been painted in years. Faded floral wallpaper curled at the edges. A single bulb hung from the ceiling, flickering like it couldn't quite decide if it should stay lit.

There were only two doors.

The one on the left was closed, marked only by a scuffed brass number: "3A."

The one on the right was slightly ajar, with a small rectangular placard beside it in worn gold lettering:

La Lumière Noire

Rédaction – Presse & Photographie

Christine exhaled slowly, adjusted her scarf, and knocked gently. A pause.

Then, from inside: "Entrez." She pushed the door open.

The space was small but alive—papers stacked like miniature skylines, photo prints clothes-pinned to lines strung across the room like laundry. The windows overlooked the street, framed by crooked shutters and sheer white curtains that diffused the gray morning light into something soft, almost theatrical.

A large wooden desk dominated the back corner, behind which sat a man in a gray vest, sleeves rolled to the elbows, cigarette smoldering in the tray beside him. His tie was loosened, his hair the color of sea salt and stubbornness.

He looked up.

She met his eyes and lifted her chin slightly. "Christine Miller. I'm here for the assignment."

He studied her for a beat. Mildly curious. Measuring.

"Étienne Duval," he said at last, in English tinted with smoke and Marseille sunlight. "So. You are the one they sent."

She didn't answer.

She let the silence hold. Let him blink first. He smiled.

Respect.

"Bon," he said, gesturing to the seat across from him. "Then let's get to work."

Christine stepped inside, letting the door swing shut behind her with a soft click.

The office was cramped but electric—a creative chaos that smelled like ink, old leather, and Gauloises cigarettes. Yellowed maps of North Africa curled at the edges on the walls, dotted with pushpins. A cork board bore headlines in French and English:

"UNREST IN CASABLANCA"

"COLONIAL MINES IN CONGO RAISE QUESTIONS"
"LIBERIA'S GHOST TRADE: WHO PROFITS?"

Black and white photos lined the walls, some blurry, others brutally sharp—children with too-old eyes, men in chains, soldiers looking everywhere but the lens. In between, glimpses of life: a laughing woman with a market basket, a jazz band mid-performance, two boys running barefoot through red dust.

Christine's eyes scanned the prints like a prayer.

This wasn't just news. It was memory, truth, and resistance printed in light and silver.

"—Mademoiselle Miller." She blinked.

Duval's voice cut across the room like a paper slice.

"You are not here to daydream," he said, not unkindly, but with no space for softness. "Sit. Listen."

Christine dropped into the wooden chair, spine straight. "Yes, sir." He tapped a folder on the desk. "You were not the first choice." She didn't flinch.

"But the first choice is in Zurich with food poisoning and the deadline doesn't care. So now, you are the first choice. Do you understand?"

"Yes," she said.

"No," he said, leaning forward, eyes narrowing. "But you will."

He opened the folder and slid a few documents toward her—train tickets, a letter of introduction, and a folded copy of La Lumière Noire with a small, bold headline:

"Whispers in the Dust: Liberia's Broken Promise"

Duval lit another cigarette, took a drag, and exhaled slowly. The smoke curled upward like punctuation.

"You're going to Liberia. You'll travel through Marseille, then Dakar, then by boat to Monrovia. There's a contact waiting for you—a man named Elias Barbour. Half-American, half-Liberian. Former dockworker turned activist. He knows who to trust. You will stay quiet, move light, and keep your lens clean. Understood?"

Christine's fingers tightened around the edge of the folder. "Yes." He nodded.

"This story is delicate. The Firestone scandal, the rumored slave labor, the rubber contracts—we are poking the Empire. The Americans don't want it printed. The French will pretend they never saw it. But the Black press here and abroad is hungry for the truth."

He slid a small envelope across the desk.

"Inside: French francs, a list of contact names, and a key. You'll pick up the rest of your equipment at a shop in Montparnasse. It's been pre-paid."

He leaned back, smoke coiling around his face. "You have five days to get the shots I need. I don't care about pretty. I care about truth."

Christine nodded once. "Then that's what you'll get."

He studied her for a long second, then tapped the ash off his cigarette.

"This assignment isn't Paris, Miller. Or New York. And it sure as hell isn't Hunter College."

He leaned forward, voice low but pointed. "You're walking into a place where secrets don't like sunlight. You're not invisible, but you will be underestimated."

His mouth quirked—not quite a smile. "Use it." Christine held his gaze.

"Be careful," he added, dragging one last time before crushing the cigarette in the ashtray. "Jokes aside, I'd hate to lose you your first time out."

He pushed the folder toward her, and just before she reached for it, he added with a dry smirk, "Don't make me send someone after you, Legs."

Christine blinked, then laughed. "That a compliment or a warning?"

"Whichever keeps you alive."

She nodded, sharp and clean. "Then I'll take it both ways."

Duval waved a hand toward the door, already moving on to the next name in his stack. "Go. Montparnasse by 3 p.m. Get your gear. The rest is waiting on the boat."

Christine stood, folder tucked under her arm, pulse ticking at her throat. She crossed the room, opened the door—then paused.

"Merci, Monsieur Duval," she said, glancing back.

He didn't look up. Just muttered, "Don't thank me yet, Legs. Not til you come back alive. And Miller—next time, skip the party shoes."

She looked down, instinctively, at the gleaming two-tones on her feet. One brow lifted. She gave a small, wry nod.

"Noted."

Then she stepped out, door swinging shut then clicking softly behind her.

Seventeen

La Rosa Negra

THE CAMPSITE — SATURDAY EVENING

The fire crackled and popped, sending sparks spiraling into the velvet night. Around it, the camp had come alive—clapping, stomping, singing. Palms slapped thighs in complex rhythms, feet pounded the earth in syncopated beats that echoed through the trees like tribal drums warning or welcoming distant souls. The rhythm shifted constantly, passed from one person to the next like a shared language older than blood.

Someone strummed a battered guitar, its voice raw and raspy with use. A hand drum kept time, deep and primal, like a heartbeat rising in anticipation. Castanets clicked like flint on stone, sharp and bright. A woman with ribbons in her braids shook a tambourine so violently that its little bells rang like wind chimes caught in a storm.

Laughter rang out. Cheers. Whoops. A rowdy harmony of voices sang a bawdy verse that made even the fire seem to grin. It was a song of mischief and mishaps—of slipping through windows and slipping off dresses, of outrunning guards and outdrinking sailors. The kind of song everyone knew the words to, and if they didn't, they clapped along anyway.

The dancers—barefoot, dust-kissed, luminous—moved with wild freedom. Some spun in time with the beat, arms flung open like wings. Others shimmied and shook with hips that spoke in tongues. It wasn't choreographed, but it wasn't chaos either. It was instinctive—body memory passed down through generations, through stories told in sweat and rhythm. This was not a rare night. This was a Tuesday.

Sofia was playing a rhythm game with two of the younger boys, drumming a pattern on an overturned bucket while giggling between taps. Carlotta lay on her side nearby, one knee bent, her elbow tucked beneath her head, a crooked smile tugging at her lips. Her boots were dusty, her dark curls loose down her back, and her belly full from whatever stew had been ladled out earlier.

For a thief with no fixed address, this was as close to paradise as it got.

Someone called out above the din—

"La Rosa!"

She didn't flinch. Didn't move. Pretended not to hear. Then came a second voice, louder. "La Rosa Negra!"

Still, she stayed silent, eyes fixed on the stars, not ready to surrender her peace.

Then came the chant—half teasing, half reverent, all rowdy:

"La Rosa! La Rosa! La Rosa!"

Carlotta sighed. The name wrapped around her like a second skin—one she hadn't chosen, but had grown into. La Rosa Negra. The Black Rose. Beautiful, barbed, and impossible to pluck without bloodshed.

She pushed up onto her elbows, shook the dust from her skirts, and let her smile twist into something different—something dangerous.

The mask slid into place.

Gone was the wary watcher at the river. In her place stood a siren forged from smoke and silk. When she stood, the firelight caught the glint in her eyes, the gleam of sweat at her collarbone, the slow curl of her hips as she moved toward the center.

The noise quieted on instinct. Anticipation rippled through the crowd like static.

She didn't speak. She didn't need to.

The guitar gave her a single note. Then another.

The drum picked up beneath it.

Slow.

Sultry.

A rhythm like honey sliding over steel.

Carlotta tilted her head, let the music move through her like possession. Her fingers teased the hem of her skirt. Her eyes scanned the firelit faces. And then—Carlotta began to sing.

> *Come close, brave fool, if you dare,*
> *The night is deep and thick with prayer.*
> *I'll kiss your coins and steal your breath,*
> *And spin you 'round the edge of death.*

Low at first—guttural, husky—the kind of sound that slithered down spines and made necks prickle. It wasn't a voice meant to soothe. It was a call. A summons. The kind of sound sirens make when they want ships to crash.

Refrain (sung like a slow chant, hypnotic):

> *Ay, la luna watches,*
> *Ay, the shadows sway,*
> *Dance with La Rosa,*
> *Or be danced away.*

Her head tilted back, throat bared to the stars, and she surrendered to the music as if possessed. Not just singing—invoking. Her voice curled around the crackling fire like smoke, like incense rising from some forgotten altar.

Every soul around the campfire stilled.

Verse 2 (softer now, intimate):

> *I danced for kings and bled for queens,*
> *Slipped knives through lies and midnight schemes.*
> *I've loved in alleyways and courts,*
> *I've burned your maps and drawn new ports.*

Then—a jingle of bells.

Her hips began to sway, slow and serpentine, the silver charms at her waist, wrists, and ankles chiming in time. The fire lit her from behind, casting shadows that flickered like spirits on the trees. Her skirts brushed the dirt, then lifted—just enough for her feet to flash, bare and sure, the flick of her ankles like punctuation to each beat.

Refrain (again, stronger):

> *Ay, la luna watches,*
> *Ay, the shadows sway,*
> *Dance with La Rosa,*
> *Or be danced away.*

She was lost in it. Loving it. Feeding off the heat, the hunger, the rhythm that surged through every body gathered. And as she danced, eyes half-lidded in pleasure, she caught the movement—

Vasco.

Approaching the fire with a few known faces and two strangers. Strangers who smelled like trouble—not locals, not family. Eyes too sharp. Weapons too clean.

Still, Carlotta didn't falter. Didn't stop. She spun once.

Refrain (louder now, defiant):

> *Ay, la luna watches,*
> *Ay, the shadows sway,*
> *Dance with La Rosa,*
> *Or be danced away.*

Then—

Stomp. Silence.

A hush fell, like the air had been pulled from the world. Around her, thieves crouched, leaned, stood still—ringing the fire like acolytes around a flame. Crickets ticked in the trees. The wind held its breath.

One beat.

Two.

Three...

Four.

Then Carlotta clapped. Once.

Twice.

A pulse. A heartbeat. The rhythm of something ancient and undeniable.

Verse 3 (beat rising):

> *I am the ghost your mother feared,*
> *the wish your father never cleared.*
> *The kiss that cuts, the vow that fades,*
> *the fire in a world of blades.*

Others joined in, clapping with her, building the tempo with reverence and rising thrill. It quickened. Grew. Became a storm.

Refrain (everyone like an anthem):

> *Ay, la luna watches,*
> *Ay, the shadows sway,*
> *Dance with La Rosa,*
> *Or be danced away.*

Final refrain (full-throated, triumphant):

> *Ay, la luna watches,*
> *Ay, the shadows sway,*
> *Dance with La Rosa,*
> *Or be danced away.*

Her feet began to move again—no longer a dance, but a declaration. Her steps were fluent, born of instinct, memory, and wildness. Her voice rose with the rhythm, rich and raw, a cry to the heavens in a language older than war. Her hair whipped around her shoulders. Her hips sang. Her arms painted the air. Her body told stories her mouth never could—of lovers lost and lovers ruined, of stolen jewels and sun-baked escapes, of heartbreak and hunger and the taste of victory.

The music pounded—drums, clapping, the tambourine like rainfall on rooftops. Voices rose to join her, caught in the frenzy she'd summoned, like the camp itself was spinning into some kind of sacred madness.

She was the storm and the lull. The dagger and the kiss. The rhythm built.

Faster. Faster. Faster— And then— A halt.

Skirts swished, freezing mid-spin. Bells fell silent.

Carlotta threw her head back and released one final note—long, impossible, and blisteringly high. It soared over the trees, over the fire, over every man and woman who'd ever doubted her.

Silence.

Then:

A roar of cheers.

Stomping feet.

Clapping hands.

Shouts of praise in every tongue the empire had tried to erase. A flower tossed from someone's cloak.

A coin flipped in tribute.

A whistle loud enough to wake the moon.

She stood in the center of it all, sweat-slick and luminous, the firelight kissing every curve of her skin.

La Rosa Negra.

The queen of thieves. Their star.

And Vasco—watching her from the edge of the firelight, awe tightening in his throat—knew he wasn't the only one who wanted to build something around her.

He was just the only one foolish enough to try.

He stepped into view like smoke unfurling—quiet, confident, uninvited.

Tall, sunburned, cloaked in a worn wool coat that had seen better storms. A crooked scar split one eyebrow. His boots were polished, oddly precise, but his eyes were feral—restless and calculating, the kind that measured everything and feared nothing.

Carlotta turned at once.

Her hand went to the blade at her hip, fingers curling around the hilt with easy promise. Around the fire, the cheers and revelry stuttered and died, like a song choked mid-note.

The spell had broken.

"You're not welcome," she said evenly.

"I don't recall asking," he replied with a faint smile.

A murmur rippled through the gathered crowd—low, dangerous, like a snake coiling in dry grass.

Strangers didn't come here. Not without invitation.

Not without consequences.

The regulars began to rise. One by one. Shadows with teeth. They closed in behind Carlotta, tightening the circle around the fire like a noose. Faces hard. Postures ready. Steel glinted in firelight—blades unsheathed, pistols thumbed, knuckles flexed for blood.

Vasco slowed his step.

Good. He wanted to know what kind of people he was dealing with—and now he knew.

Cutthroats. Survivors.

And her? Their queen.

He held his ground, but tilted his head slightly toward the two familiar faces behind him.

"They invited me," he said, voice calm. "I come in peace."

No one moved. No one bought it. Especially not Sofia.

"That's the bastard who almost got us caught at the market," she hissed, rising to her feet. "Why would you bring him here?"

Her words cracked like a whip.

The tension snapped tighter.

Gasps. Growls. Half a dozen blades drawn in a breath. Someone spat into the dirt. Someone else cocked a crossbow.

Vasco held up both hands in mock surrender. "Peace, señorita. I come with coin. And a proposition."

Carlotta didn't blink. "You'll need better bait."

"I've seen you and the girl in the city," he said, eyes on her. "Clever fingers. Silver tongues. Very convincing act."

His gaze flicked to Sofia, who had gone utterly still. "You made quite an impression."

She said nothing, but the flare in her eyes spoke volumes.

The air was sharp with danger, the kind that made men sweat before the first drop of blood was drawn.

"I'm not here to cause trouble," Vasco said. "Just the opposite. I'm here to offer you a job."

Carlotta arched a brow, unimpressed. "We already have one."

"Not like this, you don't." He stepped closer to the firelight, slow and deliberate.

The fire caught on the curve of his belt buckle—a flash of silver, clean and bright beneath the travel-worn wool. And just beneath it, the hilt of a blade too fine for any dock rat. It shimmered like something that had drawn blood in candlelight, not mud.

Not noble.

Not military either. Sea-worn but rich.

A privateer, then. Or worse.

"Name's Vasco," he said. "Recently docked from Cartagena. Delivered a vessel to a local lord—Montoya, if you must know."

That name landed like a stone.

A few murmurs scattered through the crowd. Not loud—but unmistakable.

Montoya.

Carlotta's jaw twitched, just once. A muscle jumped along her temple.

Vasco noted it. Filed it away.

"He paid well," he continued, quickening his pace—words tumbling just fast enough to dodge the rising temperature around him. "But they kept the lion's share, as nobles do. And now he's throwing a masquerade in a weeks' time. Big spectacle. Fireworks, champagne, gold leaf invitations—all to celebrate some fool crossing the Atlantic in search of dragon's teeth and river gods."

He said it in a single breath.

Just fast enough to get it out before they turned on him.

He could feel it—how tightly the moment was wound. Like a wire between teeth.

La Rosa Negra hadn't taken her eyes off him. Still as a blade before it strikes. If anyone was going to slice him down where he stood, it would be her. The others would follow. That much he knew.

And that's what made this next part so dangerous. And necessary.

He schooled his face into a half-grin—confident, maybe a little cocky—but beneath it, his heart kicked like a mule. He lifted the wineskin one of his companions had offered around and raised it to the fire, casual as anything.

"Thought I might attend," he said. A beat passed.

Then: "And thought, perhaps, I'd bring friends."

His smile widened, but it didn't quite reach his eyes. Not anymore. He was watching her too closely now.

Because he realized—again, too late—he'd underestimated her.

She didn't laugh.

Didn't bite.

Didn't blink.

He made a silent note not to make that mistake a third time.

Carlotta was unpredictable. Wild. Dangerous in ways no map or plan could anticipate.

And yet—this was the way it had to be. If he could get her to bite, the rest would fall in line. Her crew would follow. The whole lot of them would be his storm to command, and when they saw what he planned to take…

They'd thank him.

Hell, they'd worship him. If they lived through it.

But first—he had to win her over.

And Carlotta de la Rosa didn't come cheap.

She laughed, but it was a blade of a sound—sharp, bright, and utterly humorless.

"You want us to rob a nobleman," she said, "*during a masquerade?*"

Vasco didn't flinch. "I want us to rob *Montoya*—who wouldn't notice if his left eye went missing, let alone a few gems."

He stepped in just close enough for the firelight to catch the gleam in his eyes.

"You wouldn't need to touch a thing. Just distract. Deceive. Sing a little. Dance." His voice dropped. "We'd handle the rest. And in return—more coin than you've seen in a year."

It was a sweet pitch. Too sweet.

Carlotta's head tilted, eyes narrowing like she could see the hooks hidden behind the honey.

"No."

He blinked, caught off guard. "You haven't even—"

"No," she said again, firmer. Sharper. "I know a trap when I see one. That much silver? That much risk?" She cut a glance toward her people, her voice like flint. "Someone ends up dead. Probably us."

For a long beat, Vasco said nothing. Just studied her.

Then that damned smile crept back in—a curl of lips that knew too much and gave nothing away.

He should've backed down. Walked away clean. But he'd never been good at quitting.

He looked around the fire—at the glint of blades, the set jaws, the narrowed eyes of those ready to gut him if Carlotta said the word. His odds weren't good. Not here. Not tonight.

Still, he tried one last card.

"Fair enough," he said lightly. "But I'll be in town until the masquerade. If you change your mind, find me at the Boar's Tooth. Ask for the man with the crooked luck."

He tipped an invisible hat to the firelight—mocking or respectful, it was impossible to tell—and turned.

He and his companions melted into the dark the way they'd come—quiet as rumors, and twice as dangerous.

But the quiet that followed didn't last long.

Sofia exhaled loudly. "Well, *that* wasn't ominous at all."

The camp didn't laugh. Not exactly. But the pressure eased. A few chuckles, the scrape of blades sheathed. Someone struck up a rhythm again, hesitant at first. A tambourine. A snap of fingers. Slowly, the music began to crawl back to life, like a heartbeat returning after a scare.

Still, no one took their eyes off the shadows for a while. Not really.

Carlotta rubbed the back of her neck, her eyes fixed on the space Vasco had vanished into.

"*Madre de Dios,*" she muttered. "I hate it when the dangerous ones are charming."

Sofia snorted. "He wasn't *that* charming."

Carlotta didn't answer. Because she was already turning it over in her mind.

The silver. The risk. The promise.

He was trouble. More trouble than he was probably worth. Still...

That kind of score could change *everything*.

No. *No.*

This was a bad idea.

She'd find a way to get herself and Sofia out of this before Vasco dragged them into a storm they wouldn't survive.

And yet...

Somewhere in the deepest part of her gut, a truth stirred.

This wasn't over. Not by a long shot.

Eighteen

The Aftermath

CASSIA | MEMPHIS, EGYPT | C. 693 BCE

CASSIA'S PRIVATE CHAMBERS

CASSIA

The side door shut softly behind her. No footsteps followed. No voice called her back.

No one had seen her slip from the champion's chambers where the previous night's celebration had been carried out. The scents of crushed dates, sweat, and sandalwood clung to her skin. She moved like a wraith through the still-slumbering palace, her steps silent on cool marble floors she no longer saw.

She didn't breathe—really breathe—until she reached her chambers.

The heavy silence swallowed her as she slipped inside and turned the latch. Safe. Alone.

She crossed the room in a trance and sank onto the chaise, tucking her knees up and pressing her back to the cold stone wall. Only then did her heart begin to hammer again, the weight of the night catching up to her in full.

Cassia pressed a hand to her chest. It wasn't shame that burned under her ribs—not exactly. It was too complicated for a single name. It was everything at once: grief, guilt, disbelief… and something dangerously close to longing.

She closed her eyes. And there it was.

The memory of his breath against her collarbone.

The reverent way his lips had parted before they touched her skin—like she was something sacred, something fragile.

The way his hands had trembled, just slightly, as they slid beneath the loosened ties of her shift.

He hadn't known what to expect.

She hadn't either.

She let her fingertips drift over her bare thigh, just above the place where his hand had rested. Slow circles. Her skin was warm. Oversensitive. Every nerve still alive with the echo of him.

His touch had been sure, but not arrogant. Warm hands that gripped her like a man drowning—not conquering, but clinging. Sliding down her back, her ribs, her side. Tracing the line of her waist to her thigh as though he were memorizing a map he already knew would be taken from him.

She remembered the rasp of his voice in the dark—low, gravel-rough. She couldn't even remember the words. Just the tone. Like worship. Like grief. Like restraint hanging by a thread.

And when she'd trembled—when she'd almost pulled away—his hands had steadied her, not with demand but comfort. His forehead had rested against hers for a moment too long. She remembered that. That stillness. That breath they shared.

She drew another slow circle on her thigh. Her skin felt softer than she remembered. His had been rough, sun-worn, callused in ways that made her shiver. He'd held her like he could come undone at any moment—and somehow, that had made her feel powerful. *Seen.*

* * *

DJEMU

The side door closed quietly behind him as he followed her into her rooms. No footsteps followed. No words. She was still unaware of his presence.

Djemu waited, his back to the door, heart wound tight with an anxious tangle of revulsion and desire. The plan had devoured him for days — a brutal calculation dressed as duty. If it worked, it would silence the court, secure the bloodline, anchor the throne. A clean, surgical solution to a decade of whispered failure. Two wives. Ten years. No heir.

But now, standing in her private chamber, silently watching her from across the room — after everything he'd seen — his insides twisted into something unrecognizable.

She hadn't just obeyed. She had surrendered.

She had opened to the man, welcomed him, moved with him like she knew him — like she wanted him — like Djemu was already dead in her heart and she had made peace with his ghost.

He could still hear it. The sound of her breath catching. The way she'd whispered, not in pain, but with need. The look in her eyes — not blank with duty but dazed with pleasure.

He had ordered it. He had watched it.

And yet... nothing could have prepared him for what it would do to him.

Cassia was perched on the edge of the chaise, the morning sun spilling through the slats of the carved shutters, catching the sheen in her unbound hair.

The morning sun?

Djemu stiffened. She should've returned hours ago. The plan had been precise — timed, controlled, clinical. She was to slip out before dawn, veil intact, her identity hidden even in absence. A necessary sin, done in the dark, and forgotten by the time the birds stirred.

But this…?

This was reckless. Brazen.

And her hair — loose and tumbling over her shoulders in tangled waves. No braid. No wrap. Not even the modest silver pin she usually wore in court. She hadn't even tried to put herself back together.

Because she didn't regret it. Because she hadn't planned to.

A flicker of memory surged — unwanted, uninvited.

The curtain had been cracked just enough. Just enough to see skin and movement. A mess of limbs, of mouths, of moans swallowed into candlelight. He hadn't meant to look. Not at first.

But once he had, he couldn't *unsee* it.

The arch of her spine.

The way she *reached* for him — for Saben — not like it was duty, but desire. Not obligation, but longing.

Her hands fisted in the sheets.

Her voice — a sound he'd never heard from her lips — broken and breathless, calling out a name that wasn't his.

No mask of compliance. No stiff resolve. Just… *abandon*.

And now here she sat, still drunk on it.

Her skin glowed. Her mouth was swollen. Her gaze unfocused — like she hadn't really come back at all.

Had she lain in his bed like that? Ever? Had she ever looked so utterly undone for *him*?

She leaned forward slightly, elbow resting on her knee, and Djemu's gaze followed the lazy arc of her fingers as they traced slow, absentminded circles on the soft skin of her upper thigh — just above where *Saben's* hand had rested less than an hour before.

Djemu was used to seeing Cassia armored in grit — sharpened, steady, forged for battle.

But she wasn't dressed for war now. She was barely dressed at all.

Wrapped in nothing but a half-loosened shift, slipping scandalously off one shoulder — the kind of slip that wasn't accidental. Not anymore.

Still soft. Still aching.

The hem was wrinkled, askew, riding high enough to bare the supple line of her thigh. Her feet were bare. Her lips — still swollen, still stained with the ghost of a mouth that wasn't his.

The ghost of a soldier. A lover.

A choice.

And Djemu — Djemu had let it happen. No.

He had ordered it. He had watched it. Plotted it.

Disguised it as duty. Played the fool.

Gods, what are you doing? The thought screamed behind his eyes. Why are you sitting like that?

That small, familiar gesture — the slow circling of her fingers against her skin — had once comforted him.

He'd seen it before. On their wedding night. Long after the ceremony, after the servants had gone, when silence stretched thick and uncertain between them. She'd curled beside him then, those same fingers drifting across his collarbone like she was tracing the edge of something she wasn't sure she wanted to keep. A bruise, maybe.

Or a boundary. Or a warning.

He remembered the warmth of her breath on his skin, the faint scent of lotus oil in her hair — subtle, ceremonial, meant for *him* alone.

He had taken it as a sign. A sliver of trust.

A private gesture not meant for the world, but for the man who wore her ring.

Something earned.

But now, watching her — wrecked and radiant in the arms of a memory that wasn't his — that same gesture turned cruel.

Had he touched her there?

Is she tracing where Saben's hands had been—just minutes ago? Is that where he kissed her?

Did she whimper beneath his mouth? Did she beg?

Did she—

Djemu's throat closed.

The jealousy came first — hot and bitter. Then shame.

Then rage.

Then something worse. Something that hollowed him out and left his insides raw and exposed:

Fear.

Not of her.

Of what she'd become without him. Of how deeply she could feel.

How freely she could give — to someone else. The bile rose so fast it nearly choked him.

Her shift had slipped farther off her shoulder. The soft linen clung to the curve of her waist, bunched high along her thigh where her fingers still moved, slow and dreamy, like she was memorizing the shape of something precious.

Something forbidden.

Something he had *sanctioned.*

Djemu couldn't breathe.

His mind conjured images he couldn't unsee — her body arching beneath Saben, lips parted in a soundless cry, the taut lines of pleasure rippling through her like worship. She had been beautiful in the candlelight, even from the sliver of shadow where he'd watched.

Too beautiful. And too free.

She hadn't looked like a woman on a mission. She hadn't looked like a wife fulfilling an order.

She had bloomed.

Her soft sighs echoed in his skull.

Was this still his wife?

He had given her away. Handpicked her lover. Scripted the lie. Offered her body to another man like a prayer for survival. A silent sacrifice to preserve the crown. To cleanse the doubt. To buy legitimacy with sweat and semen.

And now here she sat — humming with afterglow, her skin flushed as if kissed by gods, her lips still marked by the mouth of another.

Untouched by regret.

She hadn't even seen him. Her gaze was fixed beyond the stone balcony, past the sunlit curve of the horizon. Somewhere far away.

Was she still with him?

Was she remembering Saben's mouth? His breath? The way he touched her — like she was sacred?

Jealousy slashed through him, sudden and bright and ridiculous. He had done this.

Chosen the man. Planned the hour.

Watched her walk into the dark like a whore in royal silk. All for him.

For them.

But she wasn't supposed to *want* it.

He had imagined cold duty. Tears.

A grim kind of bravery.

He'd told himself she'd come back torn, emptied out, clinging to him for comfort in the aftermath.

Instead, she returned full. Quiet.

Radiant.

And smiling.

His stomach turned.

Was she replaying it now?

The sound of Saben's voice in the dark? The rough reverence of his hands?

Had she whispered for more? Had she *begged*?

Djemu pressed a hand against the doorframe to steady himself. Had he made the right choice?

Or had he gambled something sacred — not just her body, but her trust — and lost it for good?

The realization curdled inside him like poison.

Because now that he saw her — sated and serene, glowing with the echo of someone else's hands — the truth lodged in his chest like a blade:

He hadn't just bartered her body. He had bartered her belief in him.

And maybe — just maybe — she wouldn't come back from that.

He stepped forward then, slowly, deliberately, shuffling his boots against the stone just enough to be heard.

Cassia's shoulders stiffened, her back pressed against the cold stone wall. She didn't meet his eyes.

Didn't have to.

Her face told the truth first — flushed cheeks, parted lips, eyes glassy with memory.

Rage simmered in his gut, slow and bitter, rising like smoke. He stepped closer.

One step. Then another. Then, quietly — "You're late."

* * *

CASSIA

Cassia opened her eyes, staring out the narrow window toward the distant Nile. Dawn had broken.

How long had she been sitting here?

She didn't feel victorious. Or ruined. She just felt… changed.

And though she'd braced for the weight of disgust or despair, what came instead was a kind of quiet sadness. Not regret.

But the soft mourning of something that was never meant to survive daylight.

But sacred things don't get traded like coin.

The thought struck like a knife.

A fresh wave of hollow sorrow washed over her, heavier than before. Not shame—she had done what was required. What was demanded. But duty did not dull grief, sharp and biting, from curling through her ribs.

Her fingers tightened against her thigh.

She had been betrayed. Not by the man who had touched her like she was holy—but by the man who had *vowed* to protect her. Who had taken her hand before gods and mortals, whispered of legacy...

...only to turn her into a bargaining chip. He had sold her.

Bartered her body like livestock.

Traded her flesh for the idea of peace, as if that were a fair exchange.

Was it worth it, Djemu?

Cassia sank lower into the chaise, the cool wall behind her offering no comfort.

Her body still thrummed with the echo of Saben's touch—his warmth, his reverence—but her thoughts shattered in a thousand broken directions.

Djemu would never know the depth of it.

He could never know.

Not this. Not how deeply it had shaken her. Not how Saben had made her feel seen.

Not how for a few stolen hours, she'd learned what *freedom* felt like.

Or how close she'd come to choosing the alternative.

Because in their world, marriage was an oath—sealed in blood, bound until death.

And she had been given a choice. Do it or die.

Return before dawn or don't return. This had been for survival.

Just survival.

Nothing more.

Footsteps. Soft, shuffling.

Cassia didn't turn. She didn't need to.

She *felt* him before she saw him—like a storm building pressure in the room.

Her spine straightened instinctively, her breath tightening in her throat.

Here we go, she thought bitterly.

Djemu stepped from the shadows and into the flickering candle-light of her private chambers, his posture rigid, his jaw locked. He looked like a man watching an animal he'd trapped—curious to see whether it would lash out or simply fold.

He studied her for too long.

And then, finally, he spoke—his tone too calm, too even. That flat, weaponized calm she knew too well.

"You're late."

Cassia said nothing.

Her eyes scanned his face.

He looked like a man who hadn't slept. His jaw was clenched tight, the line of his mouth pinched in restraint. Shadows pooled under his eyes, and something bitter and unspoken sat heavy in his gaze. His body was stiff, too still—like if he let himself move, he might shatter.

Emotion flickered. Was that jealousy? Rage?

Or was it just guilt, trying to hide behind arrogance? "You enjoyed it," he said.

Cold. Steely.

The words dripped with accusation, but were quiet enough not to carry through the walls. Still—sharp enough to slice.

Cassia blinked, stunned for a breath.

Are you fucking serious?

She stood. Slowly. Deliberately. Not defiant.

Not afraid.

Just cold. Steel forged in betrayal.

Her fingers curled into fists at her sides. She was done backing down.

"You sent me to him like an offering," she said, voice quiet but hard enough to draw blood.

"You dressed me in another woman's scent and told me to lie down with a stranger. And now you're angry I didn't cry through the whole thing?"

He flinched. Just slightly.

"You were starstruck," he hissed, stepping forward. His eyes raked over her like he was searching for evidence of something he didn't want to find.

"You're glowing."

Cassia laughed. Once. Cold and joyless. Her voice dropped to frost.

"You want me to be broken? Fine. I'll play that part too. But how dare you accuse me of dishonoring you—after what you asked of me?"

He blinked.

Wavered.

And for a single breath, he looked… lost.

Cassia felt it: a flicker of disbelief. The briefest urge to pity him. Djemu recovered quickly. The flicker of vulnerability vanished, replaced by something colder. Not regret. Not even anger. Just that brittle, brittle arrogance he wore like armor — but now it felt thinner, more desperate. The mask of a man who'd seen too much, felt too much, and would rather torch the truth than admit it ever touched him.

Cassia stared at him. Blinked once. Slowly.

He just stood there. Staring. Judging. Seething thoughts swirling in his eyes.

Unbelievable. He actually thought this was a win. And now he was using it against *her*?

Cassia rose to her full height—slow, deliberate, unafraid. Every inch of her was composed, lethal.

Her voice came low and steady, the kind that left bruises long after it passed.

"You sent me to him like a gift no one asked for. Coated me in another woman's scent. Told me to go quietly. To be soft. Please him, you said."

Her tone sharpened, slicing the space between them.

"Hide my face. Fuck him. Leave before he wakes—you said it yourself."

She took a step closer, the audacity in it burning. "And now you're angry it worked?"

She could feel it—how close she was to ruin. If he knew the truth… if he knew what had really passed between her and Saben, what she'd let happen, what she'd wanted—he'd bury her in a cell beneath the palace and forget her name. And no one would stop him.

But that wasn't the whole of it, was it? He hadn't just sent her to seduce.

He'd sent her with a vial of hemlock sewn into her sleeve if she failed.

Do it, or die… by my own hand.

Return before dawn or don't return at all.

She had to stand her ground — fight back. Or else she would be powerless for the rest of her life.

No. This was it. It was now or never. This had to work.

Djemu's mouth twisted, jaw clenched tight enough to splinter bone.

"You were glowing when you came back," he spat.

"Dripping with it. Don't insult me by pretending you hated it." Cassia laughed.

Sharp. Brittle.

A sound without warmth, without mercy.

"Is that what you're jealous of?" she said, tilting her head, voice soft and deadly.

"That someone else touched me and I didn't flinch?" That made Djemu flinch.

Good.

She stepped closer now, each word cutting to the quick.

"You think I wanted it? That I enjoyed it?" Her voice lowered, roughened by something darker.

"I did what you asked. What you demanded of me. It's not my fault your fragile ego can't handle the demands your position requires."

"Let me say this clearly, husband—" she leaned in, voice a razor's edge,

"I played the part. I told him the lies. I got the seed. And I left with my dignity still intact."

Her voice dropped to a whisper, and somehow it cut even deeper. "But don't confuse survival with pleasure. You wouldn't know the difference if it choked you."

That did it.

The words hit like a blade to the gut—and Djemu snapped.

The back of his hand cracked across her face so hard the sound echoed in the hallway.

Cassia hit the floor, knees and palms smacking stone, the metallic taste of blood blooming in her mouth.

Pain rang through her jaw—but she didn't cry out. Didn't even move.

He bent over her, slow and deliberate, one hand twisting in her hair, wrapping the loose tendrils around his fist like reins. His face hovered just above hers, breath sharp and sour.

"You go too far," he hissed. His tone was soft. Mockingly tender. Rotten with false sweetness. "Little dove."

Little dove — no affection, it was a leash. A joke. A threat wrapped in silk.

Cassia met his eyes, even as his grip twisted tighter, pain flaring at the base of her skull.

She didn't wince.

She wouldn't.

But her voice dropped low.

Measured.

Clipped.

"He didn't recognize me. He was drunk. Barely awake. That's why I was late."

Each line was sharper than the last, cut clean from bone.

"It was awkward. I did what you asked."

A beat.

Not long — just enough to feel the weight of it. He sneered — but there was a tremor in it.

She felt it.

And something in her shifted.

Her breath hitched — not from pain. Not even from fear. From fury.

Because he was bluffing.

Because he thought shame could control her.

Because he thought this would break her.

And so, with blood still fresh on her lip, she smiled. Then let the words fly, low and final:

"Congratulations, Djemu. Not only did you turn your wife into a whore—you failed at that too."

He froze.

The silence that followed didn't soothe. It tightened.

It crushed.

It crackled like the space between lightning and thunder. Cassia let it.

She didn't flinch. Didn't blink.

Didn't beg.

Just held his eyes with every ounce of loathing she'd spent years burying under silk and silence.

Because even if he killed her —

He actually thought this was something he could use against her.

Cassia rose slowly — measured, deliberate, but still unsteady. Every inch of her was taut, coiled, dangerous.

Djemu released his grip, stepping back just enough to keep his distance.

Not out of mercy. Out of caution.

The silence between them thickened, charged. Fury simmered in the air — hers and his. But he did not strike again.

She caught the flicker in his eyes — a hint of doubt, maybe fear, or perhaps calculation. He hadn't anticipated this. He hadn't counted on what she'd become.

Cassia didn't know what she expected now. To break? To feel hollow and discarded like a pawn tossed aside? And yet — here she stood.

Unflinching.

Refusing to fold.

The silence was heavy enough to crush bone. Djemu's jaw tightened. His shoulders stiffened. His eyes darkened — sharper now, colder.

"Gods," he muttered, voice rough and low.

For a moment, he looked smaller. Not in kindness — but as a man facing the consequences of his own making.

"Cass...," His voice faltered. "A way to avoid the court's judgment," he said slowly, voice almost breaking. "To keep the throne."

His gaze locked on hers — unguarded, raw. "I thought it would be simpler."

Cassia's fingers tightened leaving half moon nail marks in her palms. A reminder that kept her grounded.

Djemu bowed his head — a flicker of something passing through him.

Not shame. Not sorrow. Calculation.

When he looked up again, his eyes were no longer searching. They were watching.

Measuring.

"If this... didn't work," he said, voice quiet, almost gentle, "We'll never have children."

A beat.

Then another.

"You've proven your loyalty."

The words were smooth. Too smooth. A verdict dressed in silk.

Dismissal.

Cassia felt it land like a door quietly closing — on her voice, on this room, on her body still sore from last night's cold demands.

But he didn't leave. He lingered. Watching.

Why are you still here?

She didn't ask. Didn't dare.

A warning rang in her chest — not loud, but steady.

Something was off. He had what he came for. So why was he still standing there?

She gave the smallest nod in return and turned from him, walking to the far window, the weight of everything trailing behind her like a blood-soaked cloak.

The air behind her remained heavy. Charged. She didn't exhale until she heard him leave. Even then, the ache stayed. Not just in her jaw, or her scalp, or the pit of her stomach. But deeper. The moment he'd walked away, he'd taken something with him.

And she didn't yet know what it was.

* * *

DJEMU

Her gaze locked on his — too steady. Too calm.

Djemu's fury flared again — white-hot, uncontainable — then narrowed into something sharper.

Harder.

Colder.

I thought it would be simpler. A transaction.

A test.

Instead, she'd made it a betrayal. Disobedience disguised as duty. And now... *she was balling up her fists? Threatening to strike HIM?*

He clocked her fingers tightening into fists like it meant something.

As if she thought she still had choices. The corner of his mouth twitched.

Cute.

And unacceptable.

Djemu bowed his head in resolution. This was no longer about fertility.

Or loyalty.

Or court optics.

This was about power.

And Cassia had just declared herself a threat.

When he looked up again, there was no softness in his face. No question.

No give.

Just precision.

And promise.

"If this... didn't work," he said quietly — almost gently, "We'll never have children."

She didn't move.

"You've proven your loyalty." Smooth. Controlled.

A verdict, not a truth.

He watched her absorb it — saw the subtle shift in her shoulders as the weight of dismissal hit.

And yet she didn't fall apart.

Interesting. She was tougher than he thought. A harder nut to crack.

*But all nuts crack... **eventually.***

Cassia turned toward the window, slow and deliberate, like retreat was some kind of victory.

Djemu watched her walk away — silent, unreadable. The lines had been drawn.

The game was in motion. She had played her piece. So had he.

He didn't say another word. He turned and walked out.

She would either be pregnant — or not. At this point, it didn't matter.

Either way, the outcome was his to shape. And Saben?

Saben had to go.

Nineteen

New Jersey Parkway

CHLOÉ | CALDWELL, NJ | 1986

GROVER CLEVELAND MIDDLE SCHOOL, ROOM 214

CREATIVE WRITING CLASS

Chloé Hall stood at the front the room, the cheap laminate of the teacher's desk behind her and thirty-two eyeballs trained on her face like she might burst into flames at any moment. She didn't want to look at her mom—seated on a metal folding chair by the window, arms crossed, face set in stone—or at Mrs. Greenblatt, who was standing off to the side like some academic referee in a cardigan.

"Go ahead, Chloé," Mrs. Greenblatt said. "Whenever you're ready."

Chloé cleared her throat. The lined loose-leaf paper in her hand was slightly crumpled at the corners from her squeezing it too hard.

"How I Got My Mom To Let Me Cut My Hair", by Chloé Hall.

We were late. For what? Not sure, but dad said we had to hurry up and get going...

She started slow, her voice a little shaky. A few of the kids near the back slouched deeper into their desks. Melanie Russo was chewing on a pencil. Trevor Morrison was making faces at his friend under the table.

But as Chloé kept reading, the room slowly quieted.

> *"...Charlie kicked the wrench that was coming toward my head. But when he did, he lost his grip on the side of the pick-up truck, and he almost fell out of the truck! I grabbed him. Pepper grabbed me. Thankfully, his leash was attached to the truck..."*

A few students blinked. Someone whispered, "Whoa."

> *"...When I was holding Charlie and leaning out of the truck, almost falling out on the pavement while we were still driving down the exit ramp, three of my braids got stuck in the wheel of the truck..."*

By the time she finished the last sentence—*"And that's how I finally convinced Mom to let me cut my hair!"*—the room was completely still.

Even Trevor Morrison, who'd been balancing a ruler on his upper lip just five minutes earlier, had gone still. Chloé's voice had quivered at the end, but now that it was over, her arms felt strangely empty—like all her words had been holding her up, and now they were gone.

She looked up.

Mrs. Greenblatt stood frozen by the whiteboard, back straight, mouth slightly open as if she wasn't sure whether to say bravo or call security.

"Well," she said finally, the word dry and flat. "That certainly was... *vivid.*"

Michelle rose from the folding chair by the windows, heels tapping against the old tile floor. Her purse stayed slung over one shoulder, but her arms were crossed tight across her chest, like she needed to hold herself back from lunging.

"Is that good enough for you?"

Mrs. Greenblatt blinked. "I beg your pardon?"

"You called me here, because you thought my daughter's original writing assignment on Haley's comment was too good." Michelle said, coolly.

But Chloé could see it—the way her mother's jaw was clenched so hard it made the muscles jump along the sides of her face. The veins in her neck stood out like cords.

"You accused her—without any evidence—of cheating."

Mrs. Greenblatt opened her mouth. Then closed it. Then opened it again, fumbling. "I—I simply asked for a conference. There is no need to blow this out of proportion."

Michelle took a step forward.

"So I took off work this morning," she said, voice rising now, eyes blazing, "and came in here, sat in this chair for over an hour, while you watched her redo it from scratch. And now, after she reads it—after she pours herself into this—in front of all these kids, your response is that it's *vivid?*"

Her voice cracked like a whip across the room.

Mrs. Greenblatt's mouth worked again, small gasps of sound escaping between her pressed lips. She adjusted the beaded chain on her glasses with shaking fingers and said, too quickly, "It's not that I'm questioning her. It's just—this story is clearly fictional. She was supposed to write a *non-fiction* essay."

The way she said it—*fictional*—made it sound like a dirty word. Chloé flinched.

She didn't want to, but it happened anyway. A flicker of shame. Of something sour and slippery that curled low in her stomach.

Because in that moment, she wasn't sure which part the teacher thought was made up: the wrench? The truck? The ripped-out braids?

Michelle crossed the room slowly. "Do you think this is made up?"

"I—I mean, yes," Mrs. Greenblatt said, flustered. "It's just not possible. Her hair got caught in a truck tire while it was moving? That doesn't make any sense. Do you even realize how long her hair would have to be for that to happen?" She paused—just a beat too long—then added, almost casually, "Besides, I thought hair like hers

didn't really grow that long." The words landed like a slap.

Chloé's ears rang. Her stomach plummeted.

Michelle inhaled—once, slow—and stepped forward. When she spoke, her voice was flat steel.

"Number one," she said, raising a single finger, "you've now called my daughter a liar. Twice. With zero evidence. Do that again and we'll be having this conversation with The Essex County Observer."

A second finger went up.

"Number two: our hair grows the same way yours does—with care, patience, and a healthy scalp. So maybe do some research before you let whatever racist tropes are rattling around in your head come out your mouth."

A third finger.

"Number three: she is telling the truth. I held a frozen bag of corn against the raw spots where her braids tore free while we waited for the Motrin to kick in."

She scanned the rows of desks. Thirty-two faces—wide-eyed, silent.

Chloé shifted. "Actually, it was peas, Mom. Frozen—"

"Young lady," Mrs. Greenblatt snapped, sharper than a stapler slam. "Do not speak unless you are spoken to in this classroom. You will follow my rules or you will be removed."

The room recoiled. Chloé blinked, startled. Her cheeks flushed with heat—equal parts humiliation and fury.

Michelle didn't blink.

It was like someone had flicked a switch. The polite, tight-lipped version of her mother was gone in an instant. Her spine straightened. Her eyes narrowed. Her fists clenched so tight her nails left little half-moons in her palms.

Chloé recognized that posture. That stillness. That pause before the storm.

She braced herself.

Please don't let this be bad. Please don't let this be too bad.

Chloé went utterly still—the way a kid does when there's no escape, no safe explanation, no winning in an argument. She folded in on herself and prayed for silence, the survival silence you learn early in a world that demands obedience and then punishes you for it.

Mrs. Greenblatt had made Mom angry. Now Mom was going to make it count.

Michelle took one step closer to the desk.

She drew in a breath so sharp it whistled between her teeth—a ragged pull meant to steady hands already curling into fists. For a heartbeat Chloé flashed back to Christmas Eve, to the meat cleaver her mother raised after Dad's slap, and the lesson branded into her bones: there is a line you do not cross with Michelle Hall.

Mrs. Greenblatt had just sprinted over it.

"Excuse me?" Michelle's voice came out low and lethal, the kind of quiet that erases every other sound in the room. "Did you just speak to my daughter as though she were a criminal for correcting a detail in her own story?"

Yup—this was bad.

"Mrs. Hall, I would appreciate it if you didn't—"

"No." The single word cracked through the air like a ruler snap. "You don't get to silence her. Not now. Not *ever.*"

A lifetime of second-guessing—of wondering whether this Blue-Ribbon district was worth the whispers, the averted gazes, the 'Where are you really from?'—rose in Michelle's throat like bile. She had dragged her kids here for opportunity and safety. All they'd received was a front-row seat to ignorance.

Caldwell was supposed to be a fresh start—better schools, safer streets, a place where grades mattered more than bruises. Instead it was a map of small cuts, each one deeper than the last. And here she was again, waiting for the next slice.

"You decided my daughter was lying the moment she handed in that Haley's Comet paper," she said, every syllable honed to a blade. "You couldn't imagine a twelve-year-old Black girl being smart enough, insightful enough, or creative enough to write something that good—so you set out to prove her a fraud."

"Mrs. Hall—"

"Shame on you." Her finger leveled at the teacher, trembling with fury—and guilt, too, because she had chosen this place.

"You stand in front of children every day, yet the only lesson you taught today was your own bias. My daughter is brilliant. She is brave. She is enough in every way you refuse to see. And how *dare* you humiliate her? In front of the *whole class* because talent doesn't look the way you expect it to. And what's worse, is I can't believe *I allowed it!*"

The classroom was stone silent. You could hear a pin drop. Not even Trevor dared to move.

Michelle exhaled slowly and turned to Chloé, softening only slightly.

"Grab your things, baby. We're leaving."

Chloé obeyed without a word. She didn't dare look up. She didn't want to see the faces of the other kids, didn't want to see Mrs. Greenblatt's shocked expression or whichever faculty member just popped their head in the door because of the yelling. Her fingers trembled as she slipped her notebook back into her backpack.

She didn't feel proud.

She didn't feel vindicated. She just felt... scared.

It was the kind of fear that blooms in your throat and settles there—thick, unmoving, impossible to swallow.

Yes, her mother had unleashed a righteous storm on Mrs. Greenblatt — and for a split second, it felt amazing. Like watching a superhero step out of a comic book and finally do what no one else ever dared.

But the force of it also told Chloé something had shifted. Something big. Something she didn't fully understand — only that she'd have to walk through it alone.

Because tomorrow, she'd still have to come back. Back to the same rows of desks. The same stares. The same kids who already hated her for being different — one of only six Black students in the entire school district.

The bullies in East Orange had been rough, sure — but no one there had ever told her to walk on the grass because "the sidewalk is for civilized people." No one had ever asked, with a smirk, if her skin would taste like chocolate if they licked her. And no one had ever actually tried.

East Orange had its cruelty, but at least she hadn't had to babysit her classmates' little siblings to help with the bills — only to hear about it the next day at school.

But she was older now. Twelve. Old enough to be helpful. And in this town, the parents seemed to trust her. She was always busy — weeknights, weekends, whenever someone needed a sitter.

Chloé figured: she could help, so she did.

Still, standing there now, in a classroom thick with judgment and silence, she had to admit—

The bullies back home had never made her feel this small. Or this alone.

She almost missed them.

Almost.

In Caldwell, there was no cousin Chad with a booming voice and long arms to make fifth-grade boys stop pulling her ponytails. No one to step in. Charlie was younger—her responsibility, not her protector. And Mom? Mom worked double shifts and carried triple the worry.

Chloé never wanted to add to it—not with school drama, not with this.

But none of that mattered now, did it?

After today, every hallway would echo with what happened in Room 214.

Faces would turn. Whispers would spiral.

And her name—always her name—would drift down the rows of lockers like confetti no one wanted to sweep.

She had tried so hard to disappear.

Now, this confrontation had painted her in neon.

Next time, Chloé thought bitterly, I'll just write about Pepper.

He's probably a safer topic than my hair, or Charles Dickens books...

...or Dad's driving.

Twenty

Enough

CELINA | NAPLES, ITALY | C. 1743

Giovanni Darling,

I haven't heard from you in days, and the dressmaker insists she's still unpaid. The landlord has come asking as well—should I be worried? Tell me if something's wrong. I miss you, my love.

—M.

THE BARESI TOWNHOME
The letter trembled in her hands. She read it once.
Twice.
A third time—each word sinking deeper, like a blade twisted slowly into soft flesh.
"I miss you, my love."
Her vision blurred. Her chest felt too tight to breathe.

She stood there, frozen in the golden spill of morning light slanting through the parlor windows. The quiet hum of the street beyond was deafening against the sudden roaring in her ears.

Then—

Something inside her cracked.

A low, strangled sound clawed its way up her throat, a cry too tangled with grief to be anything human. It rose, scraped raw against her chest, and tore through her lips like an animal in a trap.

She shrieked—loud, guttural, a sound ripped from somewhere ancient and instinctive. A scream that hadn't known language. Only betrayal.

The porcelain teacup flew from her hand as if it had burned her—an extension of the fury that now possessed her bones. It struck the mantle with a sharp crack, exploding into delicate white shards. Tea arced across the room in a russet splash, staining the pink velvet of the chaise and dripping down the rose-hued wallpaper like blood.

She gasped—rage had no breath to spare. Her hands, trembling and savage, found the edge of the nearest table and shoved. China clattered and shattered against the hearth, the fragments skipping and spinning across the marble tile like broken teeth.

A silver candlestick caught her eye—polished, innocent, useless. She grabbed it and hurled it toward the mirror above the fireplace. It missed by inches, striking the carved molding with a brutal clang before tumbling to the floor in a graceless spin.

Her chest heaved. Her palms stung. Her ears rang with the sound of her own fury. Still, the ache inside her roared louder.

"Liar!" she screamed. "Liar, liar—you said—you said—"

Her voice dissolved in sobs as she sank to her knees amidst the broken porcelain, her skirts pooling around her like the remains of a ruined gown.

He had promised. Promised to love her. To teach her.

To protect her.

To believe in her art.

He had said he wouldn't stray again. That she could trust him. That she mattered.

And she *believed* him.

But he had gone. And stayed gone. Four days.

No word.

No note.

No knock at the door.

Just absence. Echoing louder than any cruelty he'd ever spoken aloud.

And this—this silk-wrapped lie—mocked her in now tear streaked ink.

A letter from another woman. Sweetly penned. Lightly perfumed.

As if Celina were nothing more than a ghost haunting the space between the words.

Celina screamed again—louder this time, hoarse and hollow. It came from somewhere deep in her belly, someplace primal.

Grief and rage collided in her throat, and she choked on the sound. Rage at herself for falling in love with him.

Rage at him for letting her.

Rage at the weight of every morning she woke up hoping he'd notice her again.

And every night she slept alone. Again.

Every time she passed him in the hall, hoping he'd see her. Want her.

Keep his promises to her.

The fury was molten now—hot and roiling. She stumbled toward the tea tray on the sideboard and swept it off with a violent cry. The silver crashed against the floor with a satisfying clang. Porcelain splintered like bone.

She didn't care.

The skirt of her dress caught on a chunk of broken china. She yanked it free and stepped through the wreckage like a woman possessed, glass shooting every which way.

He had said she *mattered.*

That he loved her.

And she had *believed* him.

That was the part that burned the worst.

Celina stumbled out the front door, skirts swirling like storm clouds around her knees. She didn't pause to lock it. She didn't care if it rattled behind her. She only cared that she was moving.

Behind her, Serafina emerged, eyes wild with concern. She hesitated only a moment before chasing after her mistress.

Celina bolted down the narrow lane, her slippers skimming the uneven stones, her breath sharp in her chest. The familiar streets of her neighborhood fell away behind her—quieter, cleaner, safer—and gave way to a grittier, darker underbelly of Naples.

Vicaria.

She had heard the name murmured on Giovanni's lips before—half-drunk, half-laughing—when he thought she wasn't listening. A district whispered about by servant girls and delivery boys alike, always with a glance over the shoulder. Known for its Camorra-run brothels and gambling dens, Vicaria pulsed with a different rhythm, one that pounded like a drum beneath her ribs.

Shuttered shops and crooked cart stalls lined the way, their broken wheels and torn canvas left to rot in the alleys. Street lamps flickered above her like dying stars, their yellow light barely piercing the heavy air. The shadows here stretched long and bent, twisting against the walls like figures with lives of their own.

From behind half-closed doors and smoky windows came raucous laughter and slurred song. The slap of dice on wooden tables. The low moan of a violin playing something lewd and aching. Men shouted in dialect too thick for her to understand, and women with painted eyes leaned in doorways, their silks and satins clinging to sweat-slick skin. Perfume and sweat clung thick in the air, intermingled with the stench of stale wine, unwashed bodies, fish guts, and something vaguely metallic—like blood or rust or both. The ground beneath her feet grew stickier, darker, as if soaked in years of secrets. Still she pressed forward, heart pounding, searching. She would find him.

This was the part of town he often stumbled home from—drunk and reeking of perfume, mumbling names she didn't recognize. She rounded a corner and froze.

There it was: a low, weathered sign above a door—"La Rosa Rossa"—painted in fading crimson. The same name she'd heard him mutter. Her heart clenched.

"Giovanni," she whispered to no one and everyone. He was close. She could feel it.

Inside, through the doorway, she glimpsed tables cluttered with half-empty glasses and gaudy lanterns. Men hunched over cards. Women in bright gowns leaned out, beckoning. A bawdy song slipped through the door on a swell of laughter, hands raised in coarse celebration.

She pressed against the doorframe, breath coming in jagged bursts. Her palms slick with sweat. She felt naked with rage and humiliation.

She wanted to scream again. To burst in and demand, Where is he? Where is my husband? Where is that bastard hiding?

The sun was still high, slanting golden fingers across the filth of Vicaria, casting everything in a misleading glow—too bright for a place like this. Too clean for the filth it tried to hide.

Celina stood frozen just outside the tavern's open doorway, her breath sawing in and out of her lungs in jagged bursts. The air reeked of stale beer and spilled perfume, of sweat and sex and desperation. Her palms were slick, her throat raw. She felt naked—stripped down to the bones of her rage, nerves exposed and quivering.

A bawdy tune spilled out from within—half-song, half-dare—rising above the crash of laughter and the rhythmic slap of dice on wood. A toast was shouted. Hands lifted in crude celebration.

Celina flinched.

She pressed one hand to the doorframe to steady herself. Beneath her palm, the grain of the wood felt sticky, like it had absorbed years of sweat and smoke and worse. She stared at the red roses painted across the tavern door. Too red. Too perfect.

Like mocking blood blossoms. Her stomach turned.

She wanted to scream again—to burst through the door like fire and demand answers. Where is he? Where is my husband? Where is that bastard hiding?

But her throat closed tight.

Instead, she stood there, shaking, rage simmering just below her skin.

One... two... three...

Celina pushed the door open with the full force of her fury, shoulder first, as if crashing through everything that had come before—the lies, the silence, the ache of not being enough. The hinges gave way with a groan, and the tavern's afternoon haze swallowed her whole.

A pair of men by the entrance—broad-shouldered, in loose shirts with dirty cravats and knives tucked casually at their hips—rose from their stools. One moved as if to stop her.

But she didn't slow.

"Don't touch me!" she snapped, voice sharp as a blade. "I'm here for my husband."

The sheer force of her rage startled him—he blinked and stepped aside, arms half-raised like he wasn't sure whether to catch her or let her burn the place down.

Inside, shadow met sunlight in strange places. Gaudy lanterns dangled above the room like cheap jewelry, casting sickly colored halos over tables littered with half-empty glasses and slumped bodies. Men hunched over cards, teeth bared in crooked grins. Smoke curled toward the rafters. Women in bright, tight gowns lounged like silk-wrapped traps, their laughter high and hollow. One of them leaned out from a back corner, her mouth painted like a wound, calling softly to a passing sailor.

She stormed past overturned stools and startled patrons, her skirts sweeping through spilled ale and pipe ash. Cards froze midair, music faltered. All eyes turned toward her, but she didn't see them. Couldn't. She was flame. She was fury.

"Giovanni!" she screamed. Heads turned.

"Giovanni Baresi—" Her voice cracked. "I KNOW YOU ARE HERE!"

She spun, scanning the corners, the booths tucked behind heavy velvet curtains, the candlelit staircase that led to the rooms above. "WHERE ARE YOU?!"

A few men laughed, nervous and low. A woman at the bar raised an eyebrow, then went back to sipping her drink, amused. The rest of the room held its breath.

Behind her, Serafina burst through the doorway, flushed and out of breath. She looked frantically at Celina, then at the two men who had stepped back in astonishment.

"Madonna Celina," she hissed, rushing forward, grabbing her mistress by the elbow. "Please—"

But Celina shook her off. "No! Don't you dare try to stop me. He beat me for asking questions when he was lying all along. He left me in a puddle of tears and... And now—now this!" Her voice cracked again, louder this time, echoing through the silence she'd forced over the room.

Serafina's voice lowered to a sharp whisper. "You'll ruin yourself in front of these people—please, let's go."

But Celina wasn't listening. She was a storm.

"Fuck these people. Fottetevi tutti, I don't give a damn what they think—addò cazzo sta 'stu marito mio?!"

And she wasn't done yet.

Celina stormed through the tavern like a wildfire, brushing past sneering mouths and startled faces. Serafina kept calling her name, trying to pull her back, but Celina had no intention of turning around. She was already halfway up the creaking stairs before anyone had the nerve to stop her.

Doors lined the dim hallway. She didn't hesitate. The first she flung open revealed a pair of lovers mid-act; the man yelped and the woman shrieked, grabbing a sheet. Celina slammed the door shut.

"Giovanni!" she screamed again, louder, fury scraping her throat raw.

Another door. A man playing dice with a half-dressed girl. Not him.

Another. Empty. Then— a familiar laugh. She knew that sound.

She found him in the back room, tucked behind velvet curtains and the haze of pipe smoke, lounging with a woman draped across his lap—carmine silk and painted lips, her laughter sticky-sweet like syrup gone sour.

The room fell silent when Celina appeared. All noise died, like the very walls held their breath.

Giovanni's head turned slowly. His face drained of color. "Celina—"

She threw the letter at him, striking his chest. "How dare you!"

The woman on his lap recoiled, but Celina barely saw her. "You said it was over! You promised me, Giovanni. You looked me in the eye—you lied!" Her voice cracked as fury shot through her like lightning. "You said you *loved* me!"

"Celina—stop, let me explain—"

"Explain? Explain?!" Her fists balled at her sides. "You beat me for going into your studio—called me an insolent child for questioning your late nights, and all the while, you were here? With her?"

The woman tried to slip away, but Giovanni stood quickly, pushing her aside.

"It was a mistake. It didn't mean anything. I'm under pressure, you don't understand what it's been like—"

Celina laughed—a jagged, bitter sound. "Oh, poor Giovanni. Working so hard you had to go fuck some whore to feel better?"

His face darkened. "Watch your tongue."

"Or what? You'll hit me again? Humiliate me like a child? As if this weren't humiliating enough?!" Her voice rose in pitch, wild and cracking. "Is that what a good wife deserves? I gave you everything! My trust, my name, my body, my love! I gave up painting—for you! AND FOR WHAT? Some flea-ridden bitch who moans when you throw coins at her?!"

Giovanni's face twisted—half shock, half insult. "What did you just say?" he hissed, stepping toward her, his voice low but shaking with fury. "You think you can speak to me like that? After everything I've done for you?"

His hand shot out—whether to grab, strike, or silence her, even he might not have known.

But she didn't flinch. Not this time.

"I didn't ask you to give up painting—"

The slap cracked across her face like a pistol shot.

Celina dropped hard—elbow scraping the floor, the impact stealing her breath. Gasps rippled through the room. A chair tipped. Serafina screamed.

Giovanni turned his back, shaking his hand as if she'd stung him. "You ungrateful little bitch," he spat. "Go ahead. Wallow in your drama. You think anyone here cares what you—"

Click.

He froze.

Turned.

And there she was. Standing.

Blood trailing from the corner of her mouth.

Eyes blazing, breath ragged—and a small flintlock pistol in her hand, cocked and pointed straight at his face.

Everything stopped.

The brothel, once alive with breath and movement, turned to stone. Men gawked. A glass hit the floor and didn't break. Even the barmaids stopped mid-step, eyes wide, mouths open. No one dared move.

Giovanni blinked. He knew that sound.

Taking a slow measured step toward her, "Celina… Celina, put that down."

She didn't speak.

"Let's not do anything foolish. Please. You've made your point." Still no response.

He tried a half-step closer. She lowered the aim.

To his groin.

Giovanni choked on a breath, hands flying to shield himself, eyes wide with animal panic.

"No—please—Celina—por Dio, please—" A pause.

Then her voice—calm, cold, clear. "Beg me not to unman you."

He dropped to his knees without hesitation.

"I'm begging you—I'm begging, Celina—please don't—please—"

She stared down at him, head tilted, like a painter considering the final stroke.

Then she lifted the pistol—just over his head.

The shot rang out, splitting the air like a scream. A chandelier rattled. Someone whimpered. Giovanni flinched and hit the floor face-down, arms over his head, sobbing like a child.

Smoke drifted between them.

Celina stood motionless, the pistol still warm in her hand.

Then she turned.

Did not look back.

And left.

Whispered Memories

I knew her fear before I knew her name.
It pulsed through the warm walls that held me.
Her sorrow was the lullaby.
Her silence was the scream.

I came because she called—
I was never meant to stay.
Not with words, but with her longing.
My breath was caught away.

Then the shadow came.
Uninvited. Violent.
And I felt it. I felt her break.

(Whispered)
Carry me not in cradle nor cry,
but in the hush where angels lie.
I was a seed, the wind let go,
to bloom again in earth below.
If this was not the time to be,
remember me in memory.

She wept for me before I was formed.
She wept with me before I was gone.
I forgive her. Though there's none to forgive.
She loved me in secret.

That was enough.

I felt the midwife's hands.
I smelt the stinging herbs.
I touched the edge of air—
and so, I turned...

(Whispered)
Carry me not in cradle nor cry,
but in the hush where angels lie.
I was a seed, the wind let go,
to bloom again in earth below.
If this was not the time to be,
remember me in memory.

I will try again.
I will bloom in another spring.
I will carry her name in silence,
All eternity, I will sing.

The stars pulled me back gently.
I was never born, but I was never unloved.

(Whispered)
Carry me not in cradle nor cry,
but in the hush where angels' lie.
I was a seed, the wind let go,
to bloom again in earth below.
If this was not the time to be,
remember me in memory...

...remember me in memory...

Twenty One

Deception, Destruction, Disgrace

CASSIA | MEMPHIS, EGYPT | C. 689
BCE

THE ROYAL CONCUBINES' CHAMBERS

Saben woke to warmth—and then, to the sudden absence of it. The bed beside him was empty. Still warm, but empty.

He sat up slowly, the linen twisted around his hips, blinking against the light that streamed in through the slatted shutters. For a moment, the silence felt sacred. Last night lingered like myrrh in the air—soft sounds, whispered truths, the way she'd said *I want you* like it meant *I trust you.*

Cassia.

The name hit him like a blow and a balm all at once. He dragged a hand down his face, exhaling hard. *Gods.*

He knew what they'd done might cost them both everything. And still—he wouldn't take a breath of it back.

She was gone now. Slipped out like a shadow. No sound. No trace of her left behind.

And yet she lingered. Everywhere.

He dressed—slower than usual. Every movement thick, as if wading through water. His limbs carried the weight of satisfaction... and something else. A tension. The taste of something too sweet, too dangerous to last.

When he stepped into the corridor, the guard posted from the night before straightened—then smirked.

"Well done, Captain," the man drawled, voice slick with implication. "Didn't think we'd see you 'til mid-day."

Saben didn't slow. Didn't look. But Ra's flame, he wanted to plant a fist in the man's smug face.

Branded.

Marked.

Images flickered in his mind like dream-flame: her skin, warm beneath his palms. The tremble in her voice. The truth in her tears. Her strength. Her mouth...

Now came the vultures.

By the time he reached the soldiers' mess, the morning crowd had already settled into their bowls and banter. A few glanced up as he entered. One sat straighter. Then another. The jeering began before he reached the bench.

"Look who found his way back from the House of Pleasure." "Careful," another called with a grin. "He reeks of linen and jasmine!"

A loud sniff. "And honeyed oil! Whew!" Laughter rippled through the hall.

"Must've been a noble's girl. One of those soft-handed ones who act like they're asleep unless they know someone's watching."

Saben sat at the edge of the long table and said nothing. He filled a bowl. Ate slowly.

His silence—like always—was taken as confirmation. Or worse, permission.

"Did you see her face?" one asked. "Bet she moaned like the priest-esses in the spring rites. All sighs and shaking limbs."

More laughter.

Someone else leaned in. "Bet she wailed loud enough to wake the gods. Oh Captain! Oh!"

Roars.

Saben didn't look up.

But the bowl in his hand was beginning to crack. More laughter. More barbs.

His spoon dropped into the bowl with a sharp clatter. Every man at the table stilled.

Saben didn't flinch. Didn't look at any of them. He just breathed—slow and steady—and said, low:

"A gentleman never tells." It wasn't a threat.

Not really. Just the truth.

Silence blanketed the table. No one laughed. And then—of course—they all did.

"He's just mad he can't dip his wick back in for more!" someone howled.

The table erupted again.

Saben pushed the bowl aside and stood. The strap of his satchel swung over his shoulder, leather brushing linen with a practiced swish. His expression gave nothing away. His movements were clean, contained. Commanding.

But inside? Chaos.

Because last night, he'd tasted something he wasn't meant to crave. Something forbidden. Something that had haunted him since boy-hood.

Not duty. Not ambition. Cassia.

Not the court mask. Not the painted smile or the political bride. The woman.

The one who trembled beneath his hands and kissed him like he was the last true thing she'd ever touch.

And whatever she'd walked back into this morning—whatever prison, whatever price—he had a sick, crawling sense it would fall on her shoulders alone.

He should leave. Collect his commission. Be grateful. Vanish. But something twisted hard in his chest at the thought.

He wasn't confused. She wasn't a mistake. She was a choice.

And now she was alone. And he—

He was supposed to walk away.

* * *

THE BARRACKS MESS HALL

He could hear the familiar chaos of the morning from outside the mess hall doors—the clatter of metal on clay, soldiers trading half-jokes and bruised stories over steaming bowls of lentils and flatbread. The air was thick with the heat of bodies and the satisfaction of victory. All of them drunk on the afterglow of last night's games and celebrations.

Djemu entered like a shadow behind the sun, his steps deliberate, measured—each one tamping down the fury still roiling in his gut.

She looked satisfied.

The image of Cassia perched on that chaise still burned behind his eyes—hair unbound, shift half-fallen, her skin warm and glowing like a woman *thoroughly touched. Claimed.*

Was that where he kissed her?

Is she tracing him still?

Did she moan his name the way she never moaned mine?

He clenched his jaw until his teeth ached, then forced it all beneath a smooth, regal mask. His eyes swept the room until they landed on Saben—sitting among the veterans like he belonged there, like nothing had changed.

The soldier had an easy smile stretched across his face, one that might have fooled anyone else. But Djemu saw it—the strain at the corners of his mouth, the flicker of tension in his eyes. He was trying to play it cool. Good. Let him squirm under the weight of what they both knew but couldn't say.

Djemu approached, voice rising just enough to cleave through the hum of the mess hall.

"Well, champion," he said, each word dressed in silk and spite. "How did you enjoy your reward?"

Heads turned. A few men smirked, elbowed each other, raised their mugs in salute. The energy shifted — ribald, rowdy.

Djemu smiled like a man who owned the room. But inside, he burned.

Every inch of him wanted to break Saben open and bleed him dry.

Instead, he leaned in — just enough for proximity, not enough for intimacy.

His voice dipped, low but audible. "I inspected the gift this morning."

The pause afterward was deliberate — letting the implications soak into the silence like oil into cloth.

"She looked well-used."

A few men chuckled without knowing why. Just a joke. Just a girl. But Djemu's eyes never left Saben's.

"Ridden hard and put away wet, as the saying goes."

A shrug. "Spoiled goods, if you ask me. Not that anyone else would want her now."

Laughter flared — scattered and shallow.

Djemu raised his goblet. "Bring the victor his spoils!"

Laughter and applause scattered across the hall. Not all of it real. Saben didn't move.

Djemu snapped his fingers, and servants immediately appeared with a tray bearing gleaming coins and a scroll sealed with the Pharaoh's mark.

Djemu's smile widened as he turned back to Saben. "Your winnings. And, of course, the right to choose your estate. Land, titles, the respect of every man here."

Then, a pause—just long enough to make Saben's skin crawl.

Djemu dipped his head, voice low again, so only Saben could hear. "She's quite the strategist, isn't she? Knows just how to play her part. The trembling hands. The grateful tears." A beat. Then, softly—

"Almost convincing."

He straightened, gaze sweeping the hall.

"But I trust she gave you a night worthy of song, yes?" It was not a question. It was a command.

The room hushed slightly, eager for his reply.

Saben's heart thundered behind his ribs. His throat tightened. The silence demanded an answer—and in the space between moments, he realized: this was his price.

His tongue felt like stone. But his voice came smooth. "Yes, my lord. A night I won't soon forget."

Laughter. Applause. Another slap on the back. The performance was complete.

"With this," Djemu announced, turning grand again, "you may choose the lands you wish to claim for your estates. May they serve you well, as you serve the crown."

The mess hall erupted into cheers and clinking mugs. Saben didn't cheer.

He didn't smile.

His eyes flicked to the bounty, then back to Djemu. And in that moment, he understood:

This wasn't a reward. It was a leash.

A gilded collar for the dog who won the fight.

A clean exit—if he had the discernment to take it.

Behind the public display, Djemu's mind raced. He was relieved—more than relieved—that Saben would soon be gone. No more competition. No more tangled threads between Cassia and the warrior. The thought was a small balm to his wounded pride.

Djemu had studied Cassia's face closely just moments before. Her honeyed eyes had been clear when she lied. Effortless. Unbothered.

Yes. She was quite the actress.

He'd figure out how to deal with her later. But first—Saben.

His departure was essential. The sooner the better. Djemu took some grim satisfaction in the fact that it was the soldier's own decision. No need to stain the halls with blood.

Their gazes locked—silent, taut, heavy with all that had been said and all that had not.

"There's nothing left for me here," Saben said, voice low and clipped, meant only for Djemu's ears. "I'll leave before sundown."

Djemu inclined his head in a slow, deliberate nod.

"Good," he said. Then, with a smile that didn't reach his eyes: "May your new lands be quiet. Uncomplicated."

A pause.

"Less demanding than your time here."

Saben didn't respond. His expression remained flat. Unreadable.

"Many thanks, my lord."

He turned, collected his satchel, and walked out—each step taut with restraint, the air behind him stilling in his wake.

Djemu watched him go, hands clasped behind his back, expression carved from stone.

Everything was going according to plan. Well, almost everything.

His wife was back where she belonged, albeit a little worse for the wear, and Saben was leaving.

He would deal with the 'heir' issue later. Time was on his side. He decided that was enough.

For now...

Letters i

CELINA | AMALFI COAST, ITALY |
C. 1743

MY DEAREST CELINA

To: Signora Celina Fiore Albani
c/o Villa Albani
Via del Mare, Amalfi

3rd of October, 1743

My Dearest Celina,

There are not enough words in this language—or any language—to carry the weight of my shame.

What you saw, what I allowed you to see… it was unforgivable. And yet, I ask your forgiveness all the same.

I was a fool. A selfish, hollow man chasing shadows while standing in the light of something real. You. You are the light, Celina. And I have taken you for granted, neglected you, wounded you. I cannot bear the echo of your absence in our home. I cannot breathe in a house that no longer carries the sound of your footsteps or the scent of your skin in the morning.

Please, let me make this right.

I have nothing to offer you now but truth. I lost myself in loneliness and expectation, in the weight of my own ego. But no silk gown, no empty praise, no distraction could ever compare to you. To the fire in your soul. The strength in your silence. The art in your very breath.

Come home, mia cara. Let us begin again. Let me be the man I once promised to be.

I am yours still, if you will have me.

Sempre tuo,
Giovanni

GIOVANNI

To: Giovanni d'Baresi
Via Santa Chiara
Napoli, Italia

7th of October, 1743

Giovanni,

You said you loved me. That I could trust you.
You lied.
You broke something that was still trying to become whole.
I don't know if I can forgive you. And I won't pretend to know if I even want to.
Do not write again unless it is to send my belongings.

Celina

CELINA, MY LOVE

To: Signora Celina Fiore Albani
c/o Villa Albani
Via del Mare, Amalfi

13th of October, 1743

Celina, My Love,

I do not deserve your silence. And yet, here I sit—waiting for it to break like a storm, even if only to scold me.

Your absence is unbearable. This house is not a home without your footsteps in it, without your voice softening the sharp edges of every room. I find myself looking for you out of habit, calling your name into stillness. I get no reply.

I know I have failed you. I know that trust is not a thing easily repaired once broken. But I am asking—not as the man who wronged you, but as the man who still loves you—please, write me back.

Tell me you are well. Tell me you hate me, if you must. Just let me hear from you. I would rather face your fury than be met with nothing.

Please come home.

Sempre tuo,
Giovanni

GIOVANNI ii

To: Giovanni d'Baresi
Via Santa Chiara
Napoli, Italia

16th of October, 1743

Giovanni,

I received your letters.

You ask if I am well. I am alive. That will suffice.

I have no desire to return to a house where I am unwelcome, unloved, and unprotected. You made your choices. I am now making mine.

Do not write again unless it concerns my dowry, legal matters, or the return of my belongings. Anything else will remain unread.

Celina

Twenty Two

Wheat or Barley

CASSIA | MEMPHIS, EGYPT | C. 693 BCE

CASSIA'S PRIVATE CHAMBERS

It had been three moons since the Nile's bright swells had crowned the earth.

Three months since Saben's heat had burned through her, leaving embers she could not quench.

And still, it lingered.

Cassia had expected it to dull — for time to bury it beneath obedience, obligations, and oaths.

The old words.

The ones she'd repeated so often, they carved grooves into her very bones.

But the memory refused to stay buried. It remained.

Sharp as ever.

Alive in the quiet hours before dawn. She dreamed of it often.

Not the full night — not always — but fragments. Impressions. Sensations.

Fingers on her waist. Breath against her throat. A wordless kind of worship.

She would wake with her heart pounding, mouth dry, his name a whisper caught on a sigh.

Sometimes, she still felt him — the echo of his touch skating down her back, across her belly — as if her body refused to forget what her mind had tried so desperately to bury.

Cassia had been marked. Claimed.

Awakened.

And now she paced her chamber like a tiger in a gilded cage.

The walls glowed with paint and gold, draped in linens that caught the morning breeze like sails on a boat going nowhere — always full, never free.

Her sandals whispered across smooth stone. She counted the steps without meaning to. She always did now.

Something in her had shifted. Stretched.

As if that night had opened a door she couldn't shut. As if her body had learned a language her mind had no words for.

She still felt him — not just on her skin, but within her. Like a song half-sung, echoing through a sacred chamber she hadn't known existed... until he filled it. And that unsettled her.

She had expected guilt. Shame. Even pain. But she had not expected the missing. The longing. She had not expected the ache — not just of the body, but of the soul.

You are not supposed to want him, she told herself.

You are not supposed to long for what is not yours.

But gods... She did.

More than she would ever admit aloud. And it was getting harder to lie to herself.

Cassia longed for him.

Not just for his strength, or his warmth, or the way his gaze had always seen through her — but for the truth she had only just begun to glimpse. In that hour. In every glance he'd ever given her. He had looked at her as if she were more than flesh. More than duty. More than name.

He'd been there from the beginning — not as her guard, not yet. His father had watched over her for years. Saben was the shadow behind the shadow — the boy who never belonged, but somehow always remained.

Their betrothal had come quietly, naturally. Two lives folding into one as if it were always meant to be.

Until it wasn't.

Until the gods — or Pharaoh — decided her beauty was currency, her future negotiable. And the life she thought would unfold before her… vanished.

She hadn't even cried then. She hadn't known what had been stolen. Not really.

But now? Now she did.

Djemu's first wife had died the year before — childbirth, they said. But whispers lingered. Not loud enough to reach Menemhat's ears, but loud enough to give Saben pause. Loud enough to make sense now.

Djemu was rising fast — the High Administrator of Temple Holdings — a title that masked just how much power it truly wielded. He controlled land. Grain. Priesthoods. Inheritance lines.

He needed an heir. And Pharaoh would not let that power go unanchored.

So he looked to Menemhat's line. And Cassia, sixteen and radiant, was chosen.

She had met Djemu only a handful of times before the betrothal was sealed. His praise was measured. His eyes, unreadable. Already powerful. Already dangerous. A man favored by the gods — or at least by Pharaoh. The match had been made by decree, not desire.

"You are not a girl," her mother had said, voice wrapped in silk and sorrow. "You are a legacy. Your name is not your own — it belongs to your house. To your blood."

It was never about her. And she hadn't fought it. Hadn't questioned the edict or mourned the boy beside her. She had done what was asked, believing it was honorable. Believing obedience was a form of love. That sacrifice was sacred. That her worth lived in how much she could give away.

She had gone to the altar wearing linens stitched with someone else's future, thinking herself loyal. And only now, four years later, did she begin to grasp the true cost. She had thought she was choosing duty. But she hadn't chosen at all. She had yielded — handed her life over not in protest, but in silence.

You are not supposed to long for what was never yours, she'd told herself.

But the truth landed like an arrow through her ribs: It was meant to be hers. She just hadn't known how to keep it. The memory should have faded — dulled by ritual, by rank, by time. But some things refused to dissolve. Some pieces of the past still clung — sharp-edged, glinting in the corners of her life.

Like the dagger.

It shimmered now, half-hidden beneath the folds of her linen wrap — the blade Saben had given her on what should have been their wedding day.

Not as a lover.

Not as a soldier. But as a promise.

He had said nothing when their match was broken. No protest. No plea. Only quiet eyes… and a dagger, pressed into her hand. He had joined her guard not out of ambition, but devotion. He had forfeited his own birthright to stay close. And she had kept the blade hidden for four years.

Still, it shimmered — a sliver of the life that might have been. A memory she could touch. A vow she could never keep.

* * *

Cassia sat alone in her chambers, the sunlight creeping in slant-wise through the latticework of the high windows, warming the polished stone in golden stripes. Outside, the palace buzzed with the rhythm of summer—voices, footsteps, the clatter of jars being filled with water—but within, time moved slower. Thicker.

She placed a hand low on her belly. Not yet rounded. But changed. She could feel it — a fullness. A quiet tension gathering just beneath her skin.

Her breasts ached. Food turned her stomach. Sleep unraveled in strange intervals, and her dreams…

Her dreams had shifted.

She hadn't bled since before the Feast of the Floods. She knew.

But knowing wasn't proof. And in this house, proof was every-thing.

A gentle knock. "Enter," she called.

The door opened just wide enough to admit a servant girl, who stepped inside carrying the small linen-wrapped tray Cassia had re-quested two days ago. Her head bowed, her pace careful.

She crossed the room to the low table near the hearth—a wide slab of alabaster carved with shallow curves for oil, incense, and offerings. Not quite sacred, but near enough. A private altar for quiet things.

The girl placed the tray there, dipped her head once more, then slipped out, leaving only the hush behind.

Cassia remained seated for a moment, unmoving, lost in thought. Then rose—slow, heavy-limbed—and crossed the room, her sandals whispering against the cool stone. She knelt beside the hearth, next to the tray, and unwrapped the linen with trembling fingers.

Inside: two small clay bowls.

One filled with barley. The other, wheat.

Each soaked in her urine, sealed, and left by the hearth's warmth to wait.

She peeled back the cloth lids.

Her heart fluttered—high and frantic behind her ribs.

And there—tender shoots, pale green and reaching—rose from the barley bowl.

Sprouted. Alive.

Pregnant.

With a son.

Her throat tightened. Her lips parted, but no sound came.

She did not move to touch the bowl. She only looked—barely breathing—as if even that small motion might unravel what she'd just seen.

A son. Saben's son.

The ache that bloomed in her chest was so wide, so deep, it nearly drowned her.

And yet—threaded through it like sunlight through gauze— Joy.

Real.

Undeniable.

Something good had come of that night.

Not a lie. Not a trap. Not a cruel entanglement. But love.

Brief. Blazing.

And real.

Cassia curled beside the tray, wrapping her arms around herself. She bowed her head, the soft linen of her sleeves catching at the edge of the bowl as if in benediction.

Her body no longer felt like a cage. It felt...

Purposeful.

Sacred.

A son.

Saben's son.

The words echoed like temple bells through her chest — a reverence, a revelation, a cry.

She pressed both hands to her belly, tears rising fast and full, unbidden.

He deserved to know.

Gods, she needed him to know — not just of the child, but of everything.

Of what had shifted in her.

Of what she had only come to understand when it was already too late.

That she had loved him. That she loved him still.

That what passed between them had not been strategy or sacrifice, but the truest thing she had ever touched.

She had left only because she had to — the house was stirring. The hour, too late. Her return had been expected hours earlier.

He kissed her once, soft and lingering, and she slipped away, hoping she'd at least catch sight of him before he rode out.

But she never got the chance.

She had hurried back through shadowed halls with her thoughts tangled behind her — too full, too new, too fragile to settle.

She hadn't *planned* to see Saben again that morning. But... some part of her had hoped. So the silence of his leaving without even looking back, left a bruise.

Was it only duty to him?

The thought pierced her deeper than she expected — but even now, some part of her refused to believe it. The way he had looked at her... the way he had held her...

It had been real. *Hadn't it?*

She wiped her face roughly with her sleeve and stood, pacing the edge of the chamber, one hand pressed firm against her belly, anchoring herself to this new truth.

She could send word. Quietly.

A message hidden in trade routes or temple deliveries. He should know he is to be a father.

He should know what they created.

But even as the hope rose, it collided with a harder truth. Would that put him in danger? Would it endanger her? The child?

She froze.

The answer came not in words, but in dread.

Djemu.

The thought of him stopped her breath cold. He would claim the child. Of course he would. The timing was perfect — just enough to be plausibly his. And the empire would believe it because it needed to.

Because it was convenient. Expected. Easy.

Because the plan had *worked.*

Her salvation, wrapped in silk and sacrifice, was also the key to her imprisonment. And there was no undoing it. No path that did not end in blood — Saben's or her own. No future for this child that was not veiled in lies.

Unless... *she made one.*

Cassia sank back to her knees before the tray. Her gaze found the barley shoots again — delicate, new, trembling toward the light.

She cupped her hand around them, shielding the green from the draft through the lattice.

He will never know the truth of his birth, she thought.

Not from the world.

But he will know it from me.

She would raise him to be good. To be *honorable.* To be *kind* in a world that too often rewarded cruelty. To be just. To be strong — not in dominance, but in compassion. To rule not with fear, but with love.

He would be the future. *Her* future. A redemption born from ruin.

He may have been born into a lie...

But this child had been *conceived in truth.* In love. And she would teach him to carry that legacy until it rang louder than the lies. Until it outlasted them.

She pressed her palm to her belly, steady now. Despite everything...

Because of everything...

Love must prevail.

Chlóe Hall - 8th Grade Report Card

Student : Chloe Hall   ID# : 545931

Date Issued : June 21, 1988   Status : Pass

Homeroom : Mrs. Greenblatt   Grade : 8th

Subject	Final Grade	Status
English	C+	Pass
Pre-Algebra	C-	Pass
Biology Prep	C	Pass
American History	D+	Summer School Required
Home Economics	B-	Pass
Physical Education	A-	Pass

Attendance

Days Absent: 7

Days Tardy: 13

Comment :

Chloe shows some creativity and verbal skill, but too often lets day-dreaming replace diligent study. She is frequently late to class and turns in assignments unfinished or missing important components, which is reflected in her below-average marks. Her handwriting remains careless and difficult to read. With consistent focus on the assigned work, timely submission of projects, and better support from home, I think Chloe might improve. I urge greater structure and attention to schoolwork outside the classroom so she does not continue to fall behind.

— Mrs. Karen Greenblatt

Twenty Three

Dead Flowers

CARLOTTA | CADIZ, SPAIN | C. 1494

SAN FERNANDO CATHERAL — TUESDAY AT DUSK

The amber-gray shadows stretched long over the cobblestones near San Fernando Cathedral, the late sun bleeding into the stone like spilled wine. From within the ancient walls, a trace of incense drifted on the breeze—sweet myrrh, rose oil, and a hint of beeswax smoke, clinging to the evening like a whispered prayer.

The streets were mostly empty now. Vespers had called the faithful inside. The market stalls were long shuttered. A washerwoman and her cart wheeled down a side alley, and a hunched old man cursed at a pigeon near the square's edge, but this block lay in a hush.

Carlotta walked alone, her boots tapping steady and soft on the stone. Her hands swung freely at her sides, one loosely holding a silk pouch knotted at the top with red cord, dangling from her fingers. Rue, lavender, and dried ginger—tincture supplies for Nena, whose ankles were swollen and whose babe kicked low and sharp. Carlotta hoped this mix would bring the woman rest. Maybe even comfort.

And there'd been enough coin left over for a sliver of willow bark, for the coughing boy with the blue lips.

She was already thinking of the fire back at camp, of the low hum of voices, of whether she had any bread left. Her mind was half on dinner, half on where to find more salt before they moved on. Not on danger. Not on watching her back.

So when something slammed into her shoulder, she gasped and twisted—

—but too late.

A hand gripped her elbow, another pressed against her back, and suddenly she was shoved off the main path, through a narrow archway behind the cathedral. Her boots slipped in the gravel. She stumbled, cursing—and then with a sharp grunt of breath, her feet lifted from the ground entirely.

"What the—!"

Her stomach slammed into a shoulder—his shoulder—as the bastard hoisted her like a sack of flour. The silk pouch went flying. The breath rushed out of her lungs.

"You motherless goat-fondling—put me down!"

She twisted violently, driving an elbow into his back. He lost his grip and stumbled forward. They toppled together into the brittle hedges and yellowing rose bushes, landing in a graceless heap.

Something glass shattered a few feet away. "Oof!"

Carlotta hit the ground with a thud, skirts flying, hair everywhere. Her chin cracked into stone, and she rolled—only to find herself sprawled with a pair of booted feet on either side of her ears. The other body was twisted the opposite way, his head at the bottom of her skirt.

She froze. Looked up. Then over her shoulder. "¡Malparido!" she howled, lurching upright. "Hijo de mil—"

She swung a leg to climb over him at the exact moment he tried to sit up.

Her boot caught him full in the face. "¡Mierda!"

He flopped backward, hands flying to his nose. "Ow—bloody hell!"

The two rough-edged men who'd lingered in the shadows now burst into laughter, doubling over against the courtyard wall.

Carlotta scrambled to her feet, brushing gravel and rose thorns from her arms and dress. "Serves you right, cabrón. Try to kidnap me? I'll break more than your nose."

"I think she did break it," one of the men wheezed, wiping tears from his eyes.

The other snorted. "There goes that pretty face."

Carlotta's eyes narrowed with grim satisfaction. "You'll have to learn to get by on your charm now. Pity."

The men cackled.

She spotted her pouch a few feet away and rushed to it, crouching quickly to examine it. She untied the cord and frowned at the dark wet stain inside.

"Damn it," she muttered, pulling out a cracked vial. "That was the last of the ginger. Bastard."

The man, still on the ground, rolled on his stomach with a wince. Blood trickled from his nose, and he dabbed at it with the edge of his sleeve. "You've got a temper, querida."

She turned, full of fire. "Don't call me that."

"You always did make an entrance."

"I'm glad you approve."

The men chuckled again. One offered Carlotta a hand, but she waved him off and stood on her own. The other moved toward her, reaching as if to restrain her again, but the man on the ground lifted a hand, stopping him.

"Easy," he said, low and amused, wiping the blood from his nose, scrambling to his feet. "You're drawing attention."

Carlotta froze. That voice.

Of all the cocky, silver-tongued sons of whores in this cursed city—

She wheeled around, eyes blazing. "Vasco."

He stood too close now, framed by the last golden light of dusk, grinning like the devil had kissed him and left her mark. His cravat was askew, one boot still scuffed from their tumble, but the charm in his expression was as smug as ever.

The two men, still snickering, peeled back into the alley with a flick of Vasco's fingers.

"Miss me?" he asked.

Carlotta didn't answer. She punched him in the chest instead. Hard.

He staggered a step, laughing. "Dios, I forgot how feisty you are."

"Touch me again and I'll gut you with your own belt buckle."

"Noted."

She inhaled sharply, dragging breath back into her lungs, trying to calm the pounding in her chest. Her hand twitched toward the blade at her thigh. She should have cut him, just for the surprise alone.

Beyond the rusted iron gate, a nun passed silently, her habit swaying gently as she made her way to prayers, unaware of the sparks thickening the air behind her.

"What do you want?" Carlotta snapped. "You."

She glared.

He relented, holding up his hands. "To talk. Just talk."

She didn't lower her guard, but she didn't bolt, either. "Make it fast."

Vasco glanced up at the cathedral's weather-worn roof. "Nice place for a confession, don't you think?"

She rolled her eyes. "I'm not here for absolution."

"No," he said, stepping in again. "You're here for herbs and charity. Sick mothers. Crying babies. You're a saint now. Rosa de las Montañas."

Her jaw tensed. "Don't call me that."

He smiled. "Carlotta, then."

She crossed her arms. "Get to the point."

He sobered. "The masquerade. It's not a robbery—it's a reclamation. That bastard owes me. And worse, he thinks he can spit in my face while holding my gold in his hands."

"So you want revenge," she said.

"I want justice. And I want you to help me take it." She laughed—sharp and humorless. "No."

"You haven't heard what I'm offering."

"I don't need to. I'm not risking my crew, or myself, for your wounded pride."

He took a step closer.

"Not pride," he murmured. "Freedom. For you. For them."

She faltered.

"Land. A boat. A new name. A chance to disappear."

She shook her head. "It's a fantasy."

"It's a choice," Vasco said, his voice low, almost gentle. "One I'm giving you."

She didn't answer.

And in the stillness, her silence sharpened—turned dangerous.

He stepped closer.

Too close.

His hand lifted—slow, deliberate—brushing a strand of hair away from her cheek. He didn't quite touch her skin.

A breath hung between them.

Then, with a wry little scoff, he dropped his hand, took a step back, and brushed the dust from his coat. He winced slightly—his smile still lingering at the edges of his bruised mouth.

"You're cute when you're mad," he murmured, almost as an afterthought.

But the humor didn't hold.

His smile faded. He adjusted his collar, glanced off toward the horizon, and when he looked back at her—he was someone else entirely.

Serious. Calculating.

Something harder behind his eyes.

"You ever hear a story," he asked, voice quieter now, "about a little girl from Cádiz? Skinny thing. Big mouth. Bigger dreams."

Carlotta crossed her arms. "I've heard a lot of stories. Most of them end badly."

"This one doesn't," he said, stepping toward her. "Not yet."

She didn't move, but the set of her jaw sharpened.

"She's orphaned young. Uncle takes her in. Not out of kindness—out of debt. Owes coin to the wrong kind of men, and she's a pretty girl. Smart, too. Quick hands. By thirteen, she's stealing from fishwives, swindling noble sons with tarot cards and gypsy tricks. By fifteen, she's queen of the docks. Smuggling rings, forged papers, whispered secrets for sale. She's not just surviving—she's building something."

Carlotta's face stayed still, but her fingers curled at her side.

"She saves every real coin she can hide. Stashes it under floorboards. Dreams of the New World. Bright skies, no masters. A name of her own. And she's so close, Carlotta. She's standing on the edge of the docks, papers in hand, the ship ready to sail."

He let the silence draw long before he continued.

"And then she gets a letter. Madrid. Tía y Tío muertos. And her cousin—young, scared, barely hanging on. So what does she do?"

Carlotta's eyes burned. "Shut up, Vasco."

"She goes. She goes because that girl meant something to her. Because even though she's spent her whole life fighting like a stray dog, there's a part of her that still remembers what it felt like to be left behind. She trades a cabin on a ship for a cot in a shack. The queen of the docks becomes the patron saint of sob stories."

"I said shut up." Her voice shook.

But he didn't.

He softened it.

"You were made for gold and gunpowder. Not busted tinctures and crying babies."

She flinched—barely. But he saw it.

Saw it in the way her throat moved when she swallowed. The way her shoulders tensed.

"You're too wild to be caged, niña de fuego. Even if it is under the stars."

She turned, lips parted with some sharp, cutting reply, but nothing came.

He seized the pause. "I've got the answer."

She blinked.

He stepped in, voice low and coaxing.

"This job. One job. That's all it'll take. It's not just about the coin—though Dios, Carlotta, it's a lot of coin. It's about your future. Her future. Get Sofia out of this shit hole of a life. Off the streets. Out of danger. Buy your own freedom. Your own land. A house. A name."

Her eyes flickered.

"Don't you see?" he asked. "This gives you everything you dreamed of. Cádiz, the ship, the sun. Or north, if that's where you want to go. But not like this—not broke and hunted and dragging a young girl behind you. This puts you ahead of it all."

He let the weight of it settle. Then cautiously, he continued.

"Montoya is hosting a ball. Two weeks from now. For the governor, for the nobles. Masked, decadent, loud as hell. The perfect place to rob him right under his nose."

Carlotta stared at him.

"No smoke bombs. No breaking windows. Just velvet gloves, quiet hands, and the right guests in the right rooms. It's a locked box in his

study. You distract, and I'll handle the rest, in and out. Done before they even notice the wine's gone dry."

She didn't speak.

Didn't move.

Didn't blink.

He leaned closer, voice soft as a confession. "Are you in?"

The silence stretched long between them.

For a moment, the garden was only wind and dusk. And then—

She looked away. Not in dismissal. In consideration.

He was making sense. This… could work.

She'd pulled off tighter jobs with fewer resources. It would be dangerous, yes—but the payout? It could change everything. For Sofia. For herself. No more city to city. No more selling dreams she didn't believe in. She'd wanted out for years now, but it always felt like something impossible. A myth.

This—?

This felt real.

She looked back at him. Studied his face. The old scar along his cheekbone. The eyes too quick, too knowing. He'd read her right—but not all the way.

"You think you know me," she said at last, voice slow and simmering.

He raised a brow. "I do."

"You don't." She stepped closer—close enough to smell his skin, the clove smoke on his collar, the blood still crusting under his nose.

"I want out of this life, yes. And you make a damn compelling argument. But you're still a pirate. A liar. And if there's one thing I've learned living by the docks, it's this—"

She jabbed a finger at his chest.

"Never trust a man who smells better than the tavern he sleeps in."

He grinned. "I only smell that good because I stole from the governor's mistress."

Before she could retort, he lifted a hand—casual as a cat—and placed it on the stone column behind her, leaning in slow. Not touching. Not quite. But close enough that the heat of him pressed in like a tide.

She arched a brow. "You're incorrigible."

"And you love it."

He said it like a fact. Like a man who knew the ground beneath him and the game he was playing.

She did not love it. Maybe.

Okay, maybe a little—but she sure as hell wasn't going to admit that to him. Or herself. Or anyone, really. It was nobody's business but hers—and right now, she decided a change in tactic was due. She wouldn't shove him or scowl or scold.

No.

She'd go brazen.

If he wanted a siren, she'd give him one—and then gut him with it.

Carlotta stepped in. Close.

So close their breath mingled in the dusky garden air. She stretched up on her toes, body brushing his, her chin tilting up, her mouth a whisper from his.

His hand faltered just slightly on the column behind her. His pupils flared, his cocky grin morphing into something darker. Hungrier.

She met his eyes. Invited him.

Her lips parted—just barely. He leaned in.

He should've known better.

Her fingers snapped up and clamped around the bridge of his nose.

"¡Mierda!" he howled, jerking back as the pain flared white-hot through his face.

She ducked under his arm in one smooth motion, skirts swishing, boots light as fox steps as she darted toward the garden gate.

"Yup," she called over her shoulder, laughing as she went. "Definitely broken. You should get that looked at."

The goons—still snickering—whirled around too late to stop her. She was already at the gate, slipping into the street, her laugh trailing behind her like perfume.

And then she was gone.

Vasco stood alone beneath the garden's crumbling archway, one hand to his bruised, aching face, the other balled into a fist of frustrated awe.

Damn that woman.

He'd once again underestimated her. Once again let his ego walk him right into her clever little snare.

Dangerous.

God, she was dangerous. In all the right ways.

Too dangerous?

Maybe. Maybe he bit off more than he could chew.

Letters ii

M IA CELINA

To: Signora Celina Fiore Albani
c/o Villa Albani
Via del Mare, Amalfi

21st of October, 1743

Mia Celina,

Five days. Five long, silent days since your reply arrived—and still I read it every morning and every night, hoping I misread the cold between the lines. But I did not.

You are gone from me. Not only from this house—but from my days, my nights, the air. I cannot breathe in this place without you. Even the walls feel changed. And your garden—your beautiful, wild garden—grieves with me. The roses have dulled. The vines curl in confusion, as though waiting for the sound of your voice, your footsteps in the dew.

I miss you. I miss the sound of your laugh, the scent of oils on your hands, the way your brush danced even when your heart was heavy. This house is too quiet without your stubbornness. Too dark without your light. I was a fool. I let shadows in, and in doing so, I lost the sun.

Come home, Celina. Not for duty or forgiveness—but because this place was never a home without you in it.

Please. Come home.

Giovanni

CELINA, SWEETHEART

To: Signora Celina Fiore Albani
c/o Villa Albani
Via del Mare, Amalfi

28th of October, 1743

Celina, My Love,

It has been twelve days since I last heard from you, and each of those days has stretched longer than the last. The house feels colder without your presence, quieter in the most aching of ways. Your laughter, once so warm in the mornings, is now a ghost in the halls. Even the garden droops without your careful hands. Serafina was right to call it your sanctuary—and without its mistress, it grieves.

I know I have wounded you. I know words are but fragile things against the weight of betrayal. Still, I ask you to read mine. To believe that my heart, though flawed, longs only for you. I have made mistakes—shameful ones—but my remorse is true. I cannot undo what has been done, but I would spend my life atoning for the pain I've caused you, if only you'd allow me. Come home, Celina. Not for duty, not for obligation—but because there is a part of this world that only you can color.

And without it, everything fades.

With all I am,

Giovanni

MUA ADORATA MOGLIE

To: Signora Celina Fiore Albani
c/o Villa Albani
Via del Mare, Amalfi

6th of November, 1743

Mia adorata moglie,

It has been three weeks since your last letter, and I have read those few lines so many times the ink may soon vanish from the page. I find myself clinging to your silence as if it might suddenly speak. But it does not.

The garden misses you. The air is still, as though it too is waiting. The lemons on the terrace have begun to sour, untouched. I pass your studio door and pause, hoping to hear the brush against canvas, your soft humming—but there is nothing. Just the emptiness your absence has carved into these walls.

Celina, I know I have wronged you. I know my words may no longer carry meaning. But still, I offer them. Not in defense, only in regret. I ache to be near you—not only to see you, but to be seen by you again. If there is any hope left, even the smallest thread, I beg you not to cut it.

I am lost without you.
Sempre tuo,

Giovanni

Twenty Four

Viva la Révolution

CHRISTINE | PARIS, FRANCE | C. 1934

ROOF TERRACE, HÔTEL LUTETIA — 12TH OF JUNE

The Hôtel Lutetia gleamed like a jewel against the early summer dusk, its limestone façade glowing gold in the last stretch of daylight. Just outside the revolving doors, beneath the flickering glow of wrought-iron sconces, a tall placard stood poised on a black lacquered easel.

Its ivory enamel surface caught the light like porcelain, and the hand-painted lettering—deep midnight blue with delicate gold drop shadows—announced the occasion in quiet, elegant authority:

PRIVATE RECEPTION
In Honor of
CHRISTINE MILLER
and the Publication of Her First Monograph
SHADOWS & LIGHT
Hôtel Lutetia | Paris | June 1934

Beneath that, in smaller script:
Invitation Only. Rooftop Terrace – 7th Floor

The edges of the sign were trimmed in brushed gold, understated but deliberate, much like the woman whose name it bore.

Inside, a string quartet tuned softly beneath a massive crystal, Art Deco chandelier. Somewhere farther in, laughter arced high toward the painted ceiling, champagne flutes clinked like wind chimes, and the hushed murmur of French and English intertwined like smoke.

The rooftop terrace—tucked above the city like a secret—was reserved for the evening's private guests. Publishers. Curators. Artists. A few veiled figures who nodded but offered no names. The crowd was buzzing, tasteful, and just drunk enough to forget the weight of the world between wars.

Near the bar, Dot twirled her coupe glass between two fingers and leaned into Malcolm's side with a laugh that carried clear across the terrace. "You are not about to tell these Parisians that story about the bishop and the horseshoe crab. I swear to God, Malcolm—"

Malcolm gave her a slow grin, all charm and gap-toothed confidence, parting the center of his slicked-down hair with a practiced sweep of his fingers. "You act like I ain't got other stories," he said, fake-wounded. "Dot, you wound me."

"You'll survive," she said, sipping her drink with a wink.

A few feet away, Mamie fanned herself with a cocktail napkin, her pearl earrings swinging with every emphatic flick. "Whew, baby—look at this. I ain't never thought I'd make it all the way to Paris unless I was reincarnated as Josephine Baker's feather boa." She let out a warm chuckle, eyes sweeping over the terrace, the skyline, the soft candlelight glowing against champagne flutes.

"You know Marjorie don't like givin' us days off, but I told her, 'You can fire me if you want to—Chrissy Miller's showin' in France, and I am gettin' on that boat.'"

She lifted her glass, glinting in the golden light. "And Lord, was it worth it. Congratulations, baby!"

"She hear you all the way over there on that balcony?" Dot teased.

"She felt me," Mamie said, tilting her glass in Christine's direction

with a grin that could brighten a blackout.

Across the terrace, Christine stood alone at the balustrade, fingertips resting on the cool stone. The sound of her friends—her anchors—reached her like a lifeline through the hush of the Paris night. She answered with a small, private smile and a tilted glass.

A toast without words. This night was hers.

A slow sip of champagne, eyes half-closed, Christine let the moment settle on her tongue: dry bubbles, gold, light.

Below, the ballroom throbbed with swing-jazz and applause, the music floating upward on a warm breeze. Up here, the air was almost still. She leaned against the wrought-iron rail and watched the Seine fling coins of silver at the moon.

Paris shimmered—lavish and dangerous—as if the whole city were holding its breath just for her.

Footsteps behind her.

The soft scratch of a match. The brief, violent flare of sulfur. A cigarette hissed to life.

"Figured I'd find you up here."

Elias stepped into view, shoulders squared beneath a dark wool overcoat with narrow lapels, the kind that held their shape through war and winter alike. His hat sat tilted low, shadowing eyes that missed nothing—keen, storm-colored things that had seen too much and gave nothing away. His jaw was square, clean-shaven, and etched with years of clenched teeth and swallowed truths.

Christine glanced sideways. "You clean up alright."

He gave a half-smile, all dry flint. "Critics are salivating, Miller. You've arrived."

"Too loud down there," she murmured, eyes fixed on the river below. "Too many compliments. I needed a minute."

She traced a finger absently along the rim of her glass. "Feels strange, being celebrated for doing what others weren't even allowed to try. As if I made it up here all by myself."

The Seine shimmered like spilled mercury under the moonlight. She didn't say it aloud, but the ache curled quietly in her chest: how many brilliant eyes had never been published? How many names never known?

Elias stood beside her in silence, the glowing tip of his cigarette the only movement between them. Then he exhaled slowly toward the stars.

"You earned it," he said. His voice didn't push, didn't press—just anchored the truth between them. "And I know you hate hearing that. But you did."

Christine didn't look at him. But she didn't look away from the truth, either.

"I brought someone," he said next, his tone shifting—low, deliberate. The way he sounded before a drop in enemy territory.

Christine angled a brow.

"She isn't here to flatter you," Elias continued. "She's here because—" A pause. Then, measured: "Well, I'll let her explain."

Christine turned.

A woman stood on the threshold of shadow and moonlight, the city's glow icing the edges of her silhouette. She wore a backless sheath of midnight silk; each step revealed the pale, impossible curve of her spine, catching starlight like a blade. Copper-red hair was pinned low in sculpted waves, a burnished halo against the dark. Her lips—ripe with Bordeaux pigment—held the glint of private amusement, as though she already knew the taste of every secret on the roof. Christine felt the recognition in her body first: a spark just under the skin, sliding quick and hot along her pulse. Carnal, a quiet part of her admitted. Immediate.

Closer now, the woman brought with her a current of scent—lush tuberose steeped in something darker: leather, smoke, the metallic hush of danger. It was intoxicating, like jasmine distilled through gunpowder.

She did not extend a hand. She simply let the space tighten between them, her gaze sweeping Christine's face as though committing it to memory.

"Christine Miller," Elias said, tipping his hat. "May I present Mademoiselle Delphine Moreau."

Delphine's eyes—green, edged in gold—never left Christine's. She smiled, slow as nightfall.

Elias touched the brim of his fedora once more. "I'll leave you two." He vanished down the stairwell, his footfalls swallowed by the hum of distant jazz.

Silence followed—the taut, humming kind that made the hair at the nape of Christine's neck rise like static.

Delphine stepped closer, her heels whispering against the stone like a secret being kept—black satin T-straps with slim, tapered heels, the sort of shoes worn only by women who knew precisely what they were doing. Christine's pulse gave a traitor's leap.

Delphine's gaze moved over Christine's face, studying every angle, then drifted lower—lingering on the long strand of pearls draped around her neck, where they curved around the side of her breast and swayed gently above the dip of her waist.

"You see everything," Delphine murmured. Her voice—God, that voice—was velvet steeped in cognac, thick with something honeyed and illicit. Loire Valley lilt, sharpened by Paris grit.

Christine's pulse stuttered.

"In your book," Delphine went on, "there's a missing frame. Rue des Martyrs. The café window. March third."

Christine's spine stiffened, lashes lowering a fraction. That frame was lost—burned out in the fixer, emulsified beyond recovery. Only she and her darkroom knew it had ever existed.

"How—"

Delphine gave a languid shrug, one elegant shoulder rising like smoke. "I have reasons to know."

A beat. Then: "The question is... do you have reasons to conceal?" Christine didn't answer at first. The hum of Paris stretched between them, wind brushing the hem of her coat, lifting the scent of

silk and smoke from Delphine's skin.

Finally, she said, quietly, "Sometimes the truth endangers people." Delphine's head tilted slightly, as if tasting the answer on her tongue. Then she stepped closer again—so close Christine could see the faint freckle at the edge of her collarbone, could feel the warmth

radiating off her skin like a secret kept just beneath the surface.

"And sometimes," Delphine murmured, voice low and rich as clove smoke, "it sets them free."

She took another step. Her dress whispered as it moved, silk brushing silk. The city stretched out behind them—lit and careless—but here on the balcony, the air had shifted. Charged. Suspended.

"Christine," Delphine said softly, "have you ever wanted to do more than just document history?"

Christine swallowed.

"To stop standing on the sidelines like a spectator?" Delphine circled her slowly now, hand trailing along the balustrade, the pads of her fingers dragging just barely as she moved. "To actually do something?"

Christine didn't speak. She couldn't.

She watched her instead—watched Delphine's body, the impossible fluidity of it, the precision, the grace. But her mind was a mess: a thunderclap of desire and defiance and heat, tangled in the smoke-trail of Delphine's perfume.

Delphine smiled like she already knew.

"You have so much potential," she said, barely above a whisper. "And you don't even know it."

She stopped in front of Christine again. Reached out.

And twirled a soft, dark-gold strand of Christine's hair around her finger, slow and luxurious, as though winding silk onto a spool. Her lips hovered close—warm breath brushing Christine's cheek, mouth poised above her own.

"Have you ever been seduced by a woman?" she whispered. Christine's breath caught. "N-no," she managed, scarcely a sound.

Delphine moved with the grace of inevitability. A light touch at Christine's elbow guided her behind the curve of a marble column—deep in shadow, yet a single step from discovery. The danger was part of the invitation.

One hand slid to the back of Christine's neck, thumb tracing her cheekbone; the other settled at her waist, fingers flexing, drawing her forward even as she leaned back. Her shoulders met the cool stone with a muffled thud.

Pinned. Held.

The air between them thrummed; Delphine was heat and pressure and promise.

Christine's knees softened, her whole body humming. "Come work for us," Delphine whispered.

Christine's pulse pounded in her ears. "Us?" she managed. "Who is us?"

A sly smile curved against Delphine's cheek. Instead of answering, she brushed her lips along the shell of Christine's ear—lightning disguised as a kiss. Christine's question melted into a shiver.

Delphine hummed, pleased. "Shh," she whispered, her fingertips tracing a slow path up the inside of Christine's forearm, soft as breath and sharp as want.

"Names can wait. But the work—we change things."

Christine's breath caught, confusion and intrigue knotting together. "Work?"

Delphine's eyes darkened. "The kind that moves in shadows. The kind that makes sure the right stories get told."

Christine swallowed hard, voice barely steady. "I'm not trained."

Delphine laughed low in her throat, wicked and warm. "You know how to get what you want from a man, don't you?"

Christine blinked—heat flooding her cheeks.

"Hide in plain sight," Delphine went on, her voice was smoldering and silky. "Make yourself small. Play harmless. Pretend you need protecting." Her mouth hovered just shy of Christine's jaw. "They never see you coming."

Christine tried to hold onto the question—who are you?—but her body betrayed her, soaking in her warmth, absorbing its promise.

"You're smart," Delphine purred, thumb tracing the rapid flutter at Christine's throat. "Talented. A woman. Passing."

Delphine breathed, lips grazing skin like a vow. "All the reasons no one would ever suspect you."

Christine swallowed hard. "Suspect me… of what?"

Delphine let the silence thicken, then pressed her mouth to the hollow just below Christine's ear and whispered, slow and sinfully clear:

"Of changing the outcome."

She pulled back, only slightly, her gaze locked to Christine's like a dare. "We don't want pretty girls who take pretty pictures, Christine. We want the ones who get into locked rooms and walk back out with evidence."

Christine's pulse kicked against her ribs like a caged thing.

Change the outcome.

The words settled over her skin the way ash settles after fire—quiet, pervasive, staining everything.

"What you're asking…" She heard her own voice, low and thick. "Is it—dangerous?"

Delphine straightened, palms flattened against the wall on either side of Christine's shoulders, bracketing her. Up close she smelled of tuberose, yes, but also something brighter and wilder—citrus peel bruised under a fingernail, the faint tang of ozone just before a storm.

"I won't lie to you," she said. "Yes. It's dangerous. You could die."

Her lips grazed the shell of Christine's ear, the words threaded with warmth. "But tell me—what is life without risk? Is it worth living if only some of us are free? If one person in the world is suffering, we are all suffering. Most people just choose not to feel it yet."

The rooftop lights flickered in Delphine's eyes—green shot with ember.

Change the outcome.

Christine felt the words echo down corridors of memory she hadn't known were there.

Fragments slid beneath her skin like film frames catching the light—loss, love, rage, hope—echoes of lifetimes collapsing into a single throb of wanting something…

Delphine's mouth curved. She saw the flicker behind Christine's eyes, that far-off look of recognition… thoughts swirling… a resonance… like a soul remembering… it's purpose… remembering itself.

"Yes," she murmured, fingertip tracing the hollow of Christine's collarbone. "Now we're getting somewhere."

Heat spiraled low and bright in Christine's belly. Thinking was suddenly impossible—every notion blurred by the hush of silk-on-silk, the thrum of blood in her ears.

The balcony air trembled with the echo of her heartbeat. Delphine cradled Christine's chin, two fingers gentle but unarguable. "Sleep with me," she breathed, lips hovering at the rapid flutter in Christine's throat—barely a touch, enough to unspool breath.

Her other hand flattened over Christine's sternum, where her heart felt ready to crack its ribs for light.

"I've never—" Christine began, voice raw.

Delphine silenced her with a fingertip to her lips, a hush of velvet and authority.

Then, softer still, the words that cleaved the night in two.

"Do you want to change the world, Christine? Leave it better than it was when you arrived?"

The question lodged like a spark in dry tinder. Every life, every loss, every sudden joy flickered behind Christine's eyes, all the choices that drew and erased lines in the sand of centuries.

Heat rose, an electric hum strung tight between them.

Delphine closed the distance, lips finding Christine's with a tenderness that cut deeper than hunger. Heat radiated outward from Christine's chest, flooding her veins, blooming under her skin in a flush that climbed her throat and spread across her back and shoulders like dawn breaking.

Delphine tasted of tuberose and something wilder—stormwater over stone. She deepened the kiss, tongue gliding against Christine's, and white-hot brilliance burst behind Christine's eyelids.

Instinct surged. Her hands moved—tentative, then bold—mapping the inward curve of Delphine's waist, the sweep of her hip, silk crushing softly between them. Cold night air needled wherever warm fingers had been an instant before.

The world narrowed to the press of mouths, the slide of palms, the sharp intake of breath that belonged to both of them.

Delphine drew back first. Night air rushed between them like cold water over fevered skin. She studied Christine's face—flushed, astonished, alight.

"Who is seducing whom?" she murmured, wonder threading the words. "This was meant to be business. But perhaps all true work begins with desire."

She brushed a curl from Christine's temple; her fingertips lingered—warm, electric—just long enough for a slim ivory card to appear, ghost-slick, between them. Delphine slid it between Christine's still-parted fingers with the ease of a practiced conjurer—so smooth it felt like an afterthought.

"Tomorrow. Midnight," she whispered, voice the low hum of a clandestine frequency. "Hôtel Constant, Rue des Trois Frères. Room 304. Bring the part of you that knows lines are only real when we agree to keep drawing them."

A final press of lips—soft, sealing—and Delphine was moving away, heels clicking toward the stairwell, black silk rippling like water behind her. The scent of tuberose and thunder lingered.

Christine remained motionless, breath shallow, heart thrumming against the calling card now warming in her palm.

One question tolled through her like a bell:

Are you ready to change the outcome?

Below, music and laughter drifted upward, Paris unaware that its future had just bent around a single kiss.

Christine pressed her fingertips to her lips, tasting starlight—and possibility.

The click of Delphine's heels faded down the stairwell, leaving only the hush of night and the distant hiss of Paris traffic. Christine stayed where she was, breath thin, palm cupped protectively over the card in her pocket, as though it might leap out and proclaim her decision for her.

Are you ready to change the outcome?

A hand appeared on the balustrade beside her, nails lacquered crimson.

"Chrissy, darling," Dot drawled, stepping into the rooftop glow. "You do realize the guest of honor has vanished? The waiters are threatening to toast your life's work with or without you."

Christine jerked slightly, caught between gravity and flight. "I—sorry. Needed air."

Dot studied her—really studied her—eyes flicking from Christine's swollen mouth to the hectic flush still warming her throat. "Air," she repeated, one brow arched. "Funny. I passed a vision in black silk on the stairs. Red hair, shoulders like sin, smile like she invented it. Looked rather... winded." Dot's grin curved. "Did your 'air' smell anything like tuberose?"

Heat rushed back to Christine's cheeks. "Dot—"

"Sweetheart," Dot cut in, lowering her voice, already reading between the lines.

Christine opened her mouth. Closed it. Then let out a shaky laugh. "It was… hotter than I expected."

Dot's eyes sparkled. "Hotter?" she echoed, delight and concern winding together in her voice. "Tell me everything."

Christine pressed a hand to her still-racing heart. "She kissed me." She let out a long, uneven breath she didn't realize she'd been holding—then giggled, breathless, a little stunned.

Dot's grin softened into something radiant. "Well, you were never the type to fall for a man and fade into linen cupboards, Christine Miller. You live for heat. Truth. The edge of things. You always have." She paused, searching her friend's face, then added, "I see it in your pictures. Your camera speaks louder than any sermon. You find what no one else is even looking for—so why shouldn't you love differently than anyone else loves?"

Christine shook her head slightly, eyes shining, still dazed. "It's not love, Dot. Lust doesn't require love, does it?"

She swallowed. "I think… I'm in lust. With a woman."

Her gaze drifted outward, to the velvet sprawl of Paris glittering beneath them. Searchlights combed the clouds. The future beat in the distance like a drum just out of sight.

And Delphine's words echoed low and dangerous through her ribs:

If one of us is suffering, we all suffer. Change the outcome. Christine's voice dropped. "Dot… something's changed."

Dot's brows lifted slightly, but she didn't press. "Is it her?"

Christine hesitated. "It's… complicated."

Dot didn't push. Just slipped her hand over Christine's and gave it a gentle squeeze.

"Well," Dot said, "whatever it is that's got your heart racing and your hands shaking? That's how you know it matters."

Christine let out a breathless laugh, surprised by the ache behind it. "Sounds like something you'd say."

Dot grinned. "Sounds like something my grandpa Henry used to say. You remember? 'The good things always draw blood first.'"

Christine swallowed. "Yeah. I remember."

Dot leaned her head against Christine's shoulder. "Just don't bleed alone, okay?"

Christine nodded, eyes still on the horizon. The city glowed like it knew too much.

After a beat, Dot added slyly, "Now tell me more about Red."

Christine smirked. "She's… impossible to ignore."

"Ohhh," Dot purred, eyes dancing. "Then I like her already. But careful, honey—passion can start a revolution…"

She looped her arm through Christine's, guiding them toward the stairs.

"…or a war."

Below them, the band slid into a bright, brassy swing number, and applause burst like fireworks. Dot tugged gently. "Come on, guest of honor. Face the music. Even revolutionaries have to cut the cake."

Christine let Dot guide her toward the stairs, yet her fingertips stayed curled around the folded card, testing its heat—its truth. At the top step she glanced back, half-expecting a silhouette in black silk. Only moonlight waited, silver and impartial.

There are no lines unless we draw them, she thought.

And somewhere deep beneath her ribcage, a quiet, unmistakable tremor answered—the first drumbeat— Vive la Révolution.

Letters iii

CELINA | AMALFI COAST, ITALY | C. 1743

ILLUSTRISSIMO SIGNORE D'ALBANI

To: The Esteemed Signore Luca d'Albani
Villa d'Albani
Amalfi

15th of November, 1743

Illustrissimo Signore,

I write to you with the utmost respect and a heart burdened with concern. It has now been many days since my wife, your beloved daughter Celina, departed our home. Though she has communicated with me only once since then, I find myself deeply uncertain as to the full nature of her grievance or what has passed between us in her heart.

As her husband, I recognize that I have not always met her expectations. There have been trials in our marriage—none I ever intended, but trials nonetheless. If she has shared details with you, I can only hope you will judge me with a father's fairness, not only through the lens of hurt but through the full measure of our shared hopes for her happiness and security.

Celina is the light of this household. Her absence is felt in every quiet corner of the day, and in each moment I once took for granted. I write to you not to cast blame, nor to demand, but to humbly request your counsel—and perhaps your help. If she is with you, I ask only that you speak with her. Encourage her to consider reconciliation, or at the very least, conversation. I long to understand what she truly needs and how I might restore the trust we once shared.

As her father, you have always been her protector and guide. I pray you might also now be the bridge that brings her home.

With deepest respect and humility,
Giovanni Baresi

SIGNORE GIOVANNI

To: Signore Giovanni Baresi
Palazzo Baresi
Napoli, Italy

16th of November, 1743

Signore,

I entrusted you with my daughter, and I do not take kindly
to seeing her returned to me pale, shaken, and silent.
Whatever has passed between you, see to it. Make yourself
right, and come collect your wife—without delay.
Do not require me to write again.

Luca d'Albani

Twenty Five

The Mango Rides The Wind

CHAHIRA DELHI, INDIA | C. 1221

THE DELHI SULTANATE

By midmorning, Chahira was starving, barefoot, and bored out of her mind. Someone—likely Darya, that jealous cow—had hidden her shoes again, and the palace kitchens were sending out only rice and gruel because of some holy fast she hadn't paid attention to.

She lay on the cushions like a dying poet, dramatically draped, belly growling, patience gone.

"I shall perish," she groaned to the ceiling. "They will find me like this. Starved, unsandaled, and full of unrealized potential."

Laleh, sprawled beside the brazier with yesterday's braids still half-intact, rolled her eyes. "You could just send a servant."

With a grunt, Chahira rolled through an avalanche of silk cushions on the low chaise—half of them skidding to the carpet with a hushed shiff.

"No. He needs to suffer," she declared, hair spilling everywhere.

"He'll love it."

She popped the lid off the little sandalwood casket she kept tucked behind the divan. She flattened a sheet of parchment across the nearest side table and, giggling under her breath, dipped the pen, composing her most ridiculous message yet.

The parrot has fled the jasmine cage.

Request deployment of the fourth crescent beneath the almond veil.

At once. The mango rides the wind.

She blew gently on the ink, letting the last flourish dry in the warm air, then folded the parchment with care—like it was something sacred.

Sliding off the chaise with practiced elegance, she crossed the room barefoot, ribbons of silk trailing behind her like gossip. A page lingered at the doorway, barely more than a boy, clutching a silver tray and looking like he'd stumbled into the wrong life.

She held out the scroll with both hands, gaze imperious. "To Prince Rashid," she said. "Urgent."

The boy blinked at her, then at the parchment, then—briefly—at her bare feet. His lips moved, uncertain. He accepted the scroll like it might explode and bowed awkwardly.

As he turned and hurried down the corridor, Chahira caught the sound of a whispered prayer—just a faint "Bismillah" under his breath.

She smiled, wicked and satisfied, and turned back to her chaise. Step one: complete.

Now for the fun part.

* * *

ELSEWHERE IN THE PALACE...

The first boy, still muttering prayers, tripped on a rug near the kitchens—parchment slipping from his tray and landing at the feet of a clerk's apprentice.

He read the first line—"The parrot has fled the jasmine cage"—and panicked.

"This is above me," he whispered, and ran it straight to the steward of correspondence.

The steward, seeing "deployment of the fourth crescent," turned pale, locked the door, and summoned a captain of the guard.

"This could be a warning from the concubines," he said grimly. "Or worse—a veiled threat from the merchant class."

The captain read it twice, made the Sign of the Evil Eye, and took it—personally—to the Vizier.

The Vizier, Ismat al-Din, read it once. Then again.

Then a third time aloud, slower this time, as if the words might rearrange themselves into something less… alarming.

The parrot has fled the jasmine cage.

Request deployment of the fourth crescent beneath the almond veil.

At once. The mango rides the wind.

By minute thirty, the word assassination had been whispered twice, the eastern garrison alerted, and a list of suspected spies requested from the Archives.

The parrot has fled the jasmine cage…

He looked up sharply. "The prince has escaped the harem?"

Request deployment of the fourth crescent—

"What is the fourth crescent? A battalion? A code for the eastern garrison?" He slapped the scroll. "What in God's name is the mango riding?"

His assistant leaned in. "The wind, my lord." "I KNOW THAT PART."

Panic set in. Scrolls flew. Secretaries were summoned. Guards exchanged uneasy glances. Another list of known spies was pulled—just to be sure.

The word assassination was whispered a few more times.

* * *

RASHID, MEANWHILE...

...was peacefully asleep in the palace library, sprawled across a divan with a book over his face and a half-eaten fig on his chest.

Suddenly, four guards and a scribe burst in like they'd come to arrest a traitor. A beat later, the Vizier stormed in behind them—robes flying like the wings of a furious heron, face thundercloud-dark.

Rashid sat up, bleary-eyed, and squinted. "What?"

"Your Highness," Ismat al-Din barked, "what is the parrot?!" With a theatrical gasp and absolutely no context, he flung a crumpled scroll at Rashid like it was a live snake—then stood back, chest heaving, as if he'd just defused a bomb.

Rashid blinked at the scroll now resting on his lap. "What?" "Your Highness," Ismat al-Din barked, "what is the parrot?!" Rashid blinked. "What?"

It took a moment. Then Rashid snorted. Then snorted again.

Then laughed so hard he slid off the divan, hit the floor, and lay there clutching his ribs like he'd been mortally wounded by joy.

"Ya Allah," he wheezed. "She did it. She actually sent it." Ismat al-Din looked murderous. "Explain yourself!" Rashid tried to breathe. "It's... it's about a flatbread roll." "A—what?"

"A honey-roasted lamb wrap. From the east wall vendor." He sat up straighter, still grinning. "She's barefoot and wants me to bring it. Someone keeps stealing her shoes."

He held up a finger, counting off. "'Fourth crescent' means extra mint." Another finger.

'The mango rides the wind' means—well, now she's just being dramatic."

Silence.

A long, painful silence.

Ismat al-Din closed his eyes like he was praying for a lightning strike.

"You've known her too long," he muttered. "She's infected your brain."

He turned on his heel and barked toward the hall:

"Stand down the garrison! Cancel the spy sweeps! It's a lamb wrap!"

Confused murmuring from the corridor. "...A what?" someone whispered.

"A lamb—" he sighed, "Never mind. Just stand down."

A nervous guard peeked around the corner. "Sir, do we still alert the Sultan?"

"No!" the Vizier snapped. "Unless he wants mint!" Another voice chimed in from deeper in the hall: "Ooh, mint! I like mint!"

Then someone else:

"Wait—mint? Is that code for explosives?"

The Vizier turned slowly, staring into the middle distance like he was trying to astrally project out of the palace.

Rashid, grinning now, shrugged. "To be fair, she does have a history with pyrotechnic poetry."

Ismat al-Din whispered something under his breath. It might have been a prayer. It might have been a curse.

"I am surrounded by idiots," he muttered. "And I am never getting promoted."

* * *

MOMENTS LATER...

Chahira's doors slammed open.

Rashid strode in like a man possessed—tray stacked high with flatbreads, sweets, fruit, and, blessedly, her missing shoes swinging from one finger.

"You almost caused a coup over a sandwich!"

She looked up from her pile of cushions with the serenity of a saint and took a delicate bite. "You brought mint. You do love me."

He pointed a finger, eyes wild. "They almost arrested you!"

She licked honey from her thumb. "For excellent taste in snacks?"

"I had to lie to the Vizier and tell him you were writing poetry!" She grinned—teeth and trouble. "I was."

He groaned, dropped the tray onto the nearest table, and collapsed beside her.

"I swear," he muttered, stealing a bite, "you're going to be the death of me."

"Well, at least you'll die happy," she said, mouth full of lamb and triumph.

Twenty Six

La Dolce Vita

CELINA | NAPLES, ITALY | C. 1744

VILLA D'BARESI, JUST OUTSIDE NAPLES — 10TH OF APRIL

The carriage creaked to a halt at the edge of the gravel drive, the late afternoon sun casting long golden stripes across the vineyard-covered hills. It was a well-appointed barouche—deep blue with a polished black canopy, its wheels still powdered with dust from the winding roads out of Amalfi.

The footman—borrowed from her father's household—hopped down and opened the door.

Inside, Celina shifted in her seat, pulling the folds of her travel cloak around her knees. She had dressed with quiet calculation: nothing ostentatious, yet undeniably refined. A dove-grey gown, tailored but softened by wear, and shoes still scuffed from Naples' stone streets—just enough to signal lineage without excess. A reminder that she belonged to a family whose name still held weight—enough, at least, to silence the gossips who remembered brothel walls and broken glass.

She lingered for a moment, gloved hand pressed to the cool windowpane, then placed it in Giovanni's outstretched palm.

Her fingers were cool. Unsure.

His were warm, eager, maybe trembling just a bit.

She stepped down carefully—boots crunching on the gravel. The skirts of her gown swept over the hem of the carriage, trailing dust like silk smoke. Behind them, two porters from the villa began unloading her trunks—there were three total, not many for a woman of her position, but enough to suggest a long stay.

Serafina stood waiting at the edge of the drive, dressed in a practical traveling skirt and kerchief, her face unreadable. She had arrived earlier by separate cart to prepare the villa, ensure the linens were fresh, and the pantry stocked. She gave the smallest nod when Celina met her eyes—no words, but an understanding passed between them like a thread tugged tight.

Giovanni led Celina up the uneven stone path. It had been freshly swept, but the wildness remained—rosemary and thyme lined the edges, brushing their ankles, their scent rising like a fragrant welcome. A pair of citrus trees arched overhead, branches heavy with lemons and pale green oranges, not yet ripe.

The villa was modest but sunlit—a whitewashed stone house with weathered green shutters and a red clay roof that caught the light like burnt honey. Laurel hedges framed the front courtyard, neatly trimmed and dotted with roses spilling from terracotta urns—pale pinks and soft whites climbing in joyful disarray. Somewhere nearby, water trickled gently from a stone fountain hidden just beyond the hedge.

Giovanni let go of her hand just long enough to step ahead. He turned, beaming.

"This way."

He grasped one of the tall double doors—weathered wood, aged to silver under the sun, with old iron hinges that groaned faintly as he pulled them open. One of the door's corners had been patched with new wood, still fresh against the older grain. A detail she noticed. A detail he hoped she wouldn't.

He held the door for her like a groom on their wedding night. "Welcome home," he said, eyes shining.

Celina didn't move for a moment.

The light spilled over the threshold—warm. Golden. Inviting. Inside, the villa was flooded with light.

Not just light—intentional light. Every shutter was pulled back, every drape tied high, so the late afternoon sun poured in through every window like spilled honey. The floors were polished terracotta, still warm from the day, their edges softened with age. The scent of lemon oil and fresh linen lingered in the air, layered with something heartier—fresh bread, herbs, woodsmoke.

The entryway was modest but precise, designed not to impress with grandeur but with comfort and charm. A pale blue rug, handwoven and slightly frayed at the corners, stretched across the floor beneath her boots. A slim table sat just inside the door, carved walnut with delicate inlay—Tuscan roses, she noted absently. On top, a small ceramic bowl held fresh-picked camellias. Their petals were blushing pink, wide open, their scent soft and familiar.

To the left, a narrow staircase curved gently upward, the banister wrapped in ivy that trailed from a vase at the base—clearly arranged just that morning. To the right, a wide arch opened into the parlor, where she glimpsed one of her paintings already hung above the hearth. A low fire had been set but not yet lit, as if waiting for her to decide whether warmth was welcome.

It was quiet. Still. Everything in its place.

Giovanni slipped in behind her, his voice warm at her ear.

"I know it isn't a palace. But it's ours. No one else. Just you, me, and your work."

Celina said nothing. But she looked.

She let herself take in every color, every smell, every arrangement meant to soothe her, to soften her.

And somewhere in her chest, hope stirred. Cautious. Fragile. But alive.

For the first time, Giovanni had been true to his word—her paintings were everywhere. Hung in places of prominence, not tucked in corners like afterthoughts.

She moved slowly through the space, her eyes catching on brushstrokes she remembered making with trembling hands. The girl who painted these had been desperate to be seen. Now, here they were—on display like treasure—and still she wasn't sure if she felt proud, or exposed.

"I prayed for months, for the chance to bring you here," Giovanni said, stepping beside her. "Your spirit, your talent... the way you bring life to a room. I know you felt stifled in the city. You were right."

He led her down a hallway to a smaller room at the back of the house.

Windows on three sides. Sunlight streaming in. A table. An easel. Her pigments, freshly arranged—some even new, richer, more vibrant.

"It's not the biggest room," he admitted, "but the light in here... it's like God himself wants you to create."

"The morning sun comes through the east windows, and in the evening it wraps around. You won't need candles until long after supper. And the garden out there—it's yours. Plant anything you want."

The garden was quiet—mostly untamed, but bursting with potential.

Bougainvillea vines climbed the sun-warmed walls in unruly waves of magenta and crimson, like they'd been trying to reach the roof tiles for years. Patches of lavender and sage pushed through the weeds, their scent stirred by a breeze that carried a trace of sea salt from somewhere far beyond the trees.

Birdsong fluttered between the branches—swifts and finches, their wings flashing as they dipped between hedges. A single butterfly coasted past her shoulder, its wings pale as parchment. She watched it disappear into a patch of chamomile, wild and yellow at the base of an old fig tree.

There were beds that had once been cared for—the structure of a true garden lay beneath the overgrowth—and as she walked the window, she recognized the bones of it. A row of crumbling stone markers for herbs, a broken trellis waiting for roses, a grapevine left untied and curling along the ground like a lazy serpent.

It reminded her of home.

Not in elegance or scale—her father's gardens were vast, manicured with servants and schedules—but in feeling. The way she and her mother used to kneel in the dirt together, hands stained with loam, whispering over seedlings as if they were secrets.

This garden was a pale comparison. But it was trying. And maybe that was enough.

Maybe this was finally her chance. To find peace. To plant her roots. To grow something that belonged to her.

She turned slowly in a circle, letting the light bathe her face, letting the silence wrap around her like a soft shawl. Behind her, the studio waited. Ahead of her, the villa. To her left, Giovanni stood watching—not intruding, not pushing, just waiting.

So far, he had been... perfect.

Since the day he'd come to collect her, Giovanni had treated her with care. Respect. Reverence, even. The man who once silenced her now listened. The hands that had hurt her now opened doors, poured tea, arranged wildflowers in the shape of her name.

It had been weeks since their reconciliation in Amalfi. He hadn't slipped once.

Maybe—just maybe—he'd changed.

Maybe she had finally made her point. Maybe demanding respect had unlocked something she hadn't known was possible: a love that earned her. That listened. That learned.

She wanted to believe it. She wanted to believe him.

She wanted to believe that she could learn to paint—not just as a girl playing in the margins, but as an artist. A wife. A woman of her own making. And that Giovanni—her teacher, her partner—would make good on his promise.

"This could work," she whispered to no one. "Maybe it really could."

For the first time in a long while, Celina allowed herself to hope. Silly girls deserve happiness too.

And maybe—just maybe—this silly girl was about to get hers. He turned to face her, his voice soft now.

"Darling, I did this for you. For us."

"I know I failed you before. I see that now. But I meant what I said—this is your time. Paint. Be free. Be everything you were meant to be."

He kissed her hands. One, then the other. She let him. She even smiled, just a little.

And for a moment—it felt real.

She wanted to believe this was the man she'd married.

The man who saw her. Who chose her. Who believed in her. And maybe—just maybe—he did.

* * *

23RD OF APRIL

Celina came down the stairs barefoot, her hair unbound, a soft linen robe tied loosely around her waist. The scent of strong coffee and warm bread drifted up from the kitchen, mingling with the faint hum of bees just beyond the open shutters.

Giovanni was already at the table, seated in his usual chair near the terrace doors, bathed in morning light. A half-eaten plate of fruit and bread rested before him, ...alongside a small cup of coffee, dark and fragrant, curling steam into the sunlight.

"Buongiorno, bellissima," he said, glancing up with a soft smile.

His tone was easy, warm. Familiar now.

She nodded and poured herself a cup of coffee, watching the cream swirl into the darkness like a wisp of fog.

"I have a meeting in town this morning," he said, tearing off a piece of bread. "A few things to take care of, but I'll be back before supper."

He rose, brushing crumbs from his lap, and stepped behind her to kiss her cheek. She turned slightly into the gesture without thinking. "I walked past your studio earlier," he continued. "That golden piece—you started it in the solarium, remember? I moved it in there.

The light in that room—it's perfect. It catches your hair like flame. I hope you'll finish it."

She gave a small laugh, still groggy. "That one's a mess."

Giovanni tilted his head, his expression thoughtful. "No, it's alive. There's something in it—energy. Movement. It breathes."

She blinked at him. "Really?"

"It's not finished," he said, as if that explained everything. "But the composition is strong. The light on the left side, where it drapes across the shoulder—you caught that perfectly. Your brushwork has changed. It's looser now. More confident."

Celina hesitated, unsure whether to accept the compliment or retreat from it. "It felt clumsy when I was painting it."

"That's because you stopped too soon." His voice was gentle, persuasive. "You're learning to see more than just shape. You're starting to see weight. Temperature. The way skin reacts to light. That's not clumsy. That's progress."

A soft blush rose in her cheeks. He noticed. Of course he noticed.

"You've always had instinct," he said, stepping closer, lowering his voice slightly. "But now you're gaining discipline. And that—when it's honed—is what separates talent from mastery."

She looked away, trying to mask the small smile that tugged at her lips. It was silly, how much she wanted his approval. How easily his praise warmed her.

He reached out, touching a loose curl that had fallen near her collarbone. "You should finish it. I've been hoping you would."

She lifted her eyes to his, surprised. "You moved it to the studio just for that?"

"I wanted you to see it differently. In real light." His smile widened. "I want you to see yourself differently, too."

He let the words hang there.

She turned them over in her mind, uncertain. Was this sincerity—or something else?

Still, part of her wanted to believe him. To lean into the warmth of his admiration. To believe that he meant it—not as a performance, not as a trap—but as a truth. Maybe the kind that had been buried under pride and silence before. Maybe now he saw her. Really saw her.

Her voice softened. "It's hard to trust myself. I keep wondering if it's just luck… or if I'm fooling myself."

"You're not," he said. "You're better than you think. You just don't know it yet."

She looked down at her cup, the coffee swirling gently with the last of the cream. Her fingers were trembling just slightly.

"I want to believe you."

"Come."

He took her hand, warm and certain around her cooler fingers, and led her out of the dining room. The morning light followed them down the corridor, filtering in through high windows and catching on the polished floors.

As they walked, he gestured gently to the walls—each adorned with one of her pieces. The watercolor of the Amalfi shoreline, framed in carved walnut. The still life of figs and earthenware she'd nearly thrown out. The oil sketch of a child's hands she had done on a whim, never meaning to finish.

"They belong here," he said, pausing before each one like a man walking through a sacred chapel. "Not rolled up in some portfolio. Not hiding behind other people's work. Here. On the walls. Alive."

She followed his gaze, her chest tight with a feeling she couldn't name.

"You hung the fig study," she murmured. "You said it lacked intention."

"I was wrong." His voice was quiet. "It's tender. And deliberate in its own way. You caught something... fleeting."

They continued on, the floor cool beneath her bare feet, her robe brushing lightly at her ankles. He paused outside the studio door—the one she now opened each morning without thinking—then turned the handle.

"I still want this room to feel like yours. Every time you walk into it."

He pushed the door open, letting the morning light spill through the three tall windows, gilding the floor in long amber stripes. The walls were whitewashed and bare, save for a few empty hooks and the tall easel near the far wall. A table by the open window held fresh brushes and neatly arranged pigments, the scent of rosemary drifting in from the garden. Her half-finished canvas waited there—the golden one.

Celina stepped inside.

The hush was immediate—a sacred quiet, like the stillness just before prayer.

She looked around slowly, taking it all in. The light. The scent of warmed citrus drifting through the open window. The tray of food—ripe figs, sweet biscuits, and a small pot of strong coffee—waiting on the side table near the easel. It wasn't extravagant, but it had been prepared with thought. With intention.

She had been in this room every day since they arrived—painting, testing her lines, adjusting to the new light. But something about the way he led her here this morning, the way he lingered in the doorway like a man delivering an offering, made her pause.

"I didn't want you to be distracted," Giovanni said, his voice soft. "I wanted you to feel... free to create howvever you saw fit."

Celina stood very still, her fingers grazing the edge of the table, trailing over the soft bristles of a new brush. One she hadn't seen before. He must've added it just this morning.

She turned his words over in her mind. Did he really mean it? Did he understand how sacred this space had become to her?

It was a thoughtful gesture.

She looked down at the tray again. Fruit. Sweets. Coffee. He'd arranged it all so she wouldn't need to leave the room. So she could lose herself in the work. Sweet. Caring. But part of her had hoped… today might be different.

She'd planted new herbs in the garden—basil, thyme, calendula—and they were finally taking root. The blossoms had just begun to open. She'd imagined they might spend the morning together outside, perhaps take a meal under the old olive tree. She wanted to tell him about the seedlings. Show him how her hands had brought something to life again.

But Giovanni remained in the doorway, smiling at her like a man who believed he had done everything right.

"Everything you need is here," he said. "I'll be back before dinner." With that, Giovanni turned and closed the door behind him, the soft click echoing in the quiet room. Celina stood still for a moment, watching the closed door as if willing it to stay open a little longer.

Then she turned slowly to take in the studio—its tall windows pouring sunlight across the floor, the painting he had moved here just for her, the new brushes resting neatly by the easel, and the tray of fruit and coffee waiting like a small kindness.

Her heart fluttered with a fragile hope.

Moved by the moment, she stepped forward and then hesitated—then, almost on impulse, she reached for the door handle, intending to follow him down the hall and tell him she appreciated it. Tell him she loved him.

But the door was locked.

She pulled gently at the handle, but no use—it wouldn't budge. "Oh no," she murmured. "The door must be jammed."

She knocked softly, then louder. "Giovanni, darling? The door is stuck. It won't open."

To her surprise, his voice came from just outside the door, calm and steady.

"It's okay, love. Just paint until I get home."

Confused, she pressed her palm against the door, her voice tentative. "But... I left my ribbon in my room. The one I use to tie back my hair—it keeps falling in my face."

His voice was soft, but the edge beneath it was unmistakable. "Cara mia, please—just paint. We must sell another piece, and the one I've chosen—it is perfect. I believe in you, amore. Show me your brilliance with the brush."

She hesitated, torn between the warmth in his words and the cold lock barring her way. Slowly, the meaning settled in.

In a quiet, tentative voice, she asked, "You truly think I could sell this painting? That my work is good enough for others to want it?"

"Yes, tesoro," he said gently but with conviction. "With the right training, and if you work hard. That is why I lock you in—not to cage you, but to help you grow. You need discipline, focus—that is the only way. Paint, amore mio. I will return tonight, and you will show me how brilliant you are with your brush."

She hesitated again, a flicker of protest rising in her throat. "But—what if I need to—"

His voice cut through the hesitation, gentle but firm. "No, cara. This is the way. You must trust me. I want to see you soar, to watch your spirit unfurl on the canvas. I've sent for food to be brought to you at regular intervals, so you will not be troubled by hunger or interruption."

There was a brief pause, then footsteps of his retreating boots echoed down the hall, fading into silence.

Alone now, Celina stood in the quiet studio, the faint scent of lavender and oil paint mingling in the air.

Locked inside.

Forgotten by the world outside.

So this is what it means to be an artist.

Twenty Seven

Greetings from Mussolini

CHRISTINE | PARIS, FRANCE | C. 1938

RUE DELAMBRE

Christine fit the key into the stubborn brass lock, gave it a twist, and leaned her weight against the deep green door until it creaked open with a sigh.

The hall beyond was dark and quiet.

She stepped inside and shut the door behind her, the soft click muffled by a rolled-up Persian rug that hadn't lain flat in years. Her eyes adjusted slowly—just enough moonlight seeping in through the transom window to pick out the shapes she knew by heart.

"Home" she sighed.

She dropped her keys in the ceramic bowl by the door—clink—and set her camera bag beside it, gently, as if it were still loaded with film.

No sound from within. No light under the bedroom door.

Sylvie must still be at work. Christine had forgotten the schedule. Again.

She crossed the threshold and turned on the small lamp on the entry table. A warm, amber glow spilled out, catching the edge of a crooked picture frame.

Her shoes came off with a groan of relief. First the right, then the left, her toes curling gratefully onto the cold, uneven wood floor, worn smooth by decades of footsteps.

"Glad to take those off," she sighed, padding toward the sitting room to the right.

The ceilings soared above her, deceptively grand for a space that wasn't much larger than a postage stamp. But the tall windows and arched doorways gave it a kind of reverent air—as if the flat itself had once been something greater, something holy. Maybe it still was.

Books lined one entire wall, leaning like old friends. The velvet loveseat bore the distinct impression of a life well lived, bohemian style. A record lay out, halfway to being played. The air smelled faintly of jasmine and garlic and the warmth that lingers after two people have laughed here recently.

Christine stood in the hush of it all and exhaled—finally, fully. She was home.

She crossed to the sitting room and flicked on the brass lamp near the window. Its soft amber light cast long shadows across the floor, catching the edges of the armchairs and the deep red rug.

She knelt at the hearth, pushing open the iron grate with the back of her wrist. The firebox still held the bones of the last fire — pale ash and charcoal fragments. She cleared a space, then stacked a few small logs on the grate, reaching for the kindling tucked neatly in the copper bucket to the right of the mantel. A match flared, bright and sudden. She held it to the paper curls, waited, then watched the flames lick upward in slow, dancing hunger.

The smell of burning wood bloomed into the room.

Christine sat back on her heels, listening to the soothing crackle as warmth began to seep through the chill. The firelight caught a few frames on the bookshelf—faces and places caught mid-laugh, sun-flared beaches, café tables, that one shot Sylvie hated because she claimed her smile looked crooked.

Her gaze paused on the photo of the two of them from last spring in Arles—Christine in her wide-brimmed hat, Sylvie in linen and bare feet, both of them soft from sunlight and wine.

It was crooked.

She frowned, leaning up to fix it. The frame had clearly been bumped. The smudge in the dust just beneath it gave that away—two faint, overlapping fingerprints in the thin layer of powder.

Christine pressed her lips together.

She smoothed the frame back into place, but the smudges stayed.

Her eyes lingered on them for a beat longer than necessary.

"Add dusting to the Saturday chores," she muttered, standing. "You're slipping, girl."

She rubbed the side of her hand against the shelf, half-heartedly wiping at the dust. The smear it left behind only made it worse.

The fire popped behind her. She exhaled.

It had been a while since she remembered dusting last. Too long, clearly. The whole flat was beginning to take on that charming-but-shabby look she associated with women in poetry and poverty. The kind of lifestyle that sounded romantic until your bathwater turned cold halfway through and your socks stuck to the kitchen floor.

She glanced around.

Bohemian, they called it. And sure—there were nights she still found it magical.

But lately, it was starting to feel like a metaphor she wasn't sure she wanted to live inside forever.

Amusing, sure.

But also… dangerous. Especially in her line of work.

Cultural icon, war correspondent, documentary photographer by day— someone else entirely when the street lamps were lit.

Christine moved through the fire lit room with the ease of some-one used to shifting shape. She knew how to blend in, how to observe without being observed. She had spent years mastering the delicate alchemy of presence and invisibility.

It was true: she was afforded access to certain... establishments... that most of her professional colleagues wouldn't even dream of frequenting.

But that was the brilliance of it all.

No one suspected her of visiting them either.

Not the foreign officers who handed her press credentials, Not the editors who slid envelopes across café tables,

Not the men who underestimated her at checkpoints or borders.

That was the secret currency she carried in her smile—the kind that didn't make noise but opened every locked door.

Let them think what they would. Let them look, and never see.

Christine stepped back from the fire and watched it catch fully now, the orange glow pulsing brighter against the room's dark bones. The flame lit up the corners, dancing shadows on the walls.

Stomach growling, she walked into the kitchen. It had been twelve hours since she'd last eaten, and a crusty piece of bread, a bite of hard cheese, and five cups of coffee weren't cutting it anymore.

Plus, the gin was burning a hole in her stomach.

She needed something—anything—to soften the blow before her empty gut revolted entirely.

She opened the refrigerator and pulled out a small plate of leftover meat and boiled potatoes. Cold, but edible. Next came a glass of milk from the bottle on the middle shelf.

She sniffed it. "Ew."

Buttermilk.

Sylvie's favorite.

Hers... less so.

Christine grimaced, but drank it anyway. As hungry as she was, even sour milk was better than the liquid acid carving out her insides.

"Bon appétit," she muttered, closing the fridge with her hip. Just then, something soft brushed against her leg.

Christine froze. "Maoowww."

Mussolini, her grey-and-white tuxedo cat, stretched up with imperial entitlement, sinking his claws gently into her wool sweater like a velvet-fanged massage therapist.

"Well hello there, dictator," she said, crouching to scoop him up.

She kissed the top of his head and hugged him close, pressing her cheek to his fur.

"How was your day today?" she murmured.

He purred in response, low and satisfied—like a tiny engine fueled by self-importance and table scraps.

She scruffed the back of his neck, and he leaned in harder, pressing the soft tuft behind his ear against her collarbone.

"Aww, yes, sir," she said, rubbing between his eyes with her thumb. "I've missed you too."

Her last assignment had taken longer than planned. Two weeks stretched into three.

Then five.

Then nine.

And just when she thought she was finally on her way home, the

U.S. consulate delayed her return to Paris for another four days. It was all about clearances, red tape, confidentiality, and national security.

Those words used to feel foreign to her—like something out of a spy novel or a conversation meant for other people.

Now they were just part of her vocabulary. Like f-stops.

Like evacuation routes.

Like lies people told themselves to feel safe.

Footsteps.

Upstairs. Christine froze.

The flat above hers had been empty for months—some sculptor gone to Marseille, or maybe prison. She couldn't remember. But there shouldn't be anyone there. Not at this hour. Not with that slow, deliberate cadence of movement overhead.

Her pulse kicked up.

One hard, echoing beat in her throat. Then another.

Who could she call?

At this hour? In this city? Elias.

Her contact. Reliable, quiet, brutal when necessary. The one who never signed his name but always showed up.

The signal.

Chalk.

Stove—drawer to the left. Thoughts gave way to instinct. Exactly as she'd been trained.

Exactly as they'd drilled it into her in that dim back room above Rue St. Denis, with the dark-out drapes drawn tight and the too-clean ashtrays.

Mark the window. White chalk, right to left. Someone would come.

They were watching.

They were always watching. That used to unnerve her.

Tonight, it made her feel… safer than she had in weeks.

She padded to the stove, eased open the left-hand drawer, and felt for the cylinder of chalk.

Powdery grains clung to her fingers as she drew it out. Breathe. Steady.

She crossed to the tall sitting-room window, lifted the sash two inches, and with one quick motion dragged the chalk right-to-left across the inside glass. A pale slash in the darkness—barely visible unless you knew to look.

Signal sent.

Elias would see it. Or someone else on the detail. Now what, Miller?

Oh, right. Scram.

The reporter in her ached to know who was blundering around upstairs, but strangers in your flat after dark—fresh off an assignment that had gone sideways in Tangier—was a bouquet of red flags even the blind could see.

Christine set Mussolini down; he trotted back toward the hearth, tail flicking like a metronome of disapproval.

She turned an ear to the ceiling.

The footsteps had moved off the bare boards and onto the central staircase—a narrow wooden switch-back that served the whole building.

Each tread gave a protesting creak as weight shifted downward. Closer.

Christine crossed to the coat tree, snatched her trench and slipped it on. In the inside pocket: her passport, spare cash, and half-spent roll of film she hadn't dared leave at the lab. She slid her Leica over her shoulder by habit, then hesitated…

Mussolini.

Damn. He'd have to fend for himself. Another creak overhead.

Voices now—two of them murmuring, languages blurring under their breath.

Time to go.

The chalk line would bring help. The alley would buy her minutes.

And if curiosity still burned after she'd caught her breath?

Well, there was a camera hanging at her hip—and she'd never yet resisted a good story. Regardless the danger.

She swiped her shoes in one hand and her keys in the other. A muffled jingle. Shit.

Quickly, as quietly was she could, she opened the front door. A shadow crossed over her face. She looked up just in time to see someone standing at the top of the stairs.

Christine's breath locked in her throat.

The shadow moved at the top of the stairs—broad shoulders, that same tilted fedora (over pajamas?), and a voice that stopped her cold.

"Chrissy!"

She blinked, stunned. "Dottie?!"

Dot grinned down at her like it was perfectly normal to appear in Paris unannounced, in the middle of the damn night, wearing silk pajamas and a feather trimmed robe.

"You didn't think I was gonna get married without my maid of honor, did you?"

Right behind her, Malcolm stepped into view, barefoot, yawning, and carrying a half-drunk glass of wine. His pajama pants were wrinkled, his shirt was buttoned crooked, and his expression said he deeply regretted every choice that led him to this moment.

He eyed Christine's coat, her keys, her wild-eyed panic.

"Honey, you look like you were about to bolt through the hedges barefoot. Everything alright down here?"

Christine couldn't move. Couldn't think.

"Well," she said faintly, "I wasn't expecting company." Dot was beaming like a lighthouse.

Malcolm was glaring like a storm cloud.

And the fire crackled in the hearth like the start of an avalanche. Dot started down the narrow staircase in her slippers, robe billowing behind her.

"Couldn't get my maid of honor to answer a cable, now could I? So I sailed across an ocean. But then you weren't here. So we called the concierge, he let us rent the flat upstairs while we waited, and—voilà! Surprise!"

She gave a dramatic little spin on the last word, her feathered robe flaring like stage curtains.

No assassins.

No secret police.

Just Dot and her feathers. Malcolm's voice, dry as dust:

"Turns out a month's rent in advance and three bottles of Armagnac buy a lot of goodwill."

"Honestly, Chrissy, who needs a big ol' Harlem wedding when you've got Paris, silk pajamas, and a half-decent bottle of red?"

Dot beamed, then gave an exaggerated shrug and winked, as if silk and wine were perfectly valid substitutes for matrimony.

Mussolini trotted into the hall, tail high—expecting to collect tribute, as fascists do. He wound around Dot's ankles with all the imperious satisfaction of a dictator being adored.

Dot bent to scratch behind his ears.

"Yes, yes, good evening, Your Excellency."

Christine exhaled a shaky laugh, stepped back, and waved them inside.

Dot swept forward in a flurry of scarf and sass and pulled Christine into a hug so tight the Leica dug into both of them.

"Good grief, woman—you're skin and bones. And covered in chalk," she added, catching sight of her dust-smudged fingers. "Art project?"

"Emergency project," Christine murmured, brushing her hands on her trench. She flicked a glance toward the chalk slash still visible on the window. Elias is going to kick in the door any minute.

"Long story."

"Try me," Dot said, one brow arching like it had questions and time.

Behind her, Malcolm cleared his throat. Dot slipped her arm through his with a dazzling smile—all sunshine and silk gloves, like she hadn't just crossed an ocean and wandered into the middle of a covert emergency.

"Let me lock back up," Christine said, crossing to the door. She slid the bolt, then turned back to her best friends—her pulse finally uncoiling from the base of her spine.

"You scared ten years off my life."

Dot grinned. "Please. You look like you've got decades to spare." Christine barked a laugh—bright and breathless—then wrapped

Dot up again, tighter this time. She breathed in the scent of sea salt, coal smoke, and whatever perfume first-class passengers were spritzing in the Queen Mary's powder rooms these days.

From the sitting room, the fire popped.

And Mussolini issued a regal mrrrow—as if to remind everyone whose flat this really was.

Dot glanced around the lamplit entry, taking in the postcards, the scarred floorboards, the soft golden hush.

"So this is the Paris love nest you wrote me about?"

Christine opened her mouth—half apology, half explanation—but Dot waved a hand.

"Don't worry, I've already had the grand tour. Sylvie showed me the whole place. Lovely girl. Sharp cheekbones. Smells like lavender and rebellion."

She gave Christine a wicked grin. "Nice to see you thriving in such… well-curated company."

Christine rolled her eyes, but her smile tugged at the corners.

A faint rap sounded at the courtyard door off the kitchen: three quick taps, a pause, two more.

Elias.

Dot's eyebrows shot up.

"I thought you said you weren't expecting company?"

"Remember that long story?" Christine said, already moving. "It just got longer."

She crossed into the kitchen, Mussolini padding at her heels like a four-legged chaperone. The courtyard door loomed ahead—glass pane fogged at the corners, the chalk mark catching the glow of the streetlamp outside like a secret.

Christine opened it.

Elias slipped inside in one fluid motion, already scanning the space. His coat was damp with rain, his jaw shadowed with a day's growth, and he carried that wired tension that meant he hadn't slept in at least twenty-four hours, and didn't plan to.

"You marked the window," he said, voice low, urgent. "What happened?"

"False alarm," Christine replied. "Mostly." Elias arched an eyebrow. "Mostly?"

Dot appeared in the doorway behind her, arms crossed, head tilted like a theater critic at intermission.

"She's the 'mostly,'" Christine added, thumbing in Dot's direction.

Dot gave Elias a polite nod. "Hi."

Elias didn't return the smile, but his nod was civil—distracted, already calculating. "We've met."

His attention flicked back to Christine. "She followed you back from Tangier?"

Dot scoffed. "I followed her from Harlem. Tangier was not on the itinerary."

Elias didn't hide his concern. "So you weren't compromised?"

"I told you," Christine said, voice cool. "It was a false alarm."

"Then why did it take nine weeks and a consulate lockdown to get home?" he snapped.

Christine didn't flinch. Her breath was measured, her voice even. A fire lit behind her eyes.

"Because I got the shot," she said.

The words landed like a wire pulled taut. The air shifted.

Silence thickened. The fire crackled in the next room. Mussolini gave a low, irritated growl from his spot on the divan, as if exhausted by everyone's drama.

Dot looked between them, something catching in her throat.

Elias's gaze sharpened.

Christine stood straighter. Not defensive. Not defiant. Just... clear. Then—

"Hi, I'm Malcolm," came a voice from the hallway, smooth as bourbon and just as slow. His drawl cut through the tension like a hot knife through butter. "Charmed, I'm sure."

Elias didn't blink. "We've met." A beat.

Malcolm shrugged. "Figured I'd reintroduce myself before the room froze solid."

The corner of Dot's mouth twitched, but Elias didn't bite. His focus locked on Christine.

"You got the shot," he said, flat.

"I got the shot," Christine repeated. "That's what I went for."

Dot's eyes narrowed. Her confusion began to set like concrete. "Wait—what happened in Tangier?"

Christine opened her mouth, but Elias cut in. "She got too close. And she nearly didn't get out."

Christine turned, already moving toward the sitting room. "You want tea, Elias?" she asked. "Or gin?"

"Gin."

Dot watched her, voice quieter now. "Christine... what really happened?"

Christine didn't look back. "I did my job."

The silence that followed was heavy—thick as smoke, sharp as glass.

Then the door creaked.

"I brought baguettes," said a voice. They all turned.

Sylvie stood in the entryway, soaked to the bone, umbrella inverted, hair matted to her cheek. A limp baguette dangled from her arm like a battle flag.

Her expression teetered somewhere between unimpressed and exhausted.

"Hi," she said. "I'm Sylvie."

Elias exhaled. "We've met."

Twenty Eight

Shadows

CARLOTTA | CADIZ, SPAIN | C. 1494

THE CAMPSITE —WEDNESDAY, JUST AFTER MIDNIGHT

Carlotta couldn't sleep.

She'd been tossing and turning in her bed for hours—willing sleep to come. But it remained a stranger to her beneath the pale moonlight leaking through the warped wooden shutters, casting uneven lines across the floor like the bars of a cage.

Outside the canvas flap that served as a curtain, someone snored—wet and heavy, the kind that rattled the silence. A dog barked once, far off, more question than warning. The night was warm but restless, and the soft chorus of crickets trembled in the brush like whispers too tired to carry secrets.

The fire in the central pit had burned low. Its embers pulsed with a dull orange glow, casting long, lazy shadows that swayed against the tent walls like ghosts in no hurry to leave.

The air smelled of ash, old bread, and lavender—someone had tucked sachets beneath the pillows again, for dreams or warding off lice, depending on who you asked. Carlotta found it cloying tonight. Everything felt too close.

She threw the covers off and swung her legs over the side of the cot, the wool blanket tangling around her ankles like a reluctant lover. Barefoot, she padded across the layered rugs and dust-cooled hides to where her cloak hung over the corner of a battered trunk. She slipped her hand into the lining—just beneath the seam of the inner fold, where she'd sewn a pocket only she knew how to find.

Her fingers closed around the coin.

She pulled it free and held it near the candlelight, letting its soft flickers catch the silver's face. The coin glinted, sharp and clean, stamped with the royal seal of Castile on one side and the faded crest of Cádiz on the other.

She turned it over in her fingers. He didn't even feel it.

Men like him never do—too busy believing they've already won.

She'd palmed it the moment his lips hovered close. One heartbeat before she crushed his broken nose for a second time.

A fair trade, she thought, smirking to herself. A little blood for a little silver.

But the smirk didn't last.

She sat cross-legged on the floor, letting the cool air settle over her skin. The coin rolled back and forth between her knuckles with practiced ease, gleaming each time it caught the firelight. It felt heavier than it should—like a promise she hadn't meant to make.

The night crept in. And with it, memory. A ship.

A fire.

The sound of her mother screaming. The way the men laughed.

She'd only been nine. She barely remembered the faces—but the smell, that she would never forget: salt and smoke and spilled wine and iron.

They weren't even after them.

Just wanted the cargo. But her father fought. Her mother begged. And she learned something that night:

Pirates don't take prisoners unless they plan to use them.

She'd survived by hiding—curled inside a barrel meant for grain.

The scent of dust and wheat clung to her skin for days.

But worse than the waiting, worse than the silence she'd wrapped herself in like a burial shroud—was the look on her mother's face.

Carlotta had seen it, just for a moment, as they dragged her away: Eyes wild. Lips torn open in a scream.

She could still hear it.

Still feel the tremble of the floorboards…

The rattle of the bed against the wall the barrel leaned against—beneath her—as footsteps passed.

Close enough to see the metal studs in their boots. She'd bitten her own hand to stay quiet.

Bit until skin tore.

Until her mouth filled with blood and grain and terror.

And when it was over, the barrel stayed closed. No one came looking for her. Not until morning, when the flames were down to smoldering coals and the only moving thing from the night before was the smoke.

Her uncle found her at dawn.

Sold what was left of the cargo. Pocketed the silver. And then…

Sold her, too.

"A good girl, clever hands—you'll be lucky to have her."

Lucky.

She'd spent the next seven years earning her way out of brothels and backroom cons. Sharpening her mind like a blade. Her body, a trap. Her silence, a weapon.

Pretty soon, she wasn't the girl they'd bought. She was the one they respected.

And men like Vasco? They were the worst kind. Too charming.

Too fast.

Too convinced you wanted what they were offering. Even when you didn't.

They smiled like saints and stole like devils. Spoke in promises they never meant to keep.

Vasco may not have touched her like the others had but he wore the same grin.

Moved with the same swagger.

And beneath that swagger, she knew—knew—was the same kind of rot.

Which meant he could never be trusted. No matter how sweet his words.

No matter how tempting the dream.

She looked down at the coin in her palm. Bright. Heavy. Full of promise.

She closed her fingers around it, knuckles white. "I won't be that girl again."

Not for Vasco.

Not for silver.

Not even for freedom.

A bark cut through the stillness. Sharp. Urgent.

Then another—closer this time.

Carlotta's head snapped up. She moved to the tent flap, peeled it back just enough to see.

Shadows.

Three... no, four figures, creeping along the edge of the wagons. No torches. No sound but the shifting of sand and the distant lap of water.

Carlotta crouched low, her fingers slipping to the blade hidden under her mattress. She tucked the coin into her bodice.

From another tent, a faint click of metal. Behind her, soft rustling—someone readying a weapon.

She wasn't alone.

The camp was awake in the dark. Silent. Watching.

She watched the figures creep closer. Her jaw clenched.

A shadow peeled away from the caravan's far side—Reyna, barefoot, knife in hand, eyes narrowed. Luis followed a heartbeat later, his long braid swinging low over his shoulder as he slinked between the wagons, machete gleaming faintly in the moonlight.

Another bark. Then a low growl.

Fernando stepped out of the shadows, a lantern in one hand, a cudgel in the other. The flame flared, catching on the edges of silver earrings, flashing in his dark eyes. He said nothing—just tilted his chin toward Carlotta's tent.

They were heading straight for her.

The intruders moved with quiet confidence, their boots soft in the sand. Coordinated. Trained. One of them lifted a hand—signal to surround.

They didn't expect resistance.

Which is why, when Carlotta slipped from her tent and landed a spinning heel kick to the ribs of the one reaching for the flap, they were caught completely off guard.

The man crumpled. Another cursed, drawing steel—but found Reyna already at his back, blade pressed to his throat.

A third stepped forward, only to find Luis in front of him, weapon raised.

Dogs howled. The camp exploded with light. Lanterns flared to life as others emerged—some with pitchforks, others with pistols, and all with murder in their eyes.

The sixth man—the only one still standing without a blade at his neck or a rib cracked—raised both hands in surrender.

"We don't want a fight," he said, voice calm. "We came for her."

Carlotta didn't flinch. "You've found me."

He nodded. "La Rosa Negra. Our employer wants an audience."

"Who's your employer?"

A pause.

Then: "Don Montoya."

A hush swept the camp like a breeze across a field of dry grass. Luis muttered a curse. Fernando made the sign to ward off evil.

Reyna's jaw tightened, but she didn't lower her blade.

Carlotta's voice didn't waver. "Montoya sends six men to sneak into my camp in the middle of the night… and wants me to believe this is only a conversation?"

"He sent us to invite you. Personally," the man said. "He wants to offer you a job."

"I don't take jobs from men who send assassins."

"No one here is going to die. We swear it."

She looked to her crew. They were tense but ready—waiting on her word.

She exhaled slowly. "Fine. I'll go."

"I'll go with you," Reyna said immediately, never taking her eyes off her prisoner.

"Me too," said Luis.

"And me," Fernando added, stepping forward.

Carlotta nodded once, a silent thanks. Then turned back to the Montoya men.

"Take us."

* * *

CASTILLO DE SANTA LEÓN

By daylight, the Castillo de Santa León was a monument—warm stone rising above the cliffs, banners fluttering from the ramparts, sunlight dancing across its tiled roofs

But at night?

At night, it was a shadow.

The sea below was a sheet of ink, moonlight broken by waves, and the castle itself—once golden and grand—now loomed in hues of bone and ash. No laughter drifted from the windows. No music echoed through the halls. The torches along the wall burned low, more for form than welcome.

Carlotta and her companions moved in silence, their footfalls swallowed by the worn stones of the outer courtyard. The guards who met them didn't speak — just nodded once and stepped aside, hands resting on hilts that glinted cold in the torchlight.

She took it all in with a thief's eye and a soldier's caution.

The garden was breathtaking — unnervingly so. Painted tiles in blues and golds shimmered beneath the moonlight, delicate vines wound through wrought iron trellises, and orange trees, heavy with blossom, leaned inward from the walls like curious courtiers. Everything was curated, manicured, serene.

Too serene.

Carlotta's fingers itched for the grit of her old knife handle.

She thought of the stony campground they'd left behind — damp, smoke-scarred, smelling of ash and boot leather. A half-collapsed tent, a broken crate doubling as a stool, water that tasted like rust. That had been home. Or something like it.

This? This was a trap wrapped in velvet and tapestries. At least the campground didn't pretend to be safe.

At least there, you knew where the edge was — and how close you stood to falling off it.

Here, the danger was perfumed. Lines hidden in the scent of jasmine under cloak of night.

Another pair of guards stood waiting.

"He'll see her alone," one of them said, eyes fixed on Carlotta.

Reyna stepped forward, blade already half-drawn. "We don't do alone."

Carlotta touched her arm. "It's fine."

Luis frowned. "You sure?"

"I'm a stone's throw away," she said, voice low. "One signal."

Fernando's expression didn't change, but his hand shifted to the knife at his belt. "We'll be listening."

"I know," Carlotta said. Then she turned to the guards. "Take me to him."

The doors to the private garden creaked open, spilling warm light into the courtyard.

She stepped through them—and vanished into the lion's den.

* * *

They passed beneath a low stone arch into a second courtyard. A fountain murmured quietly in its center—white marble, veined with time. It rose like a chalice, wide-brimmed and elegant, carved with olive branches and the faces of saints who did not look especially forgiving. Water trickled from their mouths into the basin below, a soft, rhythmic burble that echoed too loudly in the hush.

The scent of orange blossom gave way to wet stone and something darker — like ink and secrets.

Carlotta slowed, her eyes scanning the carved reliefs along the courtyard walls. The symmetry was maddening. Every corner, every line, measured. Nothing out of place.

That unsettled her more than chaos ever could.

She glanced up at the balconies above. Shadows watched them from behind carved screens.

So this is how kings sleep soundly, she thought. Not by trusting the world — but by caging it beautifully.

And now she was in the cage. The guards stepped aside.

Carlotta moved toward the fountain, boots whispering against the stone path. Moonlight glazed the marble, silvering the whole garden with a quiet kind of menace.

He was waiting there. Montoya.

Younger than she expected. Maybe thirty-five, maybe less. Smooth skin, dark eyes sharp enough to slit a throat. He wore no jacket, no sword, no badge of rank—just an embroidered linen shirt open at the neck and soft boots meant for comfort, not war.

A man at ease.

A man in control.

He turned when she approached, one brow lifted in amusement. "Come closer, little flower. I won't bite..." His smile sharpened. "Unless you'd like me to."

Of course. Another arrogant, self-centered male.

She stepped closer, but kept her weight evenly balanced, her hand near her hip.

He flipped a coin into the air with two fingers — a casual, almost lazy gesture. It caught the moonlight mid-spin, a quick silver flare, before arcing straight toward her.

She caught it cleanly, without looking. Muscle memory. Reflex.

Her fingers closed around the cool weight.

Automatically, she brought it to her mouth and bit down—It was real.

Silver. Familiar weight. Familiar markings. Her stomach turned.

Another one. Like Vasco's. Her jaw tensed.

She looked up slowly, the coin positioned between her fingers like a weapon she hadn't yet decided to throw.

Montoya leaned a hip against the fountain. "Let me tell you a story," he said, eyes on hers.

Carlotta stifled an inward groan.

What is it with these men and their damn stories?

Still, she said nothing. Just watched him, coin pressed against her palm.

"There was a boy once," Montoya began, tone smooth as poured wine. "Son of a merchant. Grew up poor, but clever. Knew how to read the tides, the books, and the men who held the purse strings. His father was drowning in debt. So the boy worked. Grew the shipping business. Paid the creditors. Earned his respect the way all men must—by becoming dangerous."

He paused to pluck a leaf from the fountain's edge, flicked it aside. "But then came the pirates."

Carlotta said nothing.

He went on. "They took a ship. A big one. Full of treasures the boy—now a man—had spent years collecting."

"So, he hired mercenaries. Paid them well. Promised more."

"And, they delivered… mostly."

She didn't move.

"They brought the ship back. The crates. The cargo. But when the coins were counted, some were missing. Not many. Just enough to insult him."

Montoya leaned in a little. "And when his men began to investigate, they found something interesting."

"A pattern."

"A man."

"A name."

"The same one who'd taken his coin, taken his silver, and thought he'd taken his silence with it."

His voice dipped. "He hadn't."

Carlotta stared back, eyes dark.

Montoya smiled. "So now the man wants his coins back."

"And justice."

"Preferably at the same time." He let the silence stretch.

Carlotta kept her face unreadable. But her fingers curled tighter around the coin.

Montoya's voice stayed calm. Polished.

"My men were there when he offered you the job. They heard everything. Saw everything. Including the moment you lifted the first coin."

His eyes flicked to her chest. "And I suspect you're still holding onto it. Clever girl."

Her heart beat faster, but her expression didn't change.

"You're in possession of stolen goods," he said. "Enough to land you and your cousin in a very unpleasant cell. Enough to make the entire smuggler camp disappear if I so desired. But—"

He smiled again, the way a knife smiles in the dark. "I'd rather make you rich."

Carlotta didn't move. Not a twitch. Not a blink. Just the quiet hum of her breath, even and steady, as if she hadn't just been threatened — not directly, but close enough to count.

Montoya watched her like a panther stalks its prey. Calm. Still. Coiled.

She'd dealt with men like him before — power didn't shout from men like that. It sat on them like a velvet cloak: soft to the eye, heavy underneath. He was the kind who said exactly what he meant — not out of honesty, but because he didn't need to lie.

Truth, for men like him, was a blade. Honed. Inevitable. And this? This was no request. It never had been.

Carlotta tilted her head, studying him — the line of his jaw, the faint hollows beneath his eyes. That weariness wasn't from the hour. It was older. Deeper.

And then — there.

A flicker. Barely a breath.

Something passed behind his gaze. Not regret — that would've been too clean. No, it was something knotted. Heavier.

Loss.

A failure still smoldering behind the polish.

She saw it. And in that moment, she saw the whole game laid out—

This wasn't just a warning. This was a trap. Vasco was the mark.

She was the bait.

The easy path to the takedown. And she?

She was losing her grip on the path she'd been trying so hard to hold.

Carlotta straightened, spine unfolding like a blade. She took one slow step forward, deliberate, unshaken.

At least, that's what she made it look like.

In truth, she was bluffing — and she knew it. Normally, she'd have this sort of man wrapped around her finger, or better yet, picking himself off the floor wondering how he lost the upper hand. But Montoya wasn't like the others. Power radiated off him in waves — too still, too silent, too certain.

He wasn't just dangerous. He was untouchable.

He was her mark in this moment — but barely. And deep down, she knew: she might not have the cards this time.

This wasn't some dockside brute or backroom magistrate. Men like Montoya didn't play fair — they wrote the rules.

He could crush her like an ant beneath his boot and no one would stop him.

No one could.

So she did what she always did when the ground shifted beneath her — she slid on the mask. Let him see only what she wanted him to. "You say I have a choice," she said, voice low, silk drawn over steel.

"That this isn't a threat."

Her eyes narrowed — a calculated gesture. Not defiance. Not yet. But not surrender either.

"But you speak like a man who's already made up his mind." She didn't blink. Didn't break.

Just watched.

Waiting to see what kind of predator she was really facing. Montoya didn't answer.

His silence was deliberate — another weapon.

Another reminder of who held the leash in this conversation. And Carlotta felt it — the shift in air, the tightening of the net. This was his game.

His board.

His rules.

And she? She wasn't a player. She was a piece.

"You want someone who'll play by your rules," she said, more hesitant now. "But I'm not one of your pawns. I don't belong to you. I don't belong to anyone."

His mouth twitched — not a smile. Something colder. Tighter. "I don't want to hire you just because you're talented," he said.

"I need someone like you because the people I trusted have already failed me."

He stepped forward a pace. The air shifted with him.

"Vasco came to you because you have a reputation. He did his homework. So did I. You're the best at what you do. And I intend to use that — to tip the scales back in my favor."

There was no flattery in his voice. Just fact.

Carlotta lifted her chin, slowly. Weighed his words like coins in her hand.

"What exactly is it you want from me, Montoya?"

He stared at her a moment — eyes dark, unreadable — and for a heartbeat, something else passed between them.

Not threat.

Not even calculation. Enjoyment.

Was he savoring this?

A long breath passed through his nose — steady, but heavier than before.

"La Rosa Negra," he murmured, almost to himself. "Now I understand why they call you that."

His voice had softened, just slightly — laced now with something like respect. Or maybe caution.

Carlotta let the name hang between them like a perfume. Or a warning.

"Most only see the rose," she said, gaze steady. "Until they feel the thorns."

She knew what she was. And she wanted him to know too. She was dangerous. And not just for her skill.

She had presence. That elusive, unsettling thing that made people shift when she entered a room. She wore it like a second skin — let it speak before she ever did.

Montoya almost smiled. Almost. Still trying to regain control.

Still gauging her angles.

Cute.

He'd had enough of cute. It was time to end the dance.

He let the silence stretch — long enough for discomfort to edge its way in — then took a step forward. A slow, deliberate movement. The sound of his boot on marble echoed against the garden walls, too loud in the stillness.

Then another step. And another.

The distance between them dissolved. Inches remained. "You see, I know everything, Carlotta."

His voice was calm. Almost conversational. But the words landed like cold stones in water.

"I know you spend your mornings in the marketplace, reading fortunes to fishwives. I know you palmed that ring off my nephew in town — two days ago. I know your cousin — Sofia, is it? — waits just beyond these walls with your loyal little band of thieves."

Her breath hitched. Just barely. But he caught it.

"I know Vasco approached you. I know you had nothing to do with this when it started. And I know... you didn't say yes."

He stopped inches from her. Close enough to see the flicker behind her steady eyes.

Fear?

No.

Readiness.

She was on alert now — hair raised, muscles coiled. Like a wild animal backed into a corner.

"You're clever. And careful. But I know your kind." His tone didn't waver. "The ones who walk between worlds. Who collect favors like gold. You think it keeps you safe."

He leaned in, voice lower now. Intimate. Too close. "But it only makes you useful."

Her breath caught in her throat — not because she was scared. Because she knew it was true.

"And being useful," he said, almost gently, "is the only thing that keeps people like you alive."

She didn't move. But her jaw tightened. That was all he needed.

He had her. Not broken — she'd never break — but cornered. And cornered was enough.

"You don't want to play my game? Fine."

He stepped around her slowly now, hands clasped behind his back.

A slow orbit. A hunter circling prey. "But let me be clear."

His voice darkened — just enough to shift the air between them. "If I walk out of this garden without your cooperation, I won't come for you. I won't touch a hair on your head." He stopped just behind her. Still. Close. Quiet.

"I'll bury the people you love in questions they don't know how to answer. And I'll let the men who do play my game ask those questions for me."

A pause.

Then, almost kindly — the final blow:

"But that won't be necessary, will it?"

The garden felt too quiet now, too full of breath she hadn't realized she was holding. The jasmine was cloying, the stone beneath her boots too warm. Montoya's words lingered like smoke — and she knew the smell wouldn't wash off anytime soon.

He'd boxed her in. She couldn't out talk him. Couldn't bluff her way out of this snare.

Not tonight.

Not with him.

So she did the only thing left.

She nodded. Once. Precise. Controlled.

"I'll do it." She said, her voice didn't shake. "But don't mistake my obedience for loyalty."

A pause.

"I'm not doing this for you. I want the silver. And my freedom." Montoya's mouth curved — not into a smile. Something colder.

Approval, maybe. Or interest.

"One job," Montoya repeated, voice smooth. "And you and your friends can walk away."

He held her gaze for a moment longer, weighing her again — not if she was strong enough, but if she was dangerous enough to be worth the risk.

Apparently, she was.

He nodded once to the guards at the archway. "You're free to go."

A soft scrape of steel as one stepped aside. Carlotta didn't thank him.

Didn't glance back.

She turned on her heel, cloak catching the moonlight, and walked out of the garden like she still owned her spine — because she did.

Even if he had just wrapped chains around it.

The stone path stretched before her, cool and shadowed. Her footsteps were quiet, but her thoughts roared.

She had agreed. She was in. But this wasn't over.

Not by a long shot.

Twenty Nine

Copper

THE KELLER PLANTATION — EARLY AUTUMN

The labor began before the first rooster's crow. Outside, the eastern sky was still a bruised violet, the stars fading one by one, when pain seized Colette like iron fetters clamping shut inside her belly. It was not like her earlier births—this one clawed, then flared into a steady burn that made her ribs hum.

She sank to her knees on the rough plank floor of the quarters, where crisp autumn air threaded through the warped boards and chilled the sweat already pooling at her back. The "birthing corner" was no more than a pallet of rushes laid over packed earth, a faded quilt thrown down in last night's urgency. No walls separated it from the rest of the room; every groan echoed through the cramped space, brushing the low rafters blackened by years of smoke.

A few strides away, the hearth did its work—oven, stove, lantern, sentinel. Its cracked brick throat cupped a nest of coals that hissed and winked, throwing thin ribbons of smoke into the ceiling and painting Colette's cheeks with shifting amber. An iron pot of water rocked gently on the trivet, releasing steam laced with sage, pennyroyal, and black cohosh.

Earlier, Lila—the plantation midwife—had crushed the herbs by hand, whispering half-remembered Creole prayers. A sprig of rosemary lay on the hearthstone to "keep the reckless spirits back," she'd said, while a length of red yarn circled Colette's wrist to guard the child from the evil eye.

The air was thick: woodsmoke, bitter herbs, the iron tang of old blood baked into the quilt, and the faint musk of lye soap lingering from yesterday's wash. Every scent seemed louder than sound—louder than the cricket ticking in the chimney, louder than the sighing wind, louder than Colette's sharp breaths.

Another contraction crashed through her, and her vision swam. She pressed one hand to the floor, feeling grit and straw bite her skin. In the half-light, she saw Lila's hands moving fast: wringing linen strips, sprinkling salt into a basin, uncorking a jar of lard for when the baby crowned.

Beyond the shack's door, the plantation stirred. A mule kicked a wall. A whip-poor-will fell silent. Faint piano scales drifted from the big house—Miss Patty practicing, unaware of the storm gathering in this room. The distance between those two worlds felt as thin as the yarn around Colette's wrist... and as wide as the James at flood.

The pain returned, harder. She leaned forward, forehead nearly brushing the floor, the quilt rasping her belly. Lila's voice came low and steady—French, English, African tones braided like sweetgrass: "Push when the fire tells you... breathe when it eases... every cry's the road getting shorter."

Colette breathed the smoke, the sage, the blood, tasted salt on her tongue, and let out a growl that rose from deep in the earth.

Outside, the horizon split open with a blade of gold. Morning was coming—indifferent, unstoppable. But here, in the flicker of coals and breath and prayer, time held still, waiting for a new life to pass through the narrow place that had already taken so many women before her.

Lila worked in quiet rhythm, her breath low, her lips moving in steady prayer. Her strong, callused hands moved with the memory of generations, knowing what to do even when words failed. "Come on now, baby," she whispered, dabbing sweat from Colette's brow with a scrap of linen soaked in cool rainwater. "You done did this before. You got more strength in you than the devil got lies."

Colette gritted her teeth. Her breath came in short, ragged gasps. Each contraction rose like a tidal wave and crashed through her, pulling something loose and primal with it. Her skin gleamed slick with sweat, her fingers scrabbling against the rough window sill, searching for something solid—air, wood, mercy.

Lila leaned in close, voice low and urgent. "Push now, chile. That baby comin' big. Head already crowned. Push, Colette, push like your mama pushed you into this world."

Colette screamed—a low, guttural cry that shook the rafters. Her body bowed. It tore. She felt it. Fire. Iron. A rending deeper than flesh, older than language.

And then—a cry. Thin and wet and real.

Lila caught the baby in both hands, lifting the slick, trembling form into the thick, smoky light. For one breathless moment, all the world was that sound—the wail of a child, new to the world and already demanding its place in it.

The infant's cry rang out like a church bell at dawn—bright, startling, a promise. Then it thinned, faltered, and settled into a fragile whimper that seemed to drain the room of breath.

Lila gathered the newborn to her breast, her strong hands suddenly unsure. Lines of worry carved deeper into her brow. "A girl," she whispered, voice wrapped in dread rather than joy.

Colette clawed for focus, head too heavy to lift. "Is...she all right?" Each syllable burned her throat.

Lila bent to study the child: tiny chest fluttering, lips dusky, eyes squeezed shut against the dim glow. She gave no answer.

The door slammed open.

Cold air and woodsmoke rolled in on muddy boot steps. Master John Keller filled the doorway—coat flapping, cheeks blotched with whiskey and wind, a grin shining through his beard.

"Where's my new son?"

Instinct propelled Colette's arms toward the baby, but Lila was already retreating, cradling the small bundle against her own ribs as if flesh and bone could form a shield.

Keller stepped forward, boots scraping over the worn floorboards, eyes narrowing as they adjusted to the dim firelight. He was expecting a son—light-skinned, strong-limbed, proof of his legacy made flesh. His gaze fell to the child, slick with blood and afterbirth, squirming weakly in Lila's arms.

And then he saw it.

Not the shine of his own pale skin reflected back, but copper-brown. Rich, unmistakable. Darker than any child he'd sired.

His smile froze.

A beat.

Another.

Something hard shifted behind his eyes—first confusion, then disbelief, then something far sharper. Betrayal twisted into rage. His jaw worked silently, thoughts clashing: She knew better. She knows who she belongs to. She is mine. Mine.

The silence thickened like smoke.

Colette struggled upright, her body trembling, bleeding. "Please," she whispered. "She ain't what you think. It—it wasn't my fault…"

His voice came low and cold. "Whose pup is that?"

Colette's vision blurred. The room tilted sideways. "I didn't want it…" she choked. "He took me. I—I don't even know his name. He come when you was gone. I tried to fight. I did. It wasn't my fault."

Keller's face contorted. Fury bloomed across his features like fire taking to dry fields. Without warning, he lunged forward and tore the infant from Lila's arms. The midwife cried out. The baby screamed louder, her small limbs flailing helplessly in the sudden cold.

"You lying whore," he snarled, spittle at the corners of his mouth. "You think I'm gonna raise some nigger bastard under my roof? Under my name?"

"Please," Colette begged, sobbing now. "Please, Massa John, she a baby—just a baby..."

Keller's boots hammered across the threshold, boards shuddering under his stride. He tucked the infant against his chest like contraband, the child's thin wails leaking from between his coat lapels. In the fire-glow his silhouette looked monstrous—wide shoulders, fist clenched around the crimson-stained blanket, bottle-shine of whiskey still on his breath. He paused just long enough to snarl over his shoulder:

"You're finished, Colette. Was in my will—no more. And you—" he flicked two fingers toward Lila "—spread the word: this one's spoiled meat."

Then the night swallowed him. The door banged against the frame, a gust of frozen air rushing in with the smell of wet earth and chimney soot. Outside, his boots receded down the yard, each step crunching the first skin of snow. The baby's cry dwindled down the row of cabins, echoing off bare pecan trees until it vanished into the silence of the big house.

Colette's legs buckled. Pain shot through her hips and belly—nothing left to hold her upright. Blood seeped anew between her thighs, warm and terrifyingly fast. She folded over, arms instinctively cradling an emptiness where her child had been moments before. Everything inside her felt scraped hollow.

Gone. She's gone. I never even saw her eyes.

Raw thought tumbled after raw thought: George is sixteen—he could be sold tomorrow.

Esther, my sweet girl, just nine, already quick with numbers and quicker with questions.

And Henry—still a baby at four. Still needing me. He promised freedom in his will...

Now he'll tear it up.

My babies will live and die in chains.

The room tilted. A low moan slipped out, half grief, half shock.

Lila was suddenly there, lowering herself beside Colette, gathering her into arms that had comforted her in secret darknesses for years. Their foreheads touched. Lila's breath smelled of pennyroyal and fear.

"He gon' sell her," Colette whispered, voice shredded.

"I'll never see my baby girl. Never."

Sobs tore loose, ragged and unstoppable. Lila rocked her, pressing the bloody cloth to Colette's brow, then to the gash at her thigh, then back again—small, futile ministrations against an ocean of hurt. Her own tears slipped silent down her cheeks, mingling with Colette's.

"Shhh," she murmured, though the sound trembled. "I got you. I got you." But in her mind she counted the terrible reckonings that lay ahead—Keller's rage, the overseer's questions, the children's terror once word spread.

The shack settled into a hush broken only by the spit of the hearth and Colette's ragged breathing. Outside, dusk bled into true night. Snow sifted across the fields, thin and soundless, cloaking the frozen rows in white—covering tracks, covering sins.

Lila leaned close, her voice barely more than breath. "We can't stay here, chile. Not now."

Colette didn't answer.

"I mean it," Lila said. "We got to run. For them babies. Ain't just you no more. He done marked you. Marked all of y'all."

Colette closed her eyes. And there they were.

George—tall and watchful—just sixteen, already bearing the weight of things no boy should have to carry.

Esther, sharp-eyed and hungry for answers, always whispering words under her breath, like they might stitch the world together if she could just say them right.

Little Henry, all soft curls and wobbling steps, running to her in dreams she never wanted to wake from.

She saw them lined up on a splintered auction block, stripped down, trembling.

Their eyes—wide, searching, afraid. Looking for her.

She saw Keller standing just off to the side, arms crossed, ledger in hand, mouth twisted into something that might have once been a smile.

Her babies. Born of violence, yes—but born of her. Born into chains, but not born to be broken.

"I can't lose 'nother," Colette murmured. "I can't bury one more child in my heart."

Lila cupped her face gently, voice low but fierce. "Then listen to me, gal."

She leaned in closer, her eyes bright like banked coals in the dark.

"Moses is coming."

Thirty

La Cerrada

THE CAMPSITE — THURSDAY JUST BEFORE DAWN

The garden gate closed behind them with a dull clang, and just like that, the illusion of civility shattered. The jasmine-sweet air faded into the scent of damp earth and the sharper tang of city stone. Carlotta didn't look back. She couldn't. If she did, she might falter.

They moved like shadows through the night, fast and quiet. No one spoke.

The city had a pulse after dark — distant voices, the clang of a gate, the whisper of wind curling through alleyways. But they avoided all of it, slipping down the side streets like water, turning sharp corners with practiced ease until the forest swallowed them whole.

It was only once the trees closed in — tall, dark sentinels flanking the winding path — that Carlotta allowed herself a breath. Not relief. Not safety. Just space. The kind of space where thoughts could twist and fester.

The silence stretched, thick and expectant. Even the forest seemed to hush around them, as if it too understood that the night had turned.

They didn't take the main road. That would've been foolish. Instead, they ducked into the woods at the eastern edge of the city, past the crumbling shrine and the split cedar tree — markers known only to the crew. Their feet padded over old pine needles and soft moss, barely making a sound. It was the rhythm of trust. Of experience. Of knowing when to shut the hell up and move.

Every member of the party — Sofia, Reyna, Luis, Fernando — kept their thoughts behind their eyes. But Carlotta could feel them thinking. Feel them watching her out of the corners of their vision. Waiting. She was the one who went in. The one who faced Montoya. And she hadn't said a word since stepping back into the shadows.

Not yet.

Not until they were clear of this stretch of woods.

Not until the air stopped crawling on her skin like ghosts she couldn't shake.

The path curved again, and finally — finally — the faint orange glow of the campfire broke through the trees. Their camp wasn't much to look at: a few low tents, some crates, a tarp strung between two trees to cover the supplies. But it was home. For now. And tonight, that meant everything.

As they stepped into the clearing, the hum of conversation stopped. Three heads turned — Emilio, Mara, and Linna — eyes sharp, shoulders tense.

Then Linna broke the silence. "Well?"

Carlotta didn't answer right away. She stepped into the firelight, its flicker catching in her dark eyes. Behind her, the others followed — quiet as smoke.

Luis dropped the satchel from his shoulder with a soft grunt. The leather creaked under the weight of its contents: rope, a pair of knives, a rolled map, and two oil-soaked torches they hadn't needed after all. He met Carlotta's gaze—half question, half challenge.

Carlotta exhaled. Finally. "Sit down," she said.

And just like that, La Cerrada assembled.

They moved as if drawn by instinct—no words, no calls, just the rustle of bodies finding their place around the fire. Packs were dropped, blades unbuckled, cloaks shrugged from shoulders and laid across stone or sand. Someone kicked the embers, coaxing flame from ash.

Luis crouched first, eyes sharp, lips tight.

Fernando leaned against a tree, arms crossed, watching everyone but saying nothing yet.

Sofia flopped down with a theatrical sigh, brushing twigs from her shirt. "Well, that was subtle."

"Could've gone worse," muttered Reyna. "Could've gone better, too."

A dozen voices sparked at once— "Who were those men?"

"Did he threaten you?" "Are we in danger now?"

"Is it true about Montoya being involved?" "Montoya? What did he want?"

Tension thickened like smoke. The murmurs overlapped—nervous, angry, curious. Fingers twitched toward blades. One of the younger ones looked like he might bolt into the trees.

But then—

"Did you say yes?"

Clear. Sharp. Quiet, but it cut through the noise like a drawn knife. It was Luis who said it—usually quiet, always watching. His voice wasn't angry or frightened, just... focused. Everyone else went still, as if they'd all been waiting for someone to ask that exact question.

Carlotta looked up from the fire, slowly. She didn't rush her answer.

Her fingers brushed the coin still tucked in her palm. Silver. Weighty. Cold.

She met Luis' gaze first, then Sofia's, then each face around the circle.

"I said I'd do it." A pause.

"But not for him."

She let the silence settle, heavy and full. "I did it for us."

For a moment, no one spoke. The fire crackled, throwing sparks into the dark. Somewhere in the brush, an owl called once and fell silent.

Then Luis shifted. His jaw clenched, hard enough to make a sound. "You were against it."

His voice was low.

"You said it was too risky. The man tried to kidnap you, Carlotta.

You cracked his nose. And now you want us to work with him?" Mara stiffened beside him.

"You kicked his ass and vanished into the night. We thought we were burning that bridge for good. What changed?"

Her eyes locked on Carlotta's. "What did Montoya say to you?"

Another voice from across the circle— "Did he threaten us?"

"Is he holding something over you?" "Tell us the truth, Jefa. We deserve that."

Fernando let out a breath, ran a hand through his hair.

"I don't like it," he muttered. "Feels wrong. Feels like a trap dressed in silver."

Mara tilted her head. "Maybe it is. But traps can catch more than rats if you know where to bite."

Carlotta stood still in the center of it—silent, unmoved, but her fingers were flexing slowly at her side. She didn't flinch from the questions. But she didn't answer right away either.

Because they weren't wrong.

She had changed her mind. And they deserved to know why.

She stepped forward, slow. Her voice was even, but there was an edge beneath it—raw and real.

"He didn't threaten me. Not exactly." A glance at Luis.

"But he made it clear. If I don't take this job…" Her eyes swept the circle.

"He won't come after me. He'll come after you."

The silence that followed wasn't empty. It was thick. Heavy.

Linna's expression shifted first—anger sharpening into something colder.

"Then we burn what he owns," she said. "Take his coin routes. Bleed his reach. Leave him exposed."

Mara shook her head. "You don't pick a fight with Montoya unless you're ready to bury yourself beside him."

A pause.

"But we could make him regret thinking we're his pawns." Her gaze grew dark.

"How?" Fernando asked flatly, arms crossed over his chest. "He holds the city in one hand and the crown in the other. You want to slap a lion while it's sleeping?"

"No," Mara said, eyes glittering. "We find the hand that holds his leash—and give it reason to tremble. Stack the odds in our favor."

Luis let out a low whistle. "We're talking about blackmail?"

"We're talking about options," she snapped. "Information. Weak spots. Even lions bleed."

Fernando leaned forward, voice low. "He's too smart to leave anything obvious lying around."

"Then we look harder," Carlotta said.

That turned a few heads.

She hadn't spoken since the group erupted — not really. But now she stepped forward into the firelight, voice calm, steady.

"We don't strike now," she said. "We listen. We learn. We play the part — until we've mapped every crack in his armor."

Sofia gave her a long, measured look. "So what's the plan?"

A shadow crossed Carlotta's face, a whisper almost lost beneath the crackling fire:

"We let him think he has us," she said, voice harder now. "Then we rob him blind."

Thirty One

Operation: Daggerfruit

CHAHIRA | DELHI, INDIA | C. 1223

BREAKFAST

The harem was abuzz with the latest scandal: A foreign princess—young, beautiful, and betrothal-ready—had arrived at court with her father's caravan.

Rumor had it she was to be offered to Prince Rashid to "tighten diplomatic ties." Chahira heard the rumor over pomegranate seeds, sweet cheese, and warm honey flatbread—the usual bribes for a quiet morning.

She paused mid-chew. "Well. That won't do." By lunch, she had a plan.

By sunset, she was wearing a licorice mustache and hiding behind a potted fig tree, muttering to herself.

"This is a terrible idea," Laleh hissed beside her, dressed as an elderly fruit seller. A tray piled high with produce wobbled in her hands, her humpback made entirely of rolled-up linens.

Chahira adjusted her veil and sniffed. "You say that about all my ideas."

"Because all your ideas are terrible."

"I'm not letting some peacock from Tirmidh swoop in and steal my prince."

"She's twelve."

"Perfect. I've got time to crush her dreams gradually."

Laleh groaned and shuffled forward, muttering about the wages of loyalty.

* * *

DINNER

The great hall blazed with lanterns. Musicians played a slow, lilting tune as noble guests drifted beneath the high arches like jeweled clouds. The foreign princess sat beside the Sultan—eyes wide, hands folded primly in her lap.

Chahira and Laleh shuffled into the center of the room, veiled and hunched, pretending to sell fruit. Their target: a small side table placed perfectly in the princess's path.

Phase One of Operation Daggerfruit was simple: Spill pomegranate juice.

Look innocent. Exit with dignity.

It all fell apart at the melon cart.

Someone bumped her elbow—possibly a palace steward, possibly fate itself.

She sneezed violently into her veil. Her tray tilted.

A papaya dropped. A pineapple rolled.

And then—tragedy—her foot landed squarely on a banana slice. She skidded.

Into a table.

Three bowls of pomegranate seeds launched into the air—

—and landed squarely on the princess. There was a gasp.

A very loud splat.

And then—a startled peacock burst from beneath the table, flapping wildly and knocking over a tray of saffron rice.

The entire hall went still.

The princess blinked. Her gown now resembled a murder scene. Someone screamed.

Someone else shouted, "Assassin!"

And Chahira—frozen mid-sprawl in a very ungraceful heap of fruit—said the only thing her brain could produce:

"...Blessings upon your house?"

* * *

MEANWHILE, ACROSS THE ROOM...

Rashid choked on his wine and coughed into his sleeve.

"By all the prophets," he muttered, rising to his feet.

He recognized her instantly. The walk. The chaos. The absolute inability to not cause a scene. Only Chahira would attempt espionage wearing a licorice mustache.

The Vizier stormed up beside him, breathless. "Highness! There's an intruder!"

"That's no intruder," Rashid sighed. "That's my... never mind."

He strode into the chaos just as the guards descended, swords drawn.

Chahira was scooting backward on her knees, holding up a kumquat like a talisman against death.

"She's with me!" Rashid barked. Everyone froze.

"She's part of a—yes, a performance. For the princess. Very... interpretive. The fruit has deep meaning. Symbolic. Powerful stuff."

A long pause.

A longer pause.

Several nobles looked horrified. One woman dropped her fig. A lute player slowly backed out of the room.

And then—

The princess, covered in pomegranate seeds and royal dignity, giggled.

"That was amazing. Do it again!"

Rashid crouched down and hauled Chahira to her feet. "You," he whispered, "are banned from fruit for a month."

"Technically," she said, batting her lashes, "you never outlawed melons."

"Don't test me."

* * *

LATER THAT EVENING...

Chahira sat on Rashid's balcony, legs curled beneath her, eating candied dates as if nothing had happened.

"You could have just asked if the rumors were true," he said, settling beside her.

"I could have," she replied, licking honey from her fingers. "But where's the fun in that?"

He eyed the sticky red stain still dotting her cheek and reached out with his sleeve to wipe it away.

"You started a diplomatic incident with a papaya."

She smiled. "And you still brought me dinner."

He sighed. "Ya Allah help me, I did."

They sat in silence for a moment, the city glittering below.

"You really thought I'd marry her?" he asked quietly.

She shrugged. "People do foolish things for power."

Rashid looked at her. "I'd burn this palace to the ground before I gave you up."

She turned, genuinely startled. Their eyes met.

"...That might be the nicest thing you've ever said to me."

"It's the stickiest thing I've ever said, that's for certain." He chuckled.

A cowbell chimed below. Rashid glanced over the balcony. "Ah, the princess is out walking her new pet goat."

Chahira smirked. "Did you hear? She named him Papaya."

June 1942

Dot—

Your note made me cry. I could almost hear the laughter in the room, the wrapping paper tearing, the way you pretend not to blush when people fawn over you. You deserved every minute of it.

I'm sorry I wasn't there, truly I wanted to be. But last minute assignment... you know how it is out here.

There's a spot here where the cobblestones are worn smooth by time. A little girl sang to herself as she walked past me today and the pigeons took flight, the whole street echoed with their wings. It felt like hope. Kiss these babies for me. Tell them their Aunt Chrissy is still out here, trying to make the world a bit safer before they inherit it.

Always,
Chrissy

Miss Dorothy E. Calhoun
228 West 136th Street
Apt. 4B
Harlem, New York City, NY USA

Thirty Two

Worth It

GIBRALTAR PROPER

She slipped the postcard through the narrow brass mouth of the post box and listened for the faint metallic swallow. Dot would receive it—sun-bleached by the Atlantic, corners curled from damp, smelling faintly of sea salt and engine oil. Christine winced as she straightened—three cracked ribs protested beneath the tight bandage, and her left arm throbbed inside its sling. She would live. It was worth it. It would always be worth it.

The shipping lanes, the oil depots in Tangier and Oran, every coded convoy schedule—photographed, developed, and packed into a thumb-sized reel now hidden in the hollow of her shoe. She was supposed to pass it discreetly to her contact in the ladies' powder room of the Tivoli Theatre.

But MI6 found her first.

They didn't arrest her. They didn't need to. The interrogation happened in plain sight, beneath chandeliers and cigarette smoke, at a linen-covered table not ten feet from a pair of Nazi officers draining their second round of steins. Christine had played the part well—just a woman laughing too loudly, flirting with a Portuguese man in a fine jacket. But across the table, beneath the cloth, that man's voice never rose above conversational. His questions cut like piano wire, careful and quiet. Her answers danced just as lightly.

A toast here. A tilt of the head there. Guns under napkins. Her fingers gripped the stem of her glass too tightly, but she smiled as if amused. It was all theater. It had to be.

Now, outside, the late-spring night tasted of river fog and grilled sardines. Her shoes—a pair of sand-colored brogues with muted suede quarters and small rubber taps—clicked softly over Lisbon's patterned cobblestones. Sensible, forgettable shoes: the kind that made her vanish into the city, the kind no one remembered. Inside the right heel, behind a leather inlay no cobbler would question, rested the second strip of undeveloped film—her real assignment, and now her final bargaining chip.

She exhaled, adjusting the sling, and allowed herself one heartbeat of quiet triumph before turning toward the shadowed mouth of the alley that led back to the pensione. Three days holed up in the safe house while her ribs began to knit and her bruises bloomed. Three days spent waiting for the French liaison's signal that it was safe to move again. A week late now. The delay in Lisbon had nearly cost her everything.

But the line had held.

The contact was waiting. The route was cleared. The next step was already in motion—to the quiet stone chapel where the exchange would take place.

Somewhere behind her, a tram bell clanged. Church bells tolled half past eight.

She adjusted her sunglasses and stepped off the curb, brogues ticking in measured cadence—neither too fast nor too slow, the practiced rhythm of someone meant to be forgotten.

Ahead, a door swung open to the left, spilling laughter and lamp-light onto the street. Three British soldiers staggered out, uniforms creased from long wear, cheeks flushed with cheap wine. One of them crooned a crooked line of something Scottish before the others shushed him, laughing.

Christine froze mid-step, half-shadowed beneath a wrought iron balcony. She waited, head lowered, until the men disappeared inside and the door latched shut behind them. Then she moved again, eyes sweeping the narrow street, cataloging every window, every move-ment. Somewhere, someone was always watching. Better that they had no reason to remember her.

The buildings shifted as she descended—stone replacing stucco, the corners more rounded, the archways older. She passed under a carved lintel, then another. Moorish filigree traced the upper bal-conies, their whitewashed curves glowing faintly in the moonlight. Christine had photographed places like this in better hours—before shadows meant danger and silence carried weight.

She caught a whisper of running water before she saw the source. A modest fountain sat in a small square just before the chapel, its basin cracked but still clean. The sound masked her steps as she passed, water lapping gently against worn stone.

The church loomed ahead—low, ancient, solid. Its front doors were closed, but that wasn't her way in.

Christine slipped along the outer wall, her fingers brushing over its rough surface. At the side, beneath a pointed archway where the plaster had peeled to reveal timeworn stone, she found the shadowed entrance. The wood was heavy beneath her hand, the iron latch colder than she expected.

She paused. Listened.

A small sliver of light spilled through the cracked door ahead, pooling in a thin line across the stone floor. She stepped quietly into the hallway, the heavy door closing behind her with a sigh more than a click.

Inside, the air was cool and dry, smelling of beeswax, old stone, and the faint ghost of incense. The room beyond had once been a sacristy—still bore the markings of its original purpose. A worn wooden wardrobe stood against one wall where vestments had once been kept. A chipped porcelain basin rested on a pedestal, its edges ringed with age. Now, it held only dust.

Candlelight flickered low and steady—just two stubby tapers placed at opposite corners of a long wooden table, their flames casting soft shadows that danced along the curved ceiling. The room had the hush of forgotten prayers, the kind that sank into mortar and stayed.

He stood with his back to her. Elias.

He was older than the last time she saw him—though maybe it had only been weeks. His hair was cropped shorter, his jawline dark with the kind of stubble that came not from fashion but from fatigue. His jacket was too thin for the night air, sleeves rolled to the elbows, hands planted on either side of a map spread across the table.

He turned the instant the door shut. And froze.

"You're late," he said quietly, but the words held no accusation—only relief, and the deep, fraying edge of worry.

Christine's breath hitched. "I was—"

"I know." He moved to her in three long strides. "They got to you."

She nodded once.

Elias exhaled like someone had just pulled a blade from his ribs. "MI6?" he asked.

"Lisbon. They were already watching the Tivoli."

"I tried to get to you." His voice dropped. "I was two streets over. I saw you with the Portuguese contact… and then nothing. No word. I couldn't make a move—" He shook his head. "They would've made you disappear."

"I know," she said quietly. "They almost did."

His eyes flicked to the sling. Then to her oversized sunglasses. She hadn't taken them off since she walked in.

He caught the angle of the bruising beneath—what the lenses couldn't fully hide. The edge of a split lip. A smear of yellowed shadow at her temple.

Her blouse was buttoned to the neck, but her movements betrayed her: guarded, tight. She was holding herself together. Barely.

"You look like hell."

"I'll live."

He looked away for a moment, jaw tight. "Did they—" He stopped. Shook his head again. "Doesn't matter. You're here."

A pause stretched between them, heavy with everything they wouldn't say here. Not now.

He gave the smallest nod—just enough.

Christine stepped forward, met his gaze. "Yeah," she said quietly. "But I got it."

Thirty Three

Masterpiece

CELINA | NAPLES, ITALY | C. 1744

VILLA D'BARESI

The light shifted across the floor as the sun climbed higher, brushing over canvases, empty brushes, a half-eaten pear on a chipped ceramic plate. Celina stood by the window, eyes tracking the line of shadow crawling up the garden wall. The scent of linseed oil clung to her skin. Again.

It had been a month.

Every day, Giovanni locked her in before leaving for "meetings," and every day she painted, just as he asked. As he commanded. She told herself it was fine. That this was what she wanted: to paint, to improve, to become something.

But it was beginning to feel like a gilded cell. Her fingers ached. Her spirit—once buoyed by the promise of love and art—now fluttered, listless and thin, inside her chest.

He hadn't come home the night before.

By the time she heard the key turn in the lock the next evening, Celina was ready—palette in hand, hair swept back with a scarf. Her painting stood on the easel by the largest window, bathed in late sunlight. Finished. Or nearly.

She was proud of it. It was good.

Maybe even better than good.

"Giovanni," she called softly as he entered. "Come see."

He looked tired—there were shadows under his eyes and his coat hung a little too loose—but he smiled, distracted. "Ah. Let's have a look."

She stepped back to give him space, watching his face for a reaction.

He nodded slowly. "It's… yes. It's good. Just what I hoped for."

Her heart fluttered, wanting more. Praise. Pride. Maybe even affection.

But he walked straight past her to the far window and pulled back the curtain. "The courier will be here by the end of the week. We'll need to have it wrapped properly."

Celina blinked. "Courier?"

He turned, caught off guard by her confusion. "For the buyer."

"The… buyer?" She stepped closer, paintbrush still in her fingers. "You sold it?"

Giovanni hesitated, then softened his voice. "Of course I did, my love. It's magnificent. I told you, didn't I? I believed in you."

Her heart stumbled. "But it wasn't even finished…"

"I told the collector it was nearly done. I knew you'd complete it."

He stepped closer, fingertips brushing lightly against the edge of the canvas. "You always rise to the occasion."

She smiled faintly, still uncertain. Her eyes drifted over the painting—her painting—now apparently belonging to someone else. A stranger.

Her heart fluttered, a strange blend of pride and disbelief unfurling inside her. "Who bought it?"

He glanced at her. "What?"

"The collector—who was it?" she asked again, her voice soft with wonder. "I'd like to send them a note, perhaps. Something small. A thank you." She gave a light, earnest laugh. "For believing in me. I mean—how rare, no? For someone to commission a work from an untrained woman? Especially one so early in her career."

"He—" Giovanni caught himself, just barely, and reached for his cuff. "—is a patron from the north," he said, brushing a speck of dust from his sleeve. "A quiet man. Private. He prefers to remain anonymous, but I'll extend your gratitude when I collect the final payment."

Her eyes lit with something innocent and warm. "It's quite forward-thinking. I'd love to know what he saw in it... what spoke to him."

Giovanni didn't answer right away.

Something in the way his shoulders straightened told her—just for a moment—that her question had pierced deeper than he'd meant to allow. But then his smile returned: smooth, practiced.

"That defeats the purpose of 'anonymous,' now doesn't it?"

Her brow creased, just slightly. "Anonymous? But... if you're collecting payment, surely you know who he is..."

He laughed—light, indulgent. As if she'd said something sweetly naïve. "Tesoro, you really don't understand how collectors work, do you?"

He stepped closer, dropped a kiss on her forehead like a period at the end of a sentence.

"He's the same man who purchased my piece a few months ago. He happened to see yours while he was at the house and asked about it."

Celina blinked. "He... saw my painting? At the townhouse?"

"Yes," Giovanni said simply, moving toward the sideboard where a carafe of wine waited. "He remembered it. Said it stayed with him. When I let him know you were back in Naples, he asked if it might be available. I told him it would be finished within a month or so."

He poured himself a glass, not bothering to ask if she wanted one.

"It's all very standard, amore. This is how things happen. You're new to this—try and keep up."

He didn't say it cruelly. In fact, his tone was soft, almost coaxing. But the words stung just the same.

Celina looked down at the canvas, her fingers resting lightly along its edge. Something inside her curled defensively—something that didn't quite have a name.

She nodded, slowly.

Then it hit her. Like morning sun breaking through clouds. Someone had seen her work. Her colors. Her strokes. Her vision.

And they wanted it.

Her heart rose to her throat. A sharp, breathless laugh escaped her lips. She turned, eyes wide, cheeks flushed pink with the bloom of pride and disbelief.

"He really wants my painting?" she asked, her voice soft but trembling with excitement. "Mine?"

Giovanni, mid-sip of wine, smiled over the rim of the glass. "Yes, yours, cara mia."

Before she could stop herself, she flung her arms around his neck, nearly knocking the glass from his hand. Her laugh rang out this time—light, musical, unguarded. She kissed him, quick and firm on the cheek, then the mouth. He stiffened just a little, surprised, then smiled against her lips.

"I don't believe it," she whispered, pulling back just far enough to see his face. "This is… oh, Giovanni, this is everything I've ever wanted. I don't even know how to thank you."

His smile deepened, smug beneath its tenderness. "Just finish it, amore. That's thanks enough."

She turned back toward the canvas, chest rising and falling with exhilaration. Her brush hand twitched, eager. She could already see the last few strokes taking shape in her mind.

Maybe—just maybe—this was the beginning. Maybe her name really would be known someday.

"I will!" she said, breathless with new purpose. "I'll finish it this week—I swear it." She turned to him, eyes shining. "And I'll include a note. Even if he wishes to remain anonymous, I can still thank him. A small letter, something simple—you'll give it to him for me, won't you?"

Giovanni tilted his head, watching her with something between fondness and calculation. Then, with a soft smile, he nodded. "Of course, my love. A thank-you note—it's charming. Very... you."

She kissed him on the cheek again, quick and joyful, before turning back toward the canvas. Her brush was already in her hand, trembling slightly with anticipation.

"My love," Giovanni said, leaning casually against the doorframe, "aren't you going to join me for supper? There's roast chicken tonight, and wine from the estate down the road. I've had a long day, and I was hoping to enjoy a hot meal—and your company."

"In a bit," she said, eyes still fixed on the painting. "Just a few more strokes. This must be perfect. It's my first real commission!"

Giovanni lingered in the doorway, watching her—his expression unreadable. After a moment, he stepped forward, slow and deliberate, voice lowering just slightly.

"A good painter knows when to strike the canvas," he said gently. "But a professional knows when to lay the brush down."

She paused, glancing over her shoulder. The tone in his voice had changed—velvet soft, but no longer coaxing. Firm. Certain.

He smiled. "The work will wait. Supper will not. And neither will I." He stepped closer, brushing a lock of hair from her shoulder. "You've earned the evening, cara mia. First, we eat. Then we rest. Husband and wife."

His hand lingered on the nape of her neck, warm and possessive. "Come. You can finish the painting tomorrow, with fresh eyes. Tonight, I want your company."

It was not a request.

Celina set the brush down carefully. The metal rim of it clicked against the glass jar—too loud in the quiet room.

She turned toward him, schooling her expression. He was smiling, but it was the kind of smile that expected obedience.

So she smiled, too. And followed.

He offered his arm with courtly polish, but she hesitated—just long enough for the air to shift between them.

His smile didn't falter. He simply stepped to her side and placed his hand gently, deliberately, at the small of her back. Not forceful. Not rushed. But firm enough that there was no question: she was to move.

She did.

They walked the corridor in silence, his hand never leaving her spine. A subtle anchor. A claim. Not so different from the way one might guide a horse—light enough to feel like suggestion, heavy enough to remind the animal of its reins.

Celina's bare feet moved soundlessly over the tiled floor, the hush of her linen gown brushing her ankles. Ahead, golden light spilled from the dining room—warm and inviting. Almost enough to make a person forget.

Almost.

She tried to shake the feeling. Tried to tell herself it was nothing—just a habit, a gesture, a husband's closeness after a long day.

But the weight of his palm lingered even after he removed it. And when he pulled out her chair, his eyes didn't leave hers.

"Sit, my darling," he said, voice velvet-smooth. "Eat well. You've earned every bite."

She sat smoothing the folds of her skirt as she took her seat. A modest spread was already laid out—grilled vegetables, a bit of fish, crusty bread still warm from the oven. A chilled bottle of Falanghina sat beside them, catching the last of the light in its glass. The food was simple, but every detail bespoke care. He wanted this night to feel... celebratory.

She took a small bite of fish, then another. "You've been busy lately."

"A man must provide," Giovanni said lightly, pouring her a glass of wine. "And a man with a wife as talented as mine must make sure the world has the privilege of discovering her."

She smiled at that—small, but genuine. "It still feels like a dream. Someone actually bought one of my paintings."

He leaned forward, resting his elbow against the table's edge. "Of course they did. You have a gift, Celina. All I did was clear the path."

She toyed with her fork, swirling it slowly. "Is that how it happened with your last piece? The one you sold while I was at home... in Amalfi?"

She paused, as if realizing something beneath her own question—already stirring a hornet's nest.

His expression remained calm, but his hand froze briefly over the wine glass. "What about it?"

"I never asked. I suppose I've just been thinking about it since... since I started painting again." She met his eyes. "Which one was it?"

He gave a small shrug. "A portrait. One of mine."

Her brow lifted. "Which one? I don't remember seeing you work on any new portraits at the townhouse."

There was a flicker—just behind his lashes. And then the smoothness returned.

"You wouldn't have seen it. It was in the studio. An older piece I never thought much of, until a collector expressed interest."

She tilted her head, frowning, then stopped short—her fork hovering mid-air—as she caught something in his glance, subtle but unmistakable. A slight tightening in his jaw. A look she didn't like.

"I thought I'd catalogued everything in the studio," she said slowly. "I was trying to remember if I left one of mine behind..."

Another pause. Shorter this time. Tighter.

"You were still learning, my love. Most of your early work was just practice—nothing you'd miss."

Something tightened in her stomach. She reached for the wine, fingers brushing the rim instead of the stem. "There was one. The boy in the window. Do you remember it? The one with the broken sandal?"

He didn't answer right away.

Then—too casually—"It didn't seem finished."

She set her glass down without drinking. "I know," she said quietly. "That's why I wanted it brought from the townhouse. I thought… maybe once this one is done, I could finish the boy in the window. It has the same tone, the same feel. Perhaps the collector would be interested in both?"

Giovanni didn't respond immediately.

He took a slow sip of his wine, eyes fixed on the tablecloth. "Darling?" she prompted.

He set the glass down carefully. "There's no point." A beat.

She blinked. "What do you mean?"

"The painting is gone."

Her breath caught. "Gone?"

Giovanni nodded, too casually. "It sold."

The words didn't land at first. They hovered in the air between them—foreign and out of place.

Celina blinked. "Sold? But… it wasn't finished."

"It didn't need to be," he said, reaching for his wine. "Not once I signed it."

She stared at him.

Silence fell—not soft, but shattering. Sharp-edged. Sudden.

Her voice, when it came, was a whisper pulled tight with disbelief. "You… signed it?"

He met her gaze without flinching. "It was in my studio. I refined the shadows. It was near enough mine."

Her fingers curled around the stem of her glass, but she didn't drink.

"That painting," she said slowly, "was the first thing I did entirely on my own. It was mine."

Giovanni leaned in, his voice velvet and maddening.

"And now someone owns it. Because I gave it a name worth buying."

The air seemed to drain from the room. Her chest rose, stalled, sank again.

He continued, unbothered. "It brought in more than you'd ever believe. That money has been feeding us. Bought this villa. Your paints. Supporting your dreams. I thought you'd be pleased."

She didn't speak.

Because pleased was a lie she couldn't even pretend to swallow.

He reached for her hand, brushing his thumb across her knuckles as if soothing a child. "You're extraordinary, my darling. But raw. Untrained. The world would eat you alive. You need time. Protection. Guidance."

Celina sat perfectly still.

Her eyes fixed on his hand—the one resting lightly over hers. The one that had dared to sign her name away.

The weight of his smile pressed down on her like a thumb against bruised skin.

"I gave your work its debut," Giovanni said, voice syrupy sweet. "And look what it did for us."

She said nothing. Only reached—slowly, unhurried—for her fork. He didn't move. Why would he? She was a delicate little painter.

His wife. His pupil.

The fork scraped gently across the plate.

"If you ever," she said softly, not looking at him, "sign your name to one of my paintings again..."

She moved fast.

The fork slammed into the table, just shy of the webbing between his thumb and forefinger. The tines quivered in the wood.

Giovanni flinched back with a sharp curse, his chair scraping against the stone floor.

"…I will carve your name off it myself," she finished. Her eyes lifted. Calm. Clear. Icy. "Through your skin."

He stared at her.

"Are you mad?" he asked, laughing once—but there was no amusement in it. Just nerves. Just disbelief. "What has gotten into you?"

She stood slowly, her hand still wrapped around the fork's handle. "You did," she said. "You got into me. In my mind. My work. My name."

She tilted her head slightly, the fork still anchored in the wood between them.

"I warned you once. Lie to me again, and I'm gone."

He stood then, sudden and sharp, one hand flying out—cracking against her cheek with a sound like splitting fruit.

Before the pain had finished blooming, she moved.

The fork was at his throat—pressed tight to the hollow beneath his jaw, trembling with the force of her fury.

He froze.

She straightened, lips parted on a hissed breath. Her face burned, but her eyes didn't water.

"Thank you," she whispered, voice low and dangerous. His throat bobbed against the tines.

She leaned in, her breath a thread of steam between them. "Now I don't have to pretend anymore."

Celina pressed the fork harder against his neck. A bead of blood welled and trickled down, warm and vivid against his skin.

His eyes flashed with rage.

In a sudden, desperate motion, Giovanni snatched a glass from the table and slammed it into the side of her head with a shattering crack.

She stumbled back, dazed, hand flying to the sting where the glass had cracked her skin.

The room spun. The pain blossomed behind her eyes. He advanced, fury unleashed like a brutal storm.

She fought to stay conscious, to hold on as long as she could.

But somewhere between the darkness and the sharp sting, she passed out.

Thirty Four

The Art of Seduction

THE BOAR'S TOOTH IN — FRIDAY AFTERNOON

The Boar's Tooth was exactly the kind of place that stayed open long past when it should've shuttered — a tangle of smoke, sweat, and the kind of laughter that always meant trouble. Music curled through the rafters like a drunk snake, and the scent of spiced meat and spilled wine coated everything in a thin layer of grime and temptation. Bar songs cracked like broken teeth, thick smoke veiled every corner, and the floor stuck to your boots when you walked — if you walked too slow.

Carlotta slipped inside like she belonged—Luis at her back — silent, armed and deadly. Her cloak pulled tight, hood low. She didn't glance at the gamblers crowded around worn dice tables or the sailors pressed shoulder-to-shoulder at the bar.

Her eyes scanned the tavern quickly — a glance, not a search. She moved like someone with purpose. Someone expected.

There.

Back corner.

She made her way toward the back — past a man passed out face-down in his stew, past two women arguing over a gold tooth and a knife, past the firelight where the air got heavier.

He was exactly where she knew he'd be — not by the fire, not by the windows. In the dark, with the game already in motion. Vasco.

Smiling like a man who still thought the world would always bend in his favor — despite the swollen, bruised mess where his nose used to be.

Carlotta paused just long enough for her gaze to linger on the damage.

"Pity," she said, tone dry. "You're not nearly as pretty as I remember."

Vasco didn't rise. Didn't even blink.

"Still breathing though." His voice was hoarse but steady. "You'll forgive me if I don't buy you a drink."

She pulled out the chair opposite him. Sat without asking. "I'm not here for drinks."

"Right." He leaned back — stiffly, she noticed. Probably still sore. "You're here to finish the job?"

She let the question hang, then tilted her head slightly. "I'm here to talk. Somewhere private."

A long silence stretched between them. His good eye studied her — not just her face, but her stance, her hands, her tone. Looking for the trap.

Finally, he motioned to one of the barmaids with a flick of two fingers.

"Upstairs," he said.

She didn't hesitate. Just rose and walked toward the stairs. Behind her, she heard the scrape of his chair, the muffled sound of one of his men whispering a warning. Vasco didn't answer.

She took the steps slowly—calculated and guarded.

Vasco was a man with a grudge, and bruised pride — and those were sometimes the most dangerous kind. When she entered the room, she didn't sit. She turned, arms crossed loosely, waiting.

The door closed behind her with a soft click. Vasco entered, slower than usual. Shut the door. Didn't lock it — a gesture, or maybe a warning.

He leaned against the wall, arms folded.

"Well?" he said. "What's changed?"

He wasn't smiling now. No swagger. No smug charm. Just quiet calculation. His eyes — dark and sharp, despite the swelling around one — swept over her like a blade. Searching.

She knew that look. He was reading her the way a sailor reads a storm. Last night, she'd made her position clear — crystal clear. No doubts. No room for negotiation.

And now here she was, standing in his room like none of that had happened?

No one did a full about face without reason. And Vasco knew better than to trust a sudden change of heart — especially from her.

So he watched. Waited. Let the silence stretch just long enough for her to feel the heat of it. Because something had happened. That much was obvious. Someone had gotten to her. Or something had changed. And until he knew what, he wouldn't make a single move.

Carlotta exhaled slowly, walked to the nearest chair, and sat — deliberate, unhurried. She crossed one leg over the other, settled back, and met his stare like someone with nowhere else to be.

The corner of his mouth twitched. Just a little. Finally, he said it again—lower this time.

"What's changed, Carlotta?"

She met his gaze. Unflinching.

"I thought about it."

Her voice was steady. Not defensive. Not apologetic. Just settled. "I took the plan apart in my head. Turned it over, piece by piece. And I couldn't find the flaw."

A beat. Then a shrug—small, but pointed. "That's the part that bothers me."

Vasco didn't move. Didn't blink. Just kept watching her with that bruised, unreadable face.

She let the pause linger… then rose.

Unfolded herself from the chair like smoke, slow and quiet. The room shifted with her.

She crossed the floor now, gaze fixed on him the way a fox watches a snare — close enough to smell the blood that hadn't quite dried beneath his bandage.

"You made it sound easy. Too easy. A payout that changes everything, a job with clean lines and no mess? No one gets a deal that tidy."

She stopped a few feet away, arms still crossed.

"So either you've started believing your own fantasies…" A tilt of her head. "Or you're not telling me everything."

That landed.

Vasco's expression didn't change—but the silence that followed did.

It grew thicker. Sharper. A thin wire pulled tight between them.

She stepped closer, lowering her voice just enough to make him lean in—even if he didn't mean to.

"I haven't said I was in. I don't trust you. So before I risk what's mine for your prize, I want the truth."

A pause.

"What aren't you telling me, Vasco?"

Vasco's mouth twitched — not quite a smile. More like a crack forming in a mask.

He pushed off the wall, slow and casual, like the tension in the room didn't cling to his skin like sweat. He stepped toward the table, running a hand through his curls with theatrical exasperation.

"I'm not hiding anything."

The picture of wounded innocence.

"I told you what happened — I did the job. I got the goods. And I didn't get paid what I was owed. All I want is what's mine."

He turned to face her again, spreading his arms like a man laying his cards on the table — even though they both knew his sleeves were full.

"I thought you'd understand. I thought maybe you'd want out of this life, too. One job — one. Easy mark for you. You'd barely have to work at all, not with that reputation of yours."

His eyes flicked over her, from boots to braid. Admiring. Calculating.

"La Rosa Negra," he said, almost reverently. "You and your little cousin could've disappeared after this. Sailed off into the horizon. Or into whatever new life that cunning little mind could conjure.

He let it hang, just long enough to imagine. Then he touched his nose — winced slightly at the contact.

"But clearly, I was mistaken. I'll find someone else."

No smile. No warmth. Just the shift of a man who had already made up his mind — to cut his losses, to walk away, to let Cadiz rot behind him.

"Too many thorns on that rosebush of yours to be useful."

She didn't answer right away. Did he mean it? Was he really done? She'd pushed — hard — but surely not past the point of no return.

Not with a haul like this on the line.

There were others, sure—greedy, reckless types always sniffing for coin.

But none with her skill. None with her crew.

And none Montoya had summoned in the middle of the night for a private meeting under moonlight.

That part mattered.

Still… she wasn't going to beg. No. No, no, no.

He had to be bluffing.

A man like Vasco — driven by revenge, by ego, by silver — didn't walk away from a score like this.

Hi jaw was set like stone. Carlotta mirrored it.

She knew what he was thinking — she'd gone too far. Pushed too hard. Questioned too much.

And now he was calculating how many days it would take to find someone else. Someone not as complicated. Not as demanding.

But not as good either.

She stepped forward, arms still crossed, voice even. "I don't apologize for vetting a deal that could cost me everything. You'd have done the same."

He said nothing.

"You were right, by the way," she went on. "About the mark. About the silver. About my reputation."

Still silence.

"And you're right about something else too. You can't do this without me."

His eyes narrowed. She'd struck a nerve — maybe pride, maybe curiosity.

She softened — not her stance, not her spine — but her tone. Just enough.

"My crew is in," she said. "I'm in. And we don't do things halfway."

He looked at her like a man trying to read the wind.

Then: "So why the change of heart?"

She gave a small shrug. "I didn't say it was a change of heart. Just... a calculated decision. My reasons haven't changed. But the job is worth the risk — now that I know the odds."

A pause.

Then, quieter: "But I need to know you're still in too. I need to know I'm not wasting my time."

His lips twitched — not a smile, not yet. "And if I say yes?"

"Then you get exactly what you asked for," she said. She stepped closer.

Close enough to smell the sea salt and blood dried into his collar. Close enough for the tension to snap taut between them.

"Me. My crew. La Cerrada de Rosas Negras."

A beat.

Then her voice dropped lower, a challenge wrapped in velvet: "Unless you're still too bruised to handle a rose with thorns." Vasco stilled.

Her words echoed in his mind like a bell tolling at sea — sharp, unmistakable.

La Cerrada de Rosas Negras. The Circle of Black Roses.

Working with him.

It was exactly what he wanted.

Not just the crew. Her. La Rosa Negra.

And here she was — standing so close, he could feel the heat rising off her skin.

Her scent cut through the rot and rum of the brothel like something wild and alive. Not flowers. Not perfume.

Just her. Salt and sun and fire.

Intoxicating.

His jaw tightened. Eyes darkened — hunger, yes, and frustration, and something else he didn't have a name for. Not yet.

He stepped forward, closing the last inch between them. Nose to nose, bruise to burn, predator to flame.

"You came here to taunt me or tempt me?" he asked, voice raw. She smiled — slow, sly, sovereign.

"What if it's both?"

He didn't move. Didn't blink.

Just stared at her like a man who'd been starving for years and suddenly found himself standing before a banquet.

But he didn't reach for her.

Not yet.

"I should throw you out," he said, voice low and rough. "You mocked me. Broke my face. Told me I was nothing. And now you're standing here—"

"Now," she cut in, eyes flickering to the bandage across his nose, "you're not quite as pretty as you were yesterday."

A sharp edge of a smirk curved her mouth.

He flinched — just barely. Pride stung, ego bruised.

But the heat in his gaze didn't falter. If anything, it deepened. "You're lucky I find scars appealing," she added softly.

He stepped forward, bracing one hand against the wall beside her. "You're lucky I don't care if you lie to me — as long as your body tells the truth."

Her pulse kicked hard. But she didn't back away.

Instead, she reached up, fingers brushing the edge of his collar. Slow. Deliberate. Testing the boundaries of what he'd allow.

"You want this," she whispered, not as a question, but a claim.

He didn't deny it.

But he didn't give in either. "I don't trust you," he said.

"Good," she murmured, rising to her toes. "Trust makes people careless. Lust, though..." She let the last word hang — thick, charged. Then her mouth was at his ear.

"...lust makes people useful." She kissed him then.

Her mouth met his with the fire of every word they'd left unsaid — days of circling each other, full of knives and tension and something deeper neither dared name. She didn't kiss like a woman asking to be taken. She kissed like a woman daring him to survive her.

And for a second — just one, flickering, breathless second — he didn't move.

Then he shattered.

He kissed her back with bruising intensity, all want and hunger and need. But she was already ahead of him, pulling him into the rhythm she set — not just with her lips, but with her whole body, pressing close, teasing retreat, shifting the balance until he was chasing her like a man in a fever dream.

She tasted like spice and dusk and something wilder — like the first draw of rum after a long storm, or the kind of danger that smelled like jasmine and smoke. Like promises not made, only taken. And he was taking now — hands sliding to her waist, then higher, then lower, unsure of what he wanted more: to possess her or to worship her.

It hit him then — not fear, not exactly, but the dizzying sense that she wasn't just the storm.

She was the sea itself.

And he had already left the shore behind.

Thirty Five

Window Shopping

THE DELHI SULTANATE

Chahira — sharp-tongued, sharp-eyed — had become something of a living legend within the palace walls. The concubines sought her out like moths to flame, drawn by her wit and daring. The viziers regarded her with cautious respect, their practiced politeness fraying whenever she spoke her mind. The young wives, hungry for rebellion beneath their veils, copied her style and whispered her clever jokes like stolen treasures.

No one could predict what Chahira might say next — only that it would be brilliant, irreverent, and wickedly funny.

Prince Rashid, of course, knew exactly what she was capable of.

That was why he hadn't said goodbye.

Officially, he was leaving on a hunting expedition — or at least, that was what the royal seal proclaimed. In truth, the Sultan's third son had little taste for bloodsport, but even less patience for the stifling court rituals. The hunt was his sanctioned escape: a brief respite from silk-robed diplomats, endless ceremonial obligations, and the suffocating boredom of palace life.

As his small entourage passed through the eastern courtyard of the palace, laughter spilled from the upper levels like birds released from a cage.

Women leaned from carved stone balconies overlooking the procession — some wrapped in gauzy veils, others bare-faced and bold, each draped in silks the color of ripe pomegranates and dusk. This part of the palace, the eastern wing, was known for its balconies—the favored haunt of the harem on lazy afternoons. Whether they had gathered by chance or made a game of it, today they watched with unmistakable purpose. Petals floated from their hands like blessings. Or invitations.

Rashid's stallion shifted beneath him, restless from the noise and perfume. The scent of crushed jasmine and orange peel hung thick in the air, stirred by a breeze that also carried the sound of delighted giggles and whispered wagers.

He glanced up, half-smiling at the show—but not stopping. Not yet. His gaze flicked from one balcony to another, eyes scanning the jeweled throng.

Where was she?

And then — a flicker of movement on the eastern veranda, just past the rose trellis.

Chahira, half-hidden behind a marble column, one elbow resting on the balustrade. Watching the spectacle unfold like a playwright observing her own farce. A single eyebrow raised. A bemused smile playing at her lips.

Instead of the customary rose, she tossed a folded slip of parchment, tied with a blue ribbon. He caught it midair, curious.

He unfolded it. A poetry card — her latest invention — inked with verse and sarcasm:

"Don't forget: swords are fun and all, but wit is sharper. Come back whole.

P.S. I hope your horse doesn't have your sense of direction."

A genuine laugh burst from him. He looked up — but she was already slipping back into the shadows, vanishing behind giggling concubines like smoke retreating into a lamp.

"Chahira," he called up, grinning. "Come to the window."

Her voice drifted down like jasmine on heat: "What kind of girl obeys a prince from that far away?"

That did it.

Without a word, Rashid swung off his horse, tossed the reins to a bewildered attendant, and strode toward the rose trellis with single-minded precision.

Gasps rippled through the balconies like dropped pearls. Then came the shrieks—some scandalized, some delighted—as the prince—third son to one of the most powerful thrones in the realm—began climbing.

Hand over hand, he scaled the trellis like some silk-turbaned outlaw, disturbing doves, brushing past thorns, and shaking loose a rain of petals as he went.

His embroidered sash caught on a rose thorn. He didn't stop.

Onlookers leaned farther over the rails, their laughter turning breathless. One woman clutched her chest like she'd just witnessed a public proposal. Another whispered, "Is he mad?" and was met with a gleeful, "Apparently."

By the time he vaulted over the balustrade and landed, boots thudding against warm marble, the women scattered like startled sparrows—half in shock, half in giddy admiration.

But not all of them.

He scanned the terrace, turning in slow, searching disbelief. Nothing.

And then—a rustle.

A flick of movement behind a carved cedar screen.

He crossed the terrace in three strides and pulled it open—

There.

She lay on a velvet chaise like a portrait: one arm draped over her brow, a cluster of grapes within reach, the picture of staged serenity.

Only the glint in her half-lidded eyes betrayed her.

"You defy me?" Rashid asked, breathless, his grin a wicked promise.

"I delay you," she replied smoothly, the tone of a cat about to knock over another goblet. "A far more elegant crime."

His laugh rang out, unguarded. Deep and unrepentant. Court formality evaporated between them like water on stone.

This—this—was what he craved. Her unpredictability. Her shameless joy. The way she made disobedience look like grace.

"You're coming with me," he said, voice low and full of intent.

"I haven't packed," she countered, brows rising in mock alarm.

"Perfect. You always bring too many scarves and too little sense."

She gasped in theatrical outrage. "A lady must prepare for all outcomes, Your Highness."

He turned toward the balcony, tossing a grin over his shoulder. "You say that as if you're a lady."

She laughed—a rich, honeyed sound that turned a dozen nearby heads. "Careful. Keep insulting me and I'll pack nothing but sarcasm."

He winked. "So… just another day, then?"

With a cluck of her tongue and a sway of her hips, she joined him. "You adore me."

"I tolerate you. Wild beasts are sometimes permitted in court."

She smiled like a dagger in silk. "And yet you feed me grapes and take me hunting. You spoil your beasts, my prince."

He leapt over the balcony rail without warning. His boots hit the ground with a heavy thud; he stumbled, caught himself, and raised his arms to the balcony.

"Your turn. Jump."

She blinked. "Have you gone utterly mad?"

"Frequently. But I always recover." He grinned, arms wide. "Come, little storm. I'll catch you."

She arched an eyebrow. "If I shatter my spine, I expect at least a poem in my honor."

"If you shatter, I shall recite one with every breath." He widened his stance, palms ready. "Or we'll die together and scandalize the poets."

That did it.

With a muttered, "This is idiotic," she climbed the rail. And jumped.

She landed in his arms with a squeal and a rush of skirts, knocking him clean off his feet. They collapsed in a heap—his turban askew, her hair unpinned, laughter tumbling louder than decorum allowed.

Gasps, giggles, and whispers bloomed from the balconies above—maids and noblewomen peeking from latticed screens, their delight like perfume on the air. Below, the hunting party tried not to look too entertained. Someone clapped. Someone else whistled.

Chahira lay sprawled across his chest, breathless with laughter. Her braid was tangled across his collar; his heart was pounding beneath her hand.

Their eyes met—amber and coal, wild and wide—and for a moment, time stilled.

"I can't believe you got me to do that," she said, breath catching.

"I'm shocked you actually did," he replied. "Your judgment is clearly defective."

She smirked. "Well, everyone's watching. We might as well give them something to talk about."

Rashid chuckled, winded by more than the fall. "You say that like gossip isn't your fuel."

"Oh, it is," she said sweetly. "But I prefer it to be earned."

Before he could reply, she leaned in. Close enough that he could smell the sweet spice of her hair. Close enough to ruin him.

"You're trouble," he murmured.

"I'm your trouble," she whispered back. And then he kissed her.

It should've been forbidden. A prince, in public, lips on a concubine? But his mouth found hers anyway—soft at first, a question in the shape of a kiss, then deeper. Hungrier. Honest.

Her breath faltered. The kiss was not rehearsed. It was not seduction.

It was surrender.

She was supposed to tease. Keep her balance. Perform desire without stepping off the ledge. But he kissed her like he meant it. His lips brushed hers, soft at first, as if seeking permission he wasn't supposed to need. Then firmer... hungry... as though something in him had been starved for too long.

When he pulled back—slow, aching—she felt an absence she couldn't anticipate.

He looked at her like a man halfway to being ruined. And the worst part?

She wanted to ruin him the rest of the way.

His thumb brushed her cheek as though he'd only just realized he had hands.

The kiss was... real.

Not the performance of passion, but the vulnerable kind. The dangerous kind.

He kissed her again. Tender. More honest this time. Like something had slipped.

Changed.

She felt it in the way his hand cradled the back of her neck, reverent and restrained all at once. She felt it in her knees, suddenly treacherous. Her thoughts spun, untethered—Oh no. No, no. Not this.

And yet her heart whispered—Yes.

Rashid broke the kiss slowly, reluctantly, as though some invisible thread still tugged him toward her. He pressed his forehead gently to hers, drawing in a breath like he'd surfaced from deep water.

In that moment, every rule he'd ever known felt far less important than the woman tangled in his arms.

She could feel it in the way his thumb traced the corner of her mouth—an unconscious tenderness that made her insides ache.

The way her pulse fluttered beneath his fingertips as his thumb rested there.

She liked it.

He was supposed to be a dalliance.

A means to safety, perhaps favor. Nothing more.

So why did she want to kiss him again, and again—until she unraveled like silk beneath his hands?

Neither of them was ready to admit it, but the fall had already begun.

Rashid rose with a breath, then steadied her for a suspended moment—two hearts caught in the quiet between laughter and longing.

Their eyes met.

Hers wide, bright, questioning.

His dark, unreadable—but far too still to be untouched.

"Are you always so reckless?" she asked, barely above a whisper.

He smiled. "Only with you."

Neither dared name the fire moving between them. Not yet.

He stepped back, balanced her gently on her feet, then mounted his stallion with the grace of a man born to war and ceremony.

In one fluid motion, he reached down and swept her up behind him.

"Are you comfortable?" he asked, voice low, rich as wine.

"Not in the least," she murmured, nuzzling closer and sliding her arms around his waist.

"Good."

She clucked her tongue. "All this trouble... You must be terribly fond of me."

"You'll suffice," he said, with a smirk that didn't reach his eyes.

"If I vanished, your world would crumble."

"And where would you go?" he laughed. "I'd see your legs broken before I let you run."

"You care that deeply?" she teased, squeezing him with affection.

He tilted his head. "Let's say... I'm invested."

Rashid raised his hand in signal—and a moment later, the hunting party surged forward, leaving the marble walls of the palace behind, and riding into the wide, waiting world.

Moses Is Coming...

COLETTE | RICHMOND, VA | C. 1859

For those longin' toward freedom...
Moses's comin'

They think I'm broken— but they must think again
 My whisper'd prayers ride upon the wind,
 Mock me, they ain't seen my end...
 I call down thunder, and...

 I was born in shadow and shame
 My lullaby and rattle— a chain.
 Won't neva trust no man's name
 I dance within the flame...

 She got fire in her eyes an' the river at her knee.
 She travel wit' the light, an' she's coming for me.
 Jesus wept while the ashes kept score
 But I'll be free on that distant shore...
 Moses's comin'

 I heard it whispered in the rushes,

Cotton fields and blood soaked thrushes
Hush lil' birdie, storm's a brewin'
Somebody's watchin' what ya doin'
The road is dark, howlin's near
Black skies conjure shadow fear
Starlit path, river's clear...

I was born in shadow and shame
My lullaby and rattle— a chain.
Won't neva trust no man's name
I call down thunder, and rain...

Bleedin' feet and back crack'd lashes
Snowy hills and railroad quilts
Braids of hope the branch she catches
Taste the freedom my love built

For names erased and stolen dreams
Our silenced screams—by any means
Souls forgotten beyond the veil
Whispered memories fragile, frail.

She got fire in her eyes an' the river at her knee.
She travel wit' the light, an' she's coming for me.

So tie up your sorrows, braid hope in tresses high.
Leave the door cracked just a little—

Moses came here. And I was ready.
I was made for the running.
And my spirit is free...

Thirty Six

Revelations

CELINA | NAPLES, ITALY | C. 1744

VILLA D'BARESI

Celina stirred.

At first, only a flicker—an eyelid twitching against the iron weight of unconsciousness. Her lashes were crusted, her skin hot and tight. One eye refused to open at all; the other squinted through bruised swelling and watery blur, straining toward the faintest thread of morning light slanting through the window's warped panes.

Where am I?

Pain answered before memory. It seared through her chest as she tried to breathe, coiling around her ribs like a serpent made of fire and glass. A whimper escaped her lips, ragged and thin. She tried to speak but found her tongue swollen, her mouth cracked and dry as dust.

She lifted a trembling hand to her face, and the touch sent lightning through her side. Broken. Cracked. Bruised. She couldn't know. She only knew the ache was *everywhere*.

"Maledizione..."

It slipped from her lips like a ghost — half curse, half prayer.

Her fingers brushed her mouth. Dried blood flaked away in her palm. Her hair was stiff with it, matted to her scalp, and something sharp pricked at her temple—slivers of glass from the wine goblet he'd thrown, perhaps. Or the mirror.

She blinked again. Her vision cleared just enough to make out the corner of the dining table, overturned. Shattered glass glittered like ice on the floorboards. Her limbs screamed with every twitch, every breath, but instinct forced her to move.

A sound.

No — a *silence*.

Something was wrong. Wronger than before.

She shifted with agonizing slowness, turning onto her side, breath catching with a dry sob. Her foot struck something.

Soft.

Unmoving.

She stilled.

Then forced herself to look.

Beneath the table — a shape. A body.

A braid unraveling. Blood soaked into fabric and floor.

"Serafina?" Her voice cracked. "Serafina—?"

No answer.

Just the hush of the morning.

The distant cry of gulls outside the window.

Celina dragged herself forward, inch by inch, nails scraping the wood. Her breath came in ragged gasps, black dots dancing at the edge of her vision.

"Serafina... amore mio, svegliati—" Her hand found the girl's face. Cold.

Her eyes—half-open, glassy. Lips parted as if frozen mid-breath.

Celina let out a sound that wasn't human — a low, guttural wail torn from the pit of her soul. It shattered the stillness. Her sobs came next, fierce and broken, shaking her already-battered frame.

"No... no... no, no, please..."

She cradled Serafina's head in her lap, rocking her as if the motion might wake her. Her tears washed through streaks of blood and food and dirt. Her voice collapsed into pleading nonsense — prayers, curses, endearments — anything to barter for the return of the girl who had stood between her and death.

Who had paid her price.

Serafina.

Her anchor. Her compass. Her only constant in the long, crumbling house of lies she'd called marriage.

And *now?*

Gone.

Slaughtered in her place.

Murdered — by him.

By the man who had once whispered love into her ear while sliding a dagger into her spine.

By the man who sold her art, her soul, her name — for coin and pride.

By the man who locked her away, paraded her when convenient, and kept her brilliance dimmed beneath his boot.

Her ribs ached as grief fought with rage, and something beneath her breastbone split. Something feral unfurled there, vast and merciless. Her shaking stopped.

The tears slowed.

And what remained… was steel.

No.

He would not take her light and silence it.

He would not take Serafina and walk away unscathed.

He would not cage her brilliance, bury her voice, extinguish her fire.

Not now. Not anymore.

She reached down and closed Serafina's eyes with trembling fingers.

A silent vow.

Then she pressed her palms to the floor, braced herself against the screaming of her body, and forced herself upright. Pain roared in protest. Blood dripped anew. But she didn't stop.

She looked toward the doorway. Toward the stairs. Toward the room where he slept off his drunken violence — no doubt snoring in twisted satisfaction.

A tremor passed through her. Not fear. Purpose.

Resolve.

He will pay.

For every lie he spoke and every bruise he left behind.

For every canvas he sold under his name — with her genius.

For every stolen moment of freedom, every humiliation, every shattered hope.

For Serafina.

This prison he built with her money—her gift—will be the one he rots in.

She pressed a trembling hand to her ribs and straightened, inch by inch, breath by shallow breath.

Her father had taught her one thing.

Not how to paint, not how to please, not how to suffer.

How to fight.

And fight she would. This ends now.

The words burned through her like a brand.

She braced against the floorboards, teeth gritted, every nerve screaming as she dragged herself upright. A few shards of glass fell from her skirts with a soft, crystalline clatter. Her gown hung in tatters, wrinkled and bloodstained, one slipper lost somewhere beneath the table. Her stocking was torn, foot bare and filthy. Her hair, once the pride of every gala and salon in Naples, was matted with blood, wine, and sweat—knotted wild against her back like a storm-tossed shroud.

She looked like a ghost.

Or worse—like a woman reborn in fire.

Each step toward the stairs was agony. Her muscles burned. Her joints screamed. Her chest felt like it would cave in with every breath. But she moved.

One step. Then another.

She clutched the railing, fingers white-knuckled against the polished wood, and climbed.

One step.

Then another.

Each one a vow.

Her breath came in short, ragged bursts. Pain lanced through her side. The stairs blurred in her vision, doubling and swimming, but she refused to stop. She would not fall again. Not now. Not when every step brought her closer to the end.

Halfway up, she caught a flicker of movement. She turned her head, and froze.

The hallway mirror. She saw herself.

And did not recognize the reflection staring back.

One eye was nearly swollen shut. The other ringed in purple and yellow. Her cheek split, crusted in blood. Her lips were torn. Her neck—Cristo santo, her neck—dark with bruises in the shape of fingers.

He had tried to strangle her. After she'd blacked out.

Her stomach turned.

She looked away, bile rising in her throat. Serafina hadn't stood a chance. Neither had she.

And still, they had stood.

They had resisted, even in the face of death. Her friend had stepped in—had dared—to intervene. And now Serafina's body lay lifeless on the floor downstairs.

She bit her lip until she tasted blood again. Tears rose, unbidden.

But she blinked them back.

No. No time for tears. Not right now. She reached the top of the stairs.

The hall was dim. The curtains drawn. Her feet dragged against the rug, and the ache in her limbs throbbed with every heartbeat.

She passed his room. He was snoring.

That sick, slurred, uneven wheeze she'd come to know—part man, part animal.

The door between their rooms stood open. Left that way. Always left that way.

Because he had instructed Serafina to leave it so. So that he might come and take what was his without fumbling with keys and locks and boundaries. So that his wife—his prized, pretty possession—was always within reach.

She hated it.

She hated him.

She hated what he'd made her. What had become of them.

Of her.

Of everything.

She stepped past the threshold and into her room, the air cold against her fevered skin. She didn't light the candle. She didn't have to. The quiet was thick. She crossed to the wardrobe, every step slow, deliberate.

He slept on. Unknowing.

Unconcerned.

Unforgiven.

She crossed the room in darkness, each step guided by instinct rather than sight.

The wardrobe creaked faintly as she opened it, the scent of cedar and lavender rising—mocking, familiar. Her gowns hung limp and lifeless, like the version of herself she'd worn for too long.

She reached past the silks. Past the velvet.

To the back panel—where the seam between the boards was just slightly uneven. Her fingers slipped into the gap, searching until they found the notch.

She pressed.

A small drawer, hidden behind false wood, slid open with a whisper.

Inside, wrapped in linen and tied with a black silk ribbon, lay the thing she had tucked away in a moment of hope.

The pistol.

A tiny flintlock, no longer than her hand. Ornate and deadly. A gift from her father the day she was married.

"For protection," he'd said, jaw tight, eyes unreadable. "May you never need it—but always know where it is."

Now her fingers closed around it like it was an extension of her own will.

Her thumb caressed the cool metal. The mother-of-pearl inlay gleamed faintly in the pale light sneaking through the curtains. One shot. A single, perfect judgment.

She checked the powder horn. Still full. The wadding was dry. She could load it by feel.

She'd done it blindfolded as a girl.

Tears welled again—not from grief this time, but from memory. From the sound of her father's voice. The feel of his hand steadying hers over the weapon.

"Never draw it in anger," he had said. "But if you do, don't hesitate."

Her hands didn't tremble. Not anymore.

She loaded the pistol with slow, reverent precision. Packed the powder. Set the ball.

Cock.

Click.

It was ready.

The fire in her chest pulsed harder now, but her breath was steady. She moved to the doorway.

Paused.

Waited.

Listened.

Still snoring.

She slipped through the opening like a shadow, skirts rustling faintly against the floor. The sun had fully risen—now slicing across the room in bright slats, painting her path in gold and dancing dust motes.

He was sprawled sideways across the bed, one arm hanging limp, his mouth slack. A wine bottle lay on the floor beside him, empty. His boots were still on.

The moonlight glinted off the streaks of blood smeared across his boots—silent testimony, still damp with Serafina's final stand.

A pig in silks.

Celina approached slowly, the pistol cradled against her chest until she reached the edge of the bed. Her bare foot stepped onto the woven rug, muffling even that final sound. She looked down at him—this man who had made himself her master, her warden, her thief.

Her executioner.

She raised the pistol.

Steady.

She placed the cold mouth of the barrel to his left eye.

He stirred.

Brow furrowing.

Then his eyes opened—cloudy, unfocused. They locked with hers.

Too late.

She leaned in, her voice low, unflinching.

"Serafina sends her regards."

New Beginnings

CHLOÉ | RAHWAY, NJ | C. 1991

RAHWAY HIGH SCHOOL, ROOM 412 CREATIVE WRITING CLASS — LATE JUNE

The bell had rung five minutes ago, the quiet hum of laughter and small talk drifted through the oversized windows of Marcy Watkins' fourth floor English classroom. The air buzzed with summer's promise—open windows, yearbooks half-signed, and the quiet thrill of nearly being done.

Mrs. Watkins stood at the front of the room, a stack of final essays in her hand and a smile that meant she'd saved something special for last.

"I'm pleased with the assignments you all handed in. For the most part, everyone did well. Your stories were very imaginative. I'm proud of you all," she smiled warmly.

"That said, Chloé," she held up the essay. "A+. If only all my students were as disciplined. You set the curve for the final!"

A soft ripple of reactions moved through the room—impressed whistles, raised eyebrows, a few exchanged glances. Chloé ducked her head, cheeks warm. She wasn't used to that kind of praise, not in front of everyone. Not like this.

Mrs. Watkins handed her paper back, then glanced at the class. "I couldn't put hers down. I read it straight through last night without stopping, and I think you'll see why. Chloé, would you mind reading it to us?"

A flutter of panic flickered in her chest—but before it could bloom into doubt, her boyfriend nudged her gently. "You got this, babe." He winked.

Kiesha shot her a thumbs-up from across the aisle. "It's soooo dope," she whispered. "You know it is."

Chloé stood. Slowly. Her knees were a little shaky, but her spine held straight.

She stepped to the front of the classroom, paper in hand. The windows rattled with the sound of a passing bus, and someone coughed in the back row. She cleared her throat, flicked her braids over her shoulder and began...

"The city of Memphis stirred long before the sun crowned the eastern horizon."

As the words floated over her lips, something inside her clicked. Settled...

"From the flat rooftops of whitewashed homes to the sandstone colonnades of sacred temples", Chloé continued, *"the morning light crept slowly, gilding the city..."*

Conversation Starters

Braids invites readers to reflect on memory, identity, and the connections that bind us across generations. Whether you're reading solo or gathering with others, these questions are designed to spark thoughtful conversation and deeper insight.

1. The concept of legacy — both inherited and created — is strong in Braids. What do you think the characters leave behind for the next generation?
2. How do race, class and gender intersect to limit or liberate the characters?
3. How are the male characters shaped by the expectations of masculinity in their respective eras? In what ways do they conform or resist these roles?
4. How do the relationships between men and women evolve across timelines in Braids? What changes and what stays the same? (What do these shifts suggest about progress, patriarchy, or partnership?)
5. What does healing look like for the characters in the book? Is healing a solitary act or a collective process?
6. Which character resonated with you the most? Why?
7. What role does silence play in the story? What's left unsaid or forgotten on purpose? What are the consequences of this silence?
8. In what ways might the novel suggest that past lives allow for the exploration or reimagining of identity beyond binary or heteronormative constraints?
9. If you could ask one of the characters a question, who would it be and what would you ask?

10. How has Braids made you reflect on your own identity, ancestry and the choices you've made in your life?

Credits

The postcard Pigeon Alley photo was taken by David Gilbert, Jr. and used with permission.

Author photo taken by Colette Oswald of Colette Oswald Photography.

Makeup by Katie Sojka of Katie Sojka Makeup.

Acknowledgements

I could fill pages and still miss someone. If your name isn't here, please know my gratitude runs deeper than these lines can hold.

To Henry—thank you for your patience, late-night listening, and unwavering belief in me. You've earned more than a medal. Maybe a bakery. I love you.

To Sharon, who reminded me that my creativity mattered. You were a mirror when I forgot what I looked like.

To Heather G, who saw the dream before I did, and whispered it back to me until I believed.

To Marsha W—the real M. Watkins—thank you for saving me all those years ago. Your legacy echoes through every page.

This book was born from the love, loss, light, and shadow of so many hands. If I could hold them all in one paragraph, I would. If you are reading this and recognize yourself in the story or in my journey—thank you. You're part of this too.

Carla Cornick is a multidisciplinary creative, storyteller, and award-winning entrepreneur based in South Jersey. A lifelong artist and innovator, her work explores themes of identity, agency, and ancestral memory through words, textiles, water- color, and performance. Her debut novel, Braids, is a deeply woven narrative that merges history, healing, and soul resonance—offering readers a powerful meditation on what it means to belong to ourselves and each other.

With roots in theater, music, fiber arts, and community building, Carla brings stories to life both on and off the page. Her art quilts and visual works have been exhibited throughout the region, and her leadership in the handmade and real estate industries has earned her awards and recognition for creativity and excellence. She is the founder of Be Your Own SHERO, a platform devoted to autonomy, authenticity, and empowered entrepreneurship.

Carla sees Braids not just as a novel, but as the next evolution of her creative voice—one that invites readers to listen more deeply to themselves, to one another, and to the stories we carry. Through her writing and speaking, she continues to spark conversations that heal, challenge, and inspire. She lives in Burlington County, New Jersey, with her husband, Henry, serves on the board of the South Camden Theatre Company and her art is represented by The Hunter Gallery in Merchantville, NJ.

Stay Connected

If Braids spoke to you, I'd truly love to hear from you.

Your reflections mean the world—and your review helps the book reach more hearts and hands.

Want to keep the conversation going?

I welcome invitations to speak with book clubs, classrooms, and community gatherings. I'm always open to soulful spaces where stories matter.

Let's stay connected:

Sign up for updates on future releases and creative offerings at:

CarlaCornick.com | BYOShero.com

Follow the journey on Instagram:

@CarlaCornickArt | @CCornickRE | @BYOShero

Explore my visual work:

Original art, fiber stories, and upcoming exhibits at CarlaCornick.com

Every reader matters. Every voice makes a ripple.

Thank you for being part of this one.

www.ingramcontent.com/pod-product-compliance
Lightning Source LLC
Chambersburg PA
CBHW060815120726
47909CB00006B/1938